O'Henry

A Josh Ingram Novel

t.g. brown

Copyright © 2013 by Terry Brown

All rights reserved. This book or any portion thereof may not be reproduced or used in any manner whatsoever without the express written permission of the publisher except for the use of brief quotations in a book review.

This book is a work of fiction. Names, characters, places, and incidents either are the product of the author's imagination or are used fictitiously, and any resemblance to actual persons, living or dead, businesses, companies, organizations, events, or locales is entirely coincidental.

Paperback ISBN 978-1-928029-01-4
Print Edition Published 2015

Visit my website at www.thrillerreads.com

For Ruby

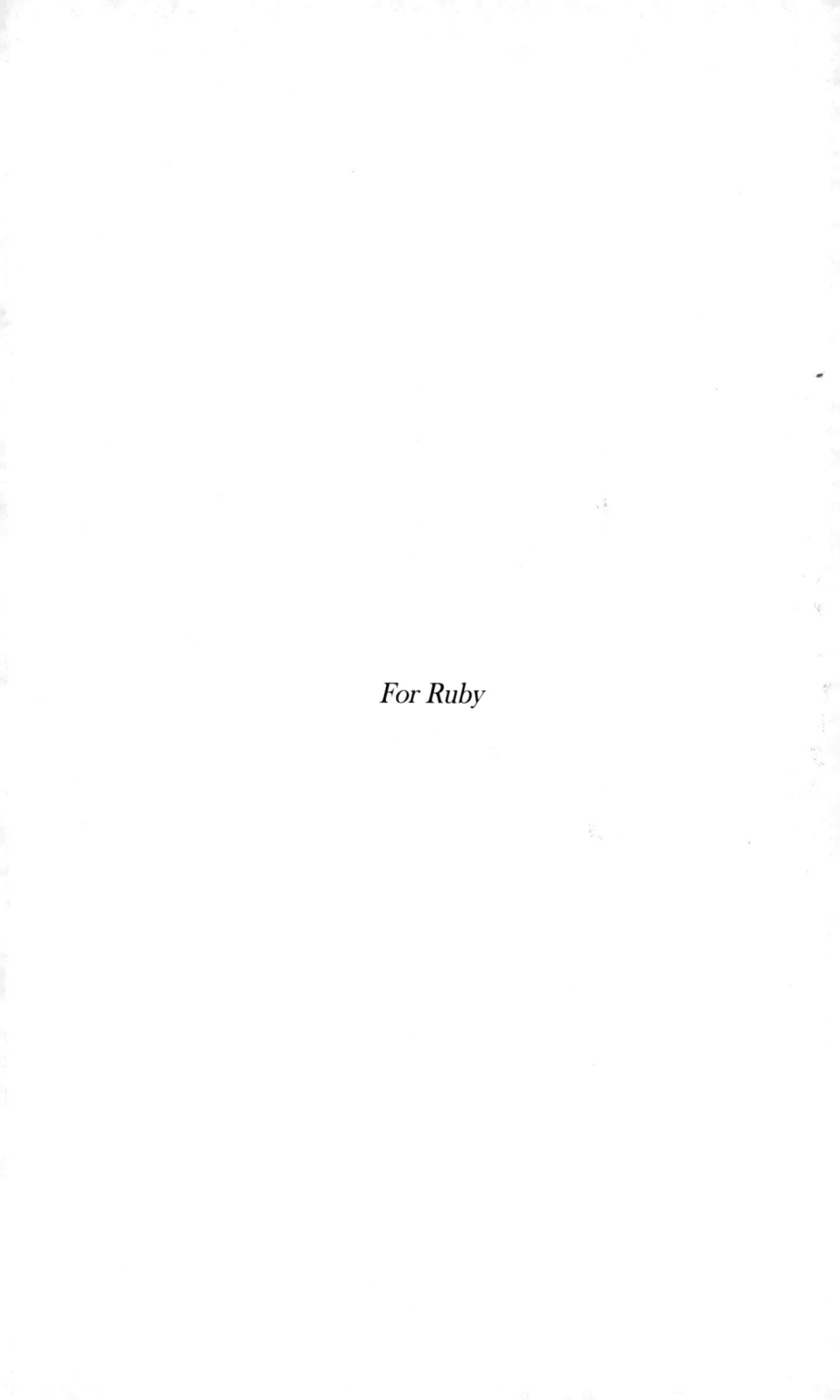

Prologue

Florida Coastline: July 27, 1968

Walter Hyter did not believe in luck; he did not believe in much at all.

With the heat of the day crested and the first hint of cool upon his sweat, Walter exhaled and slumped back, resting his head against the boathouse windowsill. He raised a bottle of cognac to his reed-thin lips and took a long satisfying draw. *Ohhh . . . so bloody good,* he thought, and put the bottle to his lips again and took another large gulp. He was about to speak, when a burp burst up into his nose and his sinuses exploded in an all-out, eye watering brandy buzz. He shook his head, snorted, and whispered to Loretta, "Such a fine mother's milk . . ." Then he leaned forward, nestled his nose in behind her ear and inhaled her scent.

Loretta sat with her legs spread across Walter's thigh, her sweaty spine and long black hair pressed against his chest, her cheap perfume swirling. Walter took another sniff and found the sugary sweetness of the rose intoxicating. He smiled and looked up into the moonlit night, then closed his eyes and said, "*Oh my lord* Governor . . . your celebrations . . . well sir . . . they are *celebratory* indeed."

The boathouse, its boards warped, its shutters set at

odd angles, sat a good three hundred yards from the governor's mansion and had been left derelict for decades. Walter had no interest in the festivities unfolding up the hill; he had what he wanted. Loretta, bought and paid for, was his for the night.

The thick, damp evening air lay heavy in Walter's lungs, and a wheeze was gathering in his throat; and yet all he could think about was how her little ass was burning a hole in his thigh. He was getting hard, *but not as hard as this goddamn bench,* he thought. The bench seat, its surface knobbed and twisted, was made from local hickory and gave no relief to his bony behind. He could feel his legs growing numb, and tingling. He knew he had to get up soon, or look like a damn fool when he did.

At first, the voices were lost to the night, filtering through the mangroves, some making it, some dropping to the forest floor. A second, much stronger wave, a jarring shrill, caught hold of Walter's senses.

"Did you hear that?" he asked.

"Hear what?" Loretta replied; her pupils dilated, her breathing slow and deliberate.

"Down by the pier—something's going on out there," he said, his eyes narrowing. "Slide yourself off me . . ."

Walter stood up and waited a few seconds for the blood to flow back into his legs, then he grabbed Loretta by the waist, pulled her body tight against his, and pressed his nose to her ear. "Don't go away . . . I'm not finished with you."

Walter followed the sounds coming from down the shoreline, keeping close to the edge of a mangrove stand. The tangled forest, skirted by a boulder-strewn beach, provided cover—cover he welcomed as he threaded his way under the soft glow of the moon. It was only when he reached the last forty feet, from the edge of the forest to the pier, that he became concerned; no trees, no rocks, just clean white sand—he would be exposed.

He could see a group of men—young men, he thought—standing near the end of the pier. He was not sure if it was the way they were moving, looking around, darting glances behind them, but they were up to no good; he'd bet on it. He paused, looked back toward the boathouse and then back at the pier, and decided to take a closer look. He crouched down low and duckwalked across the white sand to the foot of the pier, and came up behind a stray mangrove.

The pier was large, jutting out into the water for a hundred feet. Its deck planks, the size of railroad ties, were gray, gnarled, and decayed. Sporadic pockmarks had hollowed into the deck surface, and where bits of earth had been allowed to collect, tufts of ryegrass fought to survive.

Walter knew the pier well; it was where he'd first stepped onto American soil. Built during the Second World War; it was hidden out of sight, far from the manor, and until the late 1950s was used to unload supplies, contraband, illegal immigrants or anything else that could be considered in poor taste to those who slept up the hill. No longer in use, other than to hold fishing derbies for local charities, the pier received little attention.

Walter pulled a thin branch down below his chin to gain a better view. He could not make out their faces, or what they were saying, but the near-full moon provided him with a clear silhouette of the scene being played out.

Two young men were standing at the end of the pier

holding up a third who appeared drunk; his head flopped to one side. Behind them stood a sturdy wooden cross measuring over seven feet tall. From one arm of the cross hung a large spring scale. Its face was like that of a grandfather clock, and from its chin hung a fourteen-inch steel hook, good for weighing marlin and shark. On the other side of the cross dangled a weathered white and blue sign that read: FISHING DERBY.

Two other young men were standing on the opposite side of the pier. The taller of the two was holding a small box in his hand. He shouted something at the boys standing in front of the scale, and then raised the box to eye level. All at once, a squabble broke out, with the boys all hollering and pointing their fingers at each other. Walter turned his good ear toward the commotion. *What in the world are you boys yapping about?*

After a few minutes, the squabbling dropped off. With no real action going on, Walter found himself getting restless, and his mind drifted back to the boathouse and his little playmate. Another long minute dragged. *Fuck this . . .* He had better things to do and was about to turn and leave, when the tall young man yelled at the top of his lungs.

Bloody hell . . . ! Walter thought . . . *I know that voice.*

The tall young man tromped across the pier, grabbed hold of the scale hook and pulled down hard, stretching the spring. He then swung the hook up in a short arc, impaling its steel into the drunk's guts, hooking him just below his ribcage.

Walter cocked his head. *Now . . . this is getting interesting. But what are . . . ?* Then it dawned on him.

Hell's bells, they're weighing the poor bastard. A few moments later, a brilliant flash lit up the end of the pier. "What?" Walter muttered, taking in a short puff of air, "it's a nigger."

A minute later, the young men unhooked the body, dragged it to the edge of the pier and dumped it into a small wooden boat tied to the dock. Walter remained in place until the tiny boat and its crew had motored clear out of sight, then he padded down to the end of the pier.

Walter was not a big man and the scale hook met him at eye level. Using his fingertips, he pinched at the dull hook. It felt syrupy, almost gummy. *Dumb idea,* he thought, and reached down to wipe the blood off onto his pants. Thinking better of it, he stepped to the edge of the deck to dip his fingers into the ocean, and almost crushed it. A pocket camera, its flashcube spent, lay wedged between two rotted deck planks.

Walter stared at it for a moment, then his upper lip stretched tight and rose across his yellowing teeth, revealing a broad, toothy grin. He got down on one knee, rinsed off his fingers, then grabbed the camera and popped off its flashcube before slipping the camera into his pants pocket.

Half walking, half jogging his way back to the boathouse, Walter could feel the camera rubbing against his thigh. He could not believe his luck.

Chapter 1

New York City: October, present day.

The sky flashed above Fresh Foods Garden Market, lighting the parking lot in short blasts of vivid white light. Shoppers scurried to their cars as gusts of wind messed with their expensive hairdos. A middle-aged man in faded blue jeans, his gut mushrooming over his belt, his tweed sport coat flapping in the wind, pressed the trunk release and tossed a couple of bags into his two-seater Italian sports car. A gray-haired woman, slouched at the shoulders with a bag boy in tow, popped the trunk to her tired four-door sedan. Across the lot a gaggle of teenage girls poured themselves into a yellow convertible, all cackling in high spirits as the top folded over them.

Trunks popped, and car doors slammed and the sky continued to roar as O'Henry walked across the tarmac. Given a choice, he would have stayed home, poured a cup of Earl Grey and cozied up to a good book. But since that was not going to happen, he took a deep breath and decided to calm himself. He gazed up and took in the sea gulls. He liked sea gulls. He liked the way they circled around the parking lot lights. He liked to see them fight and squawk over scraps of food. But he wasn't fond of the rain, or the wind for that matter. And he sure as hell didn't like being out in the public domain, especially on such a night. Yet he had to be there. *Really, what choice do I have? It's her night to buy groceries.*

A fine sheet of rain whipped along by a strong gust rolled across the parking lot, slapping O'Henry in the face. Hail, shaped like split peas, pelleted and peppered him and stung his eyes. *I should have stayed home. Why bother coming out? All this unnecessary exposure, mingling with the general populace. What is gained? After all, a trial run is just that, I'm not taking her, not tonight. Taking her . . . soon . . . yes I will.*

As for tonight, he knew why he had come. Few things in life could match the thrill of observing the chosen one, the perfect one, going about her day-to-day living. It brought with it a level of clarity, an intimacy that he found refreshing, exhilarating. He had long ago concluded it the ultimate high.

The rain cranked up a notch and pounded straight down onto the tarmac, instantly boiling on its surface. O'Henry turned up his collar, removed a pair of kid leather gloves from his coat pocket and leaned his long awkward frame into the rain. A fresh sizzle and clap of thunder rocked the sky.

Without warning, a headlight grazed his overcoat, tearing off a button and throwing his coat flap open.

O'Henry stood motionless, staring down at the tarmac. He did not look back, or so much as raise an eyebrow toward the offending car. He was not in the least bit interested in the two tons of metal and plastic that had brushed against him. What consumed him lay at his feet. His gloves—half submerged in the muddy water—were no longer clean. His jaw muscles twitched and adrenaline spilt into his arteries, and for a split second he considered scooping them out of the toxic, infested soup. "Not happening," he said, the words curdling in his throat. He turned and headed toward the store.

Careful to use the heel of his hands, he pushed an empty grocery cart into the store, through a pair of sliding glass doors. A few feet in, he stopped and let the cart come to a rest next to a display of wooden crates filled with potatoes, corn, turnips, and squash. He tore off two tissue-thin plastic bags from a dispenser, slipped them over his hands and sighed. *Grocery stores,* he thought, *bacteria breeding caldrons of muck, loose fungi oozing and spewing spores, infecting everything. Look at them milling about, disgusting, dirty little humans pawing and sniffing at this and that.* Then he stopped in his tracks, cocked his head and felt a thrill run through him. *She's here.*

With his hands safe inside the plastic bags, his panic ratcheted down, and a glorious liberation swept over him. He strolled up aisle one, down aisle two, reading labels as though he cared if his coffee was French Roast or Italian. As he passed the magazine section, he slowed, his gaze fixed on a young woman sipping from her coffee cup while reading an issue of Atlantic Cottages. *You've been out running my dear, haven't you? Oh, I know you have. I can smell it on you.*

He crossed over to aisle three and parked his cart next to a shelf chock-full of canned corned beef. He checked his hands and smiled. The thin plastic was not hindering his grasp at all. So he picked out a bright red and yellow can of corned beef, and noted it came all the way from Argentina.

As he placed the colorful can into his cart, he caught a glimpse of a woman and her two offspring coming down the aisle toward him. He cringed. Adults were tolerated in controlled circumstances, but not this bag of red-necked pus and certainly not her unwashed and underdeveloped genetic blueprints. He shuddered as they squeezed up next to him, feeling their disease crawl upon his flesh. *Too close—you're too damn close.* He could feel the pressure building, his blood pumping into his head. He needed them all to move away, especially the brats, they were the worst: unpredictable, they could at any given moment reach out and touch him. *Bugger off! Get away from me— you simple-minded little cretins!* Then he turned to the woman and said in a tranquil voice, "Madam, have you no concept of social distance?"

"What?" she asked, looking startled, her jaw slack, eyes questioning.

He caught a whiff of her stale tobacco breath and gagged; her putrid essence had entered his body. *This is too much,* he thought, and felt his throat tighten. *Take control, you cannot be sick, not now . . . you must—*

Suddenly, a long, hard dry-heave swept over him, and he buckled and grabbed onto the cart for support. The woman glared at him, then noticed his hands and looked up, a scowl on her face.

"And what the fuck are you gawking at?"

The woman gasped and took a step back, grabbed her children by their hands and dragged them down the aisle; her cart left stranded.

O'Henry watched as the woman and her small brood scuttled away, hand in hand; their collective movements clumsy like that of a land crab. And, as they faded from his view, so did his nausea. He let out a sigh and shifted his gaze, and not more than ten feet away was the chosen one. She was reaching for a box of cookies. "Excellent," he whispered, and again felt the flutter of the thrill; threads of excitement whipping around in his mind, lashing out at memories, sending tremors through to his core until his hands began to tremble. *Not good form old boy . . .* He was taking her too soon, he knew it, but deep inside, he also knew it was worth the risk. He had a timetable to keep.

Some things had changed, and changed a lot, yet the question he'd asked himself so many years ago still remained valid today: Why does a woman feel safe, parading her little package up and down the aisles, picking out this and that for dinner for her loving family, when in reality, she isn't safe at all. . . . He glanced up and said in a hushed voice, "And you're not safe, are you, Jennifer?"

Jennifer was busy reading the contents on a jar of peanut butter.

Having her so close and watching her go about her life, so alive and vulnerable, caused a belly rush to stir inside him. He forced his gut muscles tight against his diaphragm, gripped the push bar and suppressed an erupting giggle. Then he stomped his foot on the floor. *It's like a fucking watering hole in here! The innocent come to drink and get nourishment, while the predator watches and waits. Oh . . . and let's not be so naïve; none of you are innocent, are you?* His gaze darted around the store, his thoughts now raging against the walls of his skull. *You smell your tomatoes and wipe the snot from your little brats' noses, and then go to church and confess, 'Oh yes, bless me father for I have sinned,' . . . but then again . . . I'm not your father . . . am I, Jennifer?*

No! he almost blurted out.

The jar of peanut butter slipped from Jennifer's hand. His arm reached out to catch it, an instinctive impulse as he still stood ten feet back, parked next to the corned beef. If it hit the floor, it would explode, and some twit on the PA would announce 'spill on aisle three.' All that unwanted attention. *And what if a shard of glass flew back and sliced into your perfect skin, what then? You would not be perfect, would you? How could you be . . . ? All my time, all my effort, wasted.* He paused, and a grin crossed his face. *Not that you have to be perfect, not like before, but oh my dear . . . old habits do die hard.*

But the jar didn't hit the floor, and it didn't explode. She'd been fast to react and caught it against her silk dress, pressing it tight against her belly. *Such reflexes, and at the end of a long day.* He sighed and made a mental note.

Then she did the unexpected. She spun her grocery cart around on its back wheels and marched in a straight line toward him. *She's onto me,* he thought, as a line of goose bumps ran across his shoulders and into his hairline. He pondered the situation, then clenched his jaws tight and pushed on toward her, his cart's front wheel pulling left and chirping like a chipmunk.

Good—she's coming straight at me, she will have to look, she will have no choice but to look into my eyes. I know you will Jennifer, you have to. Another step. *Look up Jennifer, look at me!* Another step. Now at his side, mere inches away, he took in her fragrance and shivered with excitement, *Oh God, look at me . . . !* But she did not look, did not so much as throw him a glance. O'Henry's face soured. *And why would she; so beautiful, so perfect . . . they're all the same . . . they've never looked . . . they've never noticed me . . . like I'm a ghost, invisible . . . like I don't exist. But I do exist, Jennifer . . .*

It started with a dull pain in his chest; his heart slogging away, its rhythm jumpy and missing beats. Then a sharp pain radiated into his neck and under his chin, and a patina of fresh sweat formed on his forehead. *So horribly unfair,* he thought.

He took a succession of deep breaths, slow and steady. He had to calm himself; he had gotten too excited, he had to pull back, he had to relax. Then as quickly as it had descended upon him, the ache began to subside and his heart returned to its normal rhythm.

Chapter 2

Standing in Louisiana's Little Bayou River, its muddy waters slapping up against his crotch, Josh Ingram was glad he had gone against Mary's advice and purchased the chest waders. When he first pulled the green boots out of the box, Mary's chin dropped. She told him that any self-respecting noodler knew to go barefoot with nothing on but maybe some old blue jeans and a T-shirt. She also told him that while he was at it, he should wipe that postage stamp smile off of his face. At times she came across as the rough-edged older sister, but he didn't mind; he'd never had one of those before and kind of liked it.

Josh was tall and lean, with a rugged air about him. His coarse black hair defied the laws of uniformity, and his steel-blue eyes carried a warmth and an intensity that was both disarming and unnerving. It was obvious his nose had been broken a number of times, with the resulting raised ridge giving off a distinct hawkish vibe. He could have been described as unforgiving, if not for his broad gentle smile.

Mary stood across from Josh, on the leeward side of the river, hidden in a clump of river reeds and cattails. She was pulling hard on a cigarette, her third smoke of the day, and had a tight grasp on a near empty mickey of Rugger's Lemon Gin. Mary always needed a smoke to get her day rolling, and she always needed a sip of gin too. Because, as she had told Josh years ago: "It tastes good." She took another puff, put the bottle of gin to her mouth and chugged back a couple of gulps, smacking her lips with loud, sloppy satisfaction.

Blocking out her antics, Josh stepped up onto a sandbar and felt the water level drop from his crotch to his knees. He took another step and the toe of his boot hit something solid. As he bent down to check it out, his lower back muscle grabbed and knotted. "Ahhh man," he muttered. It wasn't the first time it had acted up and he knew if he waited, chances were it would soon release its grip. Bent over and clutching his knees with both hands, he waited while Mary, not twenty feet away, continued with her annoying morning ritual.

Mary was short in stature, five-foot-one, wiry, and walked like a lumberjack. Her hair was clipped to just below her ears, and her generous nose sat below her black smoky eyes.

After a long minute of listening to Mary, and satisfied a full spasm had once again been averted, Josh reached down and stuck his hands into the murky water. "Hey Mary—I have something here. I think it's a log . . . and it has a hole under it," he said, with a hint of excitement in his voice. "Whoa—something just nibbled at my fingers."

Josh could hear Mary sloshing around in the reeds.

"Don't go messing with it, I'm coming right over," she said. "I'll show you how it's done." She slipped her mickey back into her vest pocket and parted the bulrushes with her arms. She had on a faded yellow T-shirt, a lightweight open green vest, and baggy blue jeans torn at the knees. She clenched her lit cigarette between her lips as she sloshed over to where Josh stood. "Now don't go getting your panties in a knot. Patience . . . that's what makes a good noodler."

She bent down, grunted, and slipped her hands into the water. "It's a fine log all right," she said, and ran her hands along the bottom of it until she found the hole. "Big hole, could be a big fish." She wiggled her fingers over the opening, the only time-tested way to get a catfish to strike. Nothing. She wiggled them again. Nothing again. She got down on her knees, grunting louder this time, and rammed her forearm deep into the nest. Josh winced in anticipation. No strike, not even a nibble. Determined, she drove her arm further in, until the river water rose to her chin. She rolled her cigarette upwards with her lips, like it was a tiny periscope. "An old hole, I got nothing moving in here," she said and smirked, just as water slapped up under her chin, some of it leaking into her mouth. She spat the water out the side of her mouth, careful to keep her smoke alive. "But—maybe that's what makes you such a fine writer, your wonderful imagination and all."

"Yeah, yeah," Josh said, and lowered his voice. "Oh . . . and speaking of that, I meant to tell you. I have to be in New York, to see Janis the day after tomorrow." He stopped, considered his options and then asked, "Any chance you'd be able to check in on Eddie for a few days?"

"Ahh yeah . . . I guess."

Josh knew that she'd just as soon not have to feed and walk Eddie and pick up his big turds. If there was such a thing as shit envy, Josh figured all the other dogs at the dog park had to be deliriously jealous. Eddie was a large chocolate lab, weighed 115 pounds, slept 23 hours a day, snored like a drunk, and shit like he was laying a pipeline across the prairies.

Mary stood up and locked eyes with Josh. The sun had just burnt through the morning mist, illuminating her face. Her cheeks had flushed to cherry red, as had the tip of her nose.

"Been nippin' at the mash have ya, my love?" Josh asked, and immediately sensed Mary's distaste. The obvious always pissed her off.

Mary's short, raven-black hair was pinned back at the bangs, revealing her latest dye job that had bled out from her hairline. Her cigarette, still lit, hung from her lower lip. With her eyes still locked on his, she took a long drag, and let the gray streams of smoke escape out of her nostrils.

Josh went on. "Ya know, if your face was a baboon's ass, people would say you're in heat."

"Oh, ain't you the funny one . . . if your face was a baboon's ass, they'd have to say your looks have improved." Some real attitude materialized in her eyes, followed by a diminutive grin that soon evaporated.

Mary was small by any noodler standards. Not the frame that would be recommended for pulling a big catfish from its underwater nest. A fully-grown man found noodling tough enough, and she barely tipped the scales at 100 pounds. But it takes more than weight on your side to be a good noodler. Mary liked to say, if you're going to stick your hand in front of a hole and wiggle your fingers hoping a fish half your size clamps down on you, you got to have nerves as hard as a coal miner's lung.

And it wasn't just the catfish you had to be worried about. All seasoned noodlers of the Deep South had their pet stories of fingers lost to snapping turtles. One particularly poignant story Mary liked to recant at Crawlies Pub after a draft or two, was that of Three Fingers Joe. A sad tale to be sure, but not as sad as his sister, Sally Two Fingers. Mary had all her digits and was proud of it.

The noodler rulebook had but one golden rule. Never noodle alone. You can get yourself dragged under, and if you do, you need your buddy there to grab you by your ankles and pull you to shore. At just over six feet two inches and 212 pounds, Josh pondered the logistics of Mary coming to his rescue, but decided to keep it to himself. Mary was like one of those scrappy little dogs, completely unaware of her limitations, and he had no intention of breaking that illusion. He liked her just the way she was.

Long before they could see the approaching vehicle, a dust cloud from its wake announced it was coming their way.

"It's a three-quarter-ton," Josh said. "It's coming fast, bad news I suspect."

"You're so full of shit. It's a half-ton," Mary responded, then added, "and, it's white with blue detailing."

"Detailing? You're so full of shit. It's a three-quarter-ton, no doubt about it, and it's blue."

After a minute, a late-model four-door sedan, brown in color, with Sheriff stenciled in yellow on the driver's door, pulled up and cut its engine. Sheriff Howard Jackson got out of the car and stretched. He was a tall man, in his late fifties, with thinning hair and a chest that had slipped to his belly. And when he'd been out drinking all night, he walked with a pronounced limp. Today Josh could see the sheriff struggling to keep a straight line as he approached.

"Morning, Josh. Mary. You two aren't easy to find," he said. "Having any luck?"

"Only thing we got so far is Josh's imagination."

The sheriff let the comment go. "Josh, I got a call from the Feds in New York this morning. It was a woman, she says they've been looking for you in a big way. She came across stressed, but she sounded darn good on the phone—called herself Rachael Tanner." He shifted his belt. "Heck, with a voice like that I could've listened to her all day."

"Well . . . she knows I'm not in the game, right, Sheriff?"

Sheriff Jackson didn't reply.

"Howard, it's the Noodle Bowl. Mary and I've been planning this since Christ was a cowboy."

"I know that, and I told her it's the Bowl, but she was real persistent. Said she had to talk to you, and if you were to give me any resistance, to tell you that . . . *O'Henry's* back." He paused, scratched at his bald spot, and a frown formed on his face. "Yeah, I think that's right. Yeah, that was his name. Anyway, she said there's more to it, but she wants to tell you in person."

"Well, you can tell her thanks but no thanks," Josh said. "And let's be clear . . . if this really is O'Henry, he stepped on stage long after I'd left the Bureau. It's been ten years, Howard. It's not my problem."

"She said they found a woman, thirty-one years of age, Harvard educated, her whole life ahead of her. Said it's this guy O'Henry's work, and it wasn't pretty. She said she could really use your help before he takes another. She said that they—that is, the FBI—messed up last time and O'Henry disappeared. Now he's back, and they're going to need the best. She told me you're the best there ever was."

Mary rolled her eyes, leaned back, her thumbs stuck in her jean pockets, and said, "Oh, you *gotta* be shitting me."

Josh said, "Come on Howard, I've not heard a word from the Bureau in all these years."

The sheriff had a blank look on his face.

"Ah, goddamnit Howard, tell her . . . tell her I'll . . ." Josh glanced over and could see a storm brewing on Mary's face. "Just give me a second, okay?" He turned to Mary.

"Don't bullshit me Josh, I know that look in your eye; you're already getting ready to commit." Mary started to cough, a dry rasping hack that came upon her at least once a day. "You're unreal, you know that? Some broad strokes your little dick, and that's all it takes to knock you off the ball. It's the Noodle Bowl, Josh. It don't come but once a year."

Josh didn't respond.

"You're an asshole, you know that?"

Josh swallowed. "Look, I'll be in New York anyway to see Janis. I could catch the eight o'clock tonight, get there a day ahead and throw my two cents worth in. End of story. No harm, no foul. And if this is O'Henry, and he takes another life, I'm not sure I'd be okay with myself if I didn't at least talk to her. Maybe it won't make a difference . . . but it'll make a difference to me."

"Yeah, yeah sure, whatever," Mary said. "You know it's going to put you back in the hole. Took you years to climb out. You sure you want to go back in?"

"Thanks Mary, but you worry too much . . ." He could see she wasn't buying it. "Hey, come on. I'll be fine."

Mary shook her head and grunted.

Sheriff Jackson glanced at Josh and grinned. "Nice waders," he said, and then climbed back into his car and drove off, leaving a trail of dust behind him.

Mary paused for a moment, rubbing the palm of her hand on her cheek. "I guess, if you're catching the eight o'clock, we'd better get your tight ass home."

Chapter 3

By the time Josh and Mary had made it back to the marina it was late afternoon. The heat of the day was nearing its peak, the sun hot and punishing. Josh stepped back into the shadow of the marina's Tackle Shop sign, to get some relief. Mary, on the other hand, didn't seem to care and let the sun pound down on her. She had moved to Nevada when she was just a kid, and Josh couldn't remember her ever complaining about the heat.

They agreed to meet back at Crawlies Pub in a few hours to grab a bite to eat, and try to get a hand or two in before he had to leave.

Mary headed over to Crawlies to arrange for an early start to the card game while Josh went in the opposite direction, to the other end of the dock, to his place.

Nine years ago, he'd bought the marina for back taxes owed to the county. It was a large, u-shaped dock with slips for harboring small to midsize sail and fishing boats, providing shelter from the open waters of the Gulf of Mexico. Crawlies was at one end of the dock. Josh's home, or shack as some would call it, was at the other end.

A number of years ago, Josh had coaxed Mary into leaving Detroit and moving south—to start her life over. His offer was a fifty percent interest in Crawlies. He had one condition: she manage it.

They had first met in Detroit, when Mary was lead detective in a serial murder case that had crossed state lines. She had a reputation as a hard ass, who would not hesitate to stomp on her superiors' egos if she thought they'd stepped out of line. Her complete lack of tolerance for authority figures greased her early retirement package and she was let go. Right from the moment he had met her, Josh knew they would be friends.

The exterior of his home had been pieced together from wood salvaged from an old barn. The surface, dull and weathered, always seemed in need of a fresh coat of stain. Josh liked the look of his place and left it alone. It was his, and he could do as he pleased.

Josh opened the door, and was greeted by Eddie, his long tail wagging, his tongue hanging out, giving Josh his signature *haven't-seen-you-in-ages* look. Josh grabbed Eddie's enormous head in his hands and scratched behind his soft, floppy ears. He changed out Eddie's water dish and filled his bowl with fresh food, then paused and smiled at his friend. Eddie had shown up at his place a little over two years ago. He was a stray, not quite a year-old, still in the clumsy stage of all paws and legs. It was obvious Eddie had not eaten in days, his ribs visible under his brown coat, and when no one came forward to claim him, Josh did.

The vet had warned Josh chocolate labs were tough to train, and she was right. After four months of working with Eddie, Josh had managed to get him to sit, and that was when Eddie wanted to. Not to be deterred, Josh registered Eddie with a dog training class at a local pet store. Each dog and owner were positioned in a large circle while the trainer stood in the center and went through the paces. A problem immediately became apparent, which turned out to be Eddie's dominant social gene; it kept dragging Josh across the floor to visit the other dogs. This did not go over well, and in the end Josh found it simpler to attend the classes without Eddie. Suffice to say, Eddie did not progress.

While his home's exterior had a tired look, the interior was in stark contrast. Walnut paneled walls and polished oak hardwood floors, custom stained to the color of deer hide, felt warm and comfortable to Josh. A small, high-end chef's kitchen occupied one end of the room. Well-used pots and pans hung from ceiling racks suspended over a six-burner gas range, and a lattice window taking up most of the kitchen's end wall provided an unencumbered view of the Gulf. And while Josh enjoyed experimenting, trying out new spices, herbs, and a variety of cooking methods, he had an unrelenting weakness for cheeseburgers and French fries. It was a part of his appetite that he tried to control, with varying degrees of success, depending on how hungry he was, and whether he was standing across the street from a burger joint. He loved full-bodied red wines, red ale beers and brandy, but preferred to drink wine in the company of others, which meant he mostly drank brandy and beer.

In the main area an overstuffed dark-brown leather chair faced a smoke-stained stone fireplace. A half-empty box of Brazilian cigars, an empty brandy snifter, and a stack of his current reads covered a round table next to his chair.

Josh dropped into his chair, poured himself a brandy, scratched Eddie behind the ears and opened his laptop to check his emails. After sifting through the usual junk, he found one from Janis, his agent, dated today and marked 'URGENT.' He thought about it, thought some more, then hit delete; with Janis, everything was urgent. The last few years he had grown tired of his protagonist, Detective Vincent Callaghan, and the idea of killing him off and ending the series kept surfacing in his mind. Killing him was easy, telling Janis was the difficult part. She'd take it hard. *Really hard,* he thought. *But ten years is a long run, and ending on a high note is better than a sour one . . . right?* Josh took a long hit of brandy. *Perhaps it's time to have that talk.*

Next came one from Arthur, dated three days ago. He smiled at the thought of getting together with his old buddy, then checked his watch, and decided he'd first book his flight to New York. The net was running slow, and after a few more draws of brandy and a number of failed attempts to secure a seat, it was clear the flight was full and he wouldn't be making the eight o'clock. There were two flights a day, and the next one wasn't until tomorrow at seven a.m. *That means we could've noodled till sundown . . . maybe even snagged my first catfish. Mary's not going to be happy.*

He opened Arthur's email:

Josh, I got something, at least I think I do. I bought a bag of books at Gilbert's auction last week, and was getting them ready for resale, and get this, I found some papers sewn into a book's leather cover. Check out the attachments; one is a contract in Spanish, and look at who signed it. I just about shit myself, has to be him I think, and the other is a picture, or rather half a picture. Pretty weird huh? Go figure.

Anyway, I'm thinking there might be an angle here. Have a look and let me know what you think. Give your detection powers some real exercise for a change.

Arthur

An 'angle' meant money. Arthur was always short of it, but he never accepted a dime of charity. Even as a kid he had been independent to the point of having trouble trusting others. Josh figured Arthur's self-absorbed, alcoholic parents were to blame. Even so, it still wasn't easy to figure Arthur. He had trouble asking for help from others, and yet to Josh, Arthur always seemed needy.

Josh sent the attachments to print, grabbed an open bag of tortilla chips and poured himself another brandy. He found the stereo remote under a stack of magazines. A red elastic band had been wrapped around it, securing a slip of paper. He removed the elastic, unraveled the paper, and hit play. Handel's *Messiah* thundered into the room, and he fumbled with the buttons until he got it turned down. He couldn't remember playing it so loud, or for that matter, what night he last played it. He read the note: Had a great time, please take care of yourself. Becky.

Mmm . . . she's never left a note before—kinda sounds like good-bye. Then it registered. She had stayed over three days ago and for some reason, she'd been hot, hotter than he could ever remember. It was as if she was making a point, not that he minded, even if her unbridled enthusiasm had played havoc with his back.

Neither of them had wanted a commitment, the occasional romp had been good enough. She lived in town, ran a soup and sandwich bistro, loved opera, wrote a weekly article for the town paper, ran in the local marathon, and had an ass that would make your teeth ache. Her visits had kept her balanced and had kept him from having to circulate in town. It had worked well, but the time between encounters was getting longer, and while not said, he knew that the time had come to move on, and she did too.

The printer finished spitting out the first attachment, a two-page contract written in Spanish, then beeped twice signaling it had finished. The second attachment hadn't come through. Josh tried a few times to get the second one to print. No success. He fiddled with the printer, yanked out the ink cartridge, put it back in again and then gave up. *I'll get Arthur to print it off tomorrow . . .* Then he folded the contract and slid it into his pocket.

Exhausted, he flopped onto the couch.

He had been asleep for over an hour when his phone rang. He picked up on the second ring, and before he could say hello, the voice at the other end spoke. "Ingram . . . it's time you woke up." Josh immediately recognized the voice, and a wave of revulsion struck deep inside of him. The voice spoke again. "Come on old chap, wake up—have a look. Your wife wants you to look at her, really she does. It is her last chance—so you'd better . . ." Blood surged into his head as he tried to force his eyes to open—then he smelled the stale scent of the root cellar. "ELLEN!" he screamed and sat up straight on the couch.

It took a few seconds until Josh realized he was alone. As he reached for the brandy snifter, he whispered, "You are so wrong Mary . . . I've not crawled out of that hole."

A minute later, the phone rang. He picked up on the third ring.

"Oh, hi Mary . . . yeah, yeah I'm all right. No, I'm okay. I'll be there in twenty."

After a quick shower, shave, and general cleanup, he was about ready to head out when he noticed a red light flashing on his phone. He hadn't heard it ring and figured it must have come when he was in the shower. He pressed play. *You have three saved messages. Two new messages. First new message:*

"Hey Josh, Arthur here. I tried Crawlies first, Mary told me you should get in tomorrow. And, she said to tell you tonight's flight is full. Sounded pissed, go figure. Like always, never know when you're coming to town . . . anyway, we have to get together and tilt a few. Be great to see you man. Oh and I wanted to let you know my angle worked. I'm meeting with a rep of The George Elhert Foundation tomorrow, and they're prepared to pay a finder's fee, that is, if they think it's legit. The fee's not a lot, but every bit helps, right? Gotta go, call me when you get to town."

Next new message:

"Josh, your father here, sorry I missed your birthday . . . again." His tongue sounded thick. "I'm not always able to tear myself from the boardroom." There was a pause for a few seconds and then his father laughed, a quiet, sad chuckle. Josh heard a paper bag being crinkled followed by a couple of large, pear-shaped chugalugs. "Sorry about that, but I have to keep my strength up. . . . Hey son, I . . ." His tongue getting thicker, his voice slurring more. "I just wanted . . ." Then there was a click, and a dial tone.

Josh put down the phone. His birthday was last summer.

Chapter 4

Josh climbed the three flights of wooden stairs to the front door of Crawlies. It was eight p.m., the place was full, and the other players were already seated at the card table. Anwar Nasser, assistant to the day cook, and Little Bob, the afternoon shift bartender, spotted him first and waved. The remaining two players, first cousins Jacob Milner and Gerald Pampas, had operated old man Milner's shrimp boat ever since high school. They made it to the marina most weekends and tried not to miss Sunday night poker.

The card table was set in a turret-like round room in the far corner of the pub. Surrounded by windows on three sides, it was the best table in the place, with an unspoiled view of the harbor lights.

The smell of fried garlic and onions sizzling in butter reminded Josh he'd not eaten much since breakfast. After ordering a 12-ounce rib-steak, baked potato and Greek salad, he tapped a sleeve of red ale and joined the others at the table. As he sat down he caught sight of Mary dealing with a couple of customers who were giving her a hard time.

Gerald, the younger of the cousins, spoke first. "Too bad about the bowl, not being able to finish and all, and coming home empty-handed. I think Mary's a little steamed."

"Yeah well, it is what it is," Josh said, keeping an eye on Mary as he took a long draw on his beer.

"Hear you're going to New York tomorrow," Little Bob said, a smirk on his enormous face. "And you're not taking the wee lass with you, I take it?" He snickered, and others joined in.

Josh scanned their faces. *What a group,* he thought. "Mary's a handful, I'll give you that, but I'd have her in my corner any time." He could see the two rowdies were not settling down, and then it happened; the biggest and loudest one shoved Mary. *Ah hell . . . now I'm gonna have to go over there.*

"I'll bet you would like to take Mary to New York," Anwar said and chuckled. No one else laughed. Anwar was the socially awkward one of the group. His heart was big as a washtub, but even after twenty years of calling America his home, he still couldn't quite fit in. Anwar stared down at the table with an embarrassed look on his face.

Josh got up from his chair and put his hand on Anwar's shoulder. "Hey Anwar, deal me a killer hand, okay buddy?" Anwar grinned and picked up a deck of cards. Josh pushed his chair back into place and walked over to Mary. "Can I be of any help?" he asked. He couldn't remember their names, but he knew of them; troublemakers from town. He hadn't seen them around for the better part of a year, which suited him just fine.

"Take a hike Ingram, ya New York City faggot," the largest one said, his triceps flexed, stretching his blue denim work shirt to its limit.

Josh looked them over, his pulse at rest, unchanged,

clocking in at sixty beats.

"Do I know you?"

"You're going to get to know us real good," the biggest one said.

Oh please, Josh thought, *no alpha dog drama, not tonight.* He scanned their faces and sighed. *Where do boneheads like you come from anyway?*

Josh would have liked to postpone to another time—and never would have been okay with him. But judging from the big man's pupil dilation, fight-or-flight had kicked in, and he wasn't leaving.

Josh's heart rate climbed a beat. The situation was starting to annoy him. "Look gentlemen, I'd just as soon not have to hurt you, so please go about your business, whatever that may be, and Goliath? Try to stay off of the steroids or your balls will end up shrinking to the size of your brain."

Mary would have said something about not trashing the place, but she'd seen Josh in action before. And in any event, it was too late to move it outdoors.

The two men glanced at each other in disbelief, then spread apart. The big man looked to be in his mid-thirties, stood six foot five, weighed 265 pounds, and could have played pro-ball. *I'll have to take him first,* Josh thought. The other man was a muscled, six-foot, 200 pounder, whose neck was as thick as his head, a stovepipe stuck on his shoulders. Stovepipe's hands were clenched, his feet planted. *Gotta be military or police training.* Josh had seen his type before; he carried the confidence of someone who'd been in a number of scraps and had always come out on the winning side.

Anwar, Little Bob, and the cousins came forward.

Mary blocked them with her arm and told them to leave it be.

Josh analyzed the situation further: the big man stood three feet to his left, stovepipe three feet to his right. And while he hadn't been in a fight in a long time, his training and hard-won experience somehow felt fresh. Instinctively, he could feel it.

Josh knew there were a few rules when confronting multiple threats. First, stay on your feet. On the floor they'll put the boots to you. Second, no holds, you'll get one opponent under control, but that leaves you wide open for attack by the other. Third, no kicking above the crotch. You can be thrown off-balance and then you're back to rule one.

Josh stared into the big man's eyes. "Last chance to leave without a permanent limp," he said, and winked.

"Fuck you, ya arrogant prick." And with that, the big man threw a wild right. Josh countered with an outward block, deflecting the arm, followed by a quick, solid elbow to the man's throat, crushing his windpipe. The big man clutched his neck and began gasping for air. Josh followed with a low, roundhouse kick catching the big man behind his legs, dropping him to his knees. Josh then pivoted on his left leg, swinging around to gather torque, and with his right foot stomped down on the back of the big man's ankle causing a loud pop, the sound resonating on the faces in the crowd. The big man fell over, howling.

Stovepipe caught Josh with a jab to his ribs. Josh sidestepped the second blow, turned and stood at ninety-degrees to his opponent, then caught Stovepipe with a direct right to his side, cracking two of Stovepipe's ribs. He then grabbed Stovepipe's arm, elbow first, and in a clean up and back motion, rotated his arm over his head, and when it had reached the end of its range of motion, he wrenched on the arm and heard a distinct *crack*. The upper arm had broken loose of the shoulder socket, and Stovepipe fell to the floor in agony. Josh spun around to see the big man stumble as he tried to get to his feet. The fight was over.

A good outcome, Josh thought. He brushed himself off, checking his hands and knuckles. No scrapes, a sore rib, but no permanent damage, and his back had held out.

He turned and saw Mary assessing him. She was not smiling.

Chapter 5

Armored to the teeth, the black sedan wound through the bucolic autumn countryside of Upper New York State. Walnut and oak trees brushed with strokes of mustard and crimson dotted the pastures. And as the sun surrendered to the night, a surreal pewter sky descended and cast its dense blanket over the hills. All of which was lost on the sole occupant in the back seat. Everyone knew the governor hated to be alone.

The sedan slowed and turned off on a dirt road, passed through a wooden gate and over an iron cattle crossing, the bulletproof tires riding hard. The road narrowed and the sedan's headlights bounced off a forest of birch and poplar that encroached from either side. The sedan continued for close to a mile, then came out into a clearing. It rolled on another thirty yards and stopped next to the last cabin at the end of a row, overlooking Pickerel Lake.

Fifty feet of brush and pine trees separated each cabin, providing more than adequate privacy, though that was a non-issue this time of year. All the other cabins had been closed up for the winter weeks ago.

The driver rushed around to the back door and opened it. The governor unfolded his long body and stood up straight. Two other men, who had been awaiting his arrival, stepped down from the back deck of the cabin to greet him.

"Is he here?" Governor Elhert asked.

Petruski and Quincy both nodded.

"He's out front," Quincy said. "Got here before us, he's sitting on the front porch. Wouldn't so much as give us the time of day . . ."

Governor Elhert raised an eyebrow and nodded. Then they all went into the cabin.

Birch logs crackled in the fireplace, and a trace of the sweet scent hung in the air. The room was small and rustic, comprised of a simple living room and compact kitchen separated by a peninsula. In the center of the room was a small, wooden table. On the table sat a video projector and a coffee pot. A dozen feet from the table, a white bed sheet had been thumbtacked to the wall and draped to the floor.

Governor Elhert threw his coat over a chair and turned to Quincy. "Okay. Bring him in, let's get this over with." The governor was a tall, almost handsome man, with a strong jawline that seemed at times more important to the media in New York than his stand on the issues.

Quincy crossed the room, opened the front porch door and turned to Demetrius. Demetrius was leaning back on the porch swing, taking in the lake, his massive legs extended and crossed at the ankles, his fingers knitted behind his head.

"The governor's arrived. He will see you now."

Demetrius stood up, his knees popping and protesting under the burden of his bulk. He was a big man, black-skinned and heavily-muscled, with a beach ball gut, and wrists so massive his cuffs had to be left unbuttoned. His eyes were large and his cheekbones were high and round, providing a soft contrast to the rest of him. He followed Quincy inside, ducking his head as he stepped through the doorway. He took a few deep breaths and hoped he didn't look too old and tired.

Governor Elhert walked up to Demetrius and shook his hand. "Demetrius, so good to see you," he said, with familiarity and candor.

"Been awhile, Governor."

"Awhile, yes it has, and please Demetrius old friend, call me William. I think it's been what, almost twenty years," Governor Elhert said, and reached for the coffee pot. "God, time does get away, doesn't it?"

"Twenty-eight years I believe," Demetrius said, surveying the room before returning his gaze to the governor.

Governor Elhert grinned, and held out a cup of coffee to Demetrius. "That long? Unbelievable. Seems just yesterday . . ." Elhert paused. "You're looking well, life next to the equator seems to agree with you."

"I guess so," Demetrius said, his gut sending him mixed signals. He smiled.

Quincy cleared his throat.

Governor Elhert glanced at Quincy. "My apologies gentlemen. You all know Demetrius from your dossiers, but Demetrius, let me introduce you: on your left, is Ronald Petruski, Deputy Chief and Head of Security."

Petruski, a short wiry man, was sucking hard on a cigarette stub, trying to get out the last bit of nicotine. He stopped, looked up, and reached out to shake hands. His slender white fingers, the tips stained burnt yellow, stood out in sharp contrast to the large, black hand extended to him.

"And to your right—"

"John Quincy, Chief of Staff and Chair of the Finance Committee," Demetrius said. "I've been out of the country, but New York is my home state, and I like to keep track of what's going on. And for that matter, would you mind telling me why are we meeting here? Not the most convenient spot."

"Quite—you're right of course," Governor Elhert said. "But we needed somewhere private, out of the media's field of view. Quincy comes here on occasion; he's a fishing buff, and this place certainly fits for being off the beaten path. So, here we are."

Quincy, a heavyset man with broad, sloping shoulders and more than ample neck fat scanned Demetrius, his eyebrows pinched at the bridge of his nose as he filed his mental notes. He reached out to shake Demetrius's hand. "Demetrius? Isn't that Greek?"

Demetrius's hand enveloped Quincy's in a soft, relaxed grip. "My old man was a truck driver, preferred to think of himself as a historian of sorts—loved the Mediterranean. He gave me the handle." He turned his attention back to the governor.

"Well, good . . . enough of the formalities," Governor Elhert said. "Demetrius, as you are no doubt hearing from the media, the race is close. We'd like to think we'll push it over the top, at least that is what I'm hearing from my people; but the reality is, the vote will be a tight one, too close for our boys and girls to call. So we are not taking any chances. A full road trip is set to start in a few weeks, and will run nonstop right up to the big day. A tremendous undertaking. If a trip to the washroom isn't on the agenda, it won't be happening." He took a sip of his coffee and added, "We simply can't let anything go wrong if we are to win, and mark my words, we will win." Then he hesitated and let out a long breath. "The reality is, we're doing all that we can to secure a margin of comfort, an edge if you will, then hold on to it until election day."

"You've never been one to let things go to chance," Demetrius said, and saw the subtlety was picked up on by the governor.

"Quite," Governor Elhert acknowledged, and paused. "There is a situation . . . a problem that may be of some concern for us. At least we in this room think we should tidy up this loose end. Not leave anything to chance, as you say."

Governor Elhert turned and faced Demetrius. "There's been an abduction," he said, letting the words hang in the air. "The victim has a shared history with my father; he was both a trusted advisor, as well as my father's close personal friend—at least that is, for most of their lives. This goes back a long way, to the early days. Back to when my father was making his mark in commerce, and later as he established himself in the political arena. Walter Hyter, 'Uncle' as we called him, showed up at our home often. My first recollection of him was in my teen years when we lived in Florida. Of course, my interests didn't stray much from tight skirts and other adolescent pursuits. And yet, I couldn't help notice this unusual little man who occupied so much of my father's time."

Cradling his cup in his hands, Demetrius waited for the governor to continue.

"Walter and my father met in college and remained friends for close to forty years. I can remember them always huddled together, scheming and planning this and that. They were inseparable. Depending on who is the one recalling their history, the story of their parting boiled down to finger-pointing. In a nutshell, a deal had gone sour and their friendship ended."

"Okay Governor, I'll bite. How does this affect you and your reelection?" Demetrius asked. "And for that matter, how do I fit into all of this?"

Governor Elhert turned to Petruski and Quincy, and gave a nod. Petruski picked up the remote and Quincy dimmed the lights.

"Have you heard of a group that call themselves the Red Panthers, out of Guatemala?" the governor asked.

"No, I don't think so, should I?"

"No, not too many have. The eggheads in the CIA claim little interest in them, not viewing them as a real danger. In any event, they're known in their own backyard, but not so well over the fence."

"A bunch of fucked-up misfits," Quincy said.

"Right." Governor Elhert acknowledged. "But misfits with a few distinctive features: they are better organized than most and have direct ties to the most senior ranks of the Guatemalan Government, and it goes without saying, they are anti-American."

Governor Elhert glanced at his subordinates and back to Demetrius.

Demetrius's voice tightened. "Governor, I know you would not be seeing me here tonight without good cause, so if you wouldn't mind, please just lay it out—spill the beans, plain and simple."

"Demetrius, please watch the screen, I think it'll help." The governor leaned toward him. "As you know, in his prime my father, was one of the most influential men in America, perhaps the most, depending on which biography you read. He was a personal friend of the Oval Office during the Cold War and before. He had many friends and of course enemies, and yet through it all he kept his most loyal advisor, Walter, by his side. In fact, Walter accompanied my father to the White House on a number of occasions. Having said that, it takes little extrapolation to figure out that this strange little man, who sat so close to my father, could have classified information that, if divulged to the wrong people or *more accurately* to those wanting to hurt this administration, could do just that."

"So, you think he's given sensitive intel to this group?"

"Goddamn terrorists," Petruski blurted out.

"Yeah right," Demetrius said without conviction. "As I was saying Governor, do you think this group now has information that will hurt your reelection?"

"Maybe, maybe not, but Walter is a loose end, or loose cannon, probably both. And 'the group' as you call them, have him at the moment, and so it behooves us to deal with them. We believe they are controllable—at a price."

Demetrius raised an eyebrow. "And you will pay it?"

"If it makes a difference to the election outcome, damn straight we will," Governor Elhert said. "Power is everything. One day you're governor of one of the largest states in the country, bigger than many countries in the world, and the next . . . well, you're on the Speaker's circuit getting paid to let people get close to you. Like an aging rock star, or perhaps a novelty act at the state fair, not sure which."

"So you pay, and what if they don't live up to their

side of the bargain and keep Walter?"

"That's where you come in, you're our insurance policy. We figure that by paying them, we will have at least bought some time. Time that you can use to find Walter. On the other hand, if they give us Walter, then all is good. And, if they are playing games, we will at least know where Walter is being held, and we can arrange an extraction, removing him from harm's way."

"Uh-huh," Demetrius said, not believing a word of it.

Governor Elhert nodded to Petruski.

"We received this a few days ago," Petruski said. "You'll note the time and date, 2:45 p.m. October 3rd, shown in red, in the bottom right-hand corner of the screen." He hit the play button and the screen lit up.

A young man in his late twenties wearing blue jeans, a crisp white T-shirt, and a black baseball cap came into view. He had a red bandana covering most of his face. "Governor Elhert, we have a friend of yours, or should I say a friend of your father's. Say hello to your Uncle Walter. Walter, you're on camera."

Walter pulled at the loose skin that hung from his jaw and frowned. "Turn down the lights, they're hurting my eyes," he said, and looked around as though he was lost and didn't understand what was happening. "I'm an old man with many problems," he pleaded, blinking into the bright lights. He dropped his gaze for a second, then zeroed in on the camera, and stuck his face in close to the lens. "Governor, I think these fine young chaps are intent on stirring up some old ashes," he said, his bloodshot, yellowing eyes straining in the bright light. He stopped, turned to his captors and cried out: "I *said* turn down the lights!"

Walter then began to rub his left knee with both hands as if he was trying to think of what to say next. He flinched as he straightened out his leg and said, "Your father was a great man, a colleague; I will not—"

"Walter, please don't do this," the lead captor said. "We all know you will give us the details, it's only a matter of time. So, let's not waste time playing these games." The lead captor waited for a few seconds and then added, "Our request is simple. You will deliver a sum of five million dollars in uncut diamonds, a small sum I think. And then we will give you your dear old uncle. It's a simple exchange, and simple is always best. Yes?"

There was a short pause, and Demetrius sensed the governor was watching him.

"Governor, we are not greedy men," the lead captor said. "We are business men such as yourself. You make deals all the time, and this time you will cut a deal with us . . ." His face soured. "Enough of this. We will call you in one week and make arrangements for the drop."

"They know nothing," Walter blurted. "The only thing these punks will get out of me is snot on their faces." He leaned in to the camera again. "Governor, rest assured, as long as the moon shines down upon the sea, they won't hear a peep out of me. Hell's bells, I'm so old, in a *flash* I could be gone, off the *hook* so to speak."

The projector went to blank white.

"What's that last bit about?" Demetrius asked.

"We have no idea," Petruski said.

"The question was for the governor."

"Not a clue," Governor Elhert said with conviction. "But having said that, one thing is for certain, any negativity against my family's name, real or not, is something we simply cannot leave to chance. Not at this stage in the game."

"Governor, it seems to me with all the resources at your disposal, discrediting an old man's ranting about some distant activity shouldn't pose a major problem," Demetrius said.

"A valid point and you could be right, but the man rode with my father for over forty years. A long time for things to happen and in the end it always boils down to the big question—what if? No. The risk is far too great, and let's be clear, Walter *will* spill his guts sooner or later."

Governor Elhert's voice then took on a sincere tone. "Demetrius I am asking for your help. I need you to locate Walter before he unlocks any skeletons that could hurt this office. I need you to provide us with the location of where they're holding him, that is all. We will take care of the rest."

"The rest?"

"My team will be sent in for the extraction, if necessary."

"Your team?"

"My team." Governor Elhert smiled.

"God knows you have the resources. Why me?"

"For the simple fact that we are a month away from election day, and this administration cannot have a tie to anything that could impede our momentum. Look, if my opponents get a whiff of anything decaying in our fridge, before you know it there'll be a leak to the press, there always is, and that's when the shit will hit the fan. No . . . it has to be this way."

"There's more to it . . . you're not laying all your cards on the table, are you Governor?"

Governor Elhert stepped in close. "Demetrius, your experience in hide-and-seek covert operations is extensive, and you're good, very good, at what you do. And you've been living in Central America for quite some time now. You know the terrain, have the contacts, and most of all I know I can trust your judgment, not to mention your willingness to be discreet." Governor Elhert smiled his acceptance speech smile. "Demetrius old friend, will you help me out?"

"I appreciate your endorsement Governor, but could it be my absence from the country for more than two decades, and my lack of contact with you all these years, that has tipped the scale?"

Governor Elhert's eyes narrowed.

"Five percent," Demetrius's voice rang out, then drained the last of his coffee. As he scanned their faces, he thought, *enough to pack it all in and get out of this stinking business.*

"Five percent?" Governor Elhert asked.

"Of the ransom," Demetrius replied.

"Two hundred and fifty grand is a lot of money, Demetrius."

"Oh, I don't know, I get the feeling that the election is worth every cent."

Governor Elhert looked to Quincy.

"It can be worked out," Quincy said.

"Well, that's it then," Governor Elhert said. "Demetrius, I'm counting on you to get the job done. We'll contact you in two days, you'll need to have made progress by that time."

"I will need resources, fifty grand up front to start, for expenses," Demetrius said.

"I will make the arrangements," Quincy spoke up.

"Also, I need the video," Demetrius said. "I trust there's a duplicate?"

"Yes, there's a duplicate," Petruski replied.

Governor Elhert said, "Okay then . . . there is one last thing Demetrius, and it should go without saying; any further communication with this office will be through Petruski, on secured lines. You and I will never speak again, for reasons which I'm certain you can appreciate." The governor passed Demetrius the DVD and shook his hand. "Don't let me down."

Demetrius made his good-byes and left the cabin.

Governor Elhert turned to Petruski. "Mark him, tag him, every move, every phone call. When he wants to take a walk, you'll know how far and why he's going. Are we clear on this?"

"Very clear, Governor."

"And, if anything, and I mean *anything* goes wrong, we've never heard of the big, black bastard, understood?" Governor Elhert said, buttoning up his coat, his face cold and calculating. "This had better be the last loose end. Too many fucking loose threads."

Chapter 6

A yellow cab eased to the curb at 288 Parklane Avenue, in central Manhattan, outside the office building of Janis Walton. Josh checked his watch; he was a full twenty-five hours early for their scheduled appointment. He'd received a text message at LaGuardia. The message was clear: Catch a cab and come straight from the airport. Take no calls and speak to no one. As he read it, he thought, *This is a first, rigid schedules are what Janis lives for, stepping off the dotted line is way out there.*

Josh climbed out of the cab and handed the driver thirty dollars for a twenty-five dollar fare.

It was quarter past nine in the morning, and the air smelled of pretzels and spent diesel fuel with a trace of burnt rubber. The street vendors had been set up for hours. Josh spotted his favorite and strolled over. He had missed certain things about New York, and Leon Gimbalinni's Coffee Stand was one of them. Gimbalinni's stainless steel wagon rested in its usual spot, its side panel glinting in the reflected light of an office window across the street. As Josh approached, the pungent aroma of fresh, strong coffee greeted him. The old cigar posters from the days of Leon's father were long gone, as was his father's wooden cart, and yet the spot where the original wagon sat had never changed. Fresh stacks of newspapers were piled on the counter and Josh knew a box of fine cigars could be found hidden underneath, on the first shelf.

Leon's eyes brightened as Josh stepped up. "Well! Mother Mary, Joseph, I don't believe it," Leon said, beaming a broad smile from under his bushy, black mustache. "You've been gone a long time. Too long, Mr. Ingram. Far too long." Then he reached out and shook Josh's hand.

Josh smiled. "Yeah, it's been ages."

"Where you been, Mr. Ingram? I'd thought you'd bought the big one. Come to think of it, I think I read it somewhere."

Josh had tried years ago to get Leon to call him by his first name, but for some reason Leon was more comfortable with Mr. Ingram; the name had stuck and Mr. Ingram he remained.

"Kind of feels like old times . . ." Josh said. He grabbed a paper, folded it, and tucked it under his arm. Then he noticed a half-healed scab over Leon's left eye.

Leon picked up on it. "Yeah, it's getting better. New competition in town." He tilted his head toward a large, van-like vendor parked fifty yards down the street. "They tried to, you know, get the spot." Leon poured a cup of coffee and handed it to Josh. "No one takes my spot," he said with pride.

As Josh started to pull some cash from his pocket, Leon raised his hand. "Please, Mr. Ingram."

Not wanting to offend his friend, Josh let the cash drop back into his pocket. "It's great to see you, Leon."

"Good to see you too, Mr. Ingram," Leon said, and reached under the counter, pulled out a couple of cigars and stuffed them into Josh's jacket pocket. "You'll need these; help keep you warm, a clipper she's sliding down from Canada."

Josh gave Leon a big grin. "Hey, you think the Giants have a shot this year?"

"I'm counting on it." Leon smiled. "Have yourself a great day, Mr. Ingram."

Josh shook Leon's hand, then turned and started up the steps to the tower.

Leon watched Josh for a moment, then poured himself a coffee and took his seat. He got himself comfortable, laid out a paper and scanned the headlines. When he reached page three, his eyes lit up and he took in a short breath. By the time he'd made it to his feet, Josh had already entered the building.

The North Tower foyer swarmed with the usual sleep deprived, caffeine addicted bunch. The express elevator opened and a horde crammed in ahead of Josh. He waited and took the next elevator, which was thankfully almost empty. In less than a minute, the elevator had reached its first stop, the 56th floor.

Josh stepped out into one of the few places on earth a writer is ever recognized, his agent's office. Two young women sat at the center of a twelve-foot-long teak reception desk shaped in the form of a crescent moon. They both looked up as he walked over from the elevator, holding their gaze on him. *I've been gone awhile, but not that long.*

"Good Morning Claire, good morning Bonnie. So tell me, what's going on?"

"Hi, Mr. Ingram," Claire said, a sadness in her tone.

Huh? Josh thought.

"Janis is waiting for you," Bonnie said. "She said you should go straight in."

Go straight in . . . ? Another first. "Thanks Bonnie." He walked to the end of the hall, took a right and stepped into Janis's office.

Janis was on the phone, and smiled when he entered, but she too had a sadness about her. She covered the phone with her hand. "I'll be just a moment, make yourself comfortable." She swiveled her chair away from Josh to face the office window. "He's here now, I'll get back to you."

She hung up, swung her chair back around, and gave a weak smile.

"What?"

"Have you read the paper?" Janis asked, looking at the one under his arm.

"Not yet . . . Why . . . ? What's up?"

"Oh, Josh. I have terrible news."

"What are you talking about?"

"Josh, please sit down." Janis pointed at a chair, looking as though she might cry.

"I'll stand—and for Christ's sake—what's going on?"

"I don't know how to tell you. It's Arthur."

"What about him?"

"He's gone."

"What do you mean, he's gone?"

"I mean," Janis's voice softened to a whisper, "I mean he's gone."

"Gone? He can't be, I'm meeting him later. What do you mean, he's gone?"

"Jesus, Josh. I mean, Arthur . . . is dead. I'm so sorry."

"Bullshit. We're having a drink together this evening."

Janis stepped closer and put her hand on his arm. "I am so sorry Josh. I wish it wasn't true."

Josh let go of his coffee cup. It hit the floor, the contents fanning out across the carpet. He knew he'd heard the words, but they weren't making sense, they didn't seem to have anything to do with him. He sat down on the arm of the chair, paused for a moment until he'd processed what she had said, and then asked, "When?"

"Yesterday, last night some time, we haven't been getting much detail from the cops. Just what's in the papers."

"How did it happen?"

"I don't know. Like I said, the police are being tight-lipped about it. The paper says foul play is suspected, but those pricks deal in half-truths, can't rely on them getting anything straight."

"Foul play? Who would hurt Arthur? He's a butterball; not a mean bone in his body. Come on! Nobody's gonna hurt him."

At that moment Arthur's death sunk in and became real. Without warning, Josh's thoughts plunged deep into a corner of his mind he thought he'd sealed off forever. A cold, calculating sector; a space without empathy, a space that understood how monsters saw the world. A corner of his mind he'd never intended to access again.

"*Good God Josh,* you just gave me the most God-awful shiver," Janis said and hesitated for a second. "I am really so sorry."

"I know you are," he said, and took notice of the mess on the carpet.

49

"Forget that." Janis picked up her phone. "Bonnie, have my car brought around."

"No . . . it's all right, thank you . . . I'll walk back. I need some time to think." Josh looked at Janis. "It'll do me good."

"Never mind, Bonnie." She hung up the phone. "Josh, if I can be of any help . . . you'll call me, right?"

"Sure. I'll be at the hotel, and if you hear thing . . . ?"

"Yes, of course," she said.

Josh left the office tower and headed back to his hotel. The moist, acrid air had turned cold and cut into the corners of his eyes.

Not a tear formed.

Chapter 7

The FBI's New York Special Crime Unit was located on the top floor of a low-rise office building in Lower East Side Manhattan. An unremarkable Cold War concrete hovel, devoid of personality, a domicile where anyone contemplating suicide would feel right at home. Row after row of gray metal desks jam-packed the room, partitioned by neck-high walls that failed to provide even a shred of privacy. A slew of dry conversations ricocheted around the bullpen, while two office runners, dressed in jeans and pale blue shirts, crisscrossed the room, darting in and out of the tight spaces.

Along the outer walls were the offices of the senior agents, each with a single window to the outside. The corner offices were for team leaders, each with two large windows and a door that locked.

Rachael Tanner closed the door to her corner office, kicked off her new shoes, plopped down on her small, low-backed sofa and rubbed her feet together. She would have loved to put her feet up on the coffee table, but today's dress choice would not allow it.

Rachael was five foot nine inches tall, athletic and lean like a runner. She carried an intensity about her that made most men uncomfortable, and a glow that kept them looking. Her fiery gray-green eyes, full lips and high cheekbones were framed by a determined jawline that left no doubt as to her resolve.

Just ten minutes, that's all I need, she said to herself, and let her head rest back against the wall. Not a minute later, she exhaled, sat up, and pressed the play button on the remote, and an old videotaped talk show came to life.

"And we're back, and tonight we have Josh Ingram, author extraordinaire, with us. A man known to us all through his seven Detective Thrillers. Is that a genre? Yes, I think so," the talk show host said, answering his own question. "So tell us Josh, where do you get your ideas? Do they come from your own experiences? Do you dig them up from your past?"

"Sometimes I do, I mean, I may take a certain incident from my past—could be significant or not so significant—then I plant it in my imagination and see what happens."

The door burst open and Riley entered Rachael's office, holding a tray with two cups of coffee. "Sorry, is this a bad time? Thought you might need a fix."

Rachael hit pause. "Thanks." She sat up straight, reached out, and wrapped her hands around a cup. "Grab a chair. I'm running some background on our Mr. Ingram."

Riley sat down directly across from her. "Sure is piss-poor timing for your team. Rumor has it you've asked Ingram to assist with the O'Henry file."

"Rumor?"

Riley grinned. "Yeah well, I overheard Kingsley going on about it on the phone, wasn't clear who he was talking to, but it's probably not that tough to figure out. . . . Kingsley has it in for you, you know."

"Yeah . . . I know."

Riley continued. "It's gonna be a little difficult to get Ingram onside now, don't you think? That is, with his friend Arthur getting hit and all."

Rachael paused and thought about how much she should say. "Sure, that's been dancing around in my head a bit—so I decided to give my old unit in Miami a call. Asked if they could use some help at this end, poke around at Arthur's crime scene. Give them my opinion, see if anything needs following up from their end. That sort of thing. The way I figure it, if I'm in the door on Arthur's file, maybe I can work something out with Ingram on O'Henry's file. . . . It's worth a shot," she said, and pushed the play button.

Riley raised an eyebrow and half smiled.

The talk show host went on. "So tell us Josh, is it true that Arthur has always been your friend, all the way back to your childhood?"

"Absolutely, we've been friends, it seems like forever. He keeps me grounded."

"It's a well-known fact that you place him somewhere in each of your novels, an Alfred Hitchcocky sort of thing. Is that a word? I don't think so." The host answering his own question again. "But c'mon, some of the predicaments you put him in, let's just say they're a bit *unbecoming*." A smirk cut at the corners of the host's mouth. "Come on Josh, fess up. Is Arthur really okay with your pranks?"

Josh pulled at his earlobe and just looked at the host, and neither spoke for a long moment. Rachael hit pause.

"Ever wonder what goes on in a mind like his?" Rachael asked.

"I did. When he was on the team. A long time ago. Sometimes . . . yeah, I wondered a lot."

She hit play.

"Yeah, it's true," Josh said to the host. "I get a kick out of including him in my novels, and some of the situations I place him in are a little unusual—writer's discretion I suppose—but we both laugh about it. He's a good-natured guy, a decent guy. I don't think many other people would've put up with me over the years."

"He doesn't mind you making him look a fool?" the interviewer asked, leaning into Josh's space. "I mean aren't you even a little afraid of getting a call from say, his lawyer?"

"You don't know Arthur," Josh replied, a cutting acidity in his voice.

The talk show host said they had to cut to a break, and when they come back, Josh Ingram would talk about his new novel. Rachael hit the pause button again.

"Not gonna drink your coffee?" Riley asked, looking her up and down.

Rachael cringed. "Oh right, thanks." Then she shifted her position on the couch, turning her bare knees away from him.

"So what do ya think about last night? Narrillo and the bookstore owner, you think there's a connection?" Riley asked.

Rachael thought about it. "A connection to organized crime? Could be. I mean, John Narrillo in New York, in a bookstore after hours, shot once in the gut and once in the chest. Not what I'd call a random event." She lifted her cup to her lips, and said, "But how a bookstore owner such as Arthur fits in? I don't see it."

It was then she noticed Riley's gaze was locked on her thighs; her black pencil dress had slid up an inch or two. She put down her cup, shifted her weight, and pulled the hem of her dress to her knees, making a clear point of her discomfort. All of which went a mile over Riley's head. *This guy is a real pig . . .*

"And what of Ingram?" Rachael asked. "You would know more about him than most. How does he fit in? He was, by all accounts, a close friend of Arthur's."

Riley's tone was defensive. "He doesn't fit in. Josh was a *friend* of Arthur's, that's all."

Strange, she thought, but decided not to press further, not now anyway. She was new to the unit and still trying to get the team to jell. Riley had his faults, no question about that, but he also had a reputation for being competent, and she knew she might need his cooperation or that of one of his team members down the road.

"So tell me, was Ingram as good as they say? I mean, his Case Solved Ratio was off the charts. It's amazing when you think his methodology was part of the curriculum at the academy. At least it was when I attended."

Riley finished off his coffee. "He was a talented guy, what can I say? He connected dots on cases when we didn't even know the dots existed. Had a sixth sense, bloody unreal at times. The best profiler the bureau ever had. But that's history, he bowed out long ago."

"Yes, of course," she said, acting as if she knew all about it. "Has Ingram made any contact since he left?"

"Not that I know of. He's kept to himself. Got totally screwed when his wife, Ellen, died. He just couldn't stay around any longer. Moved to somewhere near New Orleans. Took to writing and has apparently done well."

"Copy that," she said, then paused for a second. "That's right, Riley. You were the one, the one who found Ingram that day in the cellar. So, what did go down? I mean, you find Ingram in the cellar, sitting cross-legged on the dirt floor, drenched in blood, the perp lying next to him, beaten to a pulp, dead. And Ingram is just sitting there, staring at his dead wife."

Riley looked away, avoiding eye contact, got up and reached for the door. Stopping, he turned to her. "You know, Ingram was just too smart for his own good. . . . But if you need a place to start with catching O'Henry, I think you've made a strategic move asking him. That is, if Ingram is still willing to help."

"Thanks," she said, and gave a faint smile.

Riley added, "Ingram was a good guy. The goddamn nightmare he went through . . . nobody would be right after that." Then he stepped out and closed the door.

Rachael put down her cup and thought for a moment, then got her assistant on the phone and asked her to track down Josh Ingram. He should have made it to town by now.

Chapter 8

The cold front arrived as Leon had said it would, and the twenty-two-minute walk from Janis's office to the hotel was just long enough for the frigid air to seep through his coat and numb his shoulders.

Josh opened his hotel room door and stepped into a blast of hot, welcoming air. He tossed his coat on a chair, sat down on the side of the bed and called room service. He ordered a double brandy, and noticed the message light was flashing on the phone. He pressed play.

"Josh . . . Rachael Tanner here. I know about Arthur, and I am so sorry about your friend. Look, I know you have a lot on your mind, I get it, but I do need to speak with you, so please, please call me. And I know I shouldn't ask this, but if at all possible, I'd like to see you tonight . . . this evening. Please call me."

Josh flopped back on the bed, and with his hands behind his head, stared up at the ceiling and tried to remember every detail of Arthur's face. All he could come up with was a vague outline; his best friend had already started to fade, and as that thought sunk in, a slow ache wrapped itself around him. Then his thoughts shifted to his father, and his father's decision to slip into the shadows. *What's he doing right now? Is he safe? I should check in on him, and soon. But not today. Then again—why the fuck not today?*

O'Henry

He heard a knock at the door. Room service dropped off the brandy, placing it next to the TV. Josh took a long draw, then punched in Rachael's number.

When she picked up, she sounded stressed, but relieved that he had called. They agreed to meet at McClinty's, a local pub, around nine p.m. Drained of energy, his insides warmed by the brandy, he reached over and set the alarm.

Chapter 9

Josh entered McClinty's Pub at ten past nine; the lighting was dim and it took a moment for his eyes to adjust. When they did, it was as though he had stepped into a warm memory. Nothing had changed: the alcoves paneled in dark walnut, the oak bar lit by copper ship lights hanging overhead, and the half-full gallon jar of pickled eggs that still sat next to the cash register.

A slow reggae tune played on the jukebox. A couple of business types with their sleeves rolled up were in the back, leaning over an eight ball table, each with cue in hand, each working out his next shot. The place was humming, drinks were flowing, and the Giants had just kicked a field goal.

The air smelled of pulled pork and stale beer, and as Josh walked past the kitchen he heard someone cry out a blue streak. A second later, a pocket of smoke wafted out from the kitchen's swinging doors, followed by a red-faced man wearing a stained apron, frantically flapping a tattered yellow rag at a smoke detector.

A hand waving from an alcove near the emergency exit caught Josh's attention. Rachael slipped off the bench seat and walked toward him. She was taller than he'd expected, moving with a confidence and grace that was hard not to notice.

"Josh, I'm so glad you made it," she said. "I know this can't be easy."

Josh half smiled. "It's all right, I needed to get out. The hotel walls were getting to me."

They sat down and the waiter came over. Rachael ordered a glass of red wine, and Josh a pint of McClinty's Red Ale.

Josh looked at Rachael and could not help but think what a striking woman she was; which was immediately followed by a pang of guilt for even having noticed on such a night. He swallowed and looked down.

"Are you okay?" Rachael asked.

"Yeah, I'm fine."

"I am so sorry about your loss."

"Thanks," he said. "We were gonna meet here tonight. Part of me still thinks he'll show. You know it just doesn't feel . . ."

"Real," she said.

"Yeah, it's not easy to think of never seeing him again."

Rachael took a minute before continuing, and then asked, "Josh, is there any reason you can think of why someone would want to harm Arthur?"

"I've been kicking that around a lot, but the answer is always the same, there can't be a reason, none whatsoever. Arthur was the most harmless guy. Always took the back seat, always avoided any type of confrontation."

The waiter dropped off their drinks, a plate of taco chips and a small bowl of salsa, and left.

Josh half raised his glass. "To Arthur."

Rachael swirled her wine, tilted her glass toward him and took a sip.

"So, how long have you been with the Special Crimes Unit?"

Rachael shifted in her seat; it was clear she was uneasy with the question. "Awhile, not too long." Her voice was tight in her throat. "I came on board five months ago. Prior to this, I'd put in seven years with the Organized Crime Unit in Miami, and had some success there. In fact, I was up for a promotion. But I'd had enough—I needed a change. So I applied for New York." She hesitated, as though unsure if she should go on. "I did get a little help. My old boss put in a good word for me, connections and all that. But still, it did surprise me when I got the job." She took another sip. "And here I am."

"Hey you gotta be good, being fast-tracked in this jungle."

"Some think so, I suppose," she said, glancing to the side.

They were halfway through their second drink when Rachael spoke up. "Josh, I have something I should tell you. This afternoon I received a call from my old unit in Miami. They asked if I would have a look at Arthur's crime scene."

Josh reflected for a second on what she said, then grimaced. "*Organized crime?* You can't be serious. This is *Arthur* we're talking about. What's organized crime got to do with him?"

"The perp that killed Arthur was identified as John Narrillo. A retired mechanic with the Carlotti family out of Miami."

Josh's brow furrowed as he put his hands on the table. "No. That's ridiculous. The mob after Arthur—bullshit."

"I know it sounds far-fetched. I'm still trying to get my

mind around it. But what we do know is that Narrillo was found dead in the parking lot of Arthur's store, with two slugs in him. Blood was found splattered in Arthur's store and on the tarmac of the store's parking lot. Arthur was found in his car, crashed up against a storm sewer a few miles from his store. Both of Narrillo's knees were broken, and the damage to Arthur's car suggests he clipped Narrillo, probably in the parking lot."

Josh drained his beer and ordered another. Clearing his throat, he asked, "Okay, so tell me . . . why would the Carlotti family have an interest in Arthur?"

"That is a big question mark," she replied.

"And Arthur and the bureau. Why is the bureau looking at him? We're talking about a mild-mannered bookstore owner. And why all the interest in a retired contractor? I just don't get it; a shitload of resources are being thrown at this . . ."

"You're right, it's not outside the box for a soldier in the mob to wind up dead, but the circumstances warrant additional scrutiny."

"Circumstances?"

"A high-profile author's best friend is murdered by a mob hitman. Let's just say, the media spotlight will be shining bright and questions will be asked."

"Ahhh Christ," Josh said, and took a deep breath. He couldn't put his finger on it, but he knew there was more to it. He took another deep breath and then changed the subject. "Tell me about yourself. What made you sign up with the Feds?"

"Good question," she said, sounding somewhat relieved at the change of pace. "Never would have thought I'd be here, sitting at this table with a shield in my pocket.

Really, I had a great upbringing and a happy family life. I was an only child, so I got all the attention. My mother, she's a doctor, family practice. My dad teaches philosophy at Cornell. We'd moved around a lot when I was quite young. We lived in Yemen for three years before moving back to the States when I was sixteen. That's when my dad landed the job at Cornell, and our family has stayed put ever since. I got my undergrad in genetics at Boston, then changed stream and went on to a Masters in Linguistics."

"Linguistics, that's a leap."

"You sound like my mother. She wanted me to go into medicine. But I'd had enough of biology, human or otherwise. I specialized in Arabic. I suppose I took to it because of my time in Yemen, and I guess, because of the challenge. A few months before I graduated, a handler approached me. The timing was right, and the idea of doing something different appealed to me. So, I signed up. It all sort of fell into place."

"Good decision?" Josh asked, taking a draw on his beer.

"It was at the time, but I wonder. . . . What about you, what's your story?" Rachael asked, clearly trying to change the focus of the conversation.

Fair enough. "My upbringing was decent enough, but not always happy. My mother suffered from depression; she was in and out of institutions for most of my childhood. On depression-free days, she was the warmest, most thoughtful person I'd ever known. Doing things for others and happy to do it. My father, he was . . . *is* a great guy. He watched over my mother and cared for her in her dark times, and there were plenty of those. My father is a lawyer. He made District Attorney before reaching forty, but his success, as it turned out . . . was his undoing."

"How's that . . . ?"

"One of his first cases as a DA involved a young man, Clyde Thornhill, who was charged with the rape and murder of a college girl. My father vehemently believed Thornhill to be guilty. But most of the evidence was circumstantial, so he had to rely on a less than perfect eyewitness to get the conviction. Thornhill received his lethal injection after nearly ten years on death row. Then a few years ago, DNA evidence turned up that cleared Thornhill. That's when my father fell apart. He couldn't live with it. He fell and never bounced back. He's lost everything, his self-respect, everything. And the worst of it is, he won't accept help from me or my kid sister."

They ordered another round of drinks, and the conversation changed to lighter topics, exchanging stories of growing up, music, films and favorite authors.

Josh could see Rachael had relaxed, and decided it was time to test the water. "Rachael, you and I both know it'll be tough for me to gain access to Arthur's file, not to mention the crime scene. And if I was to get at them, I'd probably have to do something illegal. I'm thinking, if I was to tag along with you . . . ?"

A hint of a smile crossed Rachael's mouth. "I'm not gonna lie, I was hoping you would ask."

Huh. I'm being played, Josh thought. "And?" he asked.

"Okay, it's a given that Arthur's death has changed your priorities. Makes sense. But I'm hoping you would consider working with me with on the O'Henry file as an advisor? We could help each other. You'd have access to Arthur's file, and I'd have your input on O'Henry. . . .

Please Josh, I need you on my team."

"There are other profilers out there, good ones. Why me?"

"Last time around there were good profilers, but other than giving O'Henry a spotlight to glow in, they didn't get far. Now he's back, and my gut is telling me our usual profilers won't make the cut.

"So, you're looking for an *un*usual profiler?"

"Yes, I guess I am." An almost playful smile broke as her eyes narrowed. "Yeah, I'm looking for an unusual profiler, and I'm thinking that might be you." Then her voice took on a more serious tone. "Josh, I know you are the best person for the job. At least that's how I feel."

"You feel? I take it your opinion is not shared by everyone on your team."

"My team is okay. It's my boss, Herrod Kingsley that's the problem. He thinks, well, he thinks you're damaged goods."

"Kingsley . . . ? You're kidding, right?" Josh studied her face. "You're serious."

"Ah, yeah," she said. "And the icing on the cake is, I wasn't Kingsley's first or second choice to run this task force. An advisory panel overrode his objection."

Josh said nothing.

"So, if I fail, it's a win-win for Kingsley. He's proven right about me. I get buried, and he gets to put his *man* in." Rachael sighed. "But I have no intention of failing, you have to understand that."

Josh tilted his head, and said, "Rachael, I have a history with Kingsley, goes way back. I caught him doing things he shouldn't have been doing." He paused and thought it over. "Look, you have a promising career ahead of you. By taking me on board, you're going to suffer some serious collateral damage."

"Screw my career, and screw Kingsley. If I'm not successful on this case, my career is flat out finished, he'll see to that. I'd rather take my chances with a team chosen by me than one chosen by that asshole." She stopped for a moment, then asked, "But is this really about you and Kingsley? Or is there something else festering in that damaged brain of yours?"

Not too far off the mark, he thought. Then a favorite saying of his father's came to him. *Time to fish or cut bait, Josh.* "Okay Rachael. Let's give it a shot, see how it goes."

Rachael was smiling when her cell vibrated in her purse. She fished it out, and as she read the message her face turned cold. She raised her gaze to Josh. "Central Park, on a bench by the reservoir. Another severed head."

Chapter 10

Josh and Rachael entered Central Park through the West 96th Street entrance, then hung a right on West Drive for less than a quarter-mile before pulling over.

Ahead of them, on the other side of a small hill, bleached halogen light flooded the night sky and reminded Josh of the crime scenes he had attended as a profiler, and how they were always cold and detached from life. It was then he realized—he was back on the job.

Yellow crime tape had been strung up along the base of the hill, a fair distance from the scene. Two young NYPD Blues were checking ID. Rachael flashed her shield and vouched for Josh, and they ducked under the tape.

As they made their way up the hill a gust of wind cut across their path, swirling wet leaves and other debris. Josh zipped his jacket and flipped up his collar. Rachael turned her shoulder to the wind, raised her hood, then removed a wad of latex gloves from her pocket and handed a pair to Josh. "You'll need these."

As they stepped onto the crest of the hill, the full crime scene came into view. In the center was a park bench lit up like a hundredth year birthday cake. But there was no large, white candle gracefully melting down and stuck to the park bench, just a woman's severed head, her hair matted from the rain, her eyes plucked out.

"Oh boy," Rachael said, and grimaced.

"He certainly has a flare for drama," Josh said.

"Yeah, he has that, the sick son-of-a-bitch."

Detective Justin Rollins of the NYPD was pacing next to the park bench, and waved to them as they approached. He was in his mid-thirties, tall, fine-boned with wispy blonde hair. "Tanner, I thought that was you," he said, his gaze shifting to Josh.

"This is Josh Ingram, Special Investigator. He's here in an advisory capacity."

The detective turned to Josh and frowned. "I've heard of you. Some kinda hotshot, right? But, you're that writer now, aren't ya?" he said, in a tone that suggested Josh should apologize.

"Correct. Now I'm assisting on a murder investigation. Maybe we should focus on that."

The detective's frown deepened, and he turned to Rachael. "Your boss, Inspector Kingsley, he's looking for you."

"Understood detective," Rachael said, paying him lip service, her attention focused on the severed head. The detective studied them both for a few seconds, then gave his head a shake and walked away. A moment later Andy Rowland, the Coroner's senior assistant investigator sauntered up, knelt by the bench, and opened his evidence kit.

Andy peered up at Rachael, a concerned look on his face. "Agent Tanner, you okay?"

"I guess so, Andy. What've we got?"

"CSI completed the grid walk and came up blank, rains washed away any potential tracks. Photos are in the can. They'll try for prints in the lab. Nothing out of the ordinary, unless one considers a chopped off head on a bench unusual."

"How's the ears and throat?" she asked.

"Just about to do that." Then he reached down and with the tip of his finger, carefully folded the women's ear over, revealing a black number eight, the size of a dime.

Rachael exhaled a short puff and turned to Josh. "The numbering has never been released to the public." She began to rub her temples with her fingertips. "Ah hell Josh, on his last killing spree, every one of O'Henry's kills were spaced out the same, six weeks plus or minus a day. Jesus, it's just been six days since number seven."

Josh knelt on one knee to have a closer look at the head. He removed one of his latex gloves, touched her gray, blood-drained face with the back of his hand and whispered, "No more dreams . . . loves or loved ones for you."

"What did you just say?" Rachael asked.

Josh looked away. "Nothing . . ." he replied.

"It seems O'Henry wants us all on the same page," Rachael said, her focus back on the numbering.

"Yeah, that and he wants all the attention he can get. He thrives on it," Josh said.

Rachael turned to the assistant coroner. "Andy, you ready? Let's take a peek."

The assistant clicked on a penlight and pulled the head's lower jaw down until the mouth opened wide, then peered inside. After a few seconds he sighed. "Oh yeah, the perp definitely enjoys screwing with us. Got something here, looks like a small plastic bag." He stuck his gloved hand into the mouth and fished around. "It's lodged in next to her tonsils, I'm gonna have to go deeper." He cleared his throat and looked up at Rachael. "Good thing I have my mother's hands."

As he forced his hand in deeper, a gob of red lipstick smeared, moving up his white latex glove like a snail's trail.

"Shit," Andy said. "I'm not snagging it. You two may not want to watch this." Taking a deep breath, he shoved his hand farther down her throat until her front teeth pierced his latex glove and began to dig into his forearm. "Ahh . . . I'm going to have to tilt it," he said, and cleared his throat again. As he tipped the head sideways there came a sucking sound like a rubber boot being pulled out of muck. "Almost there . . ." Then he gave a final push, and with his free hand he plucked the plastic bag out from the base of the woman's neck.

Rachael blinked her eyes and looked away. Josh tapped her on the shoulder, and they stepped over to an old oak tree to get some protection from the wind.

The assistant coroner followed close on their heels. He put on a fresh pair of dry gloves, opened the plastic bag and withdrew a two-inch square of folded, white paper. He carefully unfolded it, then held it so both Josh and Rachael could read the typed message:

A wife of noble character who can find?

Thought I'd give you a little something to think about. But look at me, where are my manners. Rachael, so good of you to drop by, and I expect Josh Ingram is now standing at your side, at least I would hope so. Oh, but he is there, isn't he?

I have always been fond of the bureau, so fun to play with, and now with you both on board, well then, what could be better. Now I must go, I have a lot to do, busy

busy is the happy bear.
Ta-ta O
P.S. tell Herrod, if he tries to change the cast of players even to the slightest degree, I shall have to extend my loving hand to his family, and for that matter, the commissioner's family as well. Why not? Let's keep the juices flowing. Keep all the rabbits on their toes.

Rachael turned to Josh. "How the hell does know about you? We've only just met."

"I don't know, but he is watching us, that much is for certain," Josh said, and then turned his attention to the immediate area, scanning for a face. A face he would recognize when he saw it. A face that didn't seem to fit, furtive or excited for all the wrong reasons.

"Oh here comes fun," Rachael said, as Kingsley made his way over to them.

Herrod Kingsley ducked under a low-hanging electrical cord, which wasn't easy. He was a big man with a substantial gut, thick legs and a barrel chest. He had on an aluminum colored trench coat that gave him the tubular look of a fifty gallon hot-water tank. His thick, black hair was slicked straight back, capping off a meaty face and squat nose. "Tanner, bring me up to speed," he said in a stern voice, before noticing Josh. "Didn't expect to see you so soon, Ingram. Finally come out of hiding. Big step for you, isn't it?" His voice lathered with sarcasm, his eyes filled with contempt.

"Hemorrhoid," Josh said.

Kingsley scowled and turned to Rachael. "If this asshole so much as impedes this investigation for one minute—he's out of here. You clear on that? The only reason he's here, is because of strings being pulled that I couldn't control."

"Probably not a smart idea to remove the asshole quite yet," she said.

The assistant coroner passed Kingsley the note.

As Kingsley read it, marbled splotches of pinkish blood surfaced of his fleshy face. "Just keep me posted," he said, and then turned to Josh, who was looking the other way. "And don't let him out of your sight. He's always been trouble, even before they hauled his ass away and threw him in that padded cell. Never in the world will I understand why they let him out." Kingsley turned back to Rachael, his voice bitter. "You got yourself a real winner here, Tanner, good choice."

Rachael was about to speak, when an NYPD Blue jogged up to them, breathing hard. "We got the media forming up all along the perimeter, Channels 3, 11 and 13. Someone's leaked it, about it being a severed head and all. Gonna be a circus."

"Oh, *Lord*. How did they find out so fast?" Kingsley asked, his gaze darting around for a moment before settling on Rachael. "Tanner, this is your mess. Deal with it." Then he craned his head like he was looking for suitable exit. "I have to get word to the mayor and the commissioner. Let them know how sick this animal really is."

As Kingsley slipped away, Josh turned to Rachael. "You knew, right?"

"Yeah I knew . . . but that was a long time ago."

Josh cocked his head to one side and studied Rachael. "At least with all the media attention, Kingsley will keep his distance. If this blows up, he'll want it all to hang on your shoulders. . . . Of course, if you catch

O'Henry, he'll take the credit."

"Naturally," Rachael said.

"And you do know O'Henry tipped off the press, right?"

"I kinda figured."

"And the spotlight is gonna be bright, the press are going to hound you for details, and O'Henry—he's gonna be listening and looking for recognition."

"I'll tell the media the truth," she said, and began to rub her hand up and down the sleeve of her jacket. "As much as they need to know. Not about him though. Not yet." Then she patted down the pockets of her jacket, inside and out, then her pants, front and back, and finally found what she was looking for. "Hah, life *is good*," she said, and pulled out a small, cylindrical object wrapped in tinfoil. She peeled back the foil, revealing a single, filter-tipped cigarette and a wooden match. She clamped her lips around the cigarette, lit it, and sucked in a long draw, then tilted her head back and closed her eyes. "And when word gets out O'Henry's back, well shit, I don't even want to think about it."

Josh took another look at the note. "Do you have a criminal psychiatrist on board?"

"One attached to the district attorney's office. Got a fair reputation. Why?"

"I'd like to run this past someone who I've found useful in the past. If he's still practicing, he could be of help. An unusual guy, but insightful."

"Aren't they all unusual, psychiatrists?" Rachael half-grinned. "Be my guest. We need all the help we can get."

Rachael's cell rang. She took the call, then hung up. "Lieutenant Arlington says they're wrapping up the investigation at Arthur's store. If we want to have a look, we have to be there tomorrow, nine a.m. sharp."

Chapter 11

The cold, moist air coated his face and dissolved the worst of the morning cobwebs. The last of the storm cells had died out at around eight a.m. *Autumn in New York, what a perfect time of the year,* Josh thought. He and Rachael were standing on a sidewalk some fifty feet from Arthur's bookstore, drinking coffee and eating glazed apple fritters.

Josh took a sip of his coffee and glanced at his watch; eight forty-six. "So tell me, what do we know about John Narrillo?"

"Narrillo . . . mean as a snake. A mechanic for the mob. Did and would do anything. Had a rep as a sadist, which served him well—certainly kept the rest of the wolf pack at bay. No one challenged him, not if they valued their health."

"And he's retired?"

She washed down the last of her fritter with her coffee. "That's right. Basically, he got old and rather than be eaten alive, they allowed him to retire. Which in itself was strange, the mob doesn't have a retirement plan, not a happy one anyway. Adolfo Carlotti, the head of the family, deemed Narrillo a friend. The story is they grew up together. So Narrillo got a pass."

"Huh . . . so, a retired hitman comes to New York

and kills a timid book dealer. How does that work?"

"Hey, all I can figure is, Narrillo had to be doing someone a favor. Had to be for a made guy. Someone high up. But you're right about Arthur. We ran him, and he's one hundred percent clean."

It numbed Josh to know that his best friend had been vetted by the FBI. "There is another piece out-of-place. A few days ago, Arthur e-mailed me. He'd bought a bag of surplus books at a wholesale book auction, and was getting them ready for resale when he discovered a contract tucked away in one of the leather jackets. He sent the contract to me as an attachment, along with a picture. I got the contract, but the picture never came through. The contract was in Spanish, signed in 1945, and consisted of a transfer of shares in a German conglomerate over to George Elhert."

Rachael's cell rang in her purse. She held up her index finger and took the call. And by the look on her face, she wished she hadn't. "Uh-huh, what time? I'll be there. Yes, he's with me now. Right, I got it." She hung up. "Sorry about that, that was Kingsley; there's an O'Henry press scrum I have to attend this afternoon."

"Kingsley is keeping close tabs on you."

"You too." Rachael smirked. "Okay . . . so you were saying, the name on the contract was George Elhert?"

"Yeah, that's right."

Josh could feel her gaze on him, then she said, "*The* George Elhert, you're talking about the Governor of Florida, George Elhert, from the sixties?"

"Yup."

"That's crazy, how could he be involved? It must be someone else with the same name. Elhert isn't that uncommon."

"You would be right, except for the fact that Arthur took it upon himself to contact Elhert's son."

"Oh my God. This just keeps getting better and better. Are you serious?"

"Yeah. My buddy, Arthur, put a call in to the Governor of New York, one William T. Elhert."

Rachael laughed, then said, "Off topic I know, but you have to wonder how the son of a notoriously corrupt father gets elected as a governor himself."

Josh hunched his shoulders, taking a moment before responding. "All Arthur wanted was to see if the contract had any value to the family. See if he could make a buck."

"And . . . ?"

"*And* the fool somehow made it through the screening around the governor. I don't know if he spoke to him in person, but he must have gotten close, because they offered him a finder's fee. That is, if the contract turned out to be authentic."

"Last April I saw the governor at a fundraising event," Rachael said, "at Blessed Hearts Hospital. He came across as a decent guy. Donated a ton of cash too, I think close to three million, for some kind of new equipment. I can still picture it; the Archbishop in his purple robes sitting next to Elhert. At the time, it crossed my mind that it was a hell of a photo op for the governor."

Her brow furrowed. "We can't tell Kingsley about this. Not now anyway. He's looking for any reason to block my involvement in Arthur's case. If he thought for a second Arthur's file could get within a football field of the governor's hallowed ground, he'd pull the plug in a heartbeat."

"Agreed. And if he found out, and if you were still somehow allowed to continue poking around, Kingsley would have his nose so far up Elhert's arse that to get a message to him, you'd have to force feed it to Elhert and wait six hours."

It was a little after nine a.m. when they entered the bookstore. Lieutenant Arlington stood ten feet away; his shoulders sloped forward, his back hunched, his hair thinning. He glanced over his shoulder and saw them and came straight over. "Tanner, let's be quick about it. We're all done here. The crime-scene guys finished late yesterday. Got a copy of Detective Whittaker's report for you, he was the responding detective on the scene." Then he took notice of Josh.

"This is Josh Ingram," Rachael said. "He's assisting us with our investigation."

The lieutenant shrugged, pointing to the back of the store. "Detectives Palmer and Redding have been briefed and can fill you in on the details."

Josh and Rachael walked over and were met by the two detectives, one was in his mid-forties, the other much younger. Detective Palmer was the taller and the younger of the two. His shoulders were broad and he appeared fit and full of energy. Detective Redding, on the other hand, was beefy around the waist and had dark gray shadows under his eyes.

Detective Redding spoke first. "Been expecting you, Agent Tanner."

Detective Palmer did a double take on Josh, and a

hint of recognition crossed his face. "You're Josh Ingram?"

"Yeah," Josh said, and wondered what was coming next.

Detective Palmer reached out to shake Josh's hand. "Wow—I gotta say, it is an honor to meet you. Love your work, sir. What are you doing here?"

"He's here at my request," Rachael said, the tone of her voice saying let's keep things moving.

Detective Palmer was not dissuaded. "You were at the Academy, in the training manual I mean. A section on profiling, written by you. Impressive stuff. I keep a copy and refer to it all the time," he said, beaming.

Detective Redding looked at Palmer and gave his head a slight shake.

Josh surveyed the room. Half the store's books were stacked in piles on the floor. An inventory count had been underway, he thought. *Man how Arthur hated that exercise.* Dust from the disturbed books bothered him the most, his allergies went wild during an inventory. Josh knew enough to keep his distance from Arthur when a count was in progress; the whining was unbearable.

Detective Redding went over the initial blood splattering and started to run though how the scene could have unfolded. "It appears the owner of the store, one Arthur Romansky—"

"Let's just go with Arthur, okay?" Josh said.

Detective Redding sighed, his face empty of expression. "So, *Arthur* entered the store, apparently unaware of the perpetrator's presence. The door had not been compromised which leads one to think the perp had a key, or found a key, or was a professional and picked the lock.

Our knowledge of him as a mechanic suggests the latter." Redding stepped between the two bookshelves and pointed to a small circle of white chalk on the floor. "A .38 caliber casing was found here. It's here we figure Arthur got his throat cut, and the attacker took one or both of the slugs." Redding pointed to a few hardbacks on the floor next to Josh's shoe. "It looks as though there was a scuffle before they went outside. There's some blood smeared on the door jamb and on the knob of the side entrance door, indicating that's where they exited." All four started walking to the door.

Josh stopped and walked back for a closer inspection of the bookshelves. He pointed to a drop of blood on the spine of a book, about ten feet away from the detective's identified spot of the confrontation. They all returned to look. Both detectives had a blank look on their face.

"Have we located the knife?" Josh asked.

"No, the area has been swept a few times and turned up nothing," Detective Redding said.

Josh's stomach turned at the thought of a knife cutting into Arthur's neck. "For the most part; I would agree with your assessment. A knife slicing through a windpipe would attract bits of blood, and the centrifugal force would cause them to coalesce on the tip of the blade. As the knife continued to arc through the air, the blood would spray out in a pattern consistent with what we have here." He again pointed to the drop of blood on the spine of the book. "The shell casing being a few feet closer to the door means Arthur was heading for the door, suspecting he wasn't alone, his gun drawn. He turned when he heard his attacker come up from behind him, and got his throat slit. Shock would have hit him hard. He would've then backed himself toward the exit, raised his gun and fired."

Josh took a few steps, knelt, and pointed to the floor. "You can see here, where the dust has been disturbed from the pressure of a body lying face down. The attacker waited here for Arthur to enter the store. . . . He was definitely sent here to kill Arthur; you can add that to your report. This was a premeditated murder," Josh said, with complete confidence.

"Face down on the floor and murder one. Come on, just like that?" Rachael said, in disbelief.

"Look." Josh pointed to the floor. "See the two bare patches, both about three inches by one inch? This is where the points of his shoes, or to be more precise, his military-style boots, scuffed the area."

"Oh please," Rachael said, clearly having trouble with it.

Detective Redding cleared his throat. "Look, I have a report to finish, so if you don't mind, I will leave you to it." At that moment Detective Palmer's cell rang, and both detectives headed for the door as he took the call.

Josh thought for a moment, then called out to Redding. "Arthur's computer, do you have it?"

Redding stopped. "Yeah, we have it, but it's been beaten to crap. Someone got pissed and took a hammer to it. Techs say the hard drive is destroyed, totally toasted."

"Oh, okay, thanks."

"Someone's covering their tracks," Rachael said.

Josh did not respond.

"So getting back to murder one. Care to explain how you see it as a certainty, and not just Arthur showing up at the wrong time?"

"It's how I see it, that's all," Josh said, but could tell

she wanted more. "Okay. So, it's night and sound carries. The perp would have heard Arthur pull into the parking lot and had sufficient time to leave out the side entrance long before Arthur came in. But the perp didn't run. He waited for Arthur to enter."

"Yeah, sure. . . . But the military boots—that's rich."

Josh didn't hear her. He was already consumed by what he saw poking out of a garbage can next to Arthur's desk. Walking over, he reached into the can and pulled out a worn, but otherwise intact, green leather dust jacket. The book's title had been partially engraved into the jacket, it was in Spanish, and the author's name was missing.

"You think it's significant?" Rachael asked.

"Mmm . . . it could be. Probably. It's out of character for Arthur. He wouldn't throw away a slice of his profit. A book's jacket adds resale value. Although this one is obviously not finished; but it is old, so who knows?"

Detective Palmer stuck his head back in the doorway. "The coroner called. The report is ready. I'm printing off a copy in the cruiser. I'll be back in a minute."

"Okay thanks," Rachael said.

Josh and Rachael continued to comb the store, checking the utility closet, the bathroom, and the back room. In the back room, Josh glanced up and noticed a small, square door that opened to the attic. He found a stepladder and pushed the door open. The attic was dark and before he could ask, Rachael passed him a flashlight. He clicked it on and saw a small gray metal box nestled next to a two-by-four. He handed the box down to Rachael and stepped down the ladder. Inside, they found three, thinly-rolled joints. Josh raised his eyebrows, then closed the box without saying a word. Rachael studied him for a moment and cocked her head . . .

Detective Palmer returned with the coroner's report, handing it to Rachael. She read it, then tried to pass it to Josh.

Josh held up his hand. "Just the highlights, okay?"

"Yeah, all right," Rachael said, and took a breath. "Arthur died from a massive loss of blood, consistent with the knife wound. Due to the lack of bruising on his skin one would expect from a car accident, his heart had stopped before he ran off the road and hit the storm sewer. Toxicology shows his blood work revealed he'd been drinking, and he had a trace of cocaine in his blood."

That last item caught Josh by surprise. *First the joints, now this.*

"As for the perp, his cause of death was internal bleeding. Damage to his internal organs is consistent with that of taking a .38 caliber to the stomach and one to the chest. The one to the chest nicked his aorta on the way out. Both his legs were fractured, as was his skull, which is consistent with getting hit by Arthur's car, but that's viewed as collateral damage. The bullets did the heavy lifting." She flipped the page. "That's it." She raised her gaze to see Detective Palmer standing there with a big grin on his face.

"Anything else?" she asked.

"Uh-huh, one other thing," Palmer said, sounding somewhat elated. "I checked with the coroner, and he confirmed the perp's footwear. He was wearing military issue combat boots."

Rachael looked to Josh. "Appears you have a fan."

Josh had to grin. "Could I get a copy of the report?"

Rachael nodded to Palmer, and he left through the

side entrance.

As Josh and Rachael reached her SUV, Detective Palmer caught them and handed her the report. Rachael started the engine. "I have to get back downtown and prepare for the press conference."

"Any chance you could drop me at the hotel?"

It was eleven a.m. by the time Josh entered his hotel room. He stretched out on the bed and tried to shut down—tried not think about Arthur's throat being slit, or about the park bench and the woman's severed head, but the unwanted thoughts were relentless, continuing to loop around in his mind. He got up to take a leak, and when he returned, he commenced counting ceiling tiles, and his thoughts turned to his father. He was way overdue to check in on him. He should have made the call a week ago, he knew it was wrong not to, still he had put it off. *I'll make the call, but not today,* he thought. Then his guilt took over . . .

"Goddamnit," he said, then sat up and grabbed his laptop. Firing it up, he typed in 'Book Specialists'. The leather dust jacket *had* to be significant. Arthur would not have chucked it. But he had. *Why? What were you doing Arthur? Were you leaving a red flag? Or is it just worthless? I don't know what you were thinking . . . but I'm going to find out.*

Chapter 12

The cab pulled over to a curb in Brooklyn's Little Poland district, next to a large, blue, rectangular trash bin. The ratty arm of a couch, the color of Swiss chard, held the lid ajar, allowing its rotted innards to taint the air. Josh stepped out of the cab and moved away from the bin.

The street was in transition. Brick row houses and shops dating back to the early nineteen hundreds lined both sides of the road. The dilapidated buildings were being scooped up and transformed into chic retail outlets and upscale boutique restaurants. As Josh crossed the street, the air became earthy, filled with the aroma of fresh breads and pastries, of sausages, and onions fried in butter. Store marquees written in Polish flanked the street, and pedestrians chattering in their mother tongue passed by Josh without a glance.

The store's name was 'Collectables' and a thick red arrow bent at ninety degrees pointed down a flight of concrete stairs that dropped just below street level. The stairs terminated at an emerald-green wooden door. The door squeaked as Josh turned the handle, and an overhead cowbell clinked his arrival.

"I'll be out in a jiffy," a voice called from somewhere in the back.

The place was lit by electric hurricane lamps that cast

anemic shadows over well-worn and seasoned books, all on display in sturdy glass cabinets. Behind the counter, a laptop tuned to the weather channel flashed a new image every few seconds. A Mississippi Delta blues song was playing on a 1970's turntable, which, to Josh, made the place feel more inviting. *It's gotta be torture sitting here all day,* he thought, *day-after-day waiting for some customer to stroll through and pull out his wallet.* All of a sudden, Josh felt the need to hang out with Eddie and take him for a long, long walk.

A toilet flushed and a moment later, a tall, celery-shaped man in his late fifties appeared, wiping his hands on his denim overalls. "Hey, it's you . . . dude, I can't believe you're here. Welcome, Josh Ingram. I'm Toby Wodzisz. I own this establishment," he said, his accent clearly Brooklynese, though remnants of Polish still clung to his words. Josh noticed the man's movements were stiff and he looked to be in considerable pain.

A shot of sympathy filled Josh. He thought of his father and how time steals one's youth, slowly stripping away confidence, leaving nothing in its wake but old age and tired memories.

"Would you mind?" Toby asked, as he stepped up and leaned over the counter next to Josh. He held his cell phone out in front of them. "My clients eat this stuff up." He clicked the picture, then straightened himself out and asked, "So, what can I do for you?"

"Your website says your specialty is Latin America. I was hoping you could help me out." Josh handed Toby the green dust jacket.

Toby pulled open a top drawer and withdrew a large magnifying glass, then proceeded to inspect the jacket. He was paying particular attention to the engravings on the front, when his mouth turned down at the corners. He carefully folded back the jacket's leather flap and asked, "May I ask where you got this?"

"A friend of mine. He came across it at a book auction."

Toby's face brightened. "Is there a book to go with it?"

"No, not so far. Still searching."

"Oh, I see," Toby said, his rheumy eyes studying Josh. "This is an old cover. Late eighteen hundreds be my guess, possibly turn of the century, hard to tell. Not many covers made in this fashion, especially with engraving tools of this sort." He held the cover up to Josh. "See these letters," he pointed to the book's title, *Un hombre tr*, "the letters *e* and *t* are quite crude and cut at odd angles. Had to be the work of an independent artisan, Spanish of course. No doubt someone spent some time on it, though. My guess, it was for a special occasion. And whoever it was for, he had to be loaded. . . . It is odd though, the title not finished and the author's name missing."

"Can you tell where the cover was made or anything about the book itself?"

"Being Spanish in origin, the jacket could be from any number of countries. My guess is Central America, maybe South. The crude angles give it away. It's like the dude had to improvise. In the territories, especially back in those days, it'd be next to impossible to replace a lost tool, they'd have to make do with whatever they had on hand." Toby pondered the dust jacket and then said: "Sorry man, not much else I can say."

"What do you think it's worth? Would you throw it away?"

"I think you know the answer to that," Toby said and his voice perked up. "As to the magnitude of its value, some jackets are worth more than the books they cover. By the turn of the nineteenth century, jackets were beginning to be viewed as works of art. The Great Gatsby, for example, if sold today without its cover, a first edition would bring in around two grand. But, sold *with* its dust jacket, *hell* it'd fetch well over five. And if the cover is in mint condition, well that'd just blow the lid off of it, wouldn't it?"

Without realizing it, Josh had started to tap his fingers on the counter.

"But to answer your question," Toby said, as a matter-of-fact. "No dealer worth his salt would throw it away. Not a chance."

Chapter 13

Melissa, a junior agent, led the way to the boardroom. Josh followed close behind, lugging two banker's boxes. After walking through a maze of gray hallways lit by fluorescent lights, they arrived at a back office that doubled as a small boardroom. Melissa unlocked the room, flashed him a smile and left.

The boxes had cut into his fingers, and Josh let out a breath as he plopped them onto the table. Each box held three thick case files on O'Henry. One file for each of the six murders he had committed during his killing spree seven years ago. Laid on top of the second box was a much thinner file. It had been created just last week and covered the murder of number seven, one Victoria Henderson.

Josh checked his watch, it was a little after two p.m. He could feel his energy level tanking and let out a long yawn. *Man, do I ever need a coffee.*

At the end of the boardroom table he noticed two more cardboard boxes. One was marked physical evidence and maps. The other box was marked field officer reports, recommendations and notes on media control. He decided to take a break.

He crossed the street to an espresso bar, ordered an extra-large bold Americano, then thought Rachael might need one and ordered a second. On his way back to the boardroom, he ran into Melissa in the hallway. She was pushing a trolley with an old percolator coffee pot on top. Next to the pot was a pile of sugar cubes, and a bowl filled with two percent milk packets.

"Oh, I thought you might want this, but I see I'm a little late."

"No, it's great, thank you," Josh said, and he meant it. It was going to be a long day. "Is Agent Tanner still around?"

"Oh yes, she's practicing—target practicing. Pretty serious about it too."

"The range, is it in the basement?"

"That's right," she said, and gave him directions.

The firing range was well insulated. There was no evidence of guns being discharged until Josh swung open the door at the foot of the stairs. Immediately he recognized the sound of a 9mm being fired, it was coming from the far end of the range. He made his way over, grabbed a pair of earmuffs from a hook on the wall, and stepped into Rachael's cubicle. She had just finished a set and her target was on its way back, attached to a wire that worked like an automatic clothesline.

"Huh, not a bad grouping," Josh said, as he placed the coffee tray onto a small table in the back corner of the booth.

"So you think you can do better?"

"I don't know. Maybe. Let's have a look at your piece." He checked it over and frowned.

"What?" Rachael asked.
"Oh, nothing."
"Nothing? C'mon . . . there's something."
"No, it's fine."
"What, you don't like my gun?"
"Hey, it's a beautiful gun, but . . ."
"But what?"
"It's just, a longer barrel would be more accurate."

Rachael grinned as she attached a fresh target and sent it to the end of the range. "You know it's not *manly* to make excuses," she said, as she added milk to her coffee.

A smile cut at the corner of Josh's mouth, and he inserted a full clip into the gun.

He let the gun rest in the palm of his hand for a few seconds, getting used to the weight and feel of it. Then without hesitating, he raised the gun, pointed it and squeezed off a single shot all in one motion. The bullet hit high, an inch from the top of the target—dead center. Rachael smirked and raised an eyebrow. Josh then fired four more shots in rapid succession, three of the shots running straight down from the first shot, forming a clean, precise line, with the last bullet hitting a good inch off to one side.

Rachael's eyes narrowed. "Now that's just creepy. No one can shoot like that. Where did you learn to shoot . . . ? Oh, let me guess, your parents found you in a circus."

Feeling a little foolish for showing off, Josh handed back her firearm. "Sorry about that, sometimes I can't help myself."

"Good to know," she said, a slight sharpness to her words. Then she hit the return button to bring the target back. "That kind of shooting takes practice. How is it that you're able to keep your edge?"

"You mean . . . since I'm prohibited from carrying a piece, ever since—"

"Look, it's really none of my business."

"No, that's all right. I'd be asking the same question, or at least I'd be thinking about it if I were you. The truth is, I practice with a friend, out in the woods. I find it therapeutic."

"Well, you must be a very happy man." Then she grabbed the target, and ran her fingers down the straight line of holes, stopping at the last hole that was an inch off-center. She looked at Josh and smiled.

"Nobody's perfect," he said.

Once back in the boardroom, Josh rolled out the largest map, a map of Manhattan onto the table. *Seven years ago* he thought, and remembered he'd been on the final draft of his third novel when the name O'Henry was first coined. A severed head had shown up, parked on the front step of O'Henry's Funeral Home—a landmark, family-owned historic site. A reporter at the time had pointed out that it was a rather odd place for a head to show up, being a funeral home and all. The story went it was a local fishmonger that piped up from the crowd, yelling, "It's O'Henry, the undertaker, he's the one to blame." Being a live broadcast, the press latched onto it and dubbed the killer O'Henry. The name was recognizable and the media could market the hell out of it. And so, O'Henry was born.

O'Henry had killed six times over a stretch of nine months, and Josh had watched it all unfold on television, as had the rest of the country. But then O'Henry vanished without a trace, and with no new decapitations to drive the headlines, the media packed up and moved on to the next big story, and O'Henry dissolved into obscurity.

Numbers one through six were marked on the large map showing the location where each of the six heads had been put on display. Josh wrote number seven where Victoria Henderson's head was found, The Manning Library, located on East 39th Street, and then he wrote number eight on Central Park, where the latest head, Jane Doe was found.

Josh tacked the map of Manhattan on the wall and set up a flip chart off to one side.

Using a red marker, he traced out each victim's neighborhood on the map and circled the numbers where the severed heads had been found. Two things were apparent. First, all the heads were placed in locations that were meant to be highly visible. And second, O'Henry had never sourced his victims from the same neighborhood twice.

Josh pulled at his earlobe. *Why put on a show for nine months and then disappear . . . ? Did you stop killing? Was that it? Or did you just change your playing field? Perhaps you found religion, or it found you. Or maybe you've been pining away in jail and just got out.* Josh thought for a moment. *One thing is clear, you still want the attention, you need it, don't you? Your ego demands it. Mastermind—my ass, I'll find you.* Then a rush of hot blood flooded his mind; it was the burn of excitement; the adrenaline rush of the hunt, and it felt good.

At the top of one of the boxes was a fat envelope, stuffed with photographs of the original six women, all with their heads intact. He remembered how the press dwelled on their looks, which at the time he had thought to be a lot of hype. Looking at them now, he couldn't help but notice the women were indeed all stunning, their faces flawless—captivating. Each woman was well-dressed, her posture displaying confidence, an inner strength. *You didn't go after the usual psycho fodder—the ladies of the night. You targeted successful women. Why . . . ?* He went back to the map and pinned each woman's photo next to her number.

Josh opened the box labeled 'physical evidence' and read the summary reports. All the bodies were found within a few days of each murder, washed up on the banks of the Hudson River. The victims' hands, feet, and teeth were all intact, and no clothing or jewelry had been removed.

You wanted the world to know who your victims were. . . . You desire the spotlight and demand to be recognized for your work. Josh smiled. *But you would only be doing that if you believed you were gifted, smarter than anyone else, smarter than those pursuing you.*

Josh rummaged to the bottom of the report box and dug out a brown cardboard accordion satchel containing the coroner's summation reports. He briefly scanned each one; he could go over them again in detail later, but he wanted confirmation. In each report there was no mention of a sexual attack, rape or attempted rape; the victims were simply decapitated.

At that moment, Josh heard a light tap on the door. He opened it. It was Rachael, and she appeared to be in a hurry.

"Making progress?" she asked.

"It's coming, be a couple more hours."

"The team is set for debrief at five, will that work for you?"

"Yeah, I'll be ready," Josh said. "Hey, you okay?"

Rachael nodded, but he could see she wasn't. He was about to ask if she wanted to take a break and join him, when she abruptly turned and walked away.

He returned to the stack of files, leaned back in his chair and started to reread the coroner's reports—slower this time. In each case, the cause of death was plain enough: severed spinal cord, severed carotid arteries, and esophagus. What caught his attention was in all cases, the cut was made in one motion and by the same instrument. A large, two-handed sword, or a butcher's meat cleaver would get the job done. But to slice through with one blow meant the killer had to be incredibly strong. A clean cut could mean there was an accomplice, someone to hold the body still. Even if he drugged the victims, which some of the toxicology reports showed traces of, a clean cut would have required someone to hold the head rigid.

Josh finished up at half past four, the rumbling of his stomach reminding him he was hungry. He walked across the street to a Deli and ordered a cheeseburger, a large order of fries with a dollop of melted cheddar and a scoop of mushroom gravy on top, and a large soda. When the food arrived, he considered all the grease and felt disgusted with his lack of willpower, and then he ate every last bit of it.

Chapter 14

By the time Josh entered the debriefing room, Rachael and her team were already settled in.

Anakin Finn, a round, red-haired Irishman, sat at one end of the table with his cell phone stuck to his ear. He was getting shit on by someone. *Gotta be his wife,* Josh thought. He had all the signs. All men know the signs: the bulging eyes, the deep, labored breaths, and the hand firmly gripped on the revolver.

Vivian Kennedy, a tall, well-proportioned, third-generation African American sat straight up, her long legs crossed at the knees. She was stirring a tea bag in her china cup as she combed the paper for yesterday's horse race results.

Michal Rogowski, in his mid-thirties, had a loose and gangly look about him. He was leaning back in his plastic chair and staring out the window.

The last member of the team, Charley Gupta, a heavyset, no-neck bruiser, comprised of equal quantities of fat and muscle, sat slouched over in his chair, a roll of toilet paper stuck over his index finger.

"Good afternoon," Rachael said, her voice loud enough to draw the room's attention. "This is Josh Ingram. As you all know, I have asked Josh to assist in an advisory capacity. He's now had a chance to look over

O'Henry's old case files and in a minute he will give us his first impressions."

Josh surveyed the room. Their faces told of long nights dealing with the dysfunctional side of society, bearing witness to the side of the human condition that is best kept out of sight. They all looked up at him, and he sensed that they were okay having him onboard, not enthusiastic, but okay. And it was clear to him that they had already warmed up to Rachael.

"Before Josh gets started," Rachael said, "Anakin, let's hear what you have."

Anakin nodded and stepped up to a flip chart. "Right . . . not much more to report on number seven, Victoria Henderson. From the follow-up interviews, her coworkers at her law firm say she was short-listed and due to become a Partner in a few years. Other than that, her funeral was yesterday, and as you know, was well attended and covered by the press.

"Victim number eight," Anakin continued. "Miss Jane Doe was found—correction; her *head* was found, Monday evening in Central Park, on a bench not far from the reservoir. An accountant by the name of Tony Lee found her. He reported he was out walking his dog around ten p.m. when the dog started acting up and edged him over to the bench. He says he didn't see anyone else in the vicinity. At that time of night, we figured there should've been other walkers out . . . but who knows, the storm was rolling in. Vivian and Michal were there again this morning checking with runners, or anyone else out for a stroll."

Rachael nodded to Vivian. "Nothing more to report so far," Vivian said.

"As for the rest of her," Anakin said. "Her body turned up this morning in the Hudson, sucked up against an intake grid to Bellcap Energy's south side generator. Again, no attempt was made by the perp to ID-proof her head or her body; teeth, hands, and feet all intact. She had on jogging clothes, but no ID. The body is with the Coroner, and we're just waiting for the preliminary report. Having said that, the head appears to have been severed by a single blow, the odds are in favor of it being a sword or large axe, even a meat cleaver. The coroner is leaning toward a sword, possibly Japanese, because of the clean, precise cut. Our artist is working on a composite sketch of her face, and it should be ready before the day is out. . . . CSI completed its work, but found no trace of any physical evidence for the perp: no footprints, no fingerprints, no fibers, nada, nothing. The single, solitary clue we have is the one the perp left for us." Anakin turned over a page of the flip chart and revealed a magnified version of the note that had been tucked into the woman's throat. "I believe everyone in this room is now familiar with this."

A wife of noble character who can find?

Thought I'd give you a little something to think about. But look at me, where are my manners. Rachael, so good of you to drop by, and I expect Josh Ingram is now standing at your side, at least I would hope so. Oh, but he is there, isn't he?

I have always been fond of the bureau, so fun to play with, and now with you both on board, well then, what could be better. Now I must go, I have a lot to do, busy busy is the happy bear.
Ta-ta O

P.S. tell Herrod, if he tries to change the cast of players even to the slightest degree, I shall have to extend my loving hand to his family, and for that matter, the commissioner's family as well. Why not? Let's keep the juices flowing. Keep all the rabbits on their toes.

"What do we know of the proverb?" Rachael asked.

"According to Michal, our resident God-fearing, guilt-ridden member of the Catholic faith, the proverb comes from The King James Bible," Anakin said. "The proverb reads: *A wife of noble character who can find? She is worth far more than rubies.*"

"Gotta be more than fifty goats," Charley said, then checked around the room for a laugh and got nothing. "Fuckin' inflation."

Awkward, Josh thought, *I'm gonna have to introduce you to Anwar.*

"Okay, so I don't get this," Vivian said. "How is it that O'Henry found out so fast that Josh was involved?"

"Good question. We don't know how, but O'Henry must have been planning this for some time," Rachael replied, and glanced at Josh. "How he knew Josh would be involved? I gotta say, we don't have a clue." Then she looked to Anakin to continue.

"That's all I have," Anakin said.

Rachael turned to Josh. "Josh, you're up."

Josh cleared his throat. "What I'm about to give is a recap of how I see things. Not the only way to see it, but I think it's a reasonable assessment of what we have on file to this point. And since none of us in this room were part of the investigation seven years ago when O'Henry was last active; I think it's best that we all get a fresh idea of who we're dealing with."

At that moment, the conference room door swung open, and Herrod Kingsley and his assistant slipped in and sat at the far end of the room. Josh resumed. "So, what do we know about O'Henry?"

Stepping up to the chart; he flipped to a fresh page and printed in black pen: ORGANIZED. "O'Henry is a classic, organized killer, he leaves nothing to chance. He is deliberate, planning out each kill. Sorting and choosing each victim according to a pre-set criterion. He transports his victims to his kill site and keeps them under control throughout the process. He executes the victim in a controlled, rehearsed manner, displaying the head at a high-traffic location for maximum impact, suggesting he enjoys the limelight.

"After the decapitation, he tosses the body away like a waste byproduct, as one would after filleting a fish. And he manages all of this without leaving behind a single piece of incriminating evidence." Josh paused. "Anyone here having trouble with what I've described?"

"Yeah, I do, cause there is always evidence left at a scene," Charley said, and blew his nose.

"Correct!" Josh said. "The perp always, always leaves something behind, either physical or psychological. To date we have not been able to find a single shred of physical evidence. Which means we're left with getting inside his mind."

Kingsley cleared his throat, as if to say, what a waste of time.

Rachael glanced at Josh, ignoring Kingsley.

Josh continued. "With any luck, as we piece together bits of information and apply our intuition, we should start to get a picture of what is crawling around in his head."

Josh printed the word: MOTIVATION. "All the chosen women are stunning, and yet, in all cases there has been no evidence to support a sexual assault or sexual mutilation. So, what is the motivation? I don't believe it's dominance, or there would be at least some sort of mutilation, sexual or otherwise, especially as he got braver with each successive kill.

"No, I think he incurred damage during his youth. Family violence, bullying, bad experiences with the opposite sex, all these things can leave scars. For a healthy mind, it copes and time heals. Not so for a mind with faulty wiring. He feels wronged and it eats at him, and the more it eats at him, the more he needs to be recognized as an important entity.

"All his kills are identical, same murder weapon used, a single, clean cut, no second or third strike, no hacking at the corpse. Why would that be important to him? Is he a clean freak who takes pride in a neat and tidy kill? Is it an evidence containment issue? Does it make him feel powerful? Does it make him feel in control? I think he takes pride in the entire execution process, from start to finish. It satisfies a deep-seated need. It validates his existence." Josh took a moment to gauge his audience.

"Is an accomplice involved?" Anakin asked, tapping his index finger on his cell phone.

"Good point, and one that has been raised in the past. It would help to explain the precise severing of the head with one stroke. Someone would need to hold the victim down and pull the chin back, thus giving the sword an unencumbered target. You're right, an accomplice is possible.

"One thing we can be certain of is, he's an attention hog. All the heads have been displayed in well-known, populated areas that demand the public's attention. Deep down, O'Henry has a massive ego that has grown twisted. His passage through puberty would have been ugly; he wouldn't have done well with the girls, especially pretty girls, which would help explain his fixation with beautiful women. By putting them on display, he's placing the world on notice that he is an important man, taking what he wants, when he wants, with impunity. His need to attract the media *is* unfortunate, it's going to make our jobs a whole lot more stressful. Particularly as the kills escalate."

Kingsley spoke up, his voice brimming with self-importance. "Can you be sure there will be more kills, and for that matter, are we even convinced it's not a copycat we're dealing with?"

"As you know, there are certain aspects of O'Henry's method that were never made public," Josh said, holding up his hand to block Kingsley's response. "Agreed—a long time has passed, and numerous theories and a few books have been written about the original six murders, and yes, it is possible that some details could've been leaked."

"And?" Kingsley asked, looking at Josh with disdain.

"I know it's him," Josh said, his throat filling with anger.

A smug look crossed Kingsley's face. "And so tell me, why did he wait seven *years* to come back onto the scene?"

Josh peered into Kingsley's eyes, laying out each word loud and slow. "Not a fucking clue."

Rachael jumped in. "He could have changed his operating territory, left the country. He could've been in jail.

There are a number of scenarios that could help explain it. But now that he is back, I think we should all just focus on catching him."

"Yeah, right," Kingsley said, and then pulled out his cell and started checking his messages.

Josh turned back to the team. "The kills will escalate, and O'Henry will make sure the media has a field day. He's a planner, and he has an agenda which at this point remains unclear."

Josh studied the group for a moment, then said, "There is one more important point. In the original six killings, no notes were left at the scene. I think O'Henry's become braver. He believes he is the smartest man in the room, and he wants to up his game—a cat and mouse thing. It makes his kills that much more satisfying.

"In summation, since he is organized and shrewd, once he has the victims in his control, we have to consider them lost forever." Josh stopped and scanned the faces of the team. "Still, there is one point of exposure, when he is most vulnerable."

"The abduction site," Vivian said.

"Yes. When he has entered the public domain to snatch up his prey, that's where we have the best chance of identifying him."

"Identifying him? Don't you mean apprehending him?" Vivian asked.

"Unfortunately, I think that ship has sailed. There is of course a slim chance he could still be caught in the act, but since kill number eight went down within a week of number seven, I'm far less inclined to think we'll catch him that way."

"Why is that?" Charley asked, and sneezed into a wad

of toilet paper.

"I think O'Henry has prepared a list. A list of his intended victims. He's done his homework, he knows his victims' schedules, he knows where and when they will be most vulnerable, and he has set his plan in motion."

"And you're saying this because?" Michal asked, his brow furrowed.

Josh turned to Michal. "The latest kill occurred just six days after Victoria Henderson's murder. It takes more than six days for a controlled selection process, after which, he still has to monitor the victim's day-to-day rituals until he's comfortable scheduling the abduction and carrying out the kill. No, he has a master plan, a list of intended victims, and a timetable to keep. And I think he's just getting started."

With that a palpable hush came over the room.

"So if we are to ID him, where might we be looking?" Michal asked.

"Yes, yes, that is the definitive question, isn't it?" Josh said, and was glad the momentum was returning to the room. "So, if we think about it, where would you look . . . ? We know all the women are beautiful. So there is a definite selection process. But how does he make his selections without raising suspicion? Ask yourself this: where do women routinely go about their lives, where they can be viewed without their internal alarm bells going off, and where their home addresses can be readily obtained?"

Josh flipped to a fresh page and started writing:

LIBRARIES

GROCERY STORES

PARKING GARAGES

CHURCH

SUBWAY

RESTAURANTS

"Since he is selecting only the most beautiful women, there is the volume aspect to be considered. He needs a constant supply. He needs to view them from both near and far, and do so without them knowing he is watching them. And he needs to know where they live so he can follow their routines and plan the abduction.

"While this isn't an exhaustive list, it does cover the typical locations a woman would be found carrying out her everyday life. If anyone wants to add to the list, please feel free to do so."

No one spoke up.

"Okay . . . let's take a closer look at each site. While each one satisfies the volume requirement for the selection process, I think we can strike a few sites off the list. First, libraries are a controlled environment, and getting close enough for observation would pose too great a risk. And women are already on high alert in a parking garage, making it difficult to observe them in detail, so let's strike that one as well. Churches are frequented by regulars, making the perpetrator highly visible, and the others will notice if one of the flock go missing. Finally, subways are too hectic, too uncontrolled, and since the perp needs to know where she lives, following a woman to her home from the subway would make him stand out like a pedophile in a playground.

"So. We are left with Grocery Stores and Restaurants."

"Maybe you should think about getting serious here," Kingsley drawled. "Even if you're correct, which I consider a *remote* concept at best, there are hundreds of these establishments in the city."

"You have a point," Josh said. "The scope of possibilities is formidable. All we are trying to do is narrow our field of inquiry, whittle down the numbers and improve the odds."

"Uh-huh," Kingsley grunted, looking not at all impressed.

"It's all we have at the moment," Josh said. "We'll create a list, make some calls and stir up some memories. And with any luck, we'll get a break."

"A lot riding on luck," Vivian said.

Josh nodded, then said, "There is one other thing. The serial killer's mind is rarely fortunate enough to have a singular affliction, and in O'Henry's case I believe he is an obsessive compulsive. His kills are ritualized, precise, each one carried out in the exact same manner. This behavior indicates that many aspects of his day-to-day life will also be repetitive and obsessive. Specific tasks in his life must be carried out in a ritualistic manner. If grit gets caught up in the cogs of his mind, the neat and precise order he cherishes above all else is disturbed, which can trigger an OCD attack, which can lead to a mistake. An attack clogs his mind and uses up a vast amount of energy. He knows if he is to be successful, he has to stick to a rigid game plan and remain in control.

"I believe it is this obsessive behavior which forces him to select his victims from the same establishment, or establishments in each neighborhood. . . . Which means we need names of the grocery stores and restaurants that are common to each of the neighborhoods he's struck so far.

Kingsley broke in. "So if you're correct, and O'Henry does have a list, we are standing at the doorway to a nightmare that's just getting underway."

Josh said nothing.

"Charley, Vivian," Rachael said, her voice animated. "See what you can find out about the grocery stores in the victims' neighborhoods that O'Henry hit seven years ago, and match them with those in Victoria Henderson's neighborhood. Take her picture along and see if anyone recognizes it.

"Anakin, check with the coroner, see if the contents of Jane Doe's stomach are available yet. We'll need an itemized list of everything she ate in the last few hours of her life. Then bang on some restaurants in her neighborhood and see what you can find."

"I'm on it," Anakin said.

"And Vivian, before you head out, light a fire under the ass of the artist and have the composite of Jane Doe done up ASAP. And make sure you tell him to sketch the eyes in, so we don't scare the shit out of our good citizens. Then call the paper and *convince* them the sketch has to run on tomorrow's front page. Let's see if we can shake up someone's memory.

"Michal, keep checking with runners, dog walkers, and anyone else who may have seen anything at the park. Anything at all.

"Josh and I will coordinate on the fly. That's it people. Let's roll."

Chapter 15

Rachael and Josh arrived at the coroner's lab a little after seven p.m. The name on the frosted glass read Cecilia Bloom, Senior Coroner. Josh pushed open the door and was hit with the smell of formaldehyde and bleach. Six stainless steel post-mortem tables lined the center of the room. Two of the tables had a body, and each body was covered by a single white sheet.

Cecilia, who was sitting at the end table, next to one of the bodies, looked up as they entered. She was eating a sardine and onion sandwich and had an open bag of sea salt and vinegar potato chips on her lap. A glass of tap water sat beside her on the counter. A ball game was playing on the radio, and it was the top of the third inning. "Tried to get them to put in cable. Somehow it didn't fly," Cecilia said, and gave a toothy grin. "My name is Cecilia Bloom, and what brings you here this fine day, my lovely?" she asked, directing all her attention at Josh.

Josh didn't know if it was her crooked buckteeth or her goofy, rodent smile, but he took an immediate liking to her. "Your charming wit of course, my lady."

Cecilia's pasty white face and neck turned arterial red. She started to laugh—and inhaled a fragment of her sandwich. Hacking and coughing she waved her long skinny arm and skeletal finger at Josh in mock disapproval.

Rachael gave Josh a look, and then asked, "Cecilia, any luck with the time of death?"

"I'm just putting the final touches on my report." She coughed up the last bit of lodged sardine, then flipped a page on her clipboard and began. "The body arrived at 9:06 this morning. Rigor had already progressed to the lower stomach muscles. That in mind, coupled with the liver temp, and after allowing for the average ambient temperature of the Hudson River this time of year . . . I place the death at between four and eight Monday morning."

"O'Henry's an early riser," Josh said.

"Seems to be," Cecilia replied, and chomped into her sandwich, a chunk of raw onion dropping from her lower lip to her lap. With her bony fingers, she pinched the onion off her lab coat and stuck it back in her mouth. The crisp onion crunched between her molars, and a grin resurfaced on her lips as she studied Josh.

"Was she dead or alive?" Josh asked.

"After the decapitation?" Cecilia asked, her grin broadening.

Josh didn't respond.

"Okay, alive," Cecilia said. "She saw it coming that's for sure. If that's what you mean."

Rachael walked around to the end of the stainless steel examination table, a frown creasing her forehead. "I don't get it. O'Henry lops the head off at sunrise, keeps it hidden somewhere all day, and then delivers it to Central Park after sunset. Seems to me that, once he's done the deed, he would want to get rid of the evidence. Once she's dead, so is the thrill."

"I agree," Cecilia said. "It'd make a lot more sense to

cut her in the afternoon . . . say, just before sundown."

"Maybe he's into ceremonial killings," Josh said. "A ritual slaughter, a break of dawn Druid thing. Or, he has to get it done before he leaves for work. He's got a busy day ahead of him and he doesn't want to be pressured for time when he gets home. Or maybe his wife works night shifts, and it would get complicated if he left it to end of the day when she was up and about."

Rachael was about to speak, when her phone vibrated in her coat pocket. She reached for it and it snagged on a thread in her pocket's lining, causing it to fly out of her hand and hit the marble floor. The battery popped out on impact, and the phone slid across the floor coming to rest under a workstation. Cecilia retrieved a mop from the closet and managed to fish out the phone and hand it back to Rachael.

Rachael replaced the battery and saw a new message waiting. She listened to it for a few seconds, then turned on the phone's external speaker, replaying the message from the start. The voice sounded as though it were altered by electronics.

"Hello Rachael, I trust the package I left for you in the park was of some interest. Redemption can be such a beautiful thing. Wouldn't you agree? Oh, I know you would, if you'd been there with me and seen it for yourself. Each time I take one, there's such a stir deep inside me, I know God must be smiling down upon me. Alas. . . In the time it takes to swat a mosquito, in a blink of an eye, their spirit is set free. It gives me goose bumps just thinking about it. I shall never tire . . ."

"Oops-a-daisy," the voice continued, now whispering. *"She just stubbed her toe. Hippity hop, hippity hop. Oh my, such a sweet thing. She's so . . . cuddly. I so wish you could be here with me, Rachael, standing at my side, seeing it for yourself."*

Rachael grimaced and closed her eyes.

"My only regret is the detours I've taken. One can take so many wrong turns in life. Such a waste, and the years go by, don't they? But nothing you should worry yourself about. No, no, not at all . . . Oh look, such a sweet family, it's the American dream. A daughter and a son so full of life and ready to step out in the world, sitting and waiting patiently for their dinner. The parents busy, making preparations for the nightly feast. Nature unfolding as it should."

The undertone of the voice then slid to sweetness. *"Rachael, you have no idea of the power that is running through me. It is exquisite . . . I only wish you could feel it too. To look at them going about their lives, never knowing what lies beyond the next bend. You know, I think I might be tempted to take one, that is, if I hadn't— Oh look the meal is ready, the mother hen with her steaming bowl of mashed potatoes. I hope she's added butter and plenty of garlic. Yummy. And papa bear, the big lug, he's right behind her with his fine roast ready for the knife."* The voice paused. *"Frankly, I never did see what she saw in him, and what's with that gray fedora with the red-feather he's always wearing? A man of his stature, does he need such a prop?"* The phone line went dead; the message had ended. Rachael turned to Josh, a strained look on her face. *"Oh God,* I think he's at the mayor's home," she said, looking like she didn't want to believe it.

Rachael punched in a number on her cell, got Anakin on the line, did a quick recap and asked him to have the call traced. "Take Charley and get over there. Have Vivian call Kingsley and let him know. And call NYPD dispatch and get a cruiser to swing past the mayor's house. Tell them to proceed with caution. Tell them a neighbor saw someone sneaking around the mayor's house, but *don't* tell them it could be O'Henry, God knows who's listening in. And call the mayor and warn him. Tell him we're not certain, but we don't want to take any chances."

"And you?" Anakin asked.

"We're on our way." She hung up.

Ten seconds later, they were back in the SUV with Rachael behind the wheel. Josh flipped on the siren and flashing lights. When they hit East Broadway the traffic slowed them to a crawl. Rachael cranked the wheel, took a side street and shot down a number of back alleys and avenues until they reached the Holland Tunnel. By the time they came out the other end, the traffic flow had improved. Rachael gunned it, and after a half-mile on Marion Blvd, the needle was tipping eighty-mph and climbing.

Up ahead road construction had traffic backed up again.

"Looks gridlocked," Josh said.

"Yup," Rachael said, and cranked the wheel with both hands, jumping the median and threading them through oncoming traffic.

Aww shit . . . ! Josh thought.

Rachael changed lanes at will, back and forth, horns

blaring, tires screeching, skidding vehicles all around them.

Then Josh saw it. A tanker truck straight ahead. The truck driver laid on his horn, the deep booming sound rattling Josh's eardrums as he pumped on his imaginary brake pedal. Seconds to impact. Josh stomped his foot to the floor, then grabbed hold of the dash, both arms extended, elbows locked. Rachael threw the SUV into a lower gear, cranked the wheel to the right, and punched the gas. The hot tires bit the pavement, and they shot over the median and slammed into the construction site. Road crew workers dove out-of-the-way as the SUV plowed through, flattening mounds of gravel, spraying crushed rock out in all directions, smashing through a number of road barriers and launching a 45-gallon drum high into the air.

A few seconds later, they burst out the other side of the construction site, the SUV's bumper, hood and fenders all contorted and scarred, but the engine was still running. Rachael gunned it again and a mile-and-a-half later took a right on Sherwood Drive, then an immediate left on Willow Crescent and rolled up to a stop, some five car lengths from the mayor's home. Steam hissed and poured out from the hood as the engine tried to shut down, banging and clunking a few times before it gave up and died.

Rachael ran for the front door and rang the bell. Anakin and Charley were just pulling up as a patrol car arrived.

Josh headed to the back of the house. At the gate he stopped, took a couple of deep breaths, and for the first time wished he was carrying his gun. He slipped into the backyard and did a quick surveillance. With its terraced gardens, old oaks, maples and elms, it had the look and size of a city park. Piles of leaves three-to-four feet high were raked up under each tree, ready for bagging. A greenhouse built to match the home's exterior was in one corner of the yard. A dim light glowed over its entrance.

Josh stepped onto the back porch and opened the screen door.

Chapter 16

The mayor's house sat on a quiet, curved crescent backing onto a wooded ravine. The house was a two-story, four-gabled brick structure, with a flat-roofed side addition that served as a den. Out front, street lamps filtered light through branches of elms and oaks bordering the sidewalk. And while the house had a substantial presence, the press had deemed it modest in comparison to those of his predecessors. The mayor had been clear from the start; he wanted his family to live as normal a life as possible.

The mayor was not in his usual loquacious mood. The day had gone rather well, but the call from the commissioner had put him off. Yet it was Tuesday night and that meant roast beef. He followed his wife from the kitchen to the dining room, and went to claim his spot at the head of the table. His wife was about to place a large bowl of mashed potatoes on the table when she stubbed her toe and almost dropped them.

"You okay?" he asked.

"Yes dear . . . a bit clumsy tonight, I'm afraid."

The mayor sat down and got comfortable, placing the cutting board and roast beef in front of him. He reached to make the first slice when the phone rang. No one dared to answer it. It was dinner time, and calls were not allowed once they were seated at the table—a family rule.

At the center of the table, three lit candles flickered. The mayor held his carving knife up to the light and inspected the blade. He valued a sharp edge; it allowed him to show off his skill as a carver, which was especially important to him when they had a visitor.

O'Henry stood outside the mayor's home, balancing himself on the top of a large earthenware flowerpot, looking into what he guessed was the study. The window had been left cracked open an inch, allowing air to escape. He flared his nostrils and inhaled, *roast beef.*

The light in the study was off, and what little light entered came in from the dining room. The two rooms were separated by a half-wall with ivory wooden pillars on either end. In the middle of the study was a wooden desk with an opened laptop, a printer, and a neat stack of paper.

O'Henry watched the family huddled around the dinner table. The mayor seemed quite content seated at the head of the table; his family gathered around him. Then, in the blink of an eye, the mayor's expression changed, and he seemed to lose interest in the meal. With the carving knife resting next to the roast, he turned to his wife. "Dear, did you call Katherine for dinner?"

"Oh, I forgot to mention, she called earlier . . . she's still at school."

The mayor's hand began to tremble. "When did she call?" he asked, trying to remain calm.

"She'll be home soon. There's a new instructor who started today. He wanted to keep the class late and have one of those, get to know you sessions." The mayor's wife checked her watch. "She should be here any minute."

The mayor sighed. "Would you mind giving her a call, see how far out she is? Just to see when she'll get here."

"Call her during dinner?" his wife asked. "*Really*, she is a big girl now."

The mayor tensed, furrowing his brow . . .

"Okay dear, I'll check with her. But you know, you are acting a little odd."

The mayor didn't respond and carved a thick slice.

His other two children were seated on either side of the table, and Lefty, the family pooch, an animal rescue mutt, was lying under the table waiting for scraps to fall.

All of a sudden, Lefty's ears straightened. He jumped up, let out a single, sharp bark and pranced into the kitchen. He sniffed around, then padded to the back door and let out a couple more barks.

The mayor flinched at the first bark.

"What is it?" his wife asked, looking annoyed. "Why are you being so fidgety tonight?"

"Lefty, gave me a start, that's all . . ."

O'Henry slid around to the back porch screen door and stopped. He was dressed in an anti-reflective, black body suit, and held a large, wicker picnic basket in his hand. He gently sat the basket down and opened the door a couple of inches. Reaching up; he released the cotter pin of the door's spring, leaving it hanging loose, then opened the door and stepped inside. He placed the wicker basket on a card table next to a row of mason jars filled with homemade dill pickles. As he unscrewed the porch light bulb, he heard a dog's bark. Quickly and silently he dropped down and slid in behind an old beer fridge.

"I'm gonna check on Lefty," the mayor said, as he rose from the table. He headed down the hall and into the kitchen and saw Lefty scratching at the door. He flipped the porch light switch from inside the kitchen, but the light did not come on. He peered into the porch, and while there was some light coming in from the kitchen, it was still too dark to see much. *A raccoon maybe. . . . Jesus, I hope not, they make such a mess.* Stepping over to the kitchen sink, he reached in and lifted out a heavy meat tenderizer. He tapped the rippled steel on the palm of his hand and felt his confidence return. He knew he shouldn't be afraid of a raccoon, but seeing a wild animal in his home, even a mouse, unnerved him. He returned to the door, grabbed the handle, and pushed the door wide open, until it nudged up against the beer fridge. He stopped in his tracks. Sirens were coming down the street. Coming fast.

The mayor stood and listened for a moment. *It's getting louder,* he thought, then turned and saw colored lights strobing across the hallway. He rushed back through the kitchen and down the hallway to the front door.

Rachael was knocking on the door when the mayor opened it. "Sorry for disturbing you Mayor, but we received a call from O'Henry. It sounded like he was right outside your home."

"You *think* he was at my home, but you're not sure," the mayor said, his voice low as he spoke through clenched teeth.

"Is everyone in your family accounted for?" Rachael asked, ignoring his anger.

His face went blank, and he turned in the direction of the dining room. "When did Katherine say she'd be home?" he called out to his wife, his voice wavering.

"Any minute now, I told you that. Why? What's going on?" the mayor's wife asked, stepping into the hall.

Rachael asked, "Have you noticed anything out of the ordinary tonight?"

"Nothing," he said. "The dog was acting a little strange, barking and scratching at the back door. That was just before you—"

"Show me the back door, now!" Rachael demanded.

The mayor didn't hesitate, leading Rachael down the hall and out through the kitchen to the back porch, his wife trailing close behind. Rachael grabbed the mayor's arm, and held her hand up, indicating that he should stay put. Stepping around him, she pushed open the screen door.

Josh was kneeling on the porch floor, petting Lefty. He glanced up as Rachael appeared. "I've checked the backyard. No sign of him."

"Oh, thank God," the mayor said, sounding relieved.

"What's that?" the mayor's wife asked as she stepped forward and pointed to the wicker picnic basket sitting next to her pickles.

Chapter 17

Josh turned to the mayor and his wife. "Mayor, I want you to take your wife and return to the front room." *If the worst is about to happen, a parent cannot have that image to deal with the rest of their lives.*

The mayor stumbled as he turned to his wife, his eyes filled with fear.

"What is it?" the mayor's wife asked, her voice wavering.

The mayor wrapped his arm around his wife's shoulders and ushered her out through the kitchen to the front room.

"Ah hell Josh . . . this is such *bullshit*," Rachael said, standing next to the fridge. She paused for a moment and just stared at the basket, then looked up and said, "All right, let's get it done . . ."

The wicker basket had been tied shut with a baby-blue checkered bow. Josh tugged on a strand of the bow and the ribbon fell to the floor. He slid off the lid and peered inside. "Ahhh . . ." he sighed and stood there for a second, then reached in and withdrew a bottle of fine red wine, a block of wrapped goat cheese, two ornate, long-stemmed wine glasses, and a fresh loaf of olive bread. He placed each item on the table before turning back to Rachael, her face drained of color.

"What?"

"Those," she said, pointing to the contents of the basket he'd laid out on the table. "Those are mine. He's been in my home."

The mayor poked his head out the back door, and upon seeing the wine and cheese, cried out, "Thank the Lord . . . !" He was about to continue, when they heard a loud commotion coming from the front yard . . .

The Channel Four news team had arrived and were busy setting up to go on air. Lead reporter Jane Taylor had her microphone in her hand and was walking toward Anakin and Charley.

Josh and Rachael ran through the house and out the front door. Josh saw Taylor and jogged over to cut her off. "Can I see you for a minute?" he asked. As they walked over to the satellite truck, he said, "Look, this is really not good timing."

"Hey, you're Josh Ingram, right?" Taylor asked. "I was gonna talk to Anakin, but I'd much rather talk with you. I know all about you. I covered you when I first started as a reporter. It's been what, twenty years?"

It had been a long time since he'd talked to a reporter. The last time he was in the spotlight, they'd made it into a freak show with him as the main attraction. The pain of that memory was ripping open old wounds, and with every word she spoke he could feel his frustration spiraling out of control. He glared at her.

She leaned back. "*Hey* . . . c'mon, take it easy. Look. I got a call from some guy, that's all. He said there was a man sneaking around the mayor's house, peeping in the windows. He said the cops were here and something was going on. It's my job to report on these things, Ingram.

You know that."

"This caller, did you get a name?"

"Well, yeah. I . . . I think he called himself O'Henry? Yeah, that's right, O'Henry. Wouldn't give me his full name though."

Josh frowned. "It's too bad you wasted your time. We got the same call and nothing is going on here, other than the mayor's a little upset with all the attention."

"Sure, okay," she said, and stared at him for a moment. Then she turned to leave, took a few steps, stopped and spun around. "Wait a minute. O'Henry, wasn't that the name of that psycho? You know, the one who disappeared years ago. . . . Sure it was." Then, the penny dropped. "Holy crap. He's the one responsible for the head in Central Park. O'Henry. He's back, isn't he?"

"Look, we don't have enough information to know for sure. You *cannot* go live with this. We are in the middle of an investigation. Give us a few days? If you can do that, I'll give you an exclusive when we collar him."

"But this is great stuff!" Taylor said. "It's a certified career-making moment. And you're asking me to sit on it?" She straightened her suit jacket and threw back her hair.

"You're on in five, four," her cameraman counted down.

"You just don't get it, do you?" Josh said.

"*Annnd* you're on."

"This is Jane Taylor of Channel Four News reporting to you live from outside the home of Mayor Andy Carothers in Newark, New Jersey. This evening our news team received word a man was seen creeping around the mayor's home. As you can see, there are a number of police officers already at the scene. Rumors are circulating that the mayor has been targeted by a serial killer who terrorized the City of New York several years ago. The killer was known as O'Henry, and the last time he rolled into town, his reign of terror lasted for the better part of a year, before he suddenly disappeared. I've just spoken with Josh Ingram, who says it is too soon to make a comment. Mr. Ingram was made famous as a lead profiler for the FBI a long time ago. Which raises the obvious question. Why would Ingram be here, if O'Henry isn't? Jane Taylor, Channel Four News."

Josh sighed. "Ahh, shit."

Rachael was standing next to Anakin's car, and looked over at Josh and threw up her hands as if to say, *what the hell just happened?* "That was a friggin' disaster," she said as she stomped over. "O'Henry's got what he wanted, full friggin' media coverage. From here on in, it's gonna be a political shit-storm."

Josh knew she was right, the carnival had begun.

"Never mind," Rachael said, sounding almost apologetic. "I have to get some rest that's all, my head is so friggin' numb. . . . And yet, what I can't figure out, is why he led us here? Why terrorize the mayor? It makes no sense."

"He's peacocking," Josh said.

"What?"

"He's strutting his stuff, showing us he's in control. He believes he's smarter than all of us. Screwing with us makes him feel superior. In short, he's telling us that he's running the show."

"I'm starting to think he is," Rachael said, as slowly rubbed her temples.

Josh could see she was near collapse and needed rest. He also knew she couldn't go home. "You can stay at my place tonight. . . . I'll take the couch. Your place isn't safe. We'll sort things out in the morning."

Rachael studied him for a moment, and cocked her head to one side . . .

Chapter 18

Josh did not sleep well. He could have blamed it on the hotel couch being too short, but he knew better. Rachael lying in his bed a few steps away had made it a long night.

He smelled fresh coffee brewing and opened one eye. Rachael was standing at the vanity sink washing out a cup. She was wearing one of the hotel's white robes, her auburn hair tied up in a ponytail. She seemed lost in thought.

"Sleep well?" he asked, sitting up and stretching.

She turned toward him, startled. "You're awake," she said, and then answered his question. "Yeah . . . sort of, but I'm finding the thought of O'Henry inside my home, going through my stuff, a bit of a challenge. How about you? You sleep well?"

"Fantastic."

She looked at him and gave him a sly grin.

Busted, he thought and cracked a smile.

"Coffee?" she asked.

"Please."

As Rachael came around the couch with a cup in her hand she took in Josh's bare chest. "Whoa . . . you've seen some action."

He gave a slight nod. His body had incurred damage

over the years. Two nearly round bullet scars decorated his torso, one on his left shoulder, the other on his collarbone. A long, faint scar ran across his chest, and one shaped like a small rectangle was carved into his lower ribcage. He grabbed his shirt off the back of a chair, put it on and stepped up to the window without saying a word.

Rachael cleared her throat. "Vivian called a few minutes ago, they've tagged our Jane Doe. Her name is Jessica Hilton, age 32, a tax accountant with Zenith, Hamilton, and Smith. Her roommate saw the sketch in the paper. She came in this morning and gave a positive ID. The roommate said the last time she saw Jessica was on Saturday night. They'd been at a bar with a group of friends. She said Jessica would never stay for more than one glass of wine, and as usual she told them she was tired and left to go home. That was around nine-thirty. The two shared an apartment in Chelsea, and the roommate said it was okay if we had a look. She gave me the address."

Rachael flashed her badge at the apartment manager, then she and Josh took the elevator to the third floor. Jessica and her roommate had the end unit. It was an upscale apartment, renovated: with new hardwood floors, white cupboards, black synthetic countertops, and high-end appliances. A stationary bicycle was set up against an exposed brick wall. Black-and-white travel photos of Jessica in various countries hung in the main room. Josh took down one of the pictures, removed it from its frame, and stuck it in his pocket.

A long hallway led to the bedrooms. There were

more photographs, showing Jessica and her roommate in different marathons, as well as a framed newspaper article covering the New York Marathon with a picture of runners crossing the Verrazano-Narrows Bridge to Brooklyn. Near the center of the article was a face circled in red. Josh couldn't tell for sure, but he thought it was her.

"Pretty girl," Rachael said.

"Very. That is, if you like the athletic, beautiful, and successful type."

Rachael's eyes narrowed.

Josh caught a glimpse of her reaction . . . *okay,* he thought.

An office was set-up in what could have doubled as a large closet. There was an Apple desktop on a small desk, a jar filled with sharpened pencils, and a digital desk clock. Everything in its place. Beside the desk stood a black metal filing cabinet. Josh tried the cabinet drawers. They were locked. After rooting around the desk, he found the key under the pencil jar.

The cabinet was filled with files, labeled A to Z. The top drawer files were each designated by a company name. Each contained a few years of financial statements, correspondence, and her billing invoice. In the lower drawer he came across her personal files. Files for utilities, telephone, cable, and receipts for major purchases. Josh pulled the file labeled Visa. Receipts for each month were stapled to that month's statement. *Huh. Old school . . . gotta be the accounting gene.* He gathered up the last six months of Visa statements and receipts, and went out to the kitchen and took a seat at the table.

He removed the staples and stacked the receipts off to one side, then scanned each statement, looking for names of restaurants and grocery stores.

Having finished with the bedrooms and the bathroom Rachael came back down the hall. "Any luck?"

"Yeah, maybe. There are three restaurants she seems to prefer. One Italian, one French and one Thai. She buys most of her groceries at Fresh Foods Garden Market, and her meat from a butcher shop called World Wide Meats."

Rachael called Vivian and gave her the names of the three restaurants and told her to take Michal along.

An electric bell chimed as Rachael and Josh entered World Wide Meats. The place smelled of spices, garlic, and onions. The front area measured no more than fifteen-by-twenty feet. Josh immediately knew it was a waste of time. The space was too tight, O'Henry wouldn't be interested in this location. There was no room to maneuver, no way to carry out an assessment.

They spoke with the owner anyway, showing him a picture of Jessica. Though the owner did not work the front often, he remembered her. "Who could forget such a beautiful woman?" He went on to tell them he hadn't seen her for a while, but then again, he worked in the back most of the time. He offered to check with his regular front-end employee and get back to them if she remembered anything.

Rachael's cell rang as they left the market. It was the coroner, Cecilia Bloom. She advised the contents of the victim's stomach; lasagna, rapini, mozzarella cheese and a variety of other Italian ingredients. Rachael called up Vivian and filled her in.

They didn't have to go far to find Fresh Foods Garden Market, it was just around the corner from World Wide Meats. It was small compared to the big box stores, but the organic selection looked reasonable, Josh thought.

He turned to Rachael. "You eat organic?"

"Yeah sometimes," she said, and a look of disbelief crossed her face. "Don't be telling me you do, because I've seen what you've been eating."

"Hey, I'm thinking I'll make an effort to treat my body better is all I'm saying."

"Well in that case, maybe I'll make us a healthy dinner. See if your system can handle it."

They took a tour of the store before circling around to the front cashier. Rachael flashed her badge, asking the woman to call the manager. A moment later, a middle-aged, big-haired blonde, stepped out of her small office.

"FBI Special Crimes Unit," Rachael said, her badge in her hand. "We are investigating a woman who is known to have shopped here."

"So what's that got to do with me?" the manager asked, looking at Josh and chewing hard on her gum, her mouth opening and closing faster than a toilet seat at a Roots and Blues festival.

Minty, she must've just popped the gum into her mouth, Josh thought, wanting to reach out and clamp her lips together. Instead, he showed her the picture of Jessica, and instantly saw recognition register on her face.

"Oh that one," the manager said. "Comes in a couple of times a week. Never spoke to her, seemed normal enough, I guess. If there is such a thing." Then she made a loud popping sound with her gum.

You are driving me nuts, Josh thought, grinding his teeth. He gave his head a quick shake, trying to break free of the image of the woman's flapping mouth, and pointed to a video box near the ceiling. "Are they all working?"

"Darn straight they are. Insurance won't even look at you if they're not in order. Why, what's up? What'd she do?" she asked, now acting as if they were going to let her in on a big secret.

Josh's voice was cold. "She was murdered a few days ago."

The manager swallowed hard. "No kidding . . ." she said, a stunned look on her face . . .

"How often do you change the video tapes?" Rachael asked.

"Once a week. Cameras take a picture four times a minute. Keep the old tapes for a month then recycle them. There's a box set up in all four corners of the store. Low tech stuff, tapes only, the owner doesn't wanna spend much on that kind of thing."

"What are your store hours?" Rachael asked.

"Twenty-four-seven," she said, and rolled her eyes. "Staffing's a bitch!" Then she waved to Beatrice on the till. "No offense."

"We'll need all the tapes currently in the video boxes and all the previous tapes you still have on hand," Rachael said.

The store manager continued to chomp away on her gum and drew a half-circle on the floor with the toe of her shoe. She was less enthusiastic now that she had to lift a finger.

Twenty minutes later they left the store with Josh holding an apple box half-filled with old tapes.

Chapter 19

A sizzle followed by a brilliant flash and immediate clap of thunder gave the preacher pause.

On cue, umbrellas began popping up, dotting the congregation like mushrooms in fresh manure. Josh turned up his jacket collar, slid his hands deep into his pockets and let the rain come down.

The preacher resumed. "Arthur was a good man, loved by family, friends, and . . ."

Josh had already tuned out the preacher's sermon and begun to scan the congregation. Three employees from Arthur's store huddled together on the outer fringe, passing a joint around, its tip brightening to a reddish glow with every toke.

Without warning the wind changed direction. A moment later, the rain cranked up and within a few seconds small streams began forming in the mud, dovetailing into a larger flow that snaked its way through the congregation.

Josh could see Arthur's mother and father, and he almost felt pity for them. *Silent and sober . . . that's gotta be a first. . . . It's amazing your son turned out as well as he did.*

Standing off to one side of his parents were his cousins, all lined up in a neat row. The hoods of their raincoats erect, their faces more irritated than sorrowed—looked like a flock of pale-faced ravens perched on a fence, waiting for Tuesday's garbage truck to arrive.

A clump of fresh dirt hit the casket. Arthur's mother had dropped the first trowel-full of wet dirt into the grave. The sound of the soil hitting the casket lid made her wobble and stumble to one knee. *Perhaps not so sober,* Josh thought.

The congregation started to file past the grave. Some tossed in dirt, others a flower, and some walked by without a glance. Josh's heart softened when he saw Janis drop in a single red rose and wipe away a tear. She didn't know Arthur that well, but she knew him enough to care.

Josh stepped to the edge of the grave. The casket glistened like a giant June bug; its back freckled with small mounds of earth and a few flowers. Rain dripped off the ebony lid, forming shallow puddles in the grave muck. *A last moment in the open air before an eternity of darkness,* he thought. A chill prickled down his spine and a deep sadness entered his heart. A knot was forming in his throat, and he whispered, "I'm gonna miss you Arthur." He sensed the line was building up behind him and said, "I guess . . . I'll see you on the other side." Then he sprinkled soil on the casket and brushed away a tear with his thumb.

By the time the last person filed past Arthur's grave, the wind had increased and sheets of icy rain whipped the congregation. Dresses clung unflatteringly to women's behinds, hats flew into the air, and the procession came to a close with a succession of car engines starting.

Two gravediggers, sheltered under a large spruce tree, buttoned up their dark-green raincoats and made their way to the grave, stomping on the earth a few times for good measure and then commenced shoveling. Josh watched them work, their motions efficient. *No doubt eager to get to their lunch break. Strange how life seems to go on and on and then the next moment, it's over.* Then he thought of Arthur's life being cut short and a rage rose up inside him.

A young woman came up behind him and said with a trace of Spanish in her voice, "I am sorry to bother you at a time such as this. And I am so sorry for your friend."

Josh turned to her, his eyes filled with anger.

The woman stopped and took a half-step back. "My name is Anna Espada," she said, a soft lilt to her voice warming her words. "Later, if you could make the time, I would like to speak with you."

Josh let out a short breath through slack lips. "I'm not so sure you'd want to talk to me."

"I do not understand."

"Yeah . . . me neither," he said and tried to smile.

She studied him and said nothing.

Josh took a moment before relenting. "Look, I'm staying at the Marriott, downtown. If you want, you can reach me there. And sorry about . . ."

"Thank you. I will," she said, giving him an understanding smile, then turned and walked away.

Josh watched as she made her way to the street. A large black sedan pulled to the curb and a man jumped from the passenger side and opened the back door, then she was gone.

Josh turned and saw Janis waiting for him by her car. He glanced back one last time at the grave and was overcome with an urge to crawl into a dark corner and go to sleep.

Chapter 20

The cargo van's interior reeked of cleanliness. O'Henry liked that. Scrubbing sparked an urge, coated his thoughts, made him strong, potent. He knew he had done a wonderful job of cleaning; everything so shiny and pure. *Hmm, nothing to do but wait,* he thought . . . then ran his tongue along his upper molars and felt a husk of popcorn imbedded in his gum line, and pondered what kind of germs were feasting on him.

He took a deep breath in through his nostrils, the caustic fragrance was addictive. He shut his eyes tight and sucked harder this time, the corrosive brew tracking in past his sinuses, then all at once he began pinching at the bridge of his nose—his sinuses were on fire. *Yes, yes, so good, so cleansing,* he thought, as his eyes began to leak. He looked into the mirror, and with his index fingers pulled down his lower lids revealing the pink flesh inside. He stopped. "What was that?" he said, and peered out into the night. *Nothing . . . nothing at all, only silence,* he concluded.

He returned to the mirror, cocked his head and tried to decide whether his eyes were more brown or green. Again, he felt it. *You are here, aren't you? I know it.* "Ah yes," he said and felt it curl into his thoughts. It had been his unwelcome companion for as long as he could remember. *Alone,* he thought, *how can such a simple word be so very cruel?*

He paused, and his face hardened. *There is business to attend to. I cannot deal with you now.* He savored being in control, it made him feel noble, and indeed he did feel noble, at least until the table tilted and his mercurial, blue-blooded thoughts slid off the edge. He let out a breath and muttered, "You should have drowned me as a child, when you had the chance, mother."

He wiped a speck of moisture from his cheek and gave his head a shake. "But you're not going home alone, are you old man?" Suddenly a tremor of excitement shot though him, and his skin began to sear as if a flame had been set upon it. He squirmed in his seat, and checked the mirror again. *Oh, I'm glowing. . . .* "I am ready for you, Jennifer."

He checked his watch; he was a full half-hour ahead of schedule. He had to slow things down. If he got too excited, he could make a mistake. And that wasn't going to happen, not tonight, not ever. So, he rolled down his window and took in the night. It was cool and smelled of fall. A dusting of leaves had gathered by the curb and the air lay motionless and soft; it was a peaceful evening. He adjusted the rearview mirror a smidgeon, making certain he captured the gate. He was calm now, able to sit and wait and ponder.

Yesterday had been triumphant. He'd never intended choosing the mayor's daughter. Of course not, the daughter was less than perfect, not that she had to be, not now, not like before. *Oh, but she was so far from it,* he thought, and shuddered. *But taunting Rachael and Josh, and having them mill about like little concerned citizens, that did add such an indescribable dimension. Better than I could've ever imagined. And then, slipping into Rachael's world, hearing the door of her apartment click behind me, knowing I was alone and could do as I pleased . . . my hands under her sheets, touching where the curve of her body molded into the mattress. Absorbing her glorious scent as I withdrew the covers. So exhilarating.*

As he checked his watch, his stomach began to growl. He was feeling more than a bit peckish. *Time to focus on the task at hand.* Just as a mother knows the scent of her own child, he knew Jennifer was his.

He had done his homework. He knew Jennifer's schedule, that she lived alone, and that when she came out of the building tonight and passed through the gate, she would have a red yoga mat under her arm.

His stomach growled again. The excitement of the hunt always made him ravenous. On the seat beside him was a small, stainless steel suitcase. He dialed off the combination to each latch and opened it. He reached in and withdrew a CD, titled *Puccini - La Boheme*, then popped it into the player and adjusted the volume down to a level he found comforting. Then he withdrew a stainless steel thermos, followed by a teacup. Next came a china plate, covered by a tiny, transparent glass dome. On the plate were two cucumber sandwiches—crusts removed. Next, came a small bowl imprinted with a pastel floral design of pink and green. Inside the bowl was a variety of sweets, each wrapped in colored foil. Lastly, he withdrew a lace tablecloth, unfolded it and laid it on the case top. He poured a cup of Earl Grey, placed the teacup on the tablecloth and munched away on his cucumber sandwich.

He loved Puccini. He felt the conductor understood

him, and he loved cucumber sandwiches because they were delicate and tasty. Halfway through the second sandwich, and part way through Puccini's first act, he saw her. *She's early.* He clicked the music off and quickly deposited everything back into the case.

Jennifer stepped out of her walkup apartments front entrance. She was a half-dozen car lengths away, the red yoga mat tucked under her arm. A narrow sidewalk led to the street and at the gate stood a mature maple and a wrought-iron street lamp.

She stopped and fumbled with the gate latch, and something dropped to the ground. She bent down and picked up what he guessed was a set of car keys. *Excellent.* Her car was parked in the lot across from him. He was certain she'd turn his way, *but then again, what if she decided to walk tonight, it's not much more than a mile from here. No, she's a busy girl, she'll take the car.*

She stood still for a moment, opened the gate and turned in his direction. "Yes," he said, and let out a muted squeal of excitement. He checked his mirrors, looking up and down the street. All was quiet. Climbing into the back of the van he slid the side door open. Then, moving to the back window, he crouched down to watch. As she closed in, his heart rate picked up, and his skin began to tingle with anticipation.

She stepped under a streetlight, now only two car lengths away. She was wearing dark-blue running tights, a gray T-shirt, and a light-blue windbreaker, the kind that breathed. Her shoulder purse dangled at her side, car keys in hand.

Seconds to go. He reached down and clicked on a tape recorder and a baby's cry drifted out of the side door.

Immediately Jennifer took notice, and he could see her trying to figure out what was going on.

Such a simple ploy, he thought, and yet he'd never found a better bait to draw a woman's protective instinct out into the open. A moment later a distraught woman's voice from inside the van joined in, begging for help. The woman's voice, heavy with a Polish accent, poured out into the night, pleading. "My child. Please, please someone help me . . ."

O'Henry slipped out the other side of the van and waited, his arms loose by his side, a syringe balancing in his hand.

Jennifer stepped closer and called out, "Who's there?"

Her voice was strained, but had an honest warmth; he liked that, she came from good stock, from a fine bloodline. He moved around to the back corner of the van and could see her leaning forward, looking to see if someone else was around. No one else was in sight. No one else could help. The baby's cry just kept coming. Jennifer edged closer to the side door, putting her hand on the side of the van . . .

The moment had come, the moment all his preparation would be rewarded.

Jennifer craned her neck to look inside. O'Henry, now right behind her, stepped forward and clamped his latex gloved hand over her face. As the needle slid into her neck, and its contents emptied into her bloodstream, a muffled scream tried to escape. Hot air puffed from her nostrils and he felt the warmth seep into his hand. A second later, she fell back into his arms.

As he laid her onto the van floor, he noticed she smelled of fresh cut cucumbers. *Fascinating.*

He slid the door closed, locked it . . . then slowly eased away from the curb.

Chapter 21

After four hours of reviewing security footage, the air in the boardroom had gotten stale and uncomfortably warm. Rachael stood up, stripped off her sweater and tossed it on the table.

Josh blinked and took a deep breath, and was thankful she could not read his mind.

He didn't know what scent she had on, but he was having serious trouble concentrating and decided to take a short break. He stepped over to open the window, then leaned back and let his mind drift back to the marina. He thought about Eddie, wondering how he and Mary were getting along. The chemistry of an attention deficit riddled lab, tormented with irritable bowel syndrome, and a short-fused, ass-kicking little woman would've been interesting to witness. He smiled and hoped they were doing okay. Then he looked over at Rachael, still glued to the tube, wound up and focused. *So beautiful.*

Rachael glanced up. "What . . . ? What's going through that damaged brain of yours?"

"Thinking."

"Thinking about what?"

"Nothing that'd interest you."

"Well then, if you could drag yourself over here, I could use some help."

Another hour had passed and still no progress. His energy level had tanked and his legs had gone into restless mode; forcing him to stretch his ankles in one direction then the other, just to relieve the tension. *Time to pull the plug . . . this is going nowhere.* And had it not been for a twinge of pain jabbing him in his lower back, snapping him out of his torpor, he would have missed it. On the screen before him was a tall man in an overcoat. He was reaching toward a shelf of canned food. There was something about the man; Josh couldn't put his finger on it, but something was wrong. The man's back was to the camera, so maybe it wasn't him, but rather the woman who faced him. Josh tried to zero in on her face, but the shot was unclear, and he couldn't make out much, other than the woman had a certain delicacy about her. The next frame was of another woman, a portly specimen. She was looking backwards over her shoulder and had two children in tow. This picture was blurred as well, but she was clearly frightened and in a hurry to get her children out of there. The next frame was again of the man, showing a partial profile of his head, and it was in focus, as was the next frame showing the delicate woman pushing her cart in the direction of the tall man, his back once more to the camera. Josh took a second look, blinked, and tilted his head. Then it clicked. "It's her. Hold that frame."

"What?"

"It's her—the head on the bench—it's Jessica Hilton."

Rachael did a double take. "Oh my God."

"Go back a few frames. I have to check something."

Rachael rolled back the tape, to where the tall man was reaching for the canned goods.

"Look at this guy's hand. What is that?"

Rachael leaned in close to the screen. "It's too dull. Can't make it out, maybe there was a film on the camera lens?"

"I don't think so . . . roll the tape a little further."

The next frame was of the pudgy woman and her children, followed by the partial profile of the man.

"Stop," Josh said. "Look, look at his eye. Around its edges, something is not right."

"Yeah," Rachael said, staring at the screen. "I guess."

"No, it's off. We need to check it out."

"Well . . . okay, sure . . ."

Josh could see she wasn't as convinced as he was, but she picked up the phone and called the lab. "We got a couple of hits. I'm sending you the tape now, we'll need blow-ups ASAP. Make them as large as you can." She turned to Josh. "We'll have the prints within the hour."

Josh nodded.

Rachael hesitated, looking as though she was deciding if she should say something, then asked, "You want to go for a walk?"

They were three blocks north and two block east before they came across an art gallery that caught their attention. The current show was by a local artist, impressionism. Oil.

After viewing the gallery for a few minutes, Rachael turned to Josh. "So tell me," and she paused for a second before asking, "Is there someone in your life?"

"Yes, there is. . . . His name is Eddie."

"Oh, okay . . . I didn't realize," Rachael said, sounding embarrassed.

"Eddie is my dog."

Rachael grinned. "You're a complete moron. Has anyone ever told you that?"

"Nope. Not today," he said, and they both laughed.

By the time they made it back and entered the debriefing room, Mark from the lab was waiting for them, holding a few prints in his hand.

"How'd they turn out?" Rachael asked.

"The picture of the woman's face and the man's profile turned out okay," Mark said. "The others, not so much."

After everyone had taken their seats, Rachael addressed the team. "As you have all heard, we have a picture of the woman in Central Park, doing her shopping at Fresh Foods Garden Market. We will put Jessica Hilton up on the screen in a moment, but first let's hear what else we have." Rachael nodded to Vivian.

Vivian cleared her throat. "There are a number of grocery store chains, but only two of them, Harmony Foods and Fresh Foods Garden Market, are located in all eight of the victims' neighborhoods. We've spoken to the staff of both Harmony and Fresh Foods in four of the eight neighborhoods and drawn blanks. So far O'Henry seems to have frequented only the one Fresh Foods store, the one you hit yesterday. We'll continue checking the remaining stores tomorrow. Then we'll start reviewing the video footage of each location.

"We've been checking the web for restaurants common to each neighborhood. We located one that has locations in three of the neighborhoods, an Italian place called Antonio's. The thing is, restaurants fold faster than a perp's alibi, so their names change a lot. The good news is, one of the Antonio's restaurants is located in Chelsea, Jessica's stomping ground. We checked it out, and one waitress thought she remembered her, although she couldn't be sure. The thing is, the place is so dimly lit you'd have trouble reading the menu, let alone O'Henry scoping out his next victim."

"Good point," Josh conceded, half listening, as he studied the eight by tens from the security tape. He clicked on the overhead and slipped the picture of the man's profile into place. The photo was now three by four feet in size. Josh stepped up close to it and gave his earlobe a light tug and thought for a moment. "Everybody. Do you all see this?" he asked, pointing at the screen. "There's a raised ridge at the corner of the man's eye, it's a different shade, darker than the rest of his skin."

Vivian picked up on it. "Is he wearing a mask?"

The team fell silent.

"Yep," Josh said. "It's O'Henry, and the *motherfucker* is wearing a mask."

"A mask?" Michal said. "It's too real."

"Yeah, you're right; it is too real, lifelike, like those used on the stage—you could be standing right beside him and you wouldn't suspect a thing. But in this case, around the eye, there's been damage."

Rachael replaced the picture, putting the one of the frightened woman onto the overhead. "No question this woman is terrified," she said, "which begs the question, what the hell happened to cause that?"

Josh was not paying attention. He was lost, thinking

about the mask.

"Perhaps she can shed some light," Rachael said. "I doubt if she paid cash, and we know the actual time she was there from the tape. Vivian—put together a list of customers who checked out up to a half-hour before and after this picture, then make some calls. Let's hope someone will remember him. Maybe we'll get a break."

"Awfully thin," Charley said and blew his nose.

"Yeah well, if you've got another angle, why don't you share it with us," Rachael snapped, her voice harsh and cold. Then she caught herself and sighed.

Charley just looked at her.

"So, at least we know O'Henry uses grocery stores for his selection process and Fresh Foods in particular," Vivian said, loud enough to catch everyone's attention, clearly trying to get back on a positive track.

Josh shook his head. "Let's face it folks; we've hit a cement wall. O'Henry has his list, and he's not going to surface again. And since he has a goddamn mask, looking backward is also a lost cause. We have to find another angle to ID him, and we have to find it fast."

The team turned to Rachael.

"Okay, people," she said. "Look, Josh may be right about looking backwards, but he could be wrong about the prepared list. If he is, O'Henry could still be out there, at this very moment, sourcing his next victim. We just don't know for sure. Since we're working in a gray area here, we have to cover our bases. What that means is, until a more promising avenue reveals itself we are going to be focusing on Fresh Foods Garden Market, going from location-to-location, leaving them copies of O'Henry's masked photo, viewing tapes, talking to people, and see if it rings any bells that could get us a lead on his next victim. And, in the event O'Henry does show up wearing the mask, which he could do since he has no way of knowing we are onto him, the store is to be instructed to call us immediately. Hey, I know it doesn't look that promising, but it's all we got." She turned to Vivian. "Vivian I want you to organize the process."

"I'm on it," she said.

"People, we have a lot of work to do," Rachael said, "so let's get at it, and hope we get lucky."

"Look everyone," Josh spoke up. "O'Henry is ultra-cautious, but anyone can make a mistake, even him . . . even me." He glanced at Rachael and raised an eyebrow. "So if you do stumble across him, do not forget he is crazy, smart, and lethal. Be careful out there."

The crew then filed out, the mood sober.

Josh's cell vibrated. *It's about time,* he thought. The message was from Oliver Wilson, lead psychiatrist at Pendrana Hospital for the Criminally Insane.

Chapter 22

O'Henry took a sharp right, rolling the cargo van onto a dirt road that ran around to the back of the main house. He continued down a short slope before carving a tight left across a wooden-planked bridge that traversed a trickle creek. He stopped in front of a set of garage doors and pressed a button on his remote.

He calculated Jennifer would be coming out of the anesthetic any minute, as she had been under for more than an hour. And while not a major issue, he preferred to have his quarry locked away, nice and snug, before they came to. They could be difficult if they came around too soon.

He loaded Jennifer into a wheelchair. *Such a treasure you are my dear,* he thought and stroked her hair. *I've done well by you.* Then he rolled the wheelchair to the far end of the garage, to the mouth of a tunnel. The tunnel was made from early 19th century red brick; its archway crowned with a Roman keystone, and stood nine feet two inches at its highest point. Oil lamps lit the passageway revealing a hard packed, amber-colored clay floor. The air was dank and smelled of wet newspapers. He wheeled her down the tunnel, and at the fifty-foot mark he came to a black-painted door situated some twenty feet below the center of the house.

O'Henry

O'Henry unlocked the door and rolled Jennifer into a narrow room with a long, white cabinet set against one wall. The narrow room emptied into a large, square-shaped chamber. Down the chamber's center hung a heavy, dark-brown curtain that divided it in two. On one side of the chamber was a cage about the size of a prison cell. He slid his arm under her thighs and lifted her out of the chair, laying her onto a single cot inside the wired enclosure. He covered her with a gray wool blanket, fluffed up her pillow, then stepped out and locked the door.

An avocado green fridge manufactured in the 1960s hummed outside the cell, a well-used microwave on top. O'Henry did a quick inventory of the fridge and made note to pick up a few microwave dinners and some bottled water. He padded toward the end of the room to another door made of firebrick-red riveted metal. A braided curtain cord hung by the door. It took him a number of pulls to get the heavy, brown curtain fully retracted. He hesitated and glanced back at Jennifer; his face weary, his eyes sad.

He stepped out and entered a hallway that led through a wine cellar. He stopped and turned a few of the bottles, wiping away dust with his gloved hand until he found the right one, a Napa Valley merlot. *Oh my, this will do,* he thought, and felt a sprinkle of joy rise up inside him. He climbed a narrow set of stairs leading straight up through a passageway. He pushed open a trap door and climbed into the kitchen.

A successful hunt always made him a hungry man; he wanted meat, and lots of it. He threw a gargantuan rib-eye onto a twelve-inch skillet, filling it to the brim, and then clicked on the TV. *A game . . . how excellent.* He poured himself a glass of wine, and then set it off to the side to breathe. He watched the players come out onto the field—good teams, good offensive lines, seasoned quarterbacks. *This is going to be such fun . . .*

Jennifer rolled her head to the side and focused. Her screams never left the room.

Chapter 23

Happy Valley Retreat was built as a fat farm in the late 70s and enjoyed a short life of unfulfilled expectations. Located 45 miles out of New York, it was too far to frequent on a daily basis, and not far enough to be thought of as a weekend getaway, so the rich and the round simply chose to ignore it. The state picked it up for a song during the '81 recession and converted it to the Pendrana Hospital for the Criminally Insane.

The building itself was large and stately. Its noble face came from the limestone quarries of Indiana, and could make one believe it housed royalty. Yet Josh knew that behind its dignified face was a head full of sick thoughts. He parked his rental and went inside.

No more than a few minutes passed before he was shown into the office of Oliver Wilson, Managing Director of Operations. Josh raised an eyebrow—Wilson's office would have made a hoarder have an orgasm. Stacks of books were heaped high in each corner. Hundreds of magazines and medical periodicals were piled here-and-there. Some of the piles had been tipped, and the magazines spread out across the floor like a lava flow. Josh had navigated to the epicenter of the room when a horrific shriek came from the hall. Distracted, he knocked over a tall stack of books next to the fireplace.

Taking note of the fireplace, Josh said, "Someone must have thought there was a lot of cash in fat." He checked his friend for a reaction.

Oliver Wilson's gaze had been fixed on his computer screen. He broke free and saw Josh. "Oh, my God. Look what the cat dragged in. Josh. Buddy. Tremendous to see you," Oliver said, his voice jumpy, like he'd been self-medicating again. Oliver reached out to shake hands and glanced at the fireplace. "Yes, it is an unusual perk, isn't it? Almost feel guilty . . . well, almost. In truth? Not even a little bit."

Josh pushed a pile of magazines off a chair and sat down.

"You look healthy . . . thinner," Oliver said, and paused. "Sorry to hear about Arthur. I know you two were close."

"Yeah, thanks man . . . Arthur, he was a great guy." Josh studied Oliver for a moment, then continued. "So, how about you, Oliver? You still seeing that psychologist, what's her name?"

"Paula. We were married last spring . . . and to answer your question, I'm doing great."

Josh said nothing.

"What's this vicious rumor I hear about you working with the Feds again?"

"Yep, it's true. We have an arrangement—sorta helping each other out," Josh said, not wanting to get into the details.

"An *arrangement*, sounds fascinating. You know, I've had a chance to go over the info you sent me on O'Henry. Can't believe the crazy bastard's back in the saddle." Oliver lowered his voice. "Crazy . . . perhaps a poor choice

153

of words to use in here. Ahh, screw'em, let's face it, they're all crazier than a shithouse rat on vacation."

"Still well-suited to your calling I see," Josh said and grinned.

Oliver reached over to a stack of files on the corner of his desk, picked the top folder, laid it down in front of him and opened it. Inside were color photographs of Jessica's head and body, a copy of the coroner's report, and a copy of the note left by O'Henry. "You know what this is of course." Oliver held up the note. "Proverb 31, Portrait of a Godly Woman."

"From King James, yeah I got that, but what of it? It doesn't add up. I mean, he desires the perfect woman and then lops her head off when he discovers she's not, what, flawless? Can't be that simple."

Oliver had the note in one hand and held up her picture in the other. "The psychotic mind sees the world through its own prism and bends that world to its choosing . . . tell me, was the head close to the body?"

"It showed up a day later in the Hudson. No attempt made to hide it or ID-proof it. He just dumped it in the river, same as the other one last week, same as the six killings years ago."

"Plucked out the eyes—the sickos like their trophies, don't they?" Oliver stared at the photo for a moment. "She would've been truly beautiful. Then again, O'Henry always did have a penchant for a pretty head."

Josh let the comment go.

"You know, I wouldn't get my tail in a knot about the bodies in the river," Wilson said. "I think it's simply an expedient place to discard them, that's all. But I have to say, this note in the head thing." He stopped and began scratching at his back, trying to get to an itch he couldn't reach. "It all seems a mite staged. Too methodical even for a control freak, which O'Henry is of course." Wilson opened the bottom drawer to his desk and withdrew a stick about eighteen-inches long with a little orange plastic hand attached to its end. He stuck the stick down the back of his shirt and scratched away. "*Oh my God*, that feels so good! Call it a hunch, but I don't think he's looking for the perfect woman. No, I think he's already found her, the perfect woman, but for some reason, he is denied her. O'Henry is insane, but he's no fool. I think this is all about him making a series of moves to claim his prize."

"If that's the case, why the seven-year sabbatical? Why wait seven years before coming back onto the scene?"

"Good question. However, I doubt that he did wait. Once the sick mind gets started down the path, the thrill of the kill is not so easy to give up. He aches for it. Even if he has his perfect woman in his sights, which I think he just might, his urge to kill is too strong to sideline him for long. It's like a narcotic. More powerful than the need for sex. Totally addictive."

Josh thought about it, and asked, "Then why draw all this attention to the killings now, putting the heads back on display?"

"Again, there has to be an obstacle in his way, or you're right, he would have taken her and be finished with it, no need for all the attention. Since we know he is an intelligent little monkey . . . my guess is, he has a plan to remove the impediment that involves cranking up the spotlight brighter than ever." Oliver opened the drawer and tossed the backscratcher in. "On the other hand, he

155

may just be enjoying all the attention; makes him feel superior, feeds his ego. Tough to nail him down . . . he is after all, a nut case."

"Anything else you can offer?" Josh asked, hoping for more, a lot more.

"Sorry. I do have one caveat for you though; if he deems you a threat to his goal, you'll be dealt with, erased if you will. Then again, that could be part of his plan. Your name *is* in the note. This would suggest you are an important piece of the puzzle. But be careful when he no longer has a need for you."

"A comforting thought."

"I wish I could be of more help. We work on them once they come through the front doors, and try to rewire them. Sometimes we make progress. Most of the time, we just try."

With that, they said their good-byes, and Josh headed back toward town. He stopped at a drive-through burger joint and got himself a double cheeseburger, fries, and a large root beer. As he munched on his fries, he thought about Arthur and the governor, and how it was all too coincidental that Arthur was killed the night before he was to meet with the family's foundation. He needed to check it out, and decided it was time to pay a visit to the governor.

He was guzzling down the last of his root beer when the hands-free rang. "Josh, Rachael here." Her voice wound tight in her throat. "We have another one."

Chapter 24

Josh rolled up next to the west-side entrance of Grand Central Station. Satellite trucks from local and a few major networks were already piled up along the west wall. Sound crews were milling about testing the electronics. Someone called out, "Nine minutes to air."

As Josh swung his legs out of the rental, his stomach did a quarter turn. The burger he'd eaten had set up camp in his guts. He had eaten bad food before so the feeling was not new to him, and he also knew what to expect; sluggishness, cramps, sweat forming in the creases of his body, and so on. *Poor timing,* he thought, but he wasn't too worried, he figured it was still in its early stage. *I'll deal with it later.* And with that thought, he pushed the discomfort to the back of his mind. It would just have to wait.

The October skies were overcast, and a steady drizzle made everything clammy. Josh could see the media was about ready to let the show begin. The techs were doing the final checks. The talent, all female, were hiding out from the rain; some under patio umbrellas, some under truck side canopies. Most were busy applying lipstick and fixing their hair. It appeared much like any other media gathering, but to Josh their actions seemed more animated than usual.

Cable 3 News was there, and Josh did a double take on a face he hadn't seen or thought of for ages. *Debra*

Kincaid . . . whoa, you look the same. It's like time hit the pause button on you. Kincaid had on a navy-blue business skirt, light-gray silk shirt and blazer. She looked fit, had a mic in her hand and was scanning the playing field. When she turned in his direction, Josh looked the other way. *What was that all about?* he asked himself. Then he turned and saw Rachael standing by the west entrance, her shoulders were hunched and she looked cold. He cut a path up the grass toward her. She and a lieutenant had just finished talking. She looked a wreck, but tried to smile as he walked up. Josh slid off his jacket and draped it over her shoulders.

"You okay?" he asked.

"O'Henry has the world's attention now," she said, a deep layer of frustration in her voice.

Josh waited for the rest.

"Another woman's head. Inside, on the floor, plopped down by the West Side Grand Staircase." She turned to him . . . "It shouldn't have leaked out. The very second we arrived, we had a full set of eight-foot high partitions put up that completely, and I mean completely, closed off the spectacle from the public. We knew we had it contained, at least for a few hours. But then somehow, some friggin' jerk got a picture of it onto the web, and now it's gone viral." She paced back-and-forth once, before continuing. "So, you know what happened next? The mayor shat on the commissioner, who then shat on Kingsley, and then Kingsley shat on me, and . . . I got no one to shit on."

All this kind of talk was making Josh queasy. The pain in his lower intestine was now much sharper than before and a tremendous urge to push came over him. He held his breath, and his facial muscles tightened and began to twitch at the hinges of his jaw.

"Josh, are you all right?"

"Yeah . . . yeah, no problem," he said, squeezing out the words, and clamping down hard.

"Well, I have to tell ya, you look like shit."

"Aww hell . . ." Josh said, his voice tightening. "I'll see you in there okay?" Then he marched straight past her up the hill, stiff-legged, clenching his butt cheeks together, and disappeared into the building.

Ten minutes later, Josh made his way over to the crime scene area. He saw Cecilia Bloom, standing next to the scene photographer. They were flipping through shots on the back of a digital camera.

Rachael was standing farther down, by the eight-foot partitions talking with the lead for the crime-scene team. He handed her a single sheet of paper, nodded, and walked away. She glanced up from the report as Josh approached.

"Feel better?" she asked.

Josh nodded, his body language saying, let's change the subject.

"CSI has done its thing. There's a number nine on her ear. We're cleared to poke around. Oh, and there's another one of these." She held up a photocopy of a note. "The original is on its way to the lab."

Rachael read the note aloud:

Special Agent Tanner, do you believe in fate? Sadly, I do not. At first, each candidate seems so promising and good, but then an errant word slips from her lips or her ill-timed gesture makes me feel awkward. As such my search goes on. *Who knows, perhaps along the way, you and I will find a whole new meaning to life, or is that death. Not really a great difference is there, one simply a reflection of the other. Oh oh . . . time to go.*

Ta-ta   O

Rachael put the note down and exhaled. "I want to kill him. No trial. No right to defend himself. Just a bullet in his brain."

"Hey, you won't get an argument from me," Josh said, and he meant it, though he wasn't sure about her. He figured Rachael still believed in fair play. He did not. There is right and there is wrong, and he did not need anyone to interpret it for him.

They entered the crime scene. Cecilia Bloom was kneeling next to the head. "Tragic isn't it?" Cecilia said, "Once the brain is gone, the head might as well be a foot, chopped at the ankle. Have a look at this." She pointed to the neck. "See the ligaments around her Adam's apple, how they're stretched? The poor woman was in the middle of a full-blown scream when the sword came down." Cecilia pushed a strand of hair back from the head's face. "I'll never get used to it," she said, and turned to Josh, her face grim. "You catch the prick. How about you don't bring him in?"

Josh rested his hand on Cecilia's shoulder and gave it a couple of light pats.

Rachael looked up from her cell to Josh. "So, what did your friend the psychiatrist say?"

"Wilson, yeah, he has a theory. He says O'Henry may have already found the perfect woman, and all this is just part of an elaborate plan to claim her."

"What do you think?"

"Who knows, anything is possible." Then he turned to Rachael. "You up for a drive tomorrow? I've set up a meeting with the governor. The contract for the share transfer is rattling around in my brain. I gotta check it out, and I need to do it in person."

Rachael didn't answer; it was clear to Josh that she was stressed, and he prepared himself for a *no*. "You know, I'll understand if you can't make it."

"I'm heading back to the office to clear up a few things," she said. "Then I'll be meeting with the team later this evening . . ." She let out a deep sigh. "But I could use some time to think. Maybe the country air will do me good."

"Is that a yes?" Josh asked, and was surprised at how bad he wanted it to be.

Rachael tilted her head. "Yes, I'd like to go for a drive with you."

Chapter 25

Josh chucked some clothes, his shaver, and a toothbrush into a small duffle bag, then left the hotel to find Rachael. She was standing by a new, dark-gray Tahoe. She tossed the keys to him. "You drive."

Before leaving town they pulled in for a quick pit stop at a gas station, filled the tank, and picked up a couple of bottles of water for the road. After about ten minutes, Rachael finally stopped clicking on her cell, and a few minutes later, she was fast asleep. Josh took a ramp onto I-95 and dovetailed into the flow of traffic heading north, to Connecticut. He took a couple of gulps of water, stretched out his legs, hit cruise, and started to mellow.

An hour later he turned off onto Dover Road and ran its length to a T-intersection, hung a left onto Seaside Drive, then hugged the Upper New York State coastline for about fifteen minutes before crossing over into Connecticut. He proceeded another couple of miles, and came to a halt at the front gate of the governor's estate.

A lone sentry manned the guardhouse, his face illuminated by a cluster of flat screens. The guard was in his thirties, wore a light-brown uniform, starched and pressed sharp at its creases. He checked their IDs, his gaze lingering on Rachael, then called it in before pressing a yellow button on his console. The gates, constructed of blackened iron, retracted slowly on well-greased rails.

Josh dropped the SUV into gear and they followed a long road that ended in a circular loop in front of the manor. The manor reminded him of a thirteenth-century Irish Cathedral, formidable and cold, yet made somewhat more welcoming by a French country facade at its entrance. They made their way up a long flight of steps, passing through a curved archway where they were met by a butler who introduced himself as Morgan. At a few inches over six feet, stooped at the shoulders, and wearing a gray cardigan sweater and polished black loafers, he looked like a butler, Josh thought.

Morgan showed them into the library antechamber where they were told the governor would be with them in a moment. Josh took notice of the stone fireplace that covered most of one wall. It had firewood set inside, complete with kindling, ready to burn. He was about to comment on it when one of two fir doors leading into the library swung open. Governor Elhert entered, wearing a tuxedo.

"Sorry to keep you waiting, and please forgive the monkey suit. I have an obligatory black tie function this evening."

Josh sensed the governor was comfortable making small talk, a talent those in powerful positions seem to master early in their career. He had a presence about him that drew one's attention to him; it was both glaring and powerful. *A natural politician.*

"The church is having a fundraiser and I'm expected to give a little talk," the governor said. "But look at me, going on about my little world. Somehow, I don't think you're here to chitchat." He glanced at his watch. "I still have some time before I have to depart, so please do come in and make yourselves comfortable." Josh and Rachael followed the governor into the library where he invited them to sit, pointing to a couple of overstuffed leather chairs, before taking his position behind a massive oak desk. Josh was about to speak when the butler showed up.

"Coffee, tea, sparkling water?" the governor asked. Both Josh and Rachael declined.

"How about some brandy? Take the sting out the day."

Rachael passed and Josh accepted.

The library was large, and elaborate and twenty feet high. Books encased the first story, with the higher rows accessed by wooden ladders that ran on brass coasters. An oak circular staircase connected to the second level, which was also lined with books. In all four corners of the second level an alcove had been built, each with a small round table, a fiddleback chair, and a reading light.

A servant entered carrying a silver tray with two snifters and a bottle of cognac. He sat the tray onto the governor's desk. The governor poured out two generous portions before handing a snifter to Josh.

"So tell me, what brings the FBI to my home?"

"Is that a Cruzan?" Josh asked, pointing to an oil painting hanging across from the staircase.

"It is that."

"Would you mind if I have a look?"

"No, not at all. You're an admirer of Cornelis?"

"Yes, some of his earlier paintings in particular, those from the Gray Period are most interesting." Josh walked over to the painting. "What a tortured soul he was. The human mind is a funny thing . . . it can play tricks on you." Josh glanced back at Governor Elhert.

"Quite right you are, the mind *is* the quintessential puzzle. Perhaps that's what makes life so unpredictable. All the beauty, all the tragedy that humans are capable of, it boggles the mind."

Rachael shifted in her chair. "Governor Elhert, I think we should tell you why we are here. We would like to ask you a few questions about Arthur Romansky. We understand you had contact with him a few days ago, just before his death."

Governor Elhert's face went blank, surprised by the abruptness of the question . . .

Huh—he's hesitated too long, Josh thought.

"Sorry, that name doesn't ring a bell. I cannot say I've heard of him."

"Arthur left me a message that he'd contacted you about a contract signed by your father," Josh said. "He said you were going to have a look at it."

Elhert's face lit up. "Yes, of course, the fellow that wished to add to my father's legacy. For a price mind you. And he's been killed. Oh, I am truly sad to hear that."

"So, you did speak with him?" Josh pressed.

"Well no, not in person. That would have been my father's foundation. The director, Annette Richards, she heads it up. She came to see me the other day to give me an update on the foundation, that's when I first heard of the contract. I was told it could have my father's signature on it, and it was dated around the time the war ended. I thought it may have some historical value. Not the most exciting news of the day, but I gave her the go-ahead to have a look and see if it was legitimate. If so, I said we could pay a small finder's fee."

Josh saw a row of book spines that seemed familiar and wandered over. He ran his hand across them. "You have them all?"

"Yes, all nine. May I ask, when is the release date expected for the tenth?"

"I haven't finished it. Soon, though not before the Christmas market . . . much to my agent's dismay. I have to say, my little detective series looks somewhat out of place against these other, more serious first editions."

"Nonsense, your books are finely crafted," Governor Elhert said. "Your partner is a gifted writer as I'm sure you are aware. A mind such as his, suffice to say, is unusual."

It was clear Rachael was stumped. "I have to confess, I haven't read any of them. Sounds as though I should."

"Yes, you should," Anton Elhert said, stepping into the room. "If you're a fan of Sir Arthur Conan Doyle's work, you'll find your Mr. Ingram's work all-consuming. Sorry to intrude, but I heard Mr. Ingram had stopped by, and took the liberty of dropping in."

Anton had a look about him that struck Josh as quite odd. His face was round to a fault, his eyes were large and set too far apart, and his mouth was tiny, disproportionate, given his broad nose and expansive face.

"I'm on my way out, Anton," Governor Elhert said, the timber of his voice harsh, leaving no doubt the intrusion by his brother did not sit well.

Anton turned to Josh and Rachael. "How long will the two of you be in town?"

"Heading back in the morning," Rachael said.

"Oh, that's a shame. Tomorrow evening is our bi-monthly family dinner, and it'll be here at my dear brother's place," Anton said, and glanced over at Governor Elhert.

Another servant entered the room, announcing the helicopter had arrived. Governor Elhert gave a sympathetic smile. "I am sorry to hear about your friend Arthur. If I can be of any assistance, please do not hesitate to ask."

"Chances are we may need to speak with you again, but *we will* need to speak with Ms. Richards," Rachael said.

"Of course, leave me your card and I'll have her call you."

Rachael placed her card in the governor's hand, and he gave her a look that lingered too long. He was smiling, she was not.

Josh sensed her annoyance and moved them toward the door.

At the doorway, the governor stopped and turned to them. "I know you're planning to head out after meeting with Ms. Richards, but as Anton said, if the two of you care to join us tomorrow evening for dinner, we would love to have you. Mother started the dinner years ago with the idea it would bring us all closer. At least that was the intention."

"Please do us the honor," Anton said. "I understand it's short notice, but sometimes the unplanned turns in one's life are the most memorable."

Josh could see Rachael was about to say no, so he cut in. "We would be honored to join your family for dinner."

"Well then, that's settled," Anton said. "Everyone will be so pleased."

"Until tomorrow," Governor Elhert said.

On the way back to their vehicle, Rachael spoke up. "Thanks for accepting on my behalf. You know I could have plans."

"Do you have plans?"

"Nothing concrete—but that's not the point."

"Yeah, you're right," Josh said. "But you know, I think the governor is hiding something. I can't put my finger on it. Not yet anyway. Call it a hunch."

"More than a hunch I'd say. Men are all the same. Walking, talking erections."

"All men?" he asked.

"All men."

Chapter 26

The town of Broadview, located two miles inland from the governor's mansion, was 176 years old, had a population of 7,386, and an economy that revolved around fishing, tourism, and baby-boomers; the latter's numbers having ballooned over the last decade, as the boomers sought refuge from the big city.

It was 11:47 a.m. when Josh and Rachael pulled up next to the Rialto Theatre in the heart of town. The day was already warming and the air smelled of bacon floating on a cloud of freshly baked bread.

The street corners, once occupied by brick and stone financial institutions, had given way to French and Italian bistros. A painter's easel stood out front of each restaurant, supporting a lunch menu framed under protective glass.

Without any difficulty they found the office of the Elhert Foundation. The address was embossed in gold leaf and was easily seen from the street. Josh and Rachael entered the reception area and found that unlike its exterior nameplate, the inside was spartan, with three plastic chairs positioned around a small, black rectangular table. A teapot covered with a flower-patterned cosy was steeping on one end of the reception counter, and a silver bell sat on the other end. A sign next to the bell, read: SERVICE.

Josh hit the bell twice. A moment later a screen door in the back closed with a thud, and a woman emerged, reeking of cigarette smoke.

She wasn't at all what Josh had expected. She was short, chunky at the waist, and her pants were far too tight, making her movements cumbersome. Her jowls drooped and her face reflected a lack of sleep, but there was still a sparkle in her eyes. She spoke first.

"Holy camoly! Josh Ingram, I'm Annette Richards, so nice to meet you." She cocked her head. "You know, you're not too far off of your cover. Shed a few pounds maybe." She reached out and shook his hand and then Rachael's.

Annette invited them both to have a seat and offered them tea.

They both declined.

"Okay, so tell me, what can I do for you?" Annette asked. "The governor's office said you have some questions you'd like to run past me."

"It concerns the conversation you had with Arthur Romansky," Josh said. "Which as it turns out, was one of his last conversations, before—"

"Oh, and that's just so awful, isn't it?" Annette said. "I know Arthur was a close friend of yours. I am so sorry for your loss."

Again, hearing Arthur's name in the past tense bothered him, but Josh sensed her feelings were sincere. "I would like you to tell me, word for word, what Arthur said to you."

Annette's expression changed, as though she was about to say oops, then she said, "Oh sweetie, I truly hope you didn't come all the way here, for that."

Josh closed his eyes, not wanting to hear the rest.

"All I can tell you is, your friend e-mailed our general office mailbag with a copy of the contract he'd come across. He said he'd be willing to part with it for a price. I thought it might be of interest and ran it past the governor. He told me if it was legit, I could spend upwards of two grand."

She grabbed the teapot and poured herself a cup, then started to cough, a wet, raspy hack. "The contract wasn't viewed as an important piece, that's for sure. But being dated at the end of the war did make it a tad more desirable. You see . . . we don't have much in the way of historical entries from that period of George's life. Almost none, to be honest. So, I rang up Arthur and we set up a time I could drive out and have a look."

"That's it?" Josh asked, feeling despair seeping in.

"I'm afraid so," Annette said, and the blood drained from her face and her jowls seemed to sag lower. "I wish I could be of more help."

Josh reached into his inside jacket pocket and retrieved his copy of the contract, unfolding it on the table, and smoothing out the creases.

"Ah, huh . . . not much there," Annette said, pointing to the contract. "Just some paperwork around a transfer of shares to George."

"And yet a couple of things do come to mind," Josh said. "The contract is in Spanish and signed in Guatemala City in the fall of 1945. And the shares being transferred are those of a conglomerate that is still in existence today. In America alone, it owns half of the citrus farms in Florida."

"Yes, but ownership of shares is not that uncommon,

is it?" she blurted, immediately looking as if she had said the wrong thing. "It is true though, the transaction did take place in Guatemala."

"Yes, and why Guatemala?" Josh asked.

Annette rubbed at her inner thigh with the palm of her hand, then pinched at the seam of her pants and gave it a tug. "The obvious connection has got to be Walter Hyter. He was George's sidekick for such a long time. As I understand it, they met sometime before George went into politics, shortly after the war. Walter always kept a place in Guatemala and one in Miami. Last I heard he'd sold his condo in Miami and returned to Guatemala. That's got to be a few years ago. He could be dead for all I know. Oh my gosh, if he isn't, he'd be close to ninety by now."

Josh's gut was sending him mixed signals. This woman couldn't be as homespun as she seemed.

"If you thought the contract had little value, why did you think it should be added to George Elhert's legacy?" Rachael asked.

"I didn't . . . I mean, I wasn't sure, but as I said, it was after the war and we don't have much information during that period for George." Her desk phone rang. She picked it up and cradled it between her pudgy shoulder and her ear. As she listened to the caller, she looked over at them and hiked up her shoulders as if to ask, was there anything else?

Josh folded the contract and stuffed it back into his pocket. When they reached the door, Annette raised her hand for them to stop, putting her other hand over the receiver. "Maybe this doesn't mean much." She reached down and pulled a loose sheet of paper from under the counter. "This came with the contract. Don't know what to think of it. Your friend Arthur told me it was in the book cover as well."

Josh took the paper from her, it was a copy of a black-and-white photo of three youths. *The one Arthur tried to send me . . .* The picture had been cut in half with serrated scissors, and showed only from the tops of their thighs down to the soles of their shoes. Josh figured they were boys, probably teenagers. Two of the boys had their runners planted on some kind of wooden walkway. The one in the middle appeared to have darker skin. His ankles were bare, and his boots dangled about a foot off the boards, like he'd jumped up a second before the camera went off.

Josh gave the picture a second look, then held it up to the ceiling light and asked, "Did the governor's office show any interest in this?"

"Half a picture of some boys' legs? Nah, I didn't even bother. What'd be the point?"

"So, you've never shown this to the governor?" Rachael asked, reinforcing the point.

"Like I said, what would be the point?" Annette frowned, her folksy demeanor gone.

Chapter 27

Rachael burnt off the rest of the day, first doing reports, then getting on the phone with each member of her team asking for updates as to what leads they had on the go.

Josh called Mary and upon hearing that she had taught Eddie how to pee off the pier, he quickly declined the details. Their conversation turned to the pending purchase of a new oven and grill for Crawlies that Mary had wanted for some time. They reviewed the specifications and compared a few units they'd had their eyes on, and decided it would be best to drive out to see the units in action before making a final choice. After that, Josh went out and bought a day pass at the local gym, worked out for close to two hours and finished with a jog around town.

By the time they reached the governor's mansion, it was dark. And even though the walk from the SUV to the front steps took less than a minute, Josh could feel his shirt starting to cling to him under his brown tweed sports coat. Rachael, on the other hand, appeared cool and comfortable in her floral dress, her powder-blue cashmere sweater hanging loose on her shoulders. Josh felt a few drops of sweat trickle down behind his ear and wondered: *Why is it that women don't sweat?*

The front entry, strangled by ivy, gave way to a set of burnt-brown double doors that swung open the moment they stepped up to the archway. A different butler greeted them this time, introducing himself as Jeffrey. He too was tall, gaunt and stooped like Morgan. His hollowed-out cheeks set below his high, angular cheekbones gave him a troubled look.

Jeffrey led them down a wide hallway ending at two massive fir doors. He bowed his head and leaned forward, pushing open the doors. Josh and Rachael found themselves facing a generous-looking dining table complete with white linens and lit candles. The table was well over twenty-feet-long and was set for dinner with everyone already seated. Their heads all turned as the doors opened.

Josh glanced at Rachael and back to those seated at the table and said, "It appears we're late, our apologies."

"Not at all," Governor Elhert said, a distinct layer of alcohol in his voice. "In fact, you're right on time. We had some family business that needed attention, but now we are ready to relax and enjoy the evening. Please, have a seat."

There were two empty chairs along one side of the table. Jeffrey seated Rachael next to a woman who Josh thought had to be Governor Elhert's wife. Josh took the remaining seat next to Rachael.

"Before we get started, I think some introductions are in order," Governor Elhert said. "Of course, Josh Ingram needs little in the way of introduction, as you are all familiar with his work, or at least you've heard Anton speak of him ad nauseam over the years. Welcome, Josh.

"Next to him is Rachael Tanner. She adds a bit of intrigue to the evening as she is a Special Agent with the FBI's organized crime division out of, Miami?" With that, a palpable hush came over the table.

Rachael glanced at Josh, her reaction visceral. There had been no mention of her background with the FBI.

Anton cut in. "My dear brother is half right, which is better than all wrong. Sadly . . . a modicum too much sauce can throw his head into a tizzy. Can it not, dear brother?"

Governor Elhert's eyes narrowed.

"Anton is right," Rachael said. "That is, you have it half right, Governor. I am with the FBI, as you well know, but I'm now a Special Agent attached to the New York office, Special Crimes Unit. But I'm thinking maybe you knew that . . ."

"Yes, I suppose I did," Governor Elhert said. And without skipping a beat he continued. "Josh, to your right is my youthful and effervescent sister, Katherine Kincade. Katherine is a self-described wine aficionado. Don't let her corner you on the subject, as there is no escape."

"You'll pay for that," Katherine said, and the table broke out into a light, guarded laughter.

"Next to her, is her husband Earl Kincade. You have no doubt seen his fleet of trucks crisscrossing the state. Hauls everything from produce to electronics.

"And to my immediate right are mother and father, Lillian and George Elhert." Lillian held up her wine glass and tipped it in their direction. George sat motionless in his chair, an IV pole attached to the back, his head bowed. He was fast asleep. Governor Elhert continued. "George, you can see, will be joining us later."

No one laughed, and Lillian's eyes crinkled as she glared at her son.

"Next to my father is Dr. Ralph Armstrong, an old friend of the family. Ralph delivered all of us children, all at home, didn't you Ralph?" Ralph, who was busy trying to wipe a stain off his shirt with his napkin, glanced up. "Ralph moved with us from Harland, Florida during the great Elhert migration of '68."

Lillian shot her son another stern look.

"Not much of a hospital in Harland in those days," Dr. Armstrong said. "Many families chose to have home births over the local hospital."

Governor Elhert turned to Anton, avoiding his mother's stare, and said, "Of course, you've already met Anton, the family genius."

Anton was in the middle of whispering a message to Margaret. He turned to Josh and Rachael and smiled, his little mouth revealing a full set of childlike teeth.

"And last, and far from least, seated next to Rachael is my lovely wife, Margaret. And there you have it, our little clan."

He was right about Margaret, Josh thought. She was lovely, striking, with a cultured look that made it difficult for him not to stare.

"Not entirely dear," Margaret said, with an undeniable edge to her voice. "We have two wonderful daughters who are both away at college."

"*Honey,*" Governor Elhert said, his mocking undertone sharp enough to cause Margaret's lips to purse. "If we are including absent offspring, let's not forget our Anton. He's quite a ladies' man I am told? Perhaps there is a hoard of little Antonians running around as we speak. Oh, but let's hope not . . . I'm not sure my brother could withstand an onslaught of paternity suits at this juncture."

Josh caught a sadness in Anton's eyes; his brother had inflicted a pain he could not mask.

"Are we *quite* done?" Lillian spoke up, her voice hard as flint. The message needed no translation. There will be no more pissing on mother's dinner table.

With that, the conversation changed pace to a smattering of topics covering health, inventions, politics, and the upcoming election. The mood in the room was warming, and yet something was off, Josh thought. It was as though it had been too well planned, almost scripted, as if he and Rachael were playing a part.

"Josh, my son tells me you are a writer," Lillian said, as she reached over and wiped some drool from George's lower lip and patted his hand. "I have to say, I have never read any of your work. Anton says you are famous. Is that true?"

"I guess I have a following, at least from those who enjoy the genre. I am seldom recognized on the street or in restaurants. And to be honest, I'm glad my privacy has, for the most part, remained intact."

"Which fiction genre is that?" Earl asked, an air of self-importance in his voice.

"Thrillers," Josh said, and could see another question coming. "More precisely, a detective series."

"Hardly just another detective series," Anton said. "Come now Josh, you are being modest. Detective Vincent Callaghan is a singularly clever fellow. Ranks right up there with the greatest detectives of our times, I dare say. Brilliant writing. One simply never knows what is coming next." A grin started to form as he turned and stared at

Rachael. "A lot like life I would think. Someone such as yourself must find every day an adventure. Never knowing what's around the next bend."

"There is more routine to the job than one would think," Rachael said.

A look of disappointment crossed Anton's face.

"Josh, may I ask what has brought you to our community?" Dr. Armstrong asked. "Research for a new a book?"

"Murder," Rachael said.

Josh raised an eyebrow at this and again the table went quiet.

"Not here in Broadview though," Rachael added. "As some of you may know, Josh's good friend Arthur was recently killed in New York. I've been asked to have a look at the case, and here we are."

"Yes, so sad about your friend, Josh," Katherine said. "Please accept our condolences on your loss."

Josh nodded.

"Frankly, I don't see a connection. I mean, why *are* you here?" Earl asked. "Tell us Mr. Ingram—are we somehow suspects?"

Josh took more than a second to respond, and the effect sent a shock wave across the table.

"*Ooo* this will cause a stir at the club, won't it mother?" Katherine giggled, now appearing to love every moment of it.

"You're not a suspect, Katherine," Josh said, "but I have to be honest in telling you this, we cannot rule out your mother."

Lillian squinted at Josh and cocked her head at a sharp angle, then grinned, and the whole table burst into laughter.

When it died down, Josh said, "At this point, we have no clue why Arthur was murdered, so we are running around, searching, hoping a lead will turn up that will give us some direction. . . . I hope we haven't been a cause for concern."

"Not at all," Katherine said. "I for one find this fascinating. Don't you, Earl, find it fascinating?" Earl raised an eyebrow and did not appear impressed.

"We really don't have a lot to go on," Josh said. "We do know that Arthur had communicated with the Elhert Foundation over a contract he'd found sewn into a book's jacket. The contract, as it turns out, has George's signature on it. Arthur was due to meet with the foundation, which as it turned out was his last appointment before he died. Not a lot to go on, I'll give you that, but this is a murder investigation and every detail must be examined, no matter how small."

"You say a contract. What sort of contract?" Anton asked, his voice animated, acting as if the table talk had all-of-a-sudden been raised to a new level.

"A transfer of some shares over to father, that occurred after the war," Governor Elhert said. "It was the fact that the contract was dated just after the war which led Annette to believe it might have some historical import."

"Which shares would they be?" Lillian asked, her gaze fixed on her son.

"Klineharber International," Governor Elhert replied.

Lillian took a deliberate breath, looking as though an old injury had been reopened. She cleared her throat. "I don't recall that name. Should I . . . ? Seriously, an *old* document about some shares. What could the foundation find of interest about that?"

You're lying through your teeth, plain as day, Josh thought.

"No doubt you're correct, Mother," Katherine said. "But you know we don't have much information about father during those years. It's a period for father that is a virtual blank."

"There is something I want to show all of you." Josh reached into his breast pocket and pulled out the half picture. He unfolded it, smoothed out the creases and threw it on the table. "My friend discovered this in the same book he found the contract in."

Josh studied their faces as they passed the photo around.

"Really, Mr. Ingram, is this some sort of joke? A half picture of some shoes," Earl Kincaid said.

"It is what it is. Just have a look at it," Josh said.

When it reached the governor, his jaw muscles flexed for a second and then returned to normal. *Was that recognition?* Josh wondered, *or was the governor even paying attention?* The picture completed its round and none of the other faces appeared interested. Anton barely even looked at it, his mind off somewhere else. Josh slipped the photo back into his pocket.

Without warning, along one side of the dining room, two pocket doors slid open and a procession of kitchen staff wheeled in a number of antique wooden carts carrying the evening's dinner. For the main course, they had a choice of prime rib, baked potato, and shiitake mushrooms, or Maine lobster, ramp butter and potato gnocchi. Josh chose the lobster and Rachael the prime rib.

The dinner conversation resumed around life in the

181

country, global warming, and a long debate over which part of the world produces the finest Shiraz.

Finally, a light desert of fresh blackberries with cream was served which balanced the load.

With their napkins laid on the table, they all rose and moved out to the veranda. A light breeze had picked up off the ocean and the air smelled of sea salt and Russian Sage. Four large clay pots, one at each of the veranda's corners, were filled with fresh cut flowers. Rachael was standing by one of the pots talking to Dr. Armstrong. Josh couldn't hear what they were saying, but her body language had become fluid and her professional veneer had evaporated. She was smiling, radiant, taking with her hands, finally having a good time.

Katherine touched Josh's arm. "She is a pretty woman, your partner. You would make a fine couple, don't you think?"

Caught off guard, Josh let on as though her comments had missed the mark, and he said nothing.

"Oh, come now, a woman knows these things even if the man is obtuse," she said, and a sly grin crossed her lips.

I'm not going down this road, Josh thought. But he'd be damned if he could think of a decent comeback to diffuse the situation.

"You're married! That's it—isn't it?" she said and started to laugh.

Her words again surprised him, but this time a dull pain worked its way into him. "I was once married. But she died."

"I am *so sorry* to hear that, and I do apologize," Katherine said. "Sometimes playing with another's mind can backfire. A hazard of the idle rich, I suppose." She turned her attention across the bay and reached out over the balcony railing and pointed. "You see that house, all lit up like a refinery? That's Anton's. When he is away he lights up the place, inside and out. A paranoid man, my older brother. He obsesses about someone breaking in. Frankly, I don't see why he worries. The security around his home is everywhere. He has it all: cameras, motion sensors, the works. I simply fail to understand men and their love for gadgets. A trait all men share, don't you think?"

Josh was only half listening, so she cranked up the volume. "Men and their toys. A quality Anton shares with his brother. An affliction steeped deep in the male genetic code, I suspect."

Josh's attention was directed at the other end of the balcony. The governor's right hand was clenched into a fist, his cellphone pressed to his ear, the conversation tense. He clicked off his cell and caught Josh staring. The governor raised his brandy snifter, holding it high into the air, then swung his other arm around as though he was bowing to an audience. Josh pointed at the governor, and the governor pointed back.

"Hello . . . ? Earth to Josh," Katherine said, nudging his elbow . . . "If you look down the bay shoreline, the next house you see, the one nestled in darkness, is mine. As you can see, the only light on is the one on my boat dock. Anything I have of value is insured, so why bother worrying about it? A fatal flaw, no doubt. Certainly Anton thinks so. Mind you, I do have an exceptional wine cellar." She took Josh's snifter from his hand and replaced it with a fresh one. "I'd like to show it to you sometime—

my wine cellar, that is. It truly is extensive . . ."

All at once Josh snapped out of it and realized he had not been listening. "I'm sorry about that, I'm afraid my mind tends to wander. I'd like to think it makes me mysterious. I think most would chalk it up to a personality defect. Not an enduring quality."

Katherine almost smiled before changing the subject. "You know, if you need to get any background information on our little village, the best source is the Vicar. He's old but he remembers everything. I could call him for you if you like, and arrange a meeting."

"And where would I find the Vicar?"

"Oh, I don't know, that is a puzzle isn't it?" she said grinning.

Josh chuckled. He was starting to have a pleasant evening and nearly missed the defeated look on Rachael's face. She was on her cell phone and staring right at him, despair in her eyes. He abruptly apologized to Katherine, begging off, telling her something had come up. Then he touched her shoulder and thanked her for the lead about the Vicar.

Rachael gestured to meet in the dining room.

Josh stepped in behind her and closed the door.

"A trooper called it in twenty minutes ago. Another head has been found . . . stuck on a stake just outside the entrance to the Hampton Bridge."

Josh flinched. "Hampton Bridge . . . isn't that . . . just a mile south of here?"

Chapter 28

Less than ten feet from the SUV, Josh's cell began to vibrate; it was Alice Whitaker. *Ahh man, now what . . . ?* He tossed the keys to Rachael and got in the passenger side.

Alice Whitaker was a caseworker for a Catholic not-for-profit that helped the homeless, including his father. Years ago, Josh believed his father would eventually come around, now he wasn't so sure. Over the last six months his father's self-prescribed punishment, to drink himself to death, had gained momentum.

Josh answered the call on the fourth ring.

"Josh, Alice here." Her voice sounded tired.

"How is he?"

"He's in the hospital. But he's okay."

Josh's heart began to pound. "What happened?"

"Someone found him in a back alley near a dumpster, on his back. I'm so sorry, Josh. But thank the Lord, he'd been rolled onto his side and didn't choke."

"How bad is he?"

A long pause. "Your father has a broken wrist, a cracked jaw, and a bunch of bruises."

Josh hesitated. "Is he going to be okay?" Knowing his father would never be okay.

"The doctor says he'll be released tomorrow. Then

he'll be back to his old haunts. He's a survivor, your old man." A pause. "But how are you holding up? I read in the paper about your friend."

"Yeah, I'm fine. I'm just trying to understand what happened. Alice, about my dad. Is everything still in order? The funds? Is he eating? Is he sleeping in his bed?" Josh caught himself rambling, and added, "At least most of time, does he sleep in his bed?"

"Your dad's got his own way of doing things. He will go a full day without food. The next day he'll boot all the others out of the kitchen, cook a tremendous stew and they'll all eat like horses. And yes, he does use his bed. Strays sometimes for a day or two, but he knows there's always a place for him. . . . Josh, you have to know the home has made a huge difference to all their lives. Now that winter is approaching he'll be staying closer to home. We'll keep an eye on him. Last month I moved a couple of his friends in from the street. He seems to get along with them best. So I want you to remember . . . he's not alone, he's got friends."

"Alice, thank you for watching over him . . . I'll check in with you next week."

He sighed as he disconnected the call.

"Hey, is everything all right?" Rachael asked.

"Yeah, I hope so."

The gravel road snaked through the river valley and cut a sharp left just before the bridge. Two patrol cars were parked at angles to the entrance, with flashers on. The colored lights bounced off the willows and the iron bridge, and made the place feel unwelcoming.

The local CSI crew had arrived a minute or so before them and were hauling boxes of equipment out to the crime scene. A couple of minutes later the crime-scene lighting was ready to go, the yellow tape in place.

The county Coroner's shiny black SUV was there, but he was nowhere in sight.

Josh and Rachael made their way over to the lead officer, a deputy sheriff from town. Rachael told him the Bureau's crime-scene team would arrive in about twenty minutes, coming in by chopper. Josh could tell from the deputy's body language that he was relieved he didn't have to take the lead.

Rachael said, "If your people can secure the area, and keep the media at bay until my crew gets here, it would be appreciated."

The deputy nodded and strode up the hill.

A local reporter from town had beaten her Channel 12 News team's satellite truck to the crime scene. She was young, in her mid-twenties, and seemed confused. She was doing a slow 360 on her heels when the crime scene lights flooded the area. Bathed in bluish-white light the staked head, not more than six feet away, was looking straight at her.

Josh saw her gasp, and her knees gave out. She stumbled sideways and tried to grab at the air for support. He was about to jog over and help, when her team descended and led her away.

A few minutes later a Bell Long Ranger helicopter touched down. The Bureau's CSI crew had arrived and quickly took over the crime scene. The photographer started clicking, while the team leader completed his walk around, crisscrossing the area, getting his first impressions.

Josh caught sight of the coroner ambling toward the crime scene. He was of average height and weight and appeared fit. He had a bright, winning smile and flashed at Rachael.

Rachael showed no interest and flashed him her ID.

"A beauty," the coroner said, staring down at the head. Then something caught his attention and he frowned, and got down onto one knee. "Huh, will you look at this." And he pointed at the eye sockets. "See how the skin tissue droops down around her eyelids?"

"Sure, I guess . . . her eyes were just plucked out," Rachael said, and put on a pair of latex gloves with a bit more force than necessary.

"No, no, no, you're missing the point, it's more than that, the tissue is . . ."

The CSI photographer gave a nod to the coroner indicating she was finished.

Rachael said, "Look, we'd like confirmation of any markings behind the ears or if there is a note in the throat. So if we could check that first . . ."

The coroner let out a long breath and forced a smile at Rachael. "Care to do the honors?" His voice now cheerful, like it was turning out to be a good day.

"You do know this was a human being," Rachael snapped.

The coroner stopped and stared at her, appearing more bruised than angry. "Hey, she's all yours," he said. "I'll be back in a few minutes. I have a call to make." Then he strode back to his SUV.

Rachael took a deep breath and glanced at Josh, then

reached down and turned the left ear back, revealing a number ten. "I don't suppose you have a set of tongs in your pocket . . . ? God I hate this," she said, then slowly opened the jaws, pulling on the head's front teeth with the tips of her fingers, careful not to touch the face and damage any possible latent prints. She inserted her hand partway in and caught hold of a small plastic bag lodged under the tongue. She withdrew it and laid it on a clipboard, then stopped and stared at Josh, her eyes narrowing.

"What?" he asked.

"The inside of her head—it's frozen." She ripped off her latex gloves and threw them on the ground. "Jesus Josh, now he's using *frozen heads* to deliver fucking messages. What kind of animal is he?"

Josh said nothing and picked up the bag with his gloved hand.

"I don't get it, why he would do this?"

"I think Wilson was right," Josh said. "O'Henry's pattern is broken. He's not looking for the perfect woman. He's already found her, and he's enacting some elaborate bullshit plan to claim her."

"I still don't see why he used a frozen head. How could it possibly fit into all of this?"

Josh considered it, then said, "The original number ten on his list must have changed her routine, or some other complication came up, and he couldn't take her. His game plan is set to a certain order of events, a timetable of sorts. So, he needed to improvise. But I'm not so concerned about why. . . . What's going to keep me up at night from hereon in—is how many?"

Rachael sighed. "God, I hope you're wrong."

Josh turned his attention back to the plastic bag, picking out what appeared to be a news clipping. It had yellowed with age and was dated Tuesday, July 30th 1968. It was from The Harland Review. The caption read:

Cranston Bridge Tragedy

Still no answers in the death of teenager Myrna Washington. Her boyfriend Tyrrell Dodge is wanted for questioning and remains at large. Sheriff Barkley has asked that everyone remain calm and let the law do its job, and cautioned: "Just because Miss Washington was colored, is no reason to start finger-pointing. I must emphasize that any unlawful acts will not be tolerated by this office."

"Appears we need to have another fireside chat with the governor," Josh said.

"Why? What could that possibly accomplish?"

"Because according to him, 1968 was the year George uprooted the family from Harland and moved them here, to Broadview."

"So you're saying the Elherts are somehow connected to this news clipping?"

"It's not what I'm saying, but for some reason O'Henry is pointing us in that direction. What's he thinking? Is anyone's guess. Maybe he's trying to mislead us. At this point there's no way to tell."

"Come on, more like he's trying to get me fired. Cause I don't think the governor is going to have good things to say about me after our next little chat."

Josh appreciated her words: '*after* our next little chat.' She had guts. "You're right of course. Now that O'Henry has drawn attention to the governor's neighborhood, the press will be all over town asking questions. Elhert is not going to want a line drawn between O'Henry and the town of Harland, where he spent his youth. Not a scenario you would want unfolding in your backyard during a reelection campaign."

Rachael groaned. "Oh jeez, thanks . . . I feel so much better." She let out a sigh. "But, what else can we do?" Josh watched her as she mulled it over, then she said, "So I guess we'll go to see the governor in the morning, and act as though it's just more routine questioning. . . . Oh Josh, I'm fucked, aren't I?"

"Let's get a drink," he said.

Chapter 29

The Broadview Hotel had been built in 1905, and boasted that President Eisenhower once slept there. A large, black-and-white photo hung next to the reception counter showing the president shaking hands with the cook. It was close to midnight when Josh and Rachael arrived. Josh was about to suggest they head to the bar when he heard the thump, thump, thump of a helicopter coming in.

A minute later Kingsley, in full-attack mode, stomped across the hotel foyer. *Was it his imagination,* Josh wondered, *or did Kingsley's face and neck look more puffy than usual?* "What happened to you?" Josh asked, seeing a blotch on Kingsley's neck the size of a bee sting, red and raised.

"None of your damn business," Kingsley said. "Just what the *hell* are you doing here, Tanner? I got a call from the commissioner an hour ago, and he was livid. He'd received a call from the governor, who said you'd been to see him today."

"Oh, that is serious," Josh said.

"Am I talking to you?"

Rachael cut in. "Did the commissioner also say we had dinner with the governor's family this evening?"

The wind in Kingsley's sails died on the spot.

"What?"

"O'Henry has struck again," Josh said. "Another head found tonight. On a stake this time, not more than two miles from here."

Kingsley, now completely defused, plopped down into a lobby chair. He took a moment, then asked, "Why would he do that? Is O'Henry now stalking the governor, for God's sakes?"

"Not a bad guess," Josh said. "More likely he's leading us somewhere."

"What does that mean?"

"There's another note," Rachael said. "This time it's a news clipping from a Florida local rag dating back to the summer of 1968, about a dead black girl and her boyfriend who went missing."

"And just how does that in any way relate to this part of the world?"

"It doesn't," Josh said. "But the news clipping is from a small town paper in Florida. A town where the Elhert family lived before moving up here."

"Elhert?" Kingsley asked, his face looking like it had received a direct blow.

"The black girl died about the same time Governor Elhert, George Elhert that is, pulled up stakes and moved the family from Harland, Florida to here," Rachael said.

"You must be insane, Tanner. You are *not* to make one more move without my authorization. Do you understand me? Am I getting through to you?"

"Uh-huh."

"Clue in, Tanner. Your career is hanging on a thread," Kingsley growled, standing up and brushing off his coat sleeves. "I have to go straight back to meet with the mayor. He's called an emergency meeting. And now this! It's one huge powder keg. Don't let it explode on you, Tanner." With that he turned and headed for the chopper.

Rachael hesitated, then fished her phone from her purse and called the governor. A few seconds later she hung up. "We're invited for morning coffee."

Josh nodded. He could see Rachael was exhausted, and the planned nightcap had lost its appeal for them both. They agreed to meet for breakfast.

Chapter 30

Josh laced up his runners and zipped up his navy blue windbreaker. *A quick jog around town,* he thought, *then out to the Atlantic and catch the sunrise.*

The absence of big box stores was refreshing; the main street still had the look and feel of small town America. Half a block downwind of the bakery, Josh inhaled as deep as his lungs would allow. As he passed by, he saw a man flipping a tray of fresh bread onto the counter, the loaves sliding out and landing upside down. He passed though old neighborhoods of small homes, their flower gardens tucked away for the winter, then through an aging business area with pawnshops, a dry cleaner, a bicycle repair shop, and a gas station.

As he sprinted the last fifty feet up a short bluff, the smell of salt-water rolled over him. He stopped on the crest, peered out over the Atlantic, and thought about his marina and his friends . . . Then he wondered if his dad was thinking of him, wishing he would get well, wishing his dad's life would again be as it once was. And he wondered if he would ever return to writing. Then he thought of the darkness O'Henry brought into the world, and he turned and headed back to town.

By the time Josh had cleaned up and arrived at the restaurant, he was hungry. It took him a few seconds to spot Rachael. She was sitting at a table that faced out onto the street. She had on a simple black dress, cut at the knees.

"Morning, you're looking rested," Josh said.

"Thanks, better than I feel, that's for sure."

The waitress stopped at their table to take their order.

Rachael ordered the yogurt with granola and dry toast while Josh went for the lumberjack special. The food fixed his blood sugar, and by the second cup of coffee, he felt the edge of the day sharpen into focus.

"So, let's recap what we have," Josh said. "Which I grant you is not that much." He paused. "A week ago, I received an email from Arthur that included a copy of a contract he wanted my opinion on. But before we had a chance to talk about it, he'd already been in touch with the Elhert Foundation, hoping to make a few bucks. The foundation agreed to have a look, but it never happened because Arthur was murdered the night before the scheduled meeting.

"We do know the contract was signed in 1945, in Guatemala, and a sizable transfer of shares in a large conglomerate were moved into George Elhert's name. Elhert later goes on to become the Governor of Florida for two full terms, and his son, now following in Daddy's footsteps, is the current Governor of New York." Josh drained the last of his cup and waited for Rachael to start.

"Okay," she said, and let out a slow breath. "O'Henry returns after seven long years of silence and picks up where he left off. No one, and I mean *no one* wants the case, as it is thought to be unsolvable, based on our previous experience with O'Henry, and with the glare of the media spotlights bearing down, there will be no place to hide. So, naturally, I get the file. Then I ask for your help, but before we can connect, your friend Arthur is killed by John Narrillo, a mechanic for the Miami mob. Narrillo gets shot in Arthur's store, twice at close range, once in the belly and once in the chest. It seems he'd been waiting in the bookstore for Arthur before they entered into their death struggle. A questionable scenario, and yet the evidence as you know suggests it happened that way. Narrillo was well placed in the mob, but had been retired for some time. Our records have him classified as inactive, so perhaps it was an ad hoc contract. But why would he come to New York to do a bookstore owner? He's a made guy and only took on large contracts. So who hired him? We know he wouldn't work outside the mob. That leaves us wondering: why would the mob want Arthur killed? Why would they worry about a small-time book dealer? And why would *anybody* pay big money to have Arthur killed?"

Rachael stopped for a moment and appeared to be pondering if she should go further, then added, "Arthur lived a normal, unremarkable life. I can't see how the mob would have had an interest in him."

"And why has O'Henry come back?" Josh asked. "Or has he always been skimming the surface? And why is he pointing us to a small town in Florida where the Elherts once lived? And what role does the death of the black girl play in all of this? Which just happened to occur the year the Elherts picked up and moved back up north.

"The common thread is the Elhert family, it has to be. Arthur contacted the foundation just before he died, and O'Henry has pointed us to Harland."

"I still don't get it—or maybe I don't want to believe it," Rachael said. "But you're right, it looks as though there is a connection to the Elhert family, at least at some level."

"There is another aspect about this that doesn't feel right," Josh said. "It's as if it's being staged, like we are being led down a path . . ."

Then Josh checked his watch. "You up for some religion?"

Chapter 31

The church was located on the outskirts of Broadview and dated back to the late seventeenth century, long before the town had come into being.

The limestone steps leading up to the entranceway were worn, with shallow impressions in them. *A lot of sinners filing in and searching for forgiveness,* Josh thought. When they reached the top stair, they stopped. The door before them was twelve-feet tall, six-feet wide, made of heavy oak and bound by iron straps. Josh expected considerable resistance, but with barely a touch of his hand the door gave way and swung open, leaving behind neither a grind nor a groan.

The church smelled of smoke, must, and spent incense. After passing through two sets of semicircular arches that formed the foundation of the bell tower, Josh and Rachael stepped out into the main congregation area.

Colored light filtering in through stained glass windows produced hues of dull blue, pink, and green that seemed to cling to everything. The exposed roof, with its ribbed stone vaulting and hand-hewn timbers had the look of a skeleton, Josh thought.

"Ever feel as though you've just be eaten?"

"What . . . did you say?" Rachael asked.

"Ah, nothing."

Dark-brown walnut pews filled the length of the room

and a red, almost burgundy, carpet ran down its center. A white-haired man dressed in a black cloak stood on a wooden stepladder. He was busy polishing the pulpit. He held an orange rag in one hand and a bottle of lemon oil in the other.

The pulpit was perched above the congregation, set off to one corner. A few candles were lit near the front that reminded Josh of the last holiday he'd taken with Ellen. They'd spent a full month touring the French countryside. It was six months before she died. Ellen was a devoted admirer of architecture and would have approved of the Church's gothic influences. She would have admired many things, had she not been taken from him. He closed his eyes and let out a breath.

A wren fluttered its wings overhead, startling Rachael. Instinctively, she grabbed Josh's arm yanking him back into the present. The bird swirled upwards to the ceiling and bounced off a slab of stained glass before finding a suitable perch on which to rest. The priest took notice that he had visitors and climbed down from his ladder. He was very old and had an advanced stoop that forced him to look down to his shoes. "May I be of help?" the priest asked, craning his head up to make eye contact.

"We're looking for Father Collins," Josh said.

"Well, you've found him, or what's left of him," he said. "What do you think of her?" He half-raised his crooked arm and swept it sideways.

"She's beautiful," Rachael said.

"Isn't she though. I've spent near half of my life tending to her. I'd like to think we are old friends." He tilted his head to the side. "An odd fellow I am, I suppose. . . ."

"Not at all," Rachael said, and glanced at Josh.

"We've come to ask a few questions about the town's history," Josh said.

"Oh yes, Katherine said you would be calling." And with that Father Collins seemed to perk up. "A spot of tea would be in order. Would it not?"

Josh and Rachael accepted the invitation and Father Collins led the way to his quarters. His kitchen was neat and tidy with a large, open fireplace made from local fieldstone. Smoke had licked at its mouth, and an empty black stew pot hung on a heavy hook over a cold fire pit. A few well-chosen paintings and artifacts were hung around the room. Not so much as to be judged as clutter, but rather to say, a good mind lives here.

As Father Collins went to place the teapot on the table, Josh noticed a slight tremble in the old man's hands. Josh was about to help but stopped himself, sensing it was a matter of pride that he manage on his own. The priest then took out a small plate of scones from the sideboard and a jar of raspberry jam from the fridge. "One always has to have something with one's tea," he said, looking over at them for approval.

Josh and Rachael nodded.

Father Collins studied them, and a kindhearted grin crossed his face. "So tell me now, what is it you need to know?"

"Katherine has told us that you know all that's gone on in your town and that you forget nothing," Rachael said.

"Katherine has always been given to exaggeration, even as a child. But oh, such a sweet little thing she was. One of those children within whom the torch of life burns bright. Always questioning everything, always at the ready to give her fiery little opinion. She helped me in the garden. Liked to get her hands dirty, she did." He caught himself, and blushed. "I must apologize. Memories of an old man."

"No apologies necessary," Rachael said.

"You know the Elhert family well . . . ?" Josh asked.

"But of course, everyone knows the Elhert family. They should, the Elherts own a large part of this town. Like any other small town, I suppose. There are always a few that pull the strings." He hesitated as though he should stop, then added, "I guess that is the order of nature, a few hold the future of the many, be it a county or country, or the world for that matter." He stopped, and a pink blush ran up his neck, settling in his cheeks. "Oh my, my, now I really must focus."

Father Collins stirred his tea and took a sip. "To answer your question, yes, I've known the family ever since I first arrived in forty-seven. Good, God-fearing people, the Elherts. I cannot recall a Sunday when at least one of the family members were not in attendance. That is to say, when they are here, residing in the county. They tended to jump back and forth between here and Florida. Privilege of the rich, I suppose. . . . But they've certainly been generous over the years. Funding restorations of the church, including a new roof in 2002. Without them, I dare say many of the youth programs would cease to exist. What can I say, the Lord brought us these good people, and we are all thankful."

Father Collins poured another round of tea, and the conversation turned to the outreach programs the church had taken on, as well as the many local community events it had spearheaded. Josh could see passion in the father, but he needed to get the conversation back on track. "If I could interrupt, I think we should tell you why we have come to see you. A good friend of mine was killed in New York a few days ago, and the last task he undertook in this world was to contact the Elhert Foundation about a contract that had come into his possession."

"Yes, your friend's name I believe was Arthur. Katherine filled me in. She said the contract had to do with a transfer of shares over to George Elhert, around the time the war ended."

"Correct," Josh said, and wondered what other information Katherine had offered the good father. "Does the share transfer ring up any old memories for you?"

"I believe it was before my time. No . . . no I can't think of anything out of the ordinary. . . . There was this fellow though, a strange sort he was, who always seemed to be at George's side. His name was Walter; he was some sort of advisor to George. . . . If a contract was involved, it would seem reasonable Walter would have his nose in it, at least in some fashion. He definitely had George's ear. Walter didn't often come to church with George though. Not a man of faith, I suspect."

"Is he still alive?" Rachael asked.

"That is an excellent question," Father Collins said, and shook his head. "He would be old now, older than me, if that's possible." He chuckled.

"Does this Walter ever come to visit George?" Josh asked.

"Oh no, their friendship took a nasty turn some years ago. Has to be close to twenty years now. It was as if one day George's little shadow just up and disappeared." Father Collins stood up and ambled over to the window, opening it and drawing back the white linen curtains. "I had asked George about it, about their breakup, about him and Walter." He turned to Josh and Rachael. "I like to know what's happening in my parish, like any good father." The words hung in the air for a moment. "George told me a business arrangement had gone sour, and that's when he and Walter decided to part ways."

"Do you remember Walter's last name?" Rachael asked.

"Oh yes, I believe . . ." he said, and deliberated for a long moment. "I know his last name was German. That much I do know for certain. It was not too long after the war when we first met. People tend to remember things such as that, him being a German and all." A glint of recognition crossed his face. "Hyter, yes that's it, Walter Hyter. I knew I'd remember," he said, looking relieved he had recalled the name. "An unusual man Walter was. . . . You know, he spoke with a slight English accent, at least back then he did anyway, which always struck me as odd."

"Do you know where this Walter Hyter fellow is now?" Josh asked.

"It's funny that we're talking about Walter," Father Collins said. "The other fellow was asking about him too."

"Other fellow?" Josh asked.

"Oh yes, a mountain of a man. Huge, and black as coal, and yet he spoke with such a soft timber to his voice, you immediately felt you could trust him. Some people can do that you know."

"Do you recall his name?" Rachael pressed.

"Yes . . . it was European I believe. Demetrius. That's it."

"And what did this *Demetrius* want?" Josh asked.

"Same as you, he wanted to know the whereabouts of Walter."

"What did you tell him?" Josh asked.

"I told him, last I heard Walter had returned to Guatemala, which makes sense, I suppose. In the early days, Walter was George Elhert's sidekick. They made a truckload of trips to Guatemala. It annoyed Lillian to no end, it did," he said and giggled. He then added, "That's George's wife, Lillian. What a spark plug she was."

"Yes, we met her yesterday," Rachael said, and instantly regretted saying it.

"Oh, of course, plight of an old man's memory. . . ." The father's cheeks turned red again, and he took a sip of tea, and then continued. "In those days Lillian had to apologize for George's absences from church on numerous occasions. It was something she did not like to do, apologize."

"I can see that," Rachael said. "She strikes me as a woman of substance."

"She was a force in her day," Father Collins said. "She has mellowed these last few years. But oh, when the children were young, she rode over them with an iron switch. Good as gold they were. I can still see Lillian dressed as though she was about to meet the Queen, marching her little troupe into Sunday school all polished and attentive. Her children seemed to fit the Elhert mold early in life, in particular, Katherine. And, to some extent, William." He paused. "Anton was another matter. He was different, a quiet boy, kept to himself. Yet, I sensed there was always more going on behind those big eyes of his. A dreamer, I suppose," he said unconvincingly. "I never really understood Anton and still don't. He comes to church on Sundays though. Not on a regular basis, mind you. A bit of a lost sheep."

"The man who asked about Walter, did he say who he worked for?" Josh asked.

"He didn't say."

Father Collins offered another round of tea, but they both declined and after a few minutes said their good-byes.

Traffic in the hotel lobby was slow when they got back. An attractive check-in girl and one of the waiters were at the end of the counter making plans for the night. Rachael went back to her room to freshen up while Josh plopped down onto a lobby couch and put a call in to Anton.

When Rachael returned, Josh said, "After we've met with the governor, I've arranged a meeting with Anton for later this afternoon."

"And?"

"And then I have to go to Guatemala. I think there's more to this contract and this German fellow, Walter. I don't know what it is . . . but I have to check it out."

Rachael sighed. "When will you be back?"

Josh could see she was annoyed. "Not long, just enough time to check if Walter Hyter is still alive, and if I'm lucky, ask a few questions. A few days at the most. I know it's a long shot, but there's not much else. If I let the trail go cold, I may never know who was behind Arthur's murder."

Rachael frowned, then her gaze shifted to her watch. They were due at the governor's.

Chapter 32

They arrived back at the mansion a few minutes after eleven. The butler led them to the courtyard where they were told the governor was having his late morning breakfast and reading the paper.

Halfway down a curved flight of steps that led into the courtyard, Josh touched Rachael's arm and they stopped. The sea was churning in the distance, and white-crested rollers were frothing on the shoreline. Both Katherine's home and Anton's could be seen nestled across the bay. The morning sun was warming his skin, and a faint perfume was drifting up from the flower garden. "I'll never figure it," Josh said. "How so much beauty and so much terror can occupy the same space and time?"

"Maybe beauty isn't appreciated without the ugly," Rachael said.

"That's a sad thought."

"It's not sad."

"Sure it is," Josh said. "It's as if you're saying I'd have to crush my big toe with a claw hammer to realize how good a pedicure feels."

"You get pedicures?"

"Maybe I do . . ."

"I received word last night," Governor Elhert called out in a voice loud enough to get their attention. "The

Sheriff called. Word is, they think it's that O'Henry fellow who's behind it all." Elhert stared at them, his look saying *tell me this is all a bunch of rubbish.*

Josh and Rachael did not respond as they walked down to the governor.

A scowl crossed Elhert's face. "Not in *my* goddamn county is this happening. I will not allow it. In two weeks we're heading to the polls. A stink like this will get stuck in the voter's heads. Negative shit. Shit that can lose you an election."

"It is O'Henry," Rachael said, her tone firm.

Elhert's gaze shifted to Josh.

He nodded.

"Ahhh hell. . . . So tell me, what could he possibly be doing here?" Governor Elhert asked, gesturing they take a seat.

"Last night, at dinner, it was mentioned your family moved here from Harland, Florida, back in '68," Josh said.

Governor Elhert raised an eyebrow. "That is correct. What of it?"

"We found this note in the throat of the severed head," Rachael said, handing it over to the governor. It's a copy. The original is on its way to our New York lab."

Elhert studied the clipping for a minute, his face stone cold. "What are you trying to say?"

"Since your family came from Harland, we thought you may be able to shed some light on the article," Josh said.

Governor Elhert paused, rubbing his hand along the edge of the table, and then looked up at them. "Yes, of course I remember," he said, then took a gulp of coffee.

"It was the summer just before we moved up here. A hellishly hot summer too, and I don't mean just the temperature. In those days racial tensions were much more visible than they are today. No veneer of civility to mask the raw emotions. In essence, it boiled down to the blacks figuring it was the whites that were to blame for the black girl's death."

"Were they?" Josh asked, without a hint of sarcasm. "*Were* the whites to blame?"

"Mmm, perhaps. Probably. Every night crowds of blacks and whites protested in the streets. Fights broke out, and people were thrown in jail. I'd just finished high school, and while I don't remember all the details, I do remember it being one colossal mess."

Josh noticed the governor glance to the side, his breathing picking up a notch. *He knows more than he's letting on.*

"Why did your father decide to move the family here, to Upstate New York?" Josh pressed.

"His second term as governor had finished, and I guess he decided to return to his roots. He'd grown up here. Something about the place you've grown up in. A sense of belonging if you will. He didn't care for the winters here though; so until his health started to go a few years ago, he and Lillian wintered in Florida."

"Do you remember how the girl from the clipping, Myrna Washington, died?" Rachael asked.

Josh could see Governor Elhert had come to a decision.

"I'm afraid I won't be able to help you with that. It was such a long time ago." He handed back the note. "Now, if you'll both excuse me, I'm due back in the city in an hour. My ride, the chopper, will be here any minute. The big kickoff to the final road trip starts next week and we have to ramp things up. Get the voters excited."

"Thank you for your time, Governor, you've been very helpful," Rachael said.

Governor Elhert then turned to Josh, and said, "You catch that son-of-a-bitch, you hear me?"

"We'll do our best."

Mabel's Diner and Bar was located on the outskirts of town. Truckers' rigs were parked along the secondary road out front, looking like a succession of gray tent caterpillars.

The diner's door handle stuck to Josh's hand and squeaked as he turned the knob. The place was packed and smelled of stale beer and cigarette smoke. The special of the day was written in pink chalk, on a blackboard. *Six Perogies, fried with sweet onions and Canadian back bacon, sour cream with chives, three eggs, $6.95.*

A flat screen over the bar, tuned to the news channel, had its volume set too high and managed to make the room feel even more congested than it was. It took Josh a moment to adjust to the dim light before noticing a couple at a front booth were preparing to leave. The man dropped a twenty and some change on the table, and they left. Josh and Rachael slipped into the booth just as a waitress hurried forward and snatched up the cash, saying she'd be back in a minute to take their order.

Rachael began rummaging around in her purse, checking one area and then another. Josh watched with interest, wondering how anything could get lost in such a small space. She didn't seem to notice him staring and withdrew her cell phone and started to check her messages.

"What?" Rachael asked, looking up at him.

He smiled. "Hungry?"

"Yes, I am."

Rachael ordered a steak sandwich, fries, side salad, and diet soda.

Josh had the special.

As Josh worked his way through the special, a ball of grease formed in his guts, and he wished he'd gone with the steak.

The TV over the bar seemed to get louder.

"Governor Elhert, do you really think the people of New York will continue to buy your country home-style approach? What I mean to say is, do you truly believe you can win over their hearts for a second term?"

"I have always loved the great state of New York. My family's roots are here. I think it's fair to say that my values of honesty and integrity were forged here, in our great state. Shoulder-to-shoulder, heart-to-heart, there is no greater force on this earth than good people working together. And there are no better people than the great people of the state of New York."

"You heard it, but will the people buy it?" the reporter said looking into the camera. "The polls show a two point spread over Samuel Jenkins, which means it's still anyone's race. Governor Elhert is hoping to broaden his demographic support in his bid for re-election and—"

The waitress grabbed the remote and flipped to the sports channel.

"So, what's your take on the governor?" Josh asked Rachael, then swallowed his last bite of perogy.

"The good and decent governor seems more concerned about the effect O'Henry could have on his campaign, than the fact that the lunatic is at his doorstep."

Josh nodded. "You just about ready? Anton will be expecting us."

Chapter 33

Josh almost missed the turnoff to Anton's estate. The stone archway at the mouth of the drive was cloaked in Boston ivy, making the opening hard to see from the road. Had it not been for the blood-red Virginia creeper woven along the rim on the arch, he would have missed it altogether. He glanced over at Rachael who was busy clicking away on her phone, lost in her cyber-world.

Josh slowed the Tahoe and passed through the entranceway while two cameras zeroed in on them. They passed a small group of gardeners dressed in faded blue coveralls; each wearing a pair of bright-yellow rubber gloves, all busy yanking out annuals, trimming trees, and working the soil for winter.

Josh drove another two hundred yards before pulling up in front of Anton's home. The air smelled of freshly cut lawns, rotted vegetation, and tilled soil.

At the base of the stairs, a silver-haired butler stood at attention. He was dressed in pressed black trousers, a white shirt, and had on a pair of freshly polished wing tips. Two mid-sized hounds, each without pedigree, came running up from behind the butler and sniffed Josh at his ankles and Rachael at her knees.

"They can be a handful at times," the butler said. "Please do come in and I will let Anton know you have arrived."

The foyer was huge. Round windows set at precise angles allowed in metered light that flooded clearly defined areas. The effect was dramatic and had the look of a Shakespearean stage. Four concrete pillars flanked a circular sunken area that required three steps down to reach its base. In the center of the circle stood a full-sized bronze statue of a wounded soldier, hunched over in a trench and tending to a fallen comrade.

The butler returned a minute later. "Anton is still in session, however, I expect he will be finished momentarily. If you would please follow me."

They proceeded down a long hallway lined with dark walnut paneling. Past an endless array of sixteenth-century Dutch oil paintings, each highlighted by a single halogen bulb. The hall emptied into an enclosed courtyard. The courtyard was vast, and as they stepped in, the strains of a violin and a viola, filled the air. The sound was emanating from the far end of the enclosure, from behind a set of tall, silk partitions. As they approached the silk wall, the butler extended his hand, palm up, and pointed to two wooden chairs.

Josh and Rachael each took a seat, and when the butler left, Josh grabbed Rachael's hand and they slipped through the curtains.

Margaret was facing them and had a violin tucked under her chin. Her eyes were closed, and a faint smile was on her lips as she swayed with the music. It was a beautiful melody, Josh thought—and she was beautiful.

Seated across from her and playing the viola was Anton, the side of his big, round head pressed against his instrument.

Margaret must have sensed them watching as she ceased playing. The trance was broken. Anton turned and saw Josh, then Rachael; a hint of surprise registering on his face. "Where did the time go?" Anton asked. "I'm afraid we were caught up in the moment, my dear," he said, and smiled at Margaret.

Margaret asked Josh, "So what do you think . . . ? Do you approve?"

"It was beautiful."

Margaret blushed. "It's all because of Anton. He plays so deeply. I simply pick up on his vibe and let it flow through me."

Anton's lips quivered, revealing the tips of his little teeth. "Margaret is too kind. Playing the way she does comes from the heart and cannot be taught. All I do is coax it out." Then he turned to Josh. "Do you play an instrument? I think you must, I sense a sympathetic ear."

Anton's intense stare made Josh uncomfortable, but he still managed half a smile. "I punish my electric guitar from time to time. Mostly, I just pound out the blues."

"The guitar . . . yes, I have always had a passion for the stringed instrument," Anton said.

Josh couldn't figure if Anton meant what he'd said, or he just tapped a charitable vein that allowed him to tolerate the lowly guitar. "That's a fine-looking instrument," Josh said, directing attention to Anton's viola.

"You have a good eye. This particular one dates back to 1821, the golden era for viola construction. An odd instrument, the viola, especially when one thinks of what it is made from." He turned the viola sideways, so Josh could get a better view. "Its top is spruce, the sides and back are maple, and it's all held together by collagen rendered from the tendons and bones of some unfortunate animal, that had the misfortune of being dropped off at a glue factory. To top it off, some deranged soul decided to string it with catgut, or rather sheep's intestines of all things. One has to ask one's self who was the first to come up with such an absurd idea and how that conversation would have gone . . .

And with that, Anton stood up and twirled his body 360 degrees, raised a limp wrist to his eyebrow and said in a nasal voice, "Wait a minute, Octavio. I have an idea . . . let's string her up with a sheep's intestine."

Margaret laughed.

Rachael glanced at Josh and gave him a *you gotta be kidding me* look.

"Now that's a man I would've liked to have met," Josh said.

"And who says it was a man?" Margaret asked.

Anton grinned, his little lips trembling. "Right you are my dear. I believe Shakespeare said it best when he wrote: 'Is it not strange that sheep's guts should hale souls out of men's bodies?' One has to ponder such things. . . . Ah, but I do go on, don't I? An impairment of having lived alone for so long. Give me a captive audience and I can't help but torture them with my poetic gibberish."

"We do have a few questions," Rachael said, her abruptness changing the mood. "You've no doubt already heard about Hampton Bridge?"

"Yes, Katherine called me," Anton said. "So unnerving to think this *O'Henry* fellow may have slipped into our little pocket of the world."

"Yes, so chilling," Margaret said. "How could anyone do such a thing?"

"We will catch him. It's only a matter of time," Josh said. "He'll make a mistake, psychopaths always do."

"Oh. I see you've pigeonholed him," Anton said, a puzzled look on his face.

"Sometimes a monster is just a monster," Rachael said.

"Come now, Ms. Tanner, do you really think *the monster* acts without reason?" Anton asked. "A touch too simplistic, really I would think you of all—"

"You both have valid points," Josh said. "Of course, we in this room are fully aware the killer rarely acts without reason. Mind you, the reason he kills can at times be somewhat difficult to understand. He has his own set of values and beliefs."

"You say he," Margaret said. "Could he not be a she?"

"To date, it has been almost entirely in the domain of the man, to be a serial killer," Josh said.

"You said almost?" Margaret asked.

"There are always exceptions," Rachael said.

"We found this in her throat." Josh handed Anton the copy of the news clipping.

Anton held the clipping in his hand for a moment before reading it. A frown crossed his face and without saying a word, he gave it back to Josh.

Rachael spoke up. "We met with the governor earlier, and he came up blank when we asked about how the girl, Myrna Washington, died. We were wondering if you would be able to help us out with what happened to her, or to the missing boy, her boyfriend. Was he ever found?"

Anton's lips tightened, it was clear he wanted to avoid answering. *What is it Anton, what are you thinking?* Josh thought. *What don't you want to tell us?*

"As I remember it, the boy was the prime suspect," Anton said. "And if my memory serves, he was never found. As to how she died, some say it was an accident, some say not. As far as I know, it was a case that was never solved, a cold case as they say." Anton winked one of his big eyes at Josh. "Now there's the seed for a story for you, Josh Ingram."

Josh did not respond.

"But there is a bigger question raised by all of this," Anton said. "Why *did* O'Henry put the clipping in the woman's throat? One would have to conclude there has to be some connection to the town of Harland. What that could be . . . I have to say, I'm at a loss."

Josh noticed Rachael's gaze was fixed on Anton's face, and Anton picked up on it.

"You're surprised the family's good looks didn't encompass all the siblings?"

"Sorry, I . . ." Rachael croaked.

"Nature can be cruel, and yet we all have to play the cards we're dealt, don't we?" Anton smiled. "Oh please, life has been good to me. I have no cause to complain."

The butler stepped into the room and nodded to Anton. "The library is ready. May I bring your guests some refreshment?"

Anton asked, "Please, would you join us? Margaret and I have a routine that includes a compulsory conversation after class. Payment I've imposed on her; to have her all to myself. If only for a few minutes."

The library had one massive two-story window that faced out onto the Atlantic. The surrounding walls were lined with ornate walnut bookcases covering the first story, above the bookcases hung giant-sized museum-quality oils. A tired fire crackled in the room's fireplace; its embers popping, blinking black to red and back again, yellow spurts of flame curling out the ends of the charred wood, a trace of sweet birch in the air.

Anton turned to Josh. "If you don't mind me asking, you've said your latest book will miss the Christmas market. Can you tell us when it is due to hit the shelves?"

"Not as soon as my agent and publisher would like. Probably not until April or May."

"It'll be worth waiting for I'm sure," Margaret said.

"Tell that to my agent," Josh replied and smiled.

The butler showed up with a tray of tea and other refreshments and passed them around.

"Josh, I have to say, this is an unexpected honor to have you sitting here," Anton said. "I have read all of your books. . . . You could say I'm a fan, a very big fan." Anton rose and gestured Josh to follow.

"I always thought I'd try my hand at writing. Regrettably, it never took. I am an enthusiastic reader though, consume a book every couple of days. I read all genres, I even reread the classics. Though I have to confess, I do have a soft spot for a good murder mystery."

Josh watched Anton, and noticed he had a certain comfort and confidence in the way he conducted himself. *Was it the result of never having to earn a buck, all the sharp edges dulled from lack of use?* Still, he couldn't help feeling compassion for him; his transition to adulthood with such a visual deficit had to have been brutal.

"Have you ever married?" Rachael asked from across the room.

A look that could only be described as a glimpse into

despair flashed in Anton's eyes, and then it was gone. Josh caught the look and wondered if Rachael had too.

"Alas, but I am destined to live alone," Anton replied and grinned, the tips of his tiny teeth protruding from beneath his lips. "I do have my dogs. Such solace can be found in their forgiving ways." He turned to Josh. "Your bio says you enjoy a good game of chess."

"I've been known to tilt a few kings in my time."

"I'm glad to hear you say that. It's unfortunate how often players feel it necessary to act timid on this point, as if timidity was a virtue. Rather unbecoming when they do I must say. So thrilling to know you are a worthy opponent. So tell me, at what stage of the game do you find it most challenging?"

"I'd be careful how you answer that," Margaret said. "By the age of twenty-three, our Anton had attained the title of Chess Master."

"Very impressive, Anton. Do you still compete?" Rachael asked.

"No no, that was ages ago. Not long after I attained the rank, I decided to step out of competition. So many other avenues in life to explore. So many experiences to enjoy."

"The end game, when the mind has to be its sharpest," Josh said with conviction.

"Oh yes, indeed." Anton's eyes brightened. "When the prey is trying to escape the inevitable. When defeat is just around the corner. It separates the men from the boys."

"Or the women from the men," Margaret said.

Anton nodded.

"There is another reason we wanted to meet," Josh

said, changing the subject. He pulled out the contract from his inside coat pocket and handed it to Anton.

"Oh yes. The Guatemala Contract. It caused quite a stir across the bay when it arrived. An old skeleton, as they say."

"How's that?" Rachael asked.

"It was our family's first taste of money. A taste of *real* money that is. All very hush, hush. Father had owned land in Guatemala for decades, but the land had not produced much, only weak cash crops of rubber and palm oil. Paid the bills, not much more. But a new crop was on the horizon. The Second World War was coming to its conclusion and certain types needed to find a place to hide. Central and South America were natural spots to squirrel oneself away."

Anton paused for a moment before continuing. "Friendly dictators for a price weren't that difficult to find, and I dare say still aren't. Guatemala seemed a logical choice, of course. Favorable climate, pretty girls, and close to the states. It worked rather well for all concerned. And while father got into the action late, he did manage to broker a number of high-ranking deals. All extremely sensitive stuff. The kind of stuff one sweeps under the carpet and then hides behind a curtain of well paid for respectability."

"You talk freely on the subject, and yet I don't think your family would share the same enthusiasm," Josh said.

"Getting one's fingers dirty early on is a road many of our great American families have traveled, so why should we be so different?" Anton shrugged.

"So the shares of the company were payment for services rendered?" Rachael asked.

"The German currency was in free fall, and to purchase American dollars would attract unwanted attention, so payment by way of shares solved the dilemma. Kept those who wished to remain out of sight, insulated."

"What about the photograph, the one that was cut in half?" Josh asked, watching closely for Anton's reaction. Anton's face took on an air of understanding, of genuine interest, and yet to Josh it seemed as if he'd been expecting the question.

"A little odd, isn't it?" Anton asked. "Why cut it in half? The obvious reason would be to conceal the identity of the boys, but why?"

"You say, boys . . ."

"Oh, come now Josh, a man of your gifts. Not much of an extrapolation to come to, is it?"

Josh smiled. "If I could impose. Could you point me in the direction of the washroom?"

"Of course." Anton nodded to the butler, who led Josh down the hall. The hallway was long and curved, and a washroom came up about halfway to its end. Josh entered, waited ten seconds, and then poked his head out. *Time to have a look around.*

He followed the hallway until it came to a door with a simple skeleton key lock. He thought about using a credit card, but tried the handle first. It opened.

The room was forty by forty feet square with windows running along the outer wall. Four exhibits occupied the space: A foxhole from the First World War with a soldier throwing a hand grenade. Another showed the tunnels of Vietnam, presented in cross-section, showing how their lives would have played out in their subterranean world. There was a work in progress of a Bosnian exhibit that appeared to be nearing completion, complete with a mass grave, skeletons and all. Lastly, he saw a 13th century catapult, every detail finished to perfection. *Amazing*, Josh thought, and found himself in complete awe of the precise nature of the work and the fine craftsmanship.

He was feeling it was time to return to the others, when at the end of room, he noticed another door. He walked over and pushed it open. There was only darkness. He searched for a light switch, running his fingers along the wall until he found a toggle switch and flipped it. This room also had exhibits, though not ones he would have expected. Without warning, he heard a footstep fall at his heels. A heavy step, not Rachael's or Margaret's. He turned to find Anton standing behind him.

"You've lost your way?" Anton asked, his tone innocent, his eyes saying otherwise.

"Yes, I took a bad turn," Josh said, half-grinning. "Still, if I hadn't I wouldn't have stumbled across all this."

"And?" Anton asked, an amused look on his face.

"Incredible."

"Yes it is. It's a passion of mine," Anton said, his voice starting to relax. "The other room is dedicated to war history. This room is dedicated to the inventions man has employed to exact the truth. And perhaps justice."

"Justice?" Josh asked.

"A bit of poetic license to call it that, I grant you. But please, allow me to give you the five cent tour." Anton walked over to the first invention and reached out and stroked its timbers. "Hard to believe that The Rack as it was called, was in use for close to 250 years throughout all of Europe. One can only speculate how many criminals there would be if it was still employed today. Such a decisive deterrent in its day."

Josh's mind slid to thoughts of joints torn apart, legs and arms hanging down from the remaining stump, attached only by threads of stretched tendons. He gave his head a shake.

Anton led the way to the next display. "Ahh . . . here we have what was known as the Chinese Iron Maiden. It was in use during the Ming Dynasty, that lasted an incredible 426 years. A particularly nasty item. In essence, it is a coffin with an iron gate at its base. Red-hot coals and cold water created a cloud of steam that entered the coffin through the gate. The occupant endured a slow death, as he or she was steamed—or rather, cooked, alive. It goes without saying, the Chinese did it in full view of the citizens. Even then, they saw the benefit of setting an example."

The last item sat across the room. Placed on a four-foot by eight-foot felt covered table, it was small, not more than six inches in length, and shaped like an iron pear. Anton picked it up. "The Pear of Anguish," he said. "It was endorsed by many pillars of society, most noteworthy were those in charge of the Inquisition. So simple in its design. The pear shape was such that it could fit into various orifices of the body, the decision as to which orifice was dependent on whether you were judged a liar, an adulteress, or a homosexual. Once inserted, the screw mechanism at the top was turned, causing the iron pear to expand. The pain was said to have been excruciating, as you can imagine, although it rarely caused death. Used primarily in conjunction with other modes of torture."

"I guess you could call it the opening act," Josh said.

Anton clicked his little teeth together and giggled. "You're a strange fellow, Mr. Ingram. Perhaps that's why I like you so much."

Josh winced without showing it and said, "What do you say we join the ladies?"

Chapter 34

By the time Josh and Rachael returned to the hotel it was late afternoon. He dropped her off by the front porch, swung around to the back and parked close to the hotel's loading dock. He killed the engine and a moment later his cell rang. He didn't recognize the number, but took the call. The man had a British accent and identified himself as Evan Bristle. He asked to meet at a local restaurant across town, saying they needed to talk as he had information about the Elhert family that Josh needed to know.

Josh left a message on Rachael's voicemail that he'd meet her later in the hotel bar, around nine o'clock.

It was a few minutes after six when Josh rolled up to the restaurant. On the marquee, the name 'Steamboat Grill' was circled by a creamy, green-colored neon light. A bright yellow wooden banner hung below the marquee and read: SHRIMP AND CRAB NIGHT.

The customer parking lot was jam-packed, and Josh found himself having to pay ten bucks to park across the street in a makeshift gravel lot. A pimply-faced kid took his ten, forcing a smile that came off more as a smirk, revealing a broken front tooth under a sparsely sown mustache.

The restaurant reeked of garlic and butter, and reminded Josh he needed to get his cholesterol checked. The lighting had been turned down, which helped to hide the torn seats and scuffed floors. On each table, there was a floating candle in a small green bowl, which had a net zero effect on the glum atmosphere. A man was standing next to an alcove located by an emergency exit—it had to be him. Bristle said he would be wearing a navy-blue blazer with a yellow rose in the lapel. *No need for that,* Josh thought. He looked so damn British, it would be like trying to hide the Duke of Windsor in a biker bar. Josh hoped it would be a brief encounter.

"Mr. Ingram, so good of you to come," Bristle said. "I do apologize about the surroundings, I had no idea what the establishment was all about until I arrived."

"Not a problem, I've sat in worse," Josh said as they shook hands and took a seat in the booth.

Josh got straight down to business. "You said you have information I should be aware of."

"Yes, I do. And I'm so glad we could meet, though our paths were bound to cross at some time. It was inevitable."

"Uh-huh," Josh said, and watched as Bristle undertook a quick survey of the room, his gaze darting around for a few moments before returning to Josh. *Just what the hell are you afraid of . . . ?*

The waiter dropped off a couple of oily menus with fingerprints smeared across them.

"I'm what is known as a tracker," Bristle said. "Part of a small mop-up crew whose sole purpose is to see that the last of the Nazi war criminals are prosecuted, and to ensure that those who helped them hide after the war are held accountable."

Josh studied the man for a moment. "I would have thought they're all dead by now."

"Indeed, almost all are. In point of fact, few are left. We've been chasing down one Frederick Goball for some time. He's one of three remaining bad boys on our list."

"And?" Josh asked.

"Goball commanded the Panax extermination camp in Poland from 1942 to 1944. Some one hundred and twenty thousand died under his watch. He made himself a *name* as a sadist. Enjoyed torturing select inmates for his own entertainment. He regarded torture as an art form and went so far as to commission an artist to immortalize his favorite scenes. And, as ghastly as it sounds, there is still today a strong black market for that specific genre."

"It's been a really long day," Josh said. "So enlighten me. Why am I here?"

"Indeed. The thing is, our Mr. Goball managed to sneak himself into Guatemala at the end of the war. It irks me to say, he was so well hidden; he died before he could be dealt with in a suitable manner. He died three weeks ago."

"And?" Josh said, seeing where the conversation was headed.

"Goball is gone, but some of those who made it possible for him to slip into Guatemala and live out his life in comfort are still alive today. Those who helped him can be still be held accountable."

Josh waited for him to continue.

"And this is where the tricky part comes in; proving it. Proving a solid connection between Goball and his facilitators. As you can imagine it has been difficult, to say the least, to connect him to those who helped him. Especially some sixty years after the fact."

The waiter returned and they both declined food, settling instead for a pint of beer each.

"What do you know about Walter Hyter and Salvador Espada?" Bristle asked.

"The name Espada, I'm not familiar with," Josh lied, remembering the woman from Arthur's funeral. "Hyter . . . yeah, I've heard some stories."

"Salvador Espada was one of Guatemala's most important writers. He and Walter Hyter were friends, so much so that he gave Hyter a signed first edition of his third book, the last book of his trilogy." Bristle frowned. "Calling it a first edition would be putting it mildly. Espada wrote all three books in longhand. The books were never put to the printing press during his lifetime. It was not until after his death that he became famous. His writings are now counted as a national treasure of Guatemala. Your friend Arthur somehow came across the hand-written third book, and now your friend is dead."

"You're saying the book carried that kind of value, that Arthur would be killed for it?"

"My God man, today it would be worth hundreds of thousands of pounds, though I doubt it was the book that Arthur was killed for. Rather for what it contained within its jacket."

Josh stared at Bristle, his face devoid of emotion.

"Let me explain. We tracked down Walter Hyter last spring. He was living in Guatemala at the time, and I believe he still is. He was, as you must know by now, George Elhert's right-hand man. That is, of course, until they split in the nineties. We have suspected for some time that Elhert made a sizable portion of his early wealth by brokering war criminals to safety after the war. But we've never had a way to pin it to him."

"So you're aware of the contract?" Josh asked.

A smile crossed Bristle's face. "As I said, we connected with Walter last spring. When we found him, he was in rough shape and clearly in desperate need of some cash. In Guatemala, no cash translates to no healthcare. He told us, and did so rather freely I must say, about the book and the contents contained within its jacket. He also told us that, as George's right-hand man he knew what George was capable of, and as such he saw value in keeping the contract as a form of insurance."

"A shrewd fellow, Hyter," Josh said.

"Very. He told us the contract evidenced payment of a huge sum of money, by way of Klineharber International shares, being transferred over to George, and that the transfer was signed by Fredrick Goball.

"According to Hyter, the book was stolen from him in the eighties and deemed lost until it showed up with your friend Arthur. That's how we found the book; for sale on the web at your friend's bookstore. We need that contract, Mr. Ingram. It ties George Elhert to Goball. It will expose Elhert for the—"

Had they been sitting at the front of the restaurant, they may have heard the tinkle of glass as it broke free of the windowpane, the shards dropping to the floor. A nanosecond later, a bullet pierced the back of Bristle's skull, exiting his forehead, spraying bits of brain and blood against the wall next to Josh, peppering his shirt and his sports coat.

Josh dropped onto the bench seat and slid to the floor.

A second later a piercing scream poured out of the waitress. Josh lunged toward her, tackling her to the floor. Looking up, he saw a man peering through the window. He couldn't make out a face, but the man was large and appeared to be talking on a cell. Then the man turned away and was gone. The waitress's sobbing under him broke his concentration. "Someone call 911!" Josh yelled.

By the time Josh made it to the front door, the man was nowhere in sight and the street was clear of people; all he saw was a mongrel chasing a tabby cat into an alley, followed by the sound of an empty bottle rolling on the pavement. A siren could be heard in the distance, and the patrons started filing out onto the street. Josh turned and knelt by the shards of glass and ran his fingers across the bullet hole. The hole was small and clean with minimal webbing. *A 9mm,* he thought. Focusing on where Bristle had been sitting, he calculated the distance and angle. *A professional.*

After an hour hanging around the police station, and having given his statement, Rachael took Josh back to the hotel. They agreed to meet at the bar after he'd had a chance to clean up.

Josh let the heat of the shower penetrate his muscles and found himself thinking about Arthur. *How did you get mixed up in all this? Was it a fluke? Were you set up? If so, who was calling the shots? And why? Why does O'Henry's name keep washing up closer and closer to yours? Is it all a coincidence? And what am I doing here? A week ago I was noodling and trying to finish my manuscript. Now, I'm left with bits of brain on my clothes and working with the Feds again.*

Finished, he dried himself off and put on a fresh pair of chinos and a light-blue cotton shirt. Then he balled up his clothes from the restaurant, jammed them into a clear plastic bag and placed them by the door for trash pickup. He picked up the phone, asked for a nine o'clock wake-up call, and flopped back onto the bed.

An hour had lapsed when the phone rang. Flat-out on his stomach and half-asleep he grabbed the receiver and put it to his ear.

Josh recognized the voice. The warm, Spanish accent left no doubt who the caller was.

"Mr. Ingram, my name is Anna Espada. I met you at your friend's funeral. I've been trying to reach you. I'm still in New York. I'm sorry for calling you at this hour, but my father has asked to see you. It's about my grandfather. We are having a reception tomorrow night at the Guatemalan embassy. Please come?"

Chapter 35

Josh crossed the lobby and entered the bar. Ten past ten and the place was dead. A sign over the bar read: Two for one: Drafts and Highballs. A sad cowboy ballad was playing on the jukebox, and a couple of old-timers were sitting next to the slots. He spotted Rachael, drink in hand, being seated at an empty booth.

Josh walked over. "Hey, sorry I'm late."

"What?" she said and checked her watch. "Oh . . . yeah . . . I couldn't relax. I needed a drink." And she held up a half-empty martini.

Josh turned to the waitress. "I'll have one of those."

"A dirty martini?"

"Yeah, sure, and maybe toss in a few extra olives," he said, as he slid in across from Rachael.

Neither of them were in the mood for a full meal, so Rachael ordered appetizers: curried crab cakes, salt and pepper chicken wings, and a basket of fries. Josh was on his second martini when he got around to filling her in on what Bristle had said at the restaurant, and the phone call he'd received inviting him to the Embassy. "Look, I know it sounds a little out there, but someone blew this Bristle fellow's brains out, which in my book tends to lend some credibility to his story."

"C'mon Josh, so what you're saying is, if the Elhert

family had the balls to take out Bristle, they would be capable of having anyone who threatened the family killed, including Arthur."

"Now that I hear you saying it, I'm not so certain I believe it myself."

"Also, why would the Elherts want to take out Arthur? They were going to pay him a small finder's fee in return for the contract. Arthur had no idea who 'Goball the Nazi' was. So, why kill him? He wasn't a threat, not even close. But then, if it's not the Elherts—who *is* behind it all?"

"I don't know. But Walter Hyter's name keeps coming up. There's something there, there has to be. Hyter had a long history with Elhert. And Espada's third book was given to Hyter, the same book that held the contract that implicates George Elhert. If that's not enough, Bristle mentioned Hyter just seconds before he was killed."

"So. I take it you're still going to Guatemala?"

"I'll be gone two days, three tops. I'm gonna stop off in Miami first. Need to have a chat with Carlotti and rattle his cage. Then on to Guatemala, find Hyter, and with any luck get some answers."

"Jesus, Josh. Carlotti is not someone you push around. He'll clip you in a heartbeat. I know that for a fact. I was there, remember? I know him. He's old school, he won't accept you snooping around. The man has secrets."

Josh could feel her studying him before she said, "Promise me you'll be respectful and live. Carlotti rules the jungle down there. You have to promise me."

"Yeah, I'll be careful," he said and tried to smile. "But if anyone is in danger, it's you. O'Henry is still on the loose . . ."

"Hey, I still have twenty-four-hour surveillance on my place. Besides, I'm a big girl, I can handle myself. And we both know you're gonna have to act fast if you're to have any chance of uncovering who's behind Arthur's death. So go. Find this Walter Hyter, and learn what you can. A couple of days will fly by. I need some time with my team anyway; go over any leads they've dug up, not to mention having to deal with the press, Kingsley, and the mayor. When you get back we'll meet in Harland and pick up where we left off."

Chapter 36

Scarlet azaleas caught in the floodlights burst color across the gray stone walls of the Guatemalan Embassy. The embassy was a mile south of Central Park, and had been fortified by a ten-foot high cinder-block wall, complete with statues and climbing vines. Guards armed with automatic rifles and pump-action shotguns paced the grounds, while the haunting notes of a tenor saxophone drifted above their heads.

A cab rolled to a stop by the front gate, letting Josh out at the curb. He could hear a light banter of Latino voices coming from behind the walls, mingled with the throaty sound of a saxophone. A distinct hum was in the air.

Two sentries in military garb, each with an earpiece and an AK47 slung over his shoulder, stood in silence at the entrance to the embassy. Josh flashed his ID and made his way through to the main hall. Immediately he sensed an abundance of wealth in the room. *Bloodlines and privilege,* he thought, and headed for a far corner, backing himself up against an ivory pillar. A server with a tray of champagne flutes cruised by, and Josh took two.

Some twenty feet away, a small gaggle of stout, potbellied men equipped with cigars and graying hair talked in muted tones, each trying to look very regal.

A five-piece ensemble started its second set. A big-boned black woman dovetailed into a jazz set, her voice, resonant and seasoned, rolled out and filled the room.

Josh scanned the crowd and couldn't help notice all the young, brown-skinned women dressed in sheer evening gowns. Each seemed to be on her own elliptical orbit, each on a path that, he sadly deduced, was set to intersect with the potbellied suitors.

A short, round-shouldered man spoke into his lapel, cocked his head, and nodded in the direction of Josh. Seconds later, two larger men came into view. All three began to move in.

"Josh," a burly voice called out from behind him. Josh swung around, coming face-to-face with a huge man. The man held out his hand and said, "Name's Demetrius."

"Let me guess, you're a Guatemalan rancher with connections," Josh said.

"Nope." Demetrius chuckled. "My sources led me here. I'm looking for someone." Then he turned the tables. "And you?"

"Invited," Josh said, and glanced at the three security guards who were closing in. "So. Who's the guilty party?"

"You are." Demetrius grinned. "Gotta pin the tail on somebody. Might as well be you." Then he tipped an imaginary hat and faded into the crowd.

The guards had now spread out, ensuring their quarry could not slip away.

The woman finished her song, then picked up the tempo with a salsa beat.

The security guards were less than twenty feet away when the lead guard lifted his hand. They all slowed to a halt.

The lead appeared to be taking instructions when Josh noticed Anna across the room. She was laughing, surrounded by a ring of young men. Josh waved, catching her attention. She said something, and all the men laughed. *Either you're very funny, or they're scared shitless of your daddy.* She said something else and again they all laughed. She then bowed out and sauntered over.

"Thank you for coming," Anna said, and waved away the lead guard. "I was hoping you would make it." She smiled, it was a smile filled with warmth, and for the first time Josh was glad he came.

"I'm planning to visit your country. Your invitation seemed like good timing."

Anna raised an eyebrow. "Oh . . . how interesting. I am returning home tomorrow."

Josh could see she was pleased.

"Business or pleasure?"

"Business, I'm afraid."

"That's a shame," she said, then grinned. "Come, I want to introduce you to my father."

She led the way to the middle of the room where they were stopped by her brother.

"Who is this?" Enrico asked, stepping in front of Josh.

The brother reeked of booze, the way an alcoholic does when his liver is failing. Josh knew the smell; it reminded him of his father.

"Where is your etiquette, Sis? Introduce me to your new friend."

Anna turned to Josh and sighed. "My apologies."

Josh extended his hand. "Josh Ingram."

Enrico kept his arm by his side. "I am Enrico. Next in

line to be the head of my family. I am my father's trusted advisor. We are men of distinction, of honor, not that *you* would understand the core of a man's existence. So, you go . . ." his voice trailed off as he staggered sideways. He grabbed a pillar and steadied himself, then turned back to Josh. "Mister, you have nothing to gain by banging my sister. So I think—" he slapped his hand once against the pillar. "It is time for you to leave these places."

Anna's face darkened as she glared at her brother.

A calm smile formed on Josh's lips, and he turned to Anna. "An enchanting fellow, your brother."

Enrico took a step toward Josh. "Fuck you, white slug."

Anna's father must have noticed the commotion, as he broke from the group he was speaking with and made his way toward them. Enrico turned and was gone before his father arrived.

"Papa, I would like you to meet Josh Ingram, the writer I told you about."

"Yes, of course, it is my pleasure, Mr. Ingram. I have not read your books, but I am told you are a talented writer."

"I try."

Anna spoke up. "Josh has come here this evening as our guest, father. I will show him around."

"Of course you will," he said, patting his daughter's hand. He turned to Josh. "Mr. Ingram, you are a man that appreciates the value of the written word—I too have a love for words. My father was not only a great writer, but a great man. He wrote three novels, perhaps a small number when compared to your work." He stopped and studied Josh for a moment, then said, "But I think you must be aware of such things?"

"I have to admit, until a few days ago I knew very little about Salvador Espada, but I understand he was a great man and left behind an important legacy for your country."

A huge smile crossed Anna's father's face. "I think I like you, Mr. Ingram. Please, please come join us on the balcony," he said, and held his open hand out to his daughter.

A servant stood at the entrance to the balcony holding a silver tray. On the tray was a box of cigars, and a crystal flask of brandy surrounded by an array of snifters.

"Would you join me in one of my few vices?" Anna's father asked, turning to the servant. The servant tilted the box to Josh.

Josh picked out a cigar, slipped his fingers under a snifter, then put the glass to his nose and inhaled. It smelled of burnt caramel—*marvelous*. The servant struck a match and held it under the cigar. Josh puffed a few times before taking a long sip of brandy.

"Such a fine thing this is," Anna's father said, looking into the brandy. "How is it you Americans say . . . ? Ah yes, comfort food." He paused for a moment, then said, "My daughter tells me your friend was killed. I am sorry for your loss. Death, it is a sad business." He took a sip of brandy and his tone became solemn. "I understand your friend had in his possession my father's third and last book. Now, once again, it has gone missing. I want you to know I have created a generous reward—"

Josh reached out and touched Anna's father's arm to stop him. "A reward won't be necessary. When I find your father's book, it will be my honor to return it to your family, back to where it belongs."

Anna's father seemed pleased; his demeanor mellowing. "The night is for living, Mr. Ingram. My house is your house."

As Anna's father left the balcony, he turned to Josh and said, "Thank you."

"My father thinks you are okay. I think maybe you are okay, too," Anna said, studying him. "You are a different sort of man . . ."

Josh cut in, wanting to change the subject. "The daughter of a dignitary must have had its moments."

"Yes, it has, although it is not as interesting as it might seem. There is boredom and lots of it. The hardest part is to be away from my family, my mother and sisters, my aunts, and my many cousins. It's a big family. I love the ranch, the ocean, but father is an important man, and if he asks me to come, I do what he asks."

"You are a good daughter."

Anna half-smiled.

"Anna, there are a few things I need to clear up in my mind."

"Okay . . . ?"

"Can you tell me how you came across Arthur? He wasn't much of a world traveler, his entire Spanish vocabulary would be strained to go beyond saying hello and goodbye."

She glanced at his snifter. "Another drink?"

"Sure, why not?"

Anna returned a minute later with a tray. On it were two large, frosted mugs of beer, a bowl filled with chunks of green mango cut thick, and a pile of sea salt three inches high. "I thought we needed a change of pace," she said, pointing to the mugs and smiled.

"Watch what I do. . . . First, you dip the mango in the salt and take a big bite," her words were now muffled, "and then quickly wash it down with the cerveza."

Josh followed her lead, sticking a large piece of green mango into the salt. As he brought it to his lips, the pungent sour scent plunged his jaw muscles into an acute salivating cramp. . . . *Be a man,* he said to himself, and then crammed the whole wedge into his mouth and began to munch away. The sour, salty juices lined his cheeks and started to leak out the corners of his mouth. He raised the frosted mug to his lips and swallowed the brine laden pulp, chasing it down with the ice-cold beer. "Like that?" He grinned.

Anna laughed and raised her glass to him. Then she reached out and put her hand to his mouth, and with her fingertips brushed off some of the salt stuck to his lips. "Are you familiar with my grandfather's books?"

"Not really," Josh said, his jaw muscles still cramping.

"He wrote three books in total, each covering a generation of our family's history. Two of the books, the first two, were passed to my father many years ago. He kept them locked in a safe in our home. Then my brother's problems took over. Drugs, and alcohol, and not so good women. My brother, he stole the books from my father and pawned them off. It was a sad time. I thought my father and mother would have him shot. They were so angry."

"Two books?"

"Yes, two books. Both were eventually tracked down and recovered."

"And the third book?"

Anna sighed. "My grandfather was a great man, but he had his weaknesses . . . as all men do. For all his brilliance, my grandfather made some unusual friends. One friend in particular, who my mother has spoken about many times, was an odd little man who came to Guatemala just after the war had ended. My grandfather and this man became best of friends, frequenting the bars and, how is it you say . . . hookers. So. One night my grandfather, in one of his drunken stupors, gave this man his third book as a sign of their deep friendship. When my mother and father found out, they begged grandfather to have it returned, but grandfather's honor would not allow him to ask for it back."

Josh took another gulp of beer. "You know, you still haven't told me how you managed to connect with Arthur."

He could see her mulling it over, then she said, "For many years, I have been in contact with a number of the larger antique book vendors in the Americas and Europe, hoping the third book would one day turn up. Then a few weeks ago, as I searched the web, plugging in my grandfather's name—there it was, his book for sale at your friend Arthur's bookstore. I called your friend, and I could tell he knew little about its history. We agreed he would sell it to me for a thousand dollars.

"But now Arthur is dead, and again the book is lost . . ." Anna stopped abruptly. "Oh, I am sorry. I keep going on and on about *a book* when you've lost your friend."

"It's all right," Josh said, then took another draw on his beer. "Any thoughts on where the book has disappeared to now?"

"My father spoke with the police, and they said the book was listed on the store's inventory. However, when my father called back to confirm it was there, they told him it was missing. That's all I know."

"Anna." A woman's voice came from behind them. "Your father requests your presence. The ceremony is about to begin."

"Please Josh, make yourself comfortable. Duty calls . . ." She turned to go, then spun around and raised her hand and touched his cheek. "Call me when you land. I want to show you my beautiful country." She withdrew a silver cardholder from her purse and handed him a card with only her name and phone number. Then she turned and walked away.

A heavy hand latched onto Josh's arm. "Don't be alarmed, and don't turn around. Meet me on the front porch in five minutes," the man said, his voice seasoned with an east coast accent.

The man was dressed in a black suit, white shirt, and navy-blue tie. He was over six feet tall and appeared fit. "You're a popular guy around here, Mr. Ingram. Seems everybody wants to get to know you."

"I suppose you're right, but I haven't been able to figure out why."

"I'm supposed to believe that . . . ? The black man that you spoke to this evening. Have you ever had contact with him before?"

"And what is it to you, if I did?" Josh asked, starting to get annoyed.

"His name is Demetrius. He's well known in some circles. A mercenary."

"And you're a boy scout?"

"Fair enough," the man said, and then reached out and shook Josh's hand. "CIA. Name's Murdock. You ever been to Guatemala, Mr. Ingram?"

Josh stared at him and said nothing.

"Seven families. They control everything that goes on in the country. These are powerful people in their world, and their word is final. Judgment stops with them. If they want you dead, you're dead. No surprise, Anna's father heads up one of the families. So my advice to you—be careful."

"And Demetrius?"

"Be mindful of him as well, he's here for a reason."

"I take it you know my travel plans?"

Murdock grinned and handed Josh his card. "Call me . . . any time."

Chapter 37

Demetrius's phone vibrated in his pocket. As he fished it out, he pulled off to the side of the road.

"You called me?" Petruski asked.

"I need a rundown on someone."

"Gotta name?"

"Yeah, Josh Ingram, the writer," Demetrius said.

"Huh . . . interesting. Is he a problem?"

"Probably not. But I need his bio. Call it a hunch."

"Not the hardest guy to get info on," Petruski said.

"Yeah, I guess not. But I need you to focus on his time in the military. That could be a tougher nut to crack. See what you can find."

"I'll get on it." Petruski hung up and put a call in to Lenny Williamson, Section Head of data retrieval for the Marines.

"Lenny. Petruski here. Need a favor. A full backgrounder on Josh Ingram, the writer . . . focusing on when he served with you boys. Need it in an hour."

Demetrius was in a bar, nursing his second highball, when the call came though.

"Go ahead," Demetrius said.

"Not as straight forward as I thought," Petruski said. "Ingram's career started off normal enough, joined the Marines and rose to the rank of Captain. He achieved 'Expert Class Marksman,' something few have done. It's documented he could nail a silver dollar at 250 yards. Then he took a transfer to Black Ops. Ran catch and release operations in the Middle East. Trained as a Black Hawk pilot, and then he did something unusual. He declined a promotion. A few weeks later, the wheels fell off, and he got six months in jail for assaulting a superior officer. Sentence could have been lighter, but he knocked out three of the officer's teeth. That's all I have. Ingram was special ops, his file is buried deep and locked tight. Whatever he was up to will never see the light of day. Watch yourself, word is this guy has incurred some damage."

Chapter 38

Hurricane Hugo was rated as a category three. Its leading edge, situated 210 miles southeast of Florida, was tracking north. It wasn't expected to hit South Carolina before morning, and as the weather reports showed, it would only lick the east coast of Florida as it passed by.

It was three p.m. when Josh landed at Miami International Airport. A hot sultry day greeted him as he stepped off the plane. He had driven south for about fifteen minutes on Peterson Road when the wind picked up and changed direction.

Five minutes later, Josh rolled up in front of Carlotti's Casino. A half-dozen light bulbs were broken on the marquee over the front door, patches of plaster had come loose from the wall, and a thick layer of fresh, red paint glistened on the front windowsills. A derelict gas station sat next to the casino. The pumps were still standing, but the garage windows had been punched out and the front door had been kicked in and hung awkwardly on one hinge. On the other side of the casino were a laundromat and a coin-operated car wash. A four-door sedan and a late model compact were out front of the laundromat. Parked in front of the casino was a full-sized black SUV. Josh parked between the rusted compact and the shiny SUV.

As Josh opened the rental car door, the wind caught it

and almost tore it from his grasp. He got out and slammed the door shut, turned up his jacket collar, holding it tight under his chin and made his way to the entrance.

Inside the casino it was warm and humid, and smelled of fried chicken, and ashtrays filled with cigarette butts. It was the slow time of the day, what the Miami casino trade called the *dead zone*. Nothing much was going on; a few pensioners were playing the slots, sipping their beer and smoking their filter tips. An old movie played on a tube TV behind the bar, and a half-dozen wooden bowls filled with peanuts dotted the counter. At one end of the bar sat a fat man slouched over a bowl of nuts. He wore a white T-shirt soiled with grease stains. He was reading a newspaper, and glanced up as Josh walked past.

The main room was quiet except for the sound of the electronic slots, pinging and beeping. A short, square-shaped woman with a ruddy complexion eyed Josh. Then she turned back to her machine and pressed another button.

A tall, slender man with narrow shoulders, his sports coat left unbuttoned, intercepted Josh. Josh flashed his ID, and they made their way across to the far end of the open area, past various gaming tables, then took a couple of steps down into a smaller room. The room contained five round felt covered poker tables. A silver-haired man sat at the middle table. He appeared to be in his sixties. His tailored suit and well-groomed appearance left no doubt who he was.

"This is Mr. Carlotti," the tall, thin man said, and walked around, positioning himself behind his boss.

"You play poker, Mr. Ingram?" Carlotti asked.

"Never was much good at it," Josh replied.

"A man of your talents? I think you would be a worthy opponent. Perhaps one day we could share a game."

"Perhaps," Josh said. "But if you don't mind, I'd like to get right down to business."

Carlotti's face soured.

Josh continued. "I'm investigating the murder of Arthur Romansky."

"Oh, I know why you have come, Mr. Ingram," Carlotti said, a crispness to his voice. "And I am most interested in how it comes to pass that a close friend of mine is found dead at this Arthur fellow's store. A bookstore owner if I'm not mistaken." He got the last word out, then with his meaty fingers reached down into his pants and shifted his balls around as if he was exploring uncharted territory. Finally satisfied, he grunted. "Fuckin' prostate. . . . A word of advice, Ingram. Don't ever get old."

"Not much chance of that happening," Josh said, and meant it.

Carlotti's gaze shifted. He lifted his shoe and crushed a cockroach with his heel. "Fuckin' parasites. The world's full of them . . ."

Josh raised both eyebrows, looking straight at Carlotti, letting him know he was looking at one.

Carlotti started to chuckle then raised his hand and wheezed. It was an old smoker's hiss, a long, dry, hacking rasp that seemed to come from deep within. "Bad habits from your youth haunt you later in life."

"That they do," Josh said, and thought, *you gotta be one haunted son-of-a-bitch.*

"You say you're investigating, so investigate," Carlotti said, an edge creeping back into his voice.

"Okay . . . what I can't figure out is how a retired

mechanic ends up in a death struggle with a mild mannered book dealer in New York City."

Carlotti shifted his weight and tilted his arse like he was about to relieve some gas, then settled back down. "A man makes many friends in his life, and unfortunately—some enemies. Who knows what connections the mechanic, as you call him, made in his lifetime? You are correct when you say he was retired. But as you know, early retirement can lead to cash flow issues. If he did take on a job, I suspect he may have needed some extra coin."

Enough of this bullshit, Josh thought, and said, "Since the mechanic *was* part of the inner circle of your organization, all arrows are pointing at you. The way I see it, you or someone high up in your organization had to give the go ahead. You're involved, I just don't know how deep."

The tall man shifted on his feet, moving as though he was thinking about pulling his piece.

"Be careful who you throw accusations at, Mr. Ingram. You could hurt an old man's feelings." The look on Carlotti's face changed, his eyes, cold and without remorse, glared at Josh. "Maybe we'll not have that game after all. . . . Now, I have other matters to attend to. Matters that concern me directly." He flicked his fingers at Josh as if he was shooing a fly. "Have a nice life, Mr. Ingram."

The tall man showed Josh to the door. The rain had started, a downpour, and Josh was soaked by the time he slipped back into the rental car. He called Rachael's cell, connecting with her on the second ring. "We need to go back and check if the Elhert family has a history with Carlotti."

"Why?" Rachael asked.

"Something Carlotti said, it's rolling around in my mind. I can't place it, but it's in there. Carlotti made a point about the friends one makes in life. It was as if his subconscious was trying to tell me something."

Rachael let out a breath and said, "Opening a file on Governor Elhert might be difficult. He is the governor. And Kingsley is gonna block it with everything he's got. His career and all. . . ." Josh could sense she was mulling it over, and then she said, "Leave it to me. I'll talk to Vivian, see if we can find a back door."

Josh smiled to himself; he was finding Rachael more attractive at every turn.

Chapter 39

October was the shoulder season in Miami, and the hotel business was as slow as any other sector in the hospitality industry.

The bartender called out last call; the bar was closing in twenty minutes. Josh sloshed some red wine around in his mouth and swallowed. He was on the short side of the bottle when he realized, he was not reaching his objective—to get drunk.

So, he poured himself another glass and gulped it down, then poured the remainder of the bottle into the glass and raised it to his lips. This time, he let the wine wash around in his mouth, chewing it, as an old friend had once told him. Tomorrow he would be in Guatemala, on the hunt, looking for Walter Hyter, but for tonight all he wanted, all he needed, was to get drunk.

It wasn't clear to him why, but suddenly he wanted to hear Rachael's voice. He fished his cell out of his pocket, and Anna's card fell out onto the table. *Oh yeah. . . .* He shoved the card back into his pants, then scrolled down to Rachael's number, pressed dial, and surveyed the room. In the corner, a young Latino was stroking his girlfriend's hair and staring into her eyes. In a booth across from him, two women in business suits were shaking hands and getting ready to leave. And behind the bar, the bartender was filling a large glass jug with tomato juice.

Rachael's phone connected and began to ring.

At the onset, the drug drew Josh into a fuller sense of well-being. It was not until he turned his head back toward the bar, and his gaze remained locked onto the checkered tablecloth, that the separation of time and space hit home.

Rachael's phone was on its fourth ring when it clicked over to her answering machine. Josh checked his phone. Had he gotten the wrong number? Her voice didn't sound right, it was as if she had stuffed her mouth full of cotton balls and someone had unplugged her.

He tried to stand and got halfway off his seat. The room seemed different, strange somehow, as if he was looking through a warped pane of glass. He craned his head ninety degrees and could see the bartender putting glasses into the dishwasher. Why was he making so much noise? And the two women were now, for some reason, speaking loud and slow.

It was then Josh knew he was screwed. He dug deep and fought for an edge his mind could hold onto. But his grasp on reality slipped and a sense of confusion took over. The room began to spin and the voices surrounding him turned bitter and garbled. Then a shot of fear pounced on his adrenal gland with such vigor his back stiffened, causing him to sit straight up. An intense belly rush shot up to his jaw, and he gasped. He swayed to the left, trying to focus on the bartender. He needed to anchor himself, he needed to bring himself back.

His lower lip went numb, and his head continued to spin. He wanted to speak, but could not find the words. He switched his gaze back to the checkered tablecloth, hoping somehow the brakes would come on. Focus, he knew he had to focus.

Two men arrived at his table. One had a tattoo of a spider's web running up the sides of his neck. The other had flames licking up from under the collar of his lumberjack shirt. Flames patted Josh on the shoulder and spoke to him as if he was a friend, and yet Josh could not understand a word of it. Then the men lifted Josh up by his armpits and walked him out through the back door. Once in the alley, Flames was left holding Josh up on his own. The other man stepped in front of Josh and grabbed his chin, tilting it up. "We have a message to deliver mate, and then you're going away for a while." The man's fist struck Josh in the ribcage. Air rushed out, and pain rushed in. Then a rapid succession of crushing blows followed until Josh's body went limp and he slumped over.

"Enough," Flames said. "We gotta deliver him alive. Don't fuck it up."

A scowl formed on the other man's face, and he kicked Josh's legs from under him. Josh hit the pavement, landing on his back, smacking his head. The jarring blow brought him out of his torpor for a few seconds. He gazed up at his attackers and squinted, trying to make out their faces.

Unsatisfied Josh had received the message, the man dealing out the punishment kicked Josh once in the guts, and Josh groaned. Flames shoved the man aside. "Settle the fuck down!"

The man just shrugged, looking more pissed than concerned. Then together they loaded Josh into a waiting cargo van.

Flames checked his watch, and gunned it. They had an hour, and not a minute more, to make the pickup site. Any allowance for error had expired. The chopper never stayed on the ground for more than a few seconds.

Chapter 40

Carlotti picked up his phone and punched in a number. "Got a visitor today . . . the writer, Ingram, dropped by. He was poking around, looking for a connection to Johnny."

"What did you tell him?" the man asked, his voice mellow.

"Wha'd'ya think I told him? Nothing, that's what I told him. But I know his type, they don't give up. Trouble gets started with guys like him, and I'd hate to see anything damage our *friendship*. But you know as well as me, once the Feds start snooping they will keep coming." Carlotti paused. "So I took care of it."

There was a long silence at the other end.

"Sounds as though you let your emotions get the better of you, Mr. Carlotti."

"Fuckin' eh I did, and it feels great."

Another pause. "The compound?" the man asked, sounding slightly annoyed.

"On his way now. Gotta say, it seemed the best place for him, and still does."

"This is rather unexpected," the man said. "I suppose . . . since you already have him, we should see what he knows. It may come in useful."

Carlotti thought about it, weighed his options and said, "This sort of thing, him being a Fed and all, is gonna carry a premium."

The man started to chuckle. "You are quite a businessman, Mr. Carlotti, I'll give you that." Then the man's voice strengthened. "Fine, suffice to say you'll be well compensated."

Carlotti sighed and leaned back in his chair. He'd heard what he needed to hear.

The man continued. "You are correct though, about him being a Fed. I'd like to know. No scratch that. I *must* know every detail he has on me. Which I suppose means a little extracurricular work for our friends. Suffice to say, there'll be an additional coupon you can all share when it's over."

"How much of a coupon?"

"Fifty points."

"Huh, yeah that's acceptable," Carlotti said. *More than fuckin' acceptable.* "I'll call the compound."

"Mr. Carlotti, I do have one condition to all this, and I want you to listen closely. Ingram is to be returned *alive* and functioning, to the exact spot where you abducted him. I still have need of him."

Carlotti mulled it over for a moment. "Yeah, yeah, okay, it'll be done. So tell me, what is it that Ingram might know about you?"

"Oh come now. I don't think you really want me to tell you . . ."

Carlotti could feel his skin crawl. Everybody has a line they won't cross. *Am I standing on it now,* he wondered, and said, "I'm thinking, this extra stuff . . . the deep extraction of information, it's gonna cost you double, a hundred points not fifty, him being high profile and all."

"Getting greedy I see . . . I guess I can live with that. Still, I must have a full report. I want all the details Mr. Carlotti. You will give me all the details, won't you?"

"It'll be handled," Carlotti said, and hung up.

Chapter 41

The cargo van rolled to a stop at the far end of RR27: a paved secondary road, orphaned when U.S. Route 1 punched through in the late twenties. The dead end was located on a flat stretch of land an hour out of Miami, near the tip of the Florida peninsula and mere seconds from the Atlantic.

Flames threw the van into reverse, cranking the wheel sharp, turning them around, then backed straight into the dead end. He killed the engine and left the lights running, illuminating about fifty yards of road ahead of them.

The first thing Josh noticed when he woke was the smell of rotten fruit. As he tried to lift his head, the muscles in his neck tensed up and a flurry of aches and pains rushed to his brain. Then he remembered—the fists and the feet. *Ahh, thank Christ the spinning has stopped,* he thought, now squinting, peering out through slit lids. *Where the hell am I?* It took a few seconds before it dawned on him that he'd been chained to a metal floor, a floor of a van, his nose pressed up against a shriveled banana peel. Then he heard a high-pitched, buzzing sound. *It's coming from outside. Insects . . . I'm in the country.*

He rolled his eyes upwards and saw two men sitting in the cab. They were jabbering away in Spanish, something about where they were going to spend the night. *Are they the ones who pounded on me?* He wasn't sure. He wasn't sure of anything. He shifted his weight to his elbow and managed to sit up, bringing on another flood of aches and pains. *C'mon, think, get control. If they wanted me dead, I'd be dead. Which means they have plans.* He tugged on the heavy cast-iron cuffs that bound his wrists. The cuffs were attached to a chain made of three-quarter inch links that ran through a heavy ring welded to the floor. He knew that other than chewing his hands off at the wrists, he wasn't going anywhere.

Not more than a minute passed before Josh heard the thump thump of chopper blades. The sound was growing louder. He managed to get to his knees, now looking straight ahead between the cab's bucket seats. The chopper's operating lights flashed on, and for a second it looked to him as though a Ferris wheel had been suspended in the air. As the chopper touched down it shifted, and the halogen headlights filled the van with a blinding, bright white light.

An adrenaline rush hit, clearing Josh's mind. *Shit. They're coming for me.* He did a quick check for broken bones, found bucket loads of pain but no permanent damage. He could move fast, if he got the chance.

The van's back cargo doors swung open and three Latinos in military garb jumped in. One slipped a black hood over Josh's head and cinched it tight. Another man attached police cuffs to Josh before removing the cast-iron cuffs and chains. Josh allowed himself to be slid across the floor to the open doors, where he knew he would have a better chance at freedom.

The second he reached the cargo doors, the leader, with his rifle ready, gave it a short, hard snap, cracking its butt on Josh's forehead. The three men scooped Josh out of the van, dragged him to the waiting chopper, where they secured him to a seat using heavy leather straps tied at his waist and neck.

The helicopter was fitted with two long, cylindrical gas tanks that would make it unnecessary to refuel. The flight to Guatemala would be at low altitude. They would travel unnoticed in the warm gulf air.

Chapter 42

Seconds after the chopper touched down on Guatemalan soil, the package was loaded onto a waiting one ton flatbed truck.

Guillermo dropped the truck into reverse, backing away from the helicopter.

It was eight a.m. and already hot under the Guatemalan sun. Sweat pooled in the crevices of Guillermo's belly fat, and his once starched T-shirt, now soaked, hung loose at its seams. A bottle of pop cooked between his thighs while a plastic Virgin Mary dangled from the rearview mirror. He glanced at his younger brother Felipe, who was riding shotgun; he seemed content, chewing away on his fingers; it helped him relax, or so he said.

Guillermo slammed the gas pedal to the floor. No one came here unless they had to. The area, once a sprawling, lawless ghetto had been cleared away last spring for a planned inner-city redevelopment project. While the project was set for completion by year-end, the first shovel had never hit the dirt. After the graft was spent, the project stalled and became yet another failed government initiative. Gangs now vied for control of the turf, and everyone knew the area was not safe.

Less than a minute passed before Guillermo took a left and exited the area. He let out a sigh and gulped down some of his warm pop. After snaking through Guatemala City, through air that smelled like burning tires and last week's garbage, through traffic lights that didn't work, through smoke that belched out of late-model cars and bright-red buses, the flatbed finally breached the outer limits of the city and picked up speed. With the air in the cab circulating better, Guillermo turned on the radio and cranked it up.

It was close to ten o'clock when the flatbed veered off the highway onto a paved secondary, then continued another two hundred yards before turning onto a dirt road that slipped into the jungle. Work crews had kept the rain forest cleared back just enough to allow one vehicle at a time to make passage. Who had the right of way was solely dependent on size.

Steam hissed from the radiator as the flatbed rattled and bounced on the dried and rutted mud. Its cargo consisted of two boxes tied down tight to the flatbed. And while the boxes didn't budge, the contents did.

Josh awoke in a fetal position, his right shoulder and hip rattling hard against the bottom of a pine box. He wasn't sure what kind of box it was, not a coffin though, he was pretty sure of that, the dimension were wrong, or at least he hoped they were wrong. He turned his head as best he could and looked up, and saw holes the size of quarters in the top of the box. Suddenly, he felt like a pet frog in the hands of a very hyperactive and black-hearted kid.

It was Africa-hot inside the box and his skin was starting to bake. Bound, gagged and cramped, he desperately wanted to scream. His shoulder ached, his ribs and hip ached, and his head smacked the side of the box as the truck claimed each new pothole. He was thinking of how much he needed to stretch his legs out when the music stopped and the military address started up again.

Every ten minutes, a scheduled address crackled from a bullhorn bolted to the roof of the truck. Ten minutes of military propaganda, followed by ten minutes of Latino music, and then the process repeated.

Josh understood every word and wished he couldn't; it made the rant that much more intolerable. The voice coming over the horn was calloused and weighted on all first syllables. The man barely stopped to catch his breath, repeating his well-worn rhetoric over and over. Josh would have found it almost humorous in another set of circumstances, *but not here, not today, not in this fucking box.*

Less than five minutes into the jungle and nearing the end of the trip, the front gate of the compound came into sight. Razor wire, wrapped in spirals and strung out along the top of a nine-foot-high chain-link fence, sparkled in the late morning sun. Sentry posts set up every hundred yards encircled the three-acre compound, as did a high-voltage wire upon which lay the remains of rats, once colorful birds, and a variety of snakes that had all taken their final breath on its electrified surface.

The main gate sentry checked Guillermo's credentials, then hit a black button the size of a fifty-cent-piece and the gates swung open. The flatbed passed through the gate, and headed for one of three buildings in the center of the compound. It was a long, metal Quonset hut with few markings or features other than fans placed near the roof at both ends of the building. A short set of wooden stairs on the north side of the hut painted army green was the only way in or out.

The truck came to a halt and the second it did the cab turned into an oven. Sweat trickled down the sides of Guillermo's face as he backed up to the east side of the hut and parked. The air outside was dead calm. "Let's move it little brother," Guillermo said.

The brothers walked around to the back of the flatbed where two guards were waiting, standing in a small patch of shade next to the hut.

With zero airflow, the temperature inside the box spiked, and Josh could feel himself beginning to dry boil. His head ached, nausea circulated in his stomach, and worst of all he'd stopped sweating. With his hands tied behind his back, he knew he would have to wait it out. Seconds later, his vision faded to black.

Guillermo unspooled the winch cable from the rear of the truck and attached it to the crate containing Josh. He pushed down on the middle of three levers and the winch's electric motor kicked in, letting off a high-pitched whining sound as it pulled the weight across the deck surface. The crate scraped and squeaked, wood on wood, until it reached the end of the flatbed. As Guillermo and his brother lifted Josh off the back of the truck, gravity took hold, and Felipe's grip slipped. He swore under his breath as his pink, gnarled fingernails started to bleed.

"I think the Gringo has gained some weight, hey little brother." Guillermo laughed.

"Not so funny, Guillermo. Let's do what we are getting paid for and go."

They placed the crate on the ground, leaving it to bake in the bright sunlight.

The second crate on the flatbed measured about half the size of Josh's crate. It had long, narrow slits carved in its top to allow air to penetrate, and was surrounded by a half-dozen bags of ice. At one end of the crate was a small door, one foot high by two feet wide, held in place by three six-inch steel pins.

The brothers carried the smaller crate over to the side of the hut, placing it on the dirt next to a boarded-up basement window. The window frame had been altered with mounting brackets screwed into place on either side. Guillermo ran his hand along the top of the crate and felt a slight vibration. He peered into one of the slits and could feel their eyes upon him, then turned to his brother and said, "I think the little angels are waking up . . ."

The sharp, pungent vapor of smelling salts snapped Josh back to the present. He was inside the building, seated in a metal chair, his wrists and ankles cuffed, his head held rigid by a thick leather harness, his field of vision locked forward. The porthole he faced peered down into another room, a floor below him. The sole occupant of the room was a man, sitting on a bench with his hands tied behind his back, a black hood over his head, held in place by a red wire wrapped around his neck.

All of a sudden, Josh sensed someone behind him. A guard leaned forward and whispered into Josh's ear. "The commander wants you to see . . ."

Startled, Josh blurted, "Fuck off!"

The guard stood there for a moment with an amused look on his face, then turned and left the room.

A half hour later the sound of footsteps from outside the hut woke the guard. He raised his head from his desk, rubbed his cheeks with the palms of his hands, and tried to look alert.

The door opened and two men in military uniforms walked in, accompanied by the commander. The commander, a heavyset woman, was wearing khaki trousers and a sweat-stained green cotton shirt. Her stringy black hair and meaty nose was flanked on either side by deep-set, dark eyes. It was clear she controlled the situation as she gestured to the two soldiers that they follow her.

They proceeded through a narrow corridor, down a flight of stairs, turned right and came to a cell where a guard was standing at attention. The guard opened the cell and stepped back to let the commander and the two soldiers enter, then he followed them in.

The three spread out, forming a half-circle around the man seated on the wooden bench. Then the guard stepped forward and removed the black hood, untying one of the prisoner's hands, leaving the other hand still attached to the bench. The man did not look up. He kept his gaze on the floor, rubbing his stomach with his free hand.

At first glance, the prisoner could've been taken for a punch drunk vagrant, Josh thought. Dark sweat lines ran across his forehead where a hat had been. His khaki trousers were ragged, his lip swollen, and a raspberry of crusted blood had formed below one nostril.

The bench he sat on was worn, and residue of dried fluids sprayed out from it in all directions, as if a wet and dirty dog had shook himself off. Flies danced and hovered over the man's knees, taking turns to feed on his drying blood.

"Major, are you with us?" The commander asked, her

tone calm and soothing. "I've brought some friends of yours, they want to hear what you have to say."

"What?" the major looked up. Josh could see he recognized the other two; one a lieutenant colonel, the other a full colonel. The major grabbed the bench seat with his free hand, squeezing it until his knuckles blanched.

"Major, it's very simple," the commander said. "We need to know a few names, that's all. We need to know who else was involved."

"I . . . I have nothing to say to you."

"Major, please. Take your time to answer. We are your friends. We are here to help you. We know you have something to share . . ."

Looking up at the commander, he pleaded, "How can you make sense of this? I will not betray my friends. These are my people."

"Major, please . . . when the most basic of instincts are on stage, I think you will find it quite easy to betray your friends." The commander removed a handkerchief from her back pocket and dabbed her brow. "In any event, enough of the drama. You will come to appreciate my words." Then she reached out and pointed to the lieutenant colonel's belt. "May I see your knife?" The lieutenant unsheathed a standard-issue combat model with a four-inch blade, razor-sharp.

With the knife in hand the commander nodded to the two officers. Then she turned and knelt by the major. She stuck the knife blade into the cloth of his pant leg, cutting upwards from his ankle to his knee. She repeated the process with the other leg, then moved around behind the major and made a long slice up the back of his shirt, peeling it wide open. With the tip of the knife she made three small punctures in the major's back, one on each shoulder blade and one at the base of his spine, forming a large triangle. With each puncture the major flinched, his free hand clenched into a fist. She followed up with a number of punctures on his legs, then wiped the blade on the major's shoulder. As blood leaked from his wounds and trickled down his skin, he began to shiver.

"That should do it," the commander said. Then she glanced up at Josh as she followed the others out of the cell, and flicked off the light.

The room was dark except for light coming in from the porthole where Josh sat and from a six-inch square peephole on the prisoner's cell door. Josh watched and waited, trying not to think of what might be coming next.

The guard, standing outside of the prisoner's cell peered in through the peephole. Striking a match against the door's hinge he lit his cigar. He sucked on the cigar a few times in rapid succession and then blew a dense puff of smoke through the peephole. Then he sat down and leaned back against the door. The bluish smoke rolled into the room and hung near the ceiling like a fishing net. "Hey, mister," the guard called out to Josh. "You mind if I smoke? I think you'll come to appreciate it. The smell that is." He chuckled.

With one hand still tied to the wooden bench, the major started to swing his head back and forth, as if to convince himself this could not be happening.

Minutes passed. The room was dead quiet except for the major's labored breathing.

A sliver of light coming from the prisoner's cell caught Josh's eye. Near the ceiling of the room he saw a boarded-up basement window. He guessed its measurements at two feet wide by one foot high. And while boards covered the opening, pinpricks of light pierced around the edges, forming tiny shafts that mingled with the cigar smoke.

The sound of another match being struck broke the silence, and again a puff of smoke entered the room from the peephole. The smoke smelled pungent, sweet, more like a pipe than a cigar, Josh thought.

A metallic, clanking sound came from outside the boarded-up window. Josh heard two men talking outside, their voices muffled. Then came the sound of metal sliding on wood, followed by a bright light that instantly broke into the room, like that of a welder's flash. Its brilliance flooded the entire room. Then, as quickly as it had come, the light disappeared. A new object had slid over the window opening. Its fit, not as tight as the previous covering, gave the window's perimeter the appearance of a rectangular lunar eclipse.

A few seconds later came squeals and high pitched screeches . . . followed by a flat, thumping sound, as though a pile of wet meat had been dumped onto the cell's dirt floor. The squealing escalated and then it was gone, dissolving into silence—only to be replaced by a musty, haystack smell that filled the room.

Josh could see the major's head shifting around, trying to see in the near dark. Within seconds the outline of a large mound appeared on the floor below the covered window. There were muted red lights, the size of peas, flashing on and off all over the pile.

"Oh Lord," the major cried. "It has eyes."

As the blood of the rats warmed on the cell floor, their squealing returned for a short spell before the room returned to silence. It started with one rat venturing out from the mound. It waddled across the room until it was within inches of the major's foot. The rat lifted its pointy head and sniffed the air, its whiskers twitching, then it squealed once and ran straight for the major's leg. Its sharp little claws dug in as it ran up the major's shin to his knee. The major swung with his free hand but missed, and the rat slipped under his pant leg and crawled up his thigh. The major thrashed about, hitting his thigh with his fist. He screamed and reached into his pant leg, screaming again as the rat's teeth sunk in to his hand. He whipped his arm sideways, chucking the rat across the room where it hit the wall with a thud and a squeal.

All at once, the mound spread across the floor. The major was now surrounded by a sea of red eyes, and they were closing in.

Chapter 43

Anton stepped into the library to see his brother looking out over the ocean. Governor Elhert turned and nodded.

"Anton, thanks for coming," Governor Elhert said, his voice drawn and weak.

You look haggard dear brother, Anton thought. Gone was his brother's posturing, his swaggered look, his arrogance, they were all parked at the curb. "William, you look exhausted. Is there something troubling you?"

"We have a problem that has been festering, something that I think you should be made aware of. You remember *Uncle* Walter?"

"Why? Has he died? I would've thought he'd fertilized a flower bed long ago."

"Unfortunately . . . we are not that lucky."

"We?" Anton whispered with a hint of surprise. *That's twice he has used 'we'.*

"Walter's been kidnapped."

"I'm not so sure I follow," Anton said, a smirk crinkling around his tiny lips. *So tell me dearest brother, how does it feel to have no control over a situation? Must be rather unsettling I would think.*

"His captors are holding him for ransom. They are threatening to have Walter share our secrets with the rest of the world." He shook his head. "Jesus, I'm heading into an election—the timing just couldn't be worse."

"Ransom . . . ? How much are they asking for?"

"Five million in uncut diamonds."

"Oh, I see. That is troubling. Are you going to pay it?"

"Yes. But that's not the end of it."

Anton raised an eyebrow, an unexpected choice of words had come from his brother. "What exactly do you mean?"

Governor Elhert walked over and closed the door, dimmed the lights and pressed play on a video recorder. "I think it's best if you see for yourself."

The player came on and the ransom demand started.

Anton watched with feigned concern, enjoying every word; after all, he *had* written the script. His gaze shifted to the governor. *How unfortunate for you dear brother, this will not end well.*

It was nearing the end of the message when Walter came back into the frame. "They know nothing," Walter blurted. "The only thing these punks will get out of me is snot on their faces." Walter leaned in to the camera. "Governor, rest assured, as long as the moon shines down upon the sea, they won't hear a peep out of me. Hell's bells, I'm so old, in a *flash* I could be gone, off the *hook* so to speak."

Governor Elhert looked to Anton, who now had a shocked look on his face.

"I know, I had the same reaction. I always wondered what had become of that camera. I consoled myself that it was lost in the weeds, ruined by rain over the years. But that little fucker had it all along." He turned to Anton. "It was such a stupid thing to do in the first place. You taking that *goddamn* picture!"

Anton's mind was racing. Walter's rant had never been mentioned. *Why was I not told? This is unacceptable! It was Ingram's job to uncover the missing half of the photo and complete the picture—that was the plan. This changes everything . . . Walter, you annoying little man, you've held the key all along.* Anton paused a moment, and then a faint smile crossed his face and he started to relax. *At least now there is certainty that I will have the completed picture . . . and yes, the diamonds too. . . .* Then he stared at the governor. *Sometimes life can be so unkind, can it not, dear brother?* Then it dawned on him. *Oh my . . . poor Mr. Ingram, with all your brilliance—you've just become redundant.*

"So, what do you intend on doing?" Anton asked his brother matter-of-factly.

"Already in progress. I've sent a mercenary to locate Walter, and when he does, the old fool will be dealt with and the past buried with him."

Anton smiled. *Not if I can help it.*

Chapter 44

Cocking his head from shoulder to shoulder, the mirror caught Walter Hyter's attention, which was a plus; sometimes Walter's vision doubled and he couldn't see a damn thing. At eighty-nine, gout and heartburn were his only constant companions. Save, of course, his fearless guard Pedro, or whatever the hell his name was, waiting on the other side of the cell door.

A shallow grin curled at the corners of Walter's mouth then gave way to a puzzled look. Pulling at the flesh that hung from his jaw, he raised an eyebrow. "Oh, you're a handsome catch, aren't you?"

He raised one arm, then the other. A thin veil of skin draped down from each. Tilting his head, he looked with interest at the spectacle. He jiggled his left arm, then his right, then both. At first the loose skin flopped gently back and forth. Picking up the pace he pumped his arms up and down. Short strokes at first, then he broke into all out flapping. "Oh, this is a pretty sight," he snorted. "A white-headed praying mantis, trying to take flight. National Geographic would love this!" Walter's grin returned for a moment and then turned sour.

"God must have some kind of sick sense of humor keeping an old goat like me going." He looked to the ceiling. "Are you laughing at me . . . ? I bet you are . . .

aren't you? You sick bastard." He lowered his gaze, and his face went blank as if he had forgotten something. He peered around the room, back up at the ceiling, then down. "Ahh . . . yes," he said, and proceeded to pick a few breadcrumbs off of his shirt.

Again, his face went blank, his gaze darting left and right. "Ah, damn!" he said, and grabbed the counter. He leaned in close to the mirror, his swollen, gnarled hands keeping him steady. Rimmed in cherry-red, his rheumy eyes stared back at him—the last remnants linking him to his past.

He sneered, pulling his upper lip to one side, revealing a bony set of stained choppers. "Should've gassed them all!" he shouted with rage, the veins on his neck inflating and pressing out against his thin, milky-blue skin. Adrenaline rushed in and out of his decaying pipes, and at that moment, he felt alive—thankful for this brief respite from the dread and tedium of advancing age, and the finality of it all.

No stranger to his outbursts, the guard shifted in his chair before settling back to his magazine.

"Leave a few of them alive, and they propagate like goddamn rabbits! Hell's bells, hard to kill out those bloody dandelions. We'd had the H-bomb, we could've fixed em good! Right, Pedro!" Walter waited for a reply and smirked, his eyes now shifting beneath his thick glasses. "Are you there, Pedro? Don't make me come out and get you, you little snot."

The guard lifted his head, said something in Spanish in a casual, uninterested manner, and went back to reading.

"Could've, would've. . . ." Walter gagged and spit in

the sink. "Fuck it . . . should've snuffed them out." His voice trailed off as he wheezed and gagged some more. Then he lowered his head down into the sink until his shoulder blades touched. Thin wisps of white hair dangled over his face and tickled his lashes as he contemplated his predicament.

It wasn't long before the stink of rotten hair and spent toothpaste reached his nose. But it was not the foul air, rather the lack of it that throttled his heart and reminded Walter of his wretched condition.

He knew what came next, and forced air deep into his lungs. He exhaled, then sucked in again. Over and over, repeating the process, trying to accelerate his oxygen uptake. *It's not helping.* All at once, a round of horrific fear pumped through his body. *Ah Christ, I'm gonna suffocate.* With his hands set wide apart on the sink counter, and his elbows locked, he dropped his voice down low. "Where's my *goddamn* oxygen!"

Chair legs scraped on the floor outside the cell, and after a moment of clanging keys the door opened. The guard held a small oxygen tank and a translucent mask in one hand. He slipped the mask over Walter's head, who was now in full panic mode, his face grayish-blue. The guard checked the fit over Walter's nose and mouth and then flipped the oxygen switch on. Grabbing both of Walter's hands he backed him away from the sink and plopped him into his wheelchair.

Secure in his chair, Walter sucked on the mask like a starving infant, his eyes wild with greed. He sucked again and again, gulping in the air. Sucking and gulping, until at last, blood packed with oxygen rushed to his head, surfacing in random pink patches on his ashen face.

Walter let his head fall back, cradled into the chair's stainless steel harness. He turned his head and his cheek touched the cool steel. His eyes, now filled with despair, grew dim and glazed over. And as he drifted off, he noticed a new occupant lying on the bunk across from him.

It was a man, his back turned to him. The man was in a restless sleep. The man had been beaten.

Then, he smelled it . . .

Chapter 45

All nine of the chicken-wire enclosures were the same size. Two-foot by two-foot cubes. Each was home to a single rooster, and each had an eight-inch, spring-loaded wire door that kept the bird locked inside. The cages were laid out in a semicircle under a large chestnut tree that protected them from the blistering Guatemalan sun.

Edwardo stuck the end of a green garden hose through the wire mesh, to the center of the cage, and let the water dribble into a red clay bowl not much bigger than an ashtray. There was one bowl per enclosure, filled twice a day, sunrise and sunset. Each rooster had its own space, which was necessary to keep the little darlings from tearing each other apart. Even though he took great pride in his 'soldiers', as he preferred to call them, Edwardo knew they would just as soon peck his eyes out if they were given the chance.

And yet, all things considered it was a good day, he decided. He enjoyed the quiet. For him it was a time to contemplate the world around him. Today, he found himself in a particularly good mood. The plan was proceeding as it should, and by week's end they would have sufficient funds to last them for the coming year. As he bent down to open a fresh bag of feed, his satellite phone rang. He answered on the second ring. "Speak to me," he said, a trace of Spanish in his voice.

"Regarding the new package," Carlotti said, his voice calm and detached. "There's been a change of plan. We want you to bury it."

Edwardo thought of asking why, then decided to let it pass. "And, the old package?"

"When the transaction is complete you are to hand him over to my men; they'll be at your doorstep, as soon as the drop has been completed. And, he is to be handed over alive . . . you got that?" Before Edwardo could protest, Carlotti had hung up.

Edwardo retrieved a pack of cigarettes from under his rolled-up shirtsleeve, lit one and took a drag. Then he placed the call.

"Status?" Edwardo asked.

"We've scheduled him for questioning this evening," the commander said.

"There's been a change of heart. We cannot keep it. I want you to dispose of it, understood? And we will need the usual proof: video, the whole works. And keep the face in focus, we want to get paid."

"It'll be done," the commander said.

Edwardo held the phone to his chest and thought for a moment before asking, "The exchange, is everything in order?"

"All the details have been taken care of. The team is ready for the drop," the commander said, sounding confident.

"Good. And one more thing . . . regarding the old package, it stays put."

The commander hesitated for a moment before answering. "You think that's wise? It is a simple exchange. We have no need of him after—"

"Correct, but our partners do. One more thing, keep it healthy and have it ready to travel."

Chapter 46

Josh woke with a jolt. A shot of pain had pierced what he had hoped was a bad dream. He rolled over and sat up, and all the events of the last twenty-four hours came back to him in a rush. Then he raised his head to see a man in a wheelchair staring back at him.

The man was no more than ten feet away. He was old and thin, not much more than a collection of bones draped in cloth, Josh thought. An oxygen mask was strapped over his nose and mouth, and a good inch of pale skin hung from his angular jaw. The old man tilted his head to one side, his gaze locked on Josh.

"What *is* that smell?" Josh asked, and then spotted two metal plates and a couple of tin cups set just inside the cell. Each plate had a small pile of rice, covered in steaming grayish-brown goop.

"Smells like crap, don't it?" the old man said as he removed his mask, his voice crackling as an old man's does. "Don't taste as bad as it looks . . . tastes worse." Then the old man slapped his knee a number of times, craning his neck forward and howling with laughter, his lower jaw wobbling in its hinge.

What the fuck . . . ? Josh watched the old man for a few seconds before it struck him. "You're Walter Hyter?"

The old man's laughter and merriment came to a

halt. He squinted. "That'd be my name. Who the hell are you?"

"Name's Josh Ingram. I've been looking for you."

"Well, congratulations sonny . . . you found me," Walter said, his voice thin, croaking in his throat and dripping with sarcasm. Walter paused, and a tormented look overtook his face. He reached down and grabbed hold of the sock on his right foot. The sock was already half off and loose fitting, and yet Walter peeled it off slow and careful, as if he was disarming a bomb.

Josh did a double take: the joint of Walter's big toe was swollen to twice its normal size, candy-apple red, the skin stretched tight and shiny.

"You ever have the gout?" Walter asked, his face scrunched up like he had bitten into a rotten pear.

"Can't say that I have."

"Lucky you . . . been with me half my life. Say it's because of a gluttonous, sinner's life. Some say so anyway. *Hell,* they're probably right." He started to grin, the tips of his decaying teeth poking out from under his lip, then he stopped. "Last night . . . you got to see the show didn't you? You know—the nibble nibble brigade . . . the little fellows with the bad table manners. Not a nice a way to go . . . . Our hosts had me watch too, when I first arrived. Supposed to impress, I guess."

Walter stood up and tried to straighten his back, but failed to get his spinal cord fully erect. He padded over to the cell door, his weight centered on his heel, his red big toe pointed at the ceiling. He reached down, picked up a tin cup and one of the metal plates, and sniffed at the food. "I've seen worse ways to kill a man. *Hell's bells* . . . wetbacks. What do they know?" He returned to his chair and plopped down. Looking at Josh he scooped up a handful of rice and gruel, and stuffed it into his mouth.

Walter munched away for a minute, still staring, then gulped down some water from his tin cup. As he lowered the cup, Josh noticed a lump of gruel had stuck to the old man's cheek.

Josh felt his gut turn, and he pointed to the watery goo.

Walter stopped chomping. "What?" he asked, then frowned, and with the cuff of his shirt brushed off the goo. "Heard them talking about you, you know," Walter said, his voice taking on a whining tone. "Been a change of plan. They've scheduled you for this evening. You've been fast-tracked. Yessiree, gonna be some harvesting tonight. You're not gonna be alone though. Gonna be you and that nigger. . . . But not me. I have myself a deal."

"Harvesting?" Josh asked.

"Pop, pop. You know," Walter said, and pointed his index finger at Josh. "Harvesting. They do it in the yard. I've seen it done." Walter tilted his head in the direction of the yard. "They got cameras and all. Not that difficult to figure out, sonny—this here is a business, and you're their cash crop. Not sanctioned by the state *I'm sure*, but you can bet your little noggin they know all about it." He pointed to the barred window. "Go ahead, have yourself a look."

Josh stepped up to the window. The yard was rectangular; the size of two tennis courts. Quonset huts covered three of the sides, and a dirt road ran along the open end. The surface of the yard was flat, hard-packed dirt. In the center of the yard sat a stage about the size of a boxing ring. Two young men in military garb were busy at one end of the stage setting up a video camera on a tripod while a third tested the microphone. A thick pole stood in the center of the stage, a foot in diameter and at least seven feet high. Sandbags had been piled up behind it, formed into a half-circle.

"The black man, who is he?" Josh asked, still looking out into the yard.

"Black man? I don't know who the *black man* is. Black man. Where did you say you came from?"

Josh looked back at Walter. "What did you say?"

"Why are you worrying about the black man anyway, when you best be worrying about you own neck?"

"Tell me about him, the black man."

Walter stuck another handful of gruel in his mouth and sneered. "Not much to tell. He came just before you. They worked him over good, went on for a long time. Thought he'd be dead, but they talked about the two of you for tonight, so I'm thinking he's still alive."

Josh could feel time was running out—he needed answers. "What do you know of a book written by Salvador Espada?"

Walter stopped his chewing. "What of it?"

"My friend, a book dealer, came across it and discovered an old contract embedded in its cover."

Walter's face went blank, then turned red. "You're a goddamn plant, aren't ya boy! Just what kind of game are you playing?"

The guard outside the cell broke free of his magazine but remained seated in his chair, and told them to keep it down. Then he got up and made his way down the hall and stepped into the washroom.

"I'm no plant, you crazy old fool. And yet, I'm your

worst goddamn nightmare if you don't start talking."

Walter clenched his jaw tight and stared at Josh, daring him.

Under other circumstances, Josh could have found the situation amusing, but not today. He looked at Walter's swollen toe, and then he looked at Walter, and the old man started to squirm. Josh removed one of his leather shoes and slowly raised it over his head—and held it there for a moment. Then he whipped it down hard, striking the side of the wheelchair, causing it to shake. Walter didn't flinch. Josh then reached down and grabbed Walter by his ankle, raising his big, red toe high into the air, forcing the old man to slide down into his chair; the back of his head now pressed against the seat. *Ah for Christ's sake, you're so damn fragile,* Josh thought. Again he raised his leather shoe high above his head and got set to strike it against Walter's gout-ridden toe. Walter's eyes bulged. Then Josh whipped his shoe down to within an inch of the swollen toe, stopped, and gave it a light tap. Walter shrieked and screamed, his face was now as red as his toe.

"You're a mean bastard, you know that? Hurting an old man."

"You don't know the half of it. Now spill your guts." Josh raised his shoe high into the air, wondering if he would follow through. But it was no contest. Tears were running down Walter's face, he'd caved. "Stop! Fine, I'll talk. Only put down your goddamn clodhopper and let an old man be."

Josh lowered Walter's foot to the floor and helped him push himself back up into his chair.

Walter took a moment before he spoke, and kept glancing at his toe. Then he looked up at Josh and smirked. "What do I care? I'm talking to a dead man."

Josh went to grab Walter's ankle.

"Okay, okay, settle down," Walter cried.

Josh waited a second before saying, "Inside the book there was a contract. What I want to know is, why would this contract be so important to the Elhert family? I know it covers a transfer of shares to George Elhert for helping a Nazi escape after the war. But that would be tough, very tough to prove."

Walter shook his head. "You don't see much, do you sonny? It isn't the contract that's got the Elherts all flustered. It's the photo."

"The half picture of the boys?"

"Is that all it is?"

"If it's not, then what of it?" Josh asked, losing his patience.

"To answer that question, you're gonna first have to find the other half."

Josh heard the clank of iron doors opening down the hall. Footsteps were coming, getting louder. "We're out of time. I need to know, the other half of the photo—where is it?"

"Well, it ain't in Guatemala, that's for sure," Walter said, still focusing his attention on his toe.

The cell door opened suddenly and three guards entered. One guard shoved an AK47 in Josh's chest while another stepped forward and pressed a 9mm handgun to his temple, while the third walked around behind him and grabbed his wrists. The guard went to slap on the cuffs when his leg brushed up against Walter's toe. Walter screamed, and the guards all turned their heads.

Josh knew this was his chance. He quickly deflected

the handgun with his forearm, then planted a head-butt to the guard's nose, crushing cartilage and dropping him to the floor. Then he swung around in a sweeping motion and round-housed the guard with the AK47 in the side of the head; the guard staggered sideways and let go of the rifle. The third guard lunged forward and wrapped his arm around Josh's neck securing him in a headlock. Josh stomped down on the guard's foot, bones crackled and the headlock loosened. Driving his elbow straight back, Josh nailed the guard in his solar plexus. Stunned and unable to breath the guard dropped to one knee, gasping, then fell to the floor. The guard who had dropped the AK47 pulled a knife and swung it at Josh, cutting a shallow line across his shirt. Josh countered with a straight right to the guard's larynx, collapsing his windpipe. Then he caught the underside of the guard's chin with an uppercut, pulverizing his teeth, and the guard went down.

Josh turned to Walter. "*Where* is the goddamn picture? And don't screw with me."

Walter shrank back in his chair. "I'll tell you, but you have to take me with you," he said, now pleading. "I'm dead here. What're you going to do, kill me? Go ahead . . . do it."

Josh looked down at Walter, and sighed. "Ahh man . . . just stay put."

Using the guards' cuffs, Josh secured the two unconscious guards to the sink, then tore strips from a bed sheet and gagged them. The guard with the crushed larynx lay dead on the floor.

Josh picked up the handgun and stuck it into his waistband, then grabbed hold of Walter's wheelchair and pushed him down the hall. Near the block's outer door, they came to a halt. A large, black man was slouched over on a wooden chair next to his cell door. It took a second for Josh to recognize the man. "Demetrius?"

Demetrius looked up. One eye had swollen shut, and a cut running from his hairline to his eyebrow oozed blood.

"Can you walk?" Josh asked.

"I can make it." Demetrius got to his feet, putting most of his weight on one foot. Josh fumbled with the guard's keys and opened the cell.

They left the cell block, carrying Walter and the wheelchair up a short flight of stairs, then proceeded down a hall, passing by a front desk that was vacant. Demetrius held open the outside door, and Josh pushed Walter out into the hot, muggy, evening air. The sun had set; it was twilight and the forest was steaming.

A late-model pickup had been left parked next to the hut, its tires were threadbare, its tailgate missing. The cab of the pickup was small, just enough room for two bucket seats and a stick shift. Josh and Demetrius lifted Walter into the back of the truck and threw his wheelchair onto the deck floor.

"I'll ride in the back with the old man," Demetrius said.

"Yeah okay," Josh said, and climbed into the cab, taking notice of a key in the ignition. He took in a quick breath and slowly let it out as he scanned the area. He could hear muted voices coming from the yard that seemed to be growing louder. The main gate was straight ahead, though to get to it, they would have to pass by the open yard. In their favor was the near darkness; he hoped it was enough. He started the pickup and checked the gauges. The gas gauge needle rested on empty. *Ah shit,* he thought, and prayed it was broken.

Josh backed the truck up, slid the transmission into first gear, and rolled to the edge of the open yard. There was a collective hum of Latino voices chattering away, and yet what stood out in his mind was the sound of the pickup's tires crumbling the brittle dirt, and the light putt-putt of the engine. As they reached the halfway-mark to the gate, Josh could see a group gathered around the stage. The commander had her hands planted on her hips and was barking out orders. Then for some reason she stopped and turned toward the pickup.

At that moment, sirens blared. Searchlights flipped on, one after another, each making a loud *pop* as electricity surged and converted to light. Guards streamed out of their huts, and a second later the pickup was awash in bright light. Josh punched the gas and the rear wheels spun on the dirt, throwing dust high into the air. The truck accelerated and fishtailed, forcing Walter and Demetrius to slide a few feet down the box toward the missing tailgate.

The pickup clocked in at 79 kilometers per hour as it crashed through the metal gates, bending and throwing twisted sheets of aluminum clear. The steering wheel suddenly felt loose in Josh's hands, the linkage had been damaged, forcing him to whip the wheel one way and then the other, a full quarter turn, back and forth, just to keep them on the road.

They hadn't gone a full kilometer when he checked the rearview mirror and saw two sets of headlights appear.

Chapter 47

The headlights were attached to army trucks. Both trucks were big, their camouflage canvas stripped off revealing an exoskeleton of metal hoops. The headlights were illuminating the treetops, making Josh think the trucks were loaded to the hilt with troops. And loaded or not, they were gaining.

Josh glanced at the gas gauge and his gut tied into a knot. "Ahh, man . . ." He turned to look out the back window. Demetrius had one arm around Walter and a hand on the wheelchair. The old man didn't look good, his bony chin tight to his chest, his lips pursed.

Josh checked the mirror, the gap was narrowing. He glanced down at the gas gauge again. The needle was still tapping on empty. Balling up his hand, he gave the gauge a few whacks. Nothing, not a goddamn thing.

Moments later, the pickup shot out of the rainforest onto a paved secondary road. Josh hit the brakes, they squealed, then locked, sending the pickup skidding sideways across the road until finally coming to a halt with its front wheels resting in some weeds. Josh turned in his seat to see Demetrius sprawled out on the deck with one arm around Walter.

The secondary road led them to the main highway where they stopped at a T-intersection. The pickup's hot engine rumbled. *Which way? Left or right?* It was the tail end of twilight, and the faint glow to the West was all but snuffed out. The West led to the Pacific Ocean. Josh cranked the steering wheel to the right and headed east for Guatemala City and the airport.

The pickup crested the first hill and was dropping out of sight when the two army trucks burst out of the jungle onto the secondary.

"Damn it!" Josh yelled, and stomped down on the gas pedal. The hill was a long, straight downward slope and the pickup quickly gained speed, the front end shaking and rattling, the tires thrashing about in the wheel wells. Josh knew he had to push it, there were no options.

He caught sight of a service road at the base of the hill that cut in on the left thirty yards before a double-arched stone bridge. Josh hit the brakes, but heard only the sound of squealing metal on metal—they were not slowing down. His heart pounded in his chest as he pulled up on the emergency brake. Nothing. Then he stomped on the brakes with both feet, raising his ass clear off the bucket seat. The brakes caught and the tires locked. In the back, the wheelchair, lying on its side, slid across the deck and smacked up against the cab. Demetrius was pounding on the back wall of the cab and shouting.

A moment later they reached the turnoff. Josh pumped the brakes and cranked the wheel. *Oh shit we're dead.* The pickup tilted to the side and spun off the highway, sliding into the mouth of the service road. He whipped the wheel in the opposite direction, and the truck straightened out just as it hit a gravel patch, spraying rocks until it slowed. He limped the pickup another hundred feet or so to a small thicket of river trees, slipped in amongst them, and killed the engine.

It was quiet now, other than the pinging of the hot engine. Josh turned and saw Demetrius tending to Walter. He could see compassion in the way Demetrius was taking care of the old man, which struck Josh as odd. He was about to get out and lend a hand when the sound of the troop trucks broke the silence. They were crossing the bridge, their undercarriages clacking as the heavy wheels bounced over the stone surface. Troops packed the back of each truck, their heads bowed into the wind, rifles slung over their shoulders.

Bought us a little time, that's all, Josh thought. He opened the glove box and rummaged around, hoping to find a flashlight or a map. He found neither, only a pair of sunglasses, some loose papers and a cell phone, an old flip model. He opened the cell. At first there was only a faint green glow coming from within, then a weak signal came up.

He fished Anna's card from his pocket and punched in her number, and breathed a sigh of relief when she picked up. She had just finished dinner with her family and was on her way out for the evening, but he could tell from her voice that she was glad he had called. He told her he was lost, running low on gas, and needed her help. He then told her something he regretted the moment it left his lips; he said he knew where the third book was. Anna hesitated for a moment and then asked for his location. She knew the bridge and told him to continue east another fifty kilometers. She'd leave the ranch immediately and meet him on the highway. When he got within five kilometers of the rendezvous point, he was to call her cell and bring her in.

Josh stepped down from the cab and saw Demetrius standing by the back of the truck, brushing himself off. Walter was out cold, lying in the middle of the box, his head resting on a sandbag.

"Nice driving," Demetrius said, his tone dry. "The old man . . . I don't think he'll make it."

Josh climbed into the truck box and checked Walter's pulse. It was weak and slow, hardly there. He looked over at Demetrius and thought about the contradictions of human nature; of how a man who has spent his life as a mercenary can also have such compassion for a complete stranger. . . . *Probably best not to mention Walter's racist leanings. What good would it do?* He slid back off the truck bed and patted Demetrius on the shoulder. "The old guy is lucky to have you."

Demetrius looked up and tried to smile.

Josh nodded, and then together they loaded Walter into the cab. Demetrius positioned Walter on his lap, putting his arm around the old man's waist, and then awkwardly yanked the door closed. Space inside the cab was tight. There was barely enough room for Josh to manage the stick shift.

At about the ten kilometer mark Josh glanced at Walter; the old man had taken a turn for the worse. His breathing looked erratic, his color a pasty-gray. "Hang in there Walter," Josh said, trying to sound upbeat, and feeling less than genuine. He needed the other half of the picture.

Walter stirred and straightened his head, looking as though he were trying to speak. But before he could utter a word, the two troop trucks passed them heading in the opposite direction. Josh watched the rearview mirror as they faded out of sight. Then all at once, it happened. Both sets of taillights went solid red. "Aw shit, they're coming back."

Demetrius grabbed the door handle. "Keep her steady. I'll get in the back."

"Here, you'll need this," Josh said and handed Demetrius the handgun.

Demetrius nodded, then shifted his butt closer to the cab door and carefully slid out from under Walter. As he opened the door a surge of air filled the cab, throwing up old receipts and a paper coffee cup. Then the door closed, and the debris dropped. He was almost in the truck box, one leg in, the other out, when the truck hit a deep pothole, throwing him up and down hard. He grabbed at the cab roof to steady himself and the gun slipped out of his hand, falling to the road. *"Shit . . . !"*

The army trucks were closing in, Josh calculated the front runner at about fifty yards back. All of a sudden they opened fire, with some of the bullets hitting, punching holes in the pickup. Demetrius ducked down low in the truck box, managed to flatten out the wheelchair, then picked it up, aimed it, and whirled it out the back. With no time for the driver to react, the chair slid under the army truck's front end, wedging itself against the right wheel well. Sparks flew, and the truck began to swerve. Then came a loud *bang* as a tubular chunk of rod from the chair punctured the front tire. The truck veered to the right and nose-dived into a shallow ditch, then flipped end over end, throwing soldiers out in all directions.

The second truck quickly replaced the first, and a few seconds later the troops opened fire. Demetrius chucked out what he could: a few sandbags and a jack, all missing their target. With nothing left to toss, he made for the cab. As he opened the passenger-side door, a bullet caught him in the back, an inch below his shoulder blade, nicking his lung, and exiting his chest just below his collarbone. He slid into the cab, planting his boots on either side of Walter, now passed out on the floor. Demetrius glanced at Josh. "I lost the gun . . ."

"Yeah, I kinda figured," Josh said, and could see the big man was hurt.

The army truck moved in closer and bullets began hitting with greater accuracy. "How bad are you?" Josh asked, just as a bullet shattered the back window of the cab.

"I'll make it."

Bullshit, Josh thought, *I have to get you to a doctor.*

The truck was now no more than thirty feet from their tail, and with bullets pounding the cab, Josh could only think of one more card to play. "Brace yourself," he yelled.

Then, he slammed on the brakes with both feet. It was as if the pickup had stopped in its tracks and gone straight into reverse. The heavy truck had no time to react—the pickup's open truck bed worked like a knife, cutting deep into the army truck's radiator. Immediately the cab of the army truck filled with great gobs of steam and it slowed and swerved off to the side of the road.

Josh let out a quick breath. He knew they couldn't relax, more troops would be coming. There was a price on their heads, and in Central America, cash was king.

The odometer clicked off forty-seven kilometers. He slowed to a stop on the side of the road and punched in Anna's number.

Chapter 48

Anna answered on the first ring. A couple of minutes later, her Isuzu Trooper SUV rolled to a stop in front of the pickup. Anna climbed out and stomped over to Josh.

"Thanks for coming," Josh said, and half-smiled, not knowing how the next few minutes would unfold.

Anna wasn't smiling.

Demetrius was leaning on the front quarter panel of the pickup, spitting blood on the dirt. His shirt was crimson from his neck to his belly, and Walter was at his feet, unconscious, his back up against the front tire.

Anna pursed her lips as she took it all in, then said, "You're on the news, you know. All the radio stations are carrying it. They're saying three criminals have escaped from the Mount Edna Detention Centre . . . armed and considered extremely dangerous." She ran her fingers through her long black hair, shook her head and punched Josh on the shoulder. "Good God Josh, I don't know why they are after you, or what you have done, *or* if you have done anything. And I certainly don't know why in the God's name I'm here! You're such an *idiot!*" Then she turned and climbed back into the Trooper and revved the engine.

All she had to do was to drop it into first gear and

leave them standing there. It wasn't her problem. *And if she did leave, who could blame her,* Josh thought.

Anna held her gaze on Josh, as though she was looking right through him. Then, in the blink of an eye, he saw it. She had made her decision. A frown surfaced, barely turning the corners of her mouth. Then came a familiar sound, the sharp clacking of door locks. "Get in," she said.

Josh put his arm around Demetrius's waist and walked him to the back of the SUV. Demetrius fell in on his back, then pushed with his feet, inching his huge body across the floor until he had himself propped up against the back seat. Then he gave Josh a pained smile. Josh could see time was running out.

By comparison, Walter weighed nothing. After strapping the old man in, Josh climbed into the front with Anna.

Anna glanced at Josh before gunning it. "You must leave Guatemala tonight. Every radio station is warning to be on the outlook for you and your two friends."

"You're right—we have to go to the airport."

"*What?* You can't do that," she said, her voice rising. "Have you lost your mind? The prison guards, the military, the police, they're all out looking for you. My God, Josh, everyone is looking for you. It's guaranteed the airport will be surrounded."

"What choice do we have? Going by land isn't an option, and even if we made it to the ocean and managed to secure a boat, the trip would last at least two days, maybe three. And my friends, as you call them, they wouldn't make it. We don't have a choice. We have to fly out." Josh thought for a moment, then said, "But you're right about the International. There's gotta be other, smaller airports close to it. There always are."

Anna gave a nod. "I know of two. One has corporate jets used by high rollers, all big corporate names. It is close to the main airport, but that airport, it too will be heavily guarded. It would be easier to take a run at the International." She hit the brakes and swerved to miss an iguana lying in the middle of the road. "The other strip . . . is not much more than a short runway, cut out of the jungle. Built around the time of the Second World War."

"Is it still in operation?"

"Yes, used as a training school. I know this for a fact. I tried for my pilot's license there. Thirty minutes in the air, and I was so sick—"

"That'll do," Josh said, no longer listening to her.

"What did you say?"

"The airstrip in the jungle. Can you find it?"

"Yes, obviously, but you won't find anyone to fly you. It's a daylight operation."

"Excellent. Let's go."

Anna frowned.

They had driven for about twenty minutes, nearing the halfway point to the airstrip, when lights appeared on either side of the road.

"What do you think . . . an accident?" Josh asked, knowing the answer.

"No, no accident. Hold on. I know these roads." She killed the lights and swerved to the left, taking them onto a side road. The road immediately dropped below the highway and switched back 180 degrees, then ran another two hundred meters before swinging right. Then she hit the lights, and they could see again. They zigzagged for close to an hour on dirt roads before pulling back onto a gravel road. Dead ahead was the airstrip with a single hangar set off to one side.

A layer of clouds had formed a low ceiling over the airstrip, and as they drove along the side of the hangar a few large droplets of rain splattered onto the windshield. By the time Anna wheeled around to the back of the hangar the rain had picked up and was now dripping off the headlights.

The hangar was built for small aircraft, consisting of a large, long, corrugated sheet roof held up by six telephone poles. On one of the poles a hooded light cast a pale glow.

The hangar was completely empty and Josh was starting to lose all hope when he saw the nose of a plane on the other side of the hangar. As they drew closer he could see it was a single engine cargo plane. *Good,* he thought, *cargos have a better range.*

"You know how to fly that?" Anna asked, looking doubtful.

"Something like it . . . it's all based on the same principle, right?"

"Yeah, right . . ." She glanced at him, giving him the *you are out of your mind* look.

Demetrius seemed to perk up once he saw the plane.

Josh threw the big man's right arm across his shoulder, helping him into the copilot seat and strapping him in before going back for Walter.

He opened the door to find Walter gasping for air. *Ah shit,* Josh thought as he grabbed Walter by his armpits and tried to straighten him up.

Walter scrunched up his face. "Come closer," he sneered as he gasped for air. "I've seen enough people die to know I'm not gonna make it . . . so I'm gonna do you a favor. I'm gonna tell you where it's hidden. Let's just say it gives a dying man comfort to know the Elhert family will not get off scot-free." He paused. "I have one condition . . ."

"Uh-huh, what's that?"

Walter let out a long, hacking cough before saying, "You cannot be weak-kneed once you know the truth."

Josh hesitated for a second, then nodded.

Walter liked that, and tried to smile. "Good, very good. . . . The photo," he said, and then wheezed and coughed up fluid before he could continue. "It's in the Manor."

"Upstate New York," Josh said. "Yeah, I've been there."

"Not there, fool. Florida," Walter whispered. "Been there all along. Tucked away right under their goddamn noses . . ." With those words his breathing changed and Josh could see Walter was fading.

"Tucked away, where . . . ?" Josh sighed as he watched the old man drift, his breathing slowing until it stopped, his vacant gray eyes staring out at nothing. Josh considered the old man for a moment, and wondered what other secrets had died with him? Then he brushed the palm of his hand over Walter's eyes, closing them one last time.

He carried Walter to the plane and loaded him onboard, laying him on the cargo floor. He turned to Anna and before he could speak—

"You don't know where the book is, do you?"

Josh grimaced. "I have a hunch, that's all . . ." then he stopped himself, and said, "You're right, I don't. But I will find it, and I *will* return it to you."

Anna just stared at him, then said, "I'll bring my truck around and point the lights down the runway. You'd better get out of here, now, while there's still time." Her voice was sad, and a little lost.

Leaning forward, she raised herself on her toes and softly kissed his lips. "Now, go . . ."

Josh slid into the pilot's seat and studied the instrument panel for a moment, then adjusted the fuel mixture, armed the battery, and pumped fuel to the engine. Then he inhaled, held his breath, and turned the key. The engine cranked a half-dozen times before it finally caught. "Yes . . . !"

The gauges all appeared to be in working order, and the gas gauge showed full . . . *ahh thank Christ*, he thought, and let out a long sigh. He looked down at the SUV, its headlights lighting up a portion of the runway. He held up his hand to say good-bye, even though he knew Anna would not see it.

Josh turned to Demetrius. The big man's head was leaning against the plane's fuselage, his eyes closed.

"I'm gonna get you to a hospital. As soon as we make US airspace, I'll put us down on the first available road. Just hang in there . . ."

Demetrius opened one eye. "You're a decent guy, Ingram, you know that? You could've left me back there. I'm of no help to you now."

Josh glanced over at Demetrius, and then pushed the throttle forward, rolling the plane into position.

As the cargo plane cleared the runway and rose above the treetops, he reached over and touched Demetrius's neck.

"*Awww, no . . .*" Josh muttered.

Chapter 49

Josh banked the cargo plane into American airspace. It was near dawn, and the arc of the sun had yet to poke up on the horizon. Hugging the waters of the Gulf of Mexico, he brought the plane in low and fast and off radar, and as he breached the coastline the plane's left wing clipped the tip of a pine tree.

He'd chosen Louisiana to touch down. He knew the back roads, they were straight and flat and went on forever, with only a small farmhouse to break the monotony every mile or so. The sky was gun barrel blue, with just enough light to see the ground. At first, it resembled a black ribbon stretching out across the land. As he got closer Josh smiled; long and straight, bleak and empty, it was a paved rural road. He dropped the landing gear and throttled down, adjusting the flaps. A crosswind was making the plane jump, but it handled well, and as it touched down he throttled back and applied the brakes.

Up ahead was a large, abandoned barn, a hog barn he guessed, its roof sagged, its walls punctuated with craggy holes that once held rows of small windows. *Perfect. Big enough to hide the plane from the road . . . and with any luck, it won't be noticed for days.* He taxied off the road and maneuvered around to the back.

Josh found a shovel lying on the ground near the

barn. Once he got through the turf layer the earth became more manageable, and he was able to dig a waist-deep grave for both Demetrius and Walter. He retrieved some old tarps from a lean-to shed, spreading them out on the ground. He laid Walter out on one and wrapped him tight. He then rolled Demetrius onto the other and wrapped him up. By the time he finished and tossed on the last shovelful of soil, he was wasted.

He sat down between the graves, wiped his brow with his shirtsleeve and tried to think of something appropriate to say. Words weren't coming easy, how could they—he'd barely known them. Then he thought of Arthur's funeral and the preacher . . .

The Lord's Prayer, it's all he knew.

He was close to the end of the prayer when he drifted off.

Then he heard a man call to him, the man wanted him to wake up. He could smell the must, seeping out of the thawing earth. He was again in the root cellar, the light dim, the candles burned to flattened puddles, his hands tied to a wooden chair. He could not move. A woman was sitting on a chair across from him, her hands and feet tied with hemp rope. A clear plastic bag had been pulled over her head and tied tight around her neck. Her face was bluish-gray and her eyes were closed. A layer of condensation had filmed on the inside of the bag, making it hard for him to see who it was. He craned his head forward, inching closer to the woman. He knew her, that much he was sure of—then her eyes cracked open. Josh awoke to find graves on either side of him, and he let out a long, deep sigh.

He took one long last look at the graves. *Life is no more than a highway running in one direction. No off ramp, no cloverleaf to turn around and try again. You have to make life count, or what's the point? But maybe that's it; there is no point to it. You simply exist.*

He turned and started walking down to the road, and had walked for about forty-five minutes before he saw a farmhouse in the distance. Ten minutes later, he was standing at the foot of the driveway. It was a sixties rancher style, the size of two doublewides. Fresh white paint had been applied to the windowsills, and garden gnomes played on the front lawn. All was quiet and the lights were out.

In the driveway sat a rusting, faded orange pickup. The driver's window was down, and Josh stuck his head in. No key. He walked around to a clothesline on the side of the house and grabbed a pair of black jeans, two sizes too big, and an extra extra large black T-shirt. He went back to the pickup and changed beside it, then popped the truck out of gear, pushed it out onto the road a hundred feet or so, and stopped. Reaching under the dash, he located the live wire and ripped it loose. Touching it to the ignition wire, he heard the engine catch. He put the truck into gear and let it idle forward for a quarter mile before he hit the lights and floored the gas. Then he retrieved the cell from his pocket. He wasn't sure there would be reception, but he punched in Rachael's number. She answered on the third ring and sounded drained of energy, until she realized who was calling.

"My God, Josh, where have you been? I've been waiting and waiting for your call." Her voice was filled with worry. "Are you all right? Where are you?"

It was good to hear her voice.

He told her the cell was about to die and he would bring her up to speed when they got together. She told him there was little in the way of development on the O'Henry file, and that Kingsley was acting stranger than ever. They agreed they would meet tomorrow in Harland and follow up on the dead black girl in the news clipping. Then the phone died.

Josh arrived in Baton Rouge at quarter past ten that morning and ditched the truck in a restaurant parking lot. He called Mary collect on a pay phone outside the diner and gave her a thumbnail sketch of what had happened in Guatemala, then walked across the street to a small park. He sat down on a bench under a large shade tree to wait. He calculated she'd show up in about two-and-half hours, then he slouched down on the bench and fell asleep.

Mary showed up a few minutes short of three hours, rolling up beside him in her late-model Pathfinder, her window down.

"Nice duds," Mary said. "Fits you like a well-used condom."

"Thanks for coming," Josh replied, letting her comment slide. "Look, I need to ask you for a favor."

"Anything for you, dear," Mary said, trying to sound cheeky, though Josh could tell she was worried. "But first, let's get some food in you. I hope you're hungry, cause I'm damn well starving."

Mary's voice sounded *off. . . . I must look far worse than I realize.*

They crossed the street and stepped into the diner. The waitress gave Josh a second look, but Mary told her everything was okay. Josh ordered the Texas scrambler with extra chilies, two side orders of hash browns, whole grain toast and a strawberry milkshake.

"Not sure I want to be in the same state as you, when that comes out," Mary said. She ordered two eggs over easy, toast and glass of chocolate milk. "So, what's the favor you want to ask of me?"

"Mary, look, I'll understand if you're not interested . . ."

Mary's eyes narrowed. "Yeah, well, I've just about had enough of fast Eddie. My God, Josh, he's a four legged shittin' machine. I've never seen anything like it."

Mary was on a roll, and Josh decided to let her run with it. When she needed to vent, it was best to let her do so, otherwise it would be a long ride home.

Then it was his turn, and he was about to fill her in when the waitress came over with their food. She apologized for it taking so long; one of the cooks had called in sick.

For a second, Josh's mind wandered, returning to Walter and Demetrius.

Mary frowned. "Hey . . . you all right?"

"Yeah, sure, I'm okay. . . . Look, Mary, I was wondering if you would come to Florida with me?" Josh could see Mary was surprised. "I could use your help, your experience. Although I'll understand if you can't make it."

Mary jumped in. "You mean I'll have to pass Eddie on to Anwar?"

Josh wasn't sure that was such a good idea, but said, "I need you to do some investigative reporting."

All at once, Mary looked deflated, sighed, and said, "Sounds kinda lame."

"Maybe. But everything seems to be pointing to Harland, a small town on Florida's West Coast. There was a suspicious death there dating back to the late sixties. A black girl, a teenager, died, and her boyfriend went missing and was never found. Foul play was suspected, with racial tensions burning on both sides of the fence, each side blaming the other. There's more to it, but someone is intent on keeping it under wraps."

"And, who brought this to your attention?" Mary asked, sounding skeptical. "Which, I might add, is some forty years after the fact."

Josh cleared his throat. "O'Henry."

"Oh Christ, Josh." Mary's toast fell out of her hand. "When do we leave?"

Chapter 50

Mary dropped Josh off by the Tackle Shop and parked the Pathfinder out front of Crawlies.

She lived above the restaurant in a one-bedroom suite. On the roof, she had built a makeshift patio that overlooked the marina. She maintained it was there she could barbecue, read, and drink gin in peace.

Josh had never seen Mary have friends over, and she never said much about her private life. She had told him her parents passed away fifteen years ago, six months apart, first her mother and then her father. He knew her sister had hooked up with a dentist, and that she and her sister hadn't spoken in years. Josh also knew Mary didn't waste time and she'd be ready to leave before he was.

When Josh opened his front door Eddie was waiting for him, his huge tail whacking against the entry wall, his body twisting back and forth. Josh grabbed Eddie's massive head and gave him a hug. "You're not getting enough exercise, are ya boy? Our lives will get back to normal soon, I promise." Then he gave Eddie another big hug.

He changed out Eddie's water and filled his food dish, then peeled off the stolen clothes and hit the shower. He stood there for close to twenty minutes and let the hot water penetrate his sore muscles. He thought of Arthur in his grave, of O'Henry's twisted mind, and wondered how it was all connected. When the water temperature cooled, he jumped out, shaved, threw on some clean clothes, packed his duffle bag and dumped it by the front door.

That's when he saw it, a brown package leaning against the umbrella stand. It was from Arthur, and he immediately knew what it was. He ripped off the wrapping paper, revealing a book, a hand-written book, signed by Salvador Espada. He quickly thumbed through it, then closed it and slid it onto the bookshelf.

He tried Rachael on her phone, and ended up leaving her a message saying he'd be staying at the Driftwood Hotel. He plopped himself down in his leather chair, poured a brandy, sifted through his emails and paid a few bills online. He called Anwar to confirm that he would be okay to take care of Eddie. He told him of a spare bag of dog food by the back landing and thanked him again for helping out, and said when he got back, they would have to crack a beer or two and get caught up. Then Josh grabbed his duffle bag and headed out to meet Mary in front of Crawlies.

A direct flight from New Orleans International Airport to Harland, Florida could have taken a couple of hours, but with the driving and the stopover in Tampa, it stretched to five. Josh and Mary stepped off the plane in Harland a few minutes after seven p.m. It had been a long day.

The airport was located two miles outside of town. The town's population stood at a shade under fifteen thousand, and had been written up as one of the last hidden coastal gems of southwest Florida.

Tourism and Taxton Industries, Inc., the town's biggest employers, powered the local economy. Taxton manufactured medium to heavyweight trucks for export to Latin America and had done so since the early seventies. It was a privately owned company, with controlling interest held by the Elhert family.

Josh tried for a new SUV but ended up having to rent a late-model four-door sedan. He met Mary at the front of the air terminal, threw their luggage in the backseat, and they headed for downtown. After checking in at the hotel, they agreed to meet back at the bar in an hour, grab a bite to eat and plan their next steps.

Josh had a bottle of brandy sent up to his room, then settled into a comfortable wicker chair on the balcony, put his feet up and was enjoying a cigar when his cell rang. It was Rachael. She was on the Long Island Expressway heading for a late meeting with Kingsley. She sounded tired and stressed. A copycat had struck last night. He'd chopped up a hooker in the Bronx and left the head at a bus stop. It was a crude hacking job, no numbering and no note. They'd caught him because he'd gone around bragging about his kill in a Bronx bar, and he's now in for psychological assessment.

"It's stirred up another media shitstorm," she said. "Kingsley has called a special meeting with the mayor and the commissioner. He's fully aware we're nearly shut down with no new leads, and he wants to underscore my lack of progress. Josh, if we don't get a break soon, I'm finished."

"Are you still coming?" Josh asked, his voice tentative.

"Yeah I am. My flight leaves in morning at 8:20, I

have a stopover, so I'll make it there just before noon."

"I'll be there. It'll be good to see you."

Rachael didn't respond, and an uneasy silence took over.

"Goddamnit, Josh . . . not a peep from O'Henry. Just when it looks like he can't get enough airtime, he falls off the map. I don't know what to think."

"He's led us here for a reason. He's a planner. He wants to show us he's in control. The more we sweat, the sweeter the victory. I know it sounds hollow, but something will give. So get yourself down here and let's get to work, okay?"

"Okay . . ." she said. "But Josh, what if he's just jerking us around? All we have is that lousy news clipping."

"At least we know he still wants us in the game."

"Yeah, I guess."

"I'll pick you up tomorrow. Hopefully, we've made some progress by the time you arrive."

"We?" Rachael asked.

"Yeah, I brought along Mary."

"Oh right, good . . ."

Josh had another brandy, then stretched out on the couch for a nap. It was around nine p.m. when he grabbed his jacket and headed for the lobby.

The hotel bar wasn't well lit and the fake kerosene lamps hanging from the ceiling didn't do much for the atmosphere. Mary was nursing a gin and tonic at the bar. She glanced at Josh as he sat down. He could tell she was on her second, maybe her third drink.

"Spoke with Rachael, she's coming in tomorrow about noon."

"Oh *good*, the FBI are coming."

"You got an issue with Rachael? Have you even talked to her?"

Mary ran her index finger around the lip of her glass. "I called her when you were gone, I was looking for you. She seemed a little chatty to me. Likes to give orders, one of those. I can tell."

Josh sighed. "Come on. I'm hungry, let's get a booth. Somewhere where we can talk."

The booths were made from stained mahogany and needed polishing, and the seats were worn. Josh chose a booth near the back. Mary ordered another gin and tonic. Josh ordered a cheeseburger, fries, and a glass of milk.

"I need you to go to the library," he said. "To go through old newspapers, both local and state. Starting from say, July 1st, 1968 onwards, checking daily for information about the black teenager that died and her boyfriend who disappeared. You'll need to look for anything that could tie the Elhert family in. And if the family name pops up, did they give quotes? And if so, what side of the fence were they on, that is, the black side or white side. Was old man Elhert screwing around in the black quarter of town? Was a black man screwing Elhert's wife? See what you can find, anything at all. We need to find a connection. There has to be one—"

"Yeah I got it," Mary said, sounding pissed off. "Jesus, Josh, I was out collaring bad guys when you were having wet dreams about your first love."

Josh stopped in his tracks and grinned. She had a point.

After a few seconds, Mary said, "You're right, there has to be a connection. I mean, why bother planting the news clipping in the first place?"

Josh nodded.

"Okay, I'll go to the library. And you and what's her name? What are you two going to do?"

"Rachael . . . mmm, I'm not sure . . . we'll figure something out," he said and grinned, and watched Mary twist in her seat.

"You're an asshole, you know that?"

"So I've been told."

Chapter 51

Josh dropped Mary off at the library at 8:36 a.m. He waited to see that she got in, then drove north two blocks, took a right off 52nd Street, left onto 50th Ave, and angle parked in front of the Kimberly Hotel. He had picked the Kimberly for breakfast on the advice of the front desk staff at the Driftwood Hotel. Kimberly was where the locals hung out.

The restaurant was long and narrow, made even more so by the various sailboat parts and fishing nets hanging on the walls. The only free table he could find was next to a serving table made from a single oak plank, a foot wide and ten feet long. The plank was loaded with pastries smothered in marmalade, scones filled with fruit, and blueberry muffins piled a foot high. Located at one end of the plank was an apple pie and a half-eaten cherry pie. Four old men, wearing coveralls and plaid shirts, were sitting across from the pies, debating about what makes a first-rate quarter horse. They had the best table, it faced out to the street. Regulars.

All four shut up and turned, watching Josh as he took a seat across from them. Josh half raised his hand as if to say hello. They all just stared at him. The one who appeared to be the oldest had a large white napkin tucked into the neck of his dark-blue plaid shirt. His ears were small, protruding at right angles to his tiny head. As he ate his cherry pie he gave Josh a slight smile, then all four returned to their debate.

A young waitress with thighs the size of hundred pound oxygen tanks shuffled over. Her oily ponytail wiggled with each swish of her thighs. She flipped over to a clean page on her order pad and asked, "What can I do yeh for?" Her voice carried a disinterested tone that was reflected in her thin smile and pursed lips.

"A couple of things," Josh replied, striving to maintain a pleasant tone. "First, I'd love some of that great-smelling coffee and a slice of cherry pie, and then I'd like some advice."

"Coffee and pie are no problem, but I'm not so sure about giving any advice," she said, and flickered her eyelids. She poured Josh a cup and dropped a couple of creamers on the table. Then she stood and stared at him, slack-jawed, mouth wide open.

Way too early for this, Josh thought, and took a breath. "Actually," he said, raising his voice, so those seated around him could hear. "I'm writing a book about unsolved crimes of the South. One in particular took place here, in the late sixties."

Thankfully, her opened-mouthed shock and *aw-shucks I'm not interested* attitude wasn't shared by the old boys. They seemed to perk up, the eldest in particular.

"It involved the death of a black teenage girl and the disappearance of her boyfriend that occurred here in the summer of '68. It was suspected the girl's death was not an accident, and as the boyfriend just up and disappeared, he became the prime suspect. No traces were ever found of him, he simply vanished into thin air."

"Look mister, I weren't even born then, so I can't help you none," the waitress said with all the enthusiasm of the next in line to get a pap smear.

"Well, I can understand that," Josh said, "although if you would pass the word around that I'm looking for information, I would be grateful." He pulled out a wad of fifties and stripped off one and placed it in her hand.

Again, her jaw dropped, but this time he could see a rush of pink bleed into her cheeks. She blinked. "Yes sir," she said, like she'd discovered her next best friend. She slipped the bill into her breast pocket and shuffled off to the next table.

Josh was on his second cup of coffee, debating if he should order another slice of pie, when the four old codgers rose from their table, their chairs squeaking and scraping. They'd said their good-byes and were filing out past Josh's table when the eldest, who was hanging back a little from the others, whispered to Josh. "Hey mister, I think I can help ya with that stuff you were talking about. About them kids. I'll meet ya around back. Give me twenty minutes to lose the fellas?"

Josh nodded. Then the old man placed his hand on Josh's shoulder and squeezed, leaving a strong scent of liniment in his wake. Josh took another refill of coffee and decided to sit back and read the local paper. He had some time to kill, so he ordered himself another slice of cherry pie.

The alley behind the hotel ran the entire length of the building to a brick wall. A set of rusting queen-sized bed springs, a bent bicycle wheel, and a broken wooden pallet leaned up against the wall. Josh tapped his shoe on the pallet, and was starting to think he'd been stood up, figuring the old guy must have changed his mind.

As he started to head back, a hushed voice called out.

"Mister, over here." The sound came from what appeared to be a crack in the side of the hotel. As Josh stepped closer he could make out a narrow separation, a hollow not more than a foot deep, in the side of the building, and from it, the old man stepped out.

"You have something for me?" Josh asked.

"About what you were saying in there," the old man said, and leaned his head toward the hotel. "About them kids . . . a hell of a thing. Took years for the town to recover."

"Yeah, I can imagine. Bad enough to happen in the city, but in a small town where everyone knows each other's business, it had to feel a lot more personal."

"You got it mister, damn near tore the town apart. Nothing like that ever happened before, not around here. Not in Harland, that's for darn sure. The place was crawling with reporters. The police, military, and FBI were all in on the manhunt, looking for that black kid. It went on for a couple of weeks. Reporters, TV channels, they came from all over the place. Volunteers swept through the countryside looking for him too. It lasted for a while, and then the reporters started to leave . . . people got bored, I guess."

"Hey, I could've got all that from the newspapers," Josh said, baiting him.

"Uh-huh, but there's more, a lot more," the old man said and shifted his gaze.

"More? Okay, so let's hear it . . ."

A fake cowering came over the old guy.

Josh reached into his pocket and withdrew a fifty. The old man eyed it and hesitated. Josh produced another fifty, and the man hesitated again.

"Hey, that's all you're getting for now, but if your information turns out to be good, I'll double it."

The old man snatched the cash out of Josh's hand and jammed it into his pants pocket. "How do I know I can trust you?"

"Trust is a bitch, isn't it?" Josh said, and could see the old man was now getting worried. "Look, what's your name? So I'll know who to ask for later, when I give you the rest of the cash." Josh reached out to shake the man's hand.

The old man didn't shake, but said, "Harold, that's my name." Then he shoved his hands hard into his pockets, as if he'd already said too much. His body stiffened. "Now, you can't go telling anyone we talked, okay mister?"

"Understood. You have my word. I won't be telling a soul."

Harold eyeballed Josh for a few seconds before he began. "Well . . . there was a fella that used to come into town and drink at the pub. Sometimes two, even three times a month, and then he'd be gone for months at a time. He wasn't much of a talker. A loner, if you know what I mean." Harold stopped and stuck his bony old finger into his ear and started to dig. "Anyway, he'd get as miserable as a lame mule when he got too much liquor in him. Liked to grab the waitresses' asses too." Harold withdrew his finger from his ear and smiled. "Gotta say, we all kinda liked to grab at little Mirtle's ass. It was as though

God was testing us. He straps two fine, and I mean fine, plump pigs to her arse and then he just sits back and watches what're we gonna do."

Josh raised an eyebrow.

"Well, you know, none of us cared too much for him, the loner that is." Another worried look crossed Harold's face. "But he'd buy a drink or two for whoever would sit and listen to him. I would've felt bad for him, if he weren't so dang mean."

"So what did he say about the dead black girl and her missing boyfriend?" Josh asked, starting to get impatient.

"Hold your horses now, I'm gettin' to it, I'm gettin' to it," he said, and then hawked up some phlegm and spat on the side of the dumpster. "You youth of today, it's always gimme gimme. No respect for your elders." Then his foot started to tap and his gaze darted around, as if he was trying to decide what he should do next. He stopped and craned his head back up. "Like I was saying, he'd drink too much and he'd get mean. I would have left, except he always bought me another drink. I guess he wanted someone to talk to. Anyway, he told me more than once he knew what had happened to those kids down at Cranston Bridge, as if he had some kind of *inside* information. Then he'd get these big, buggy eyeballs like he was trying to squeeze out a loaf, and then he'd shut right up and go all silent-like. No sense trying to talk to him after that. Didn't bother me none. I liked it when he went quiet."

"That's all you have?" Josh felt his heart sinking. "Don't suppose there's a name?"

Harold shook his head. "Not his whole name, but his first name was Albert, and he had a scar that ran down one side of his face. Clipped off a bit of one of his nostrils, ugly son of a gun."

"Any idea where he is now?"

"Don't know for sure, but he never lived in town. I know that cause he'd brag about living in the country, under the stars. Partial to peeing in the bushes, that sort of thing."

"When did you see him last?"

"Two, no . . . three months ago. He'd come to town and got drunk as usual. Same as always."

Josh could see Harold was finished. "Look, if you think of anything else, call me." He took Harold's hand, turned it palm up, and wrote down his cell number. "Call me, okay?" Josh said, wanting to drive home the point. Then he reached into his pocket and gave Harold another fifty. "I'll make it worth your while if you can remember anything else."

Harold wandered off in the direction of the bar, counting his cash.

Chapter 52

The librarian was tall and thin as a ruler. Her movements were slow and arthritic, and as she got closer, Mary could see her knuckles were swollen and the ends of her fingers had grown crooked. Mary smiled, reached out and gently shook her hand.

"Hi, I'm Mary. I'm assisting Josh Ingram, and we're-"

"Josh Ingram, yes, I've heard all about it," the librarian said, her voice soft, but excited. "You've caused quite a stir in town. We don't get many big name writers here." She caught herself, and smiled. "Correction, we never get *any* famous writers here. I'm Elizabeth Reynolds, the librarian. Friends call me Lizzy."

Mary wasn't sure why, but she took an immediate liking to Lizzy, and a second later an idea came to her. She thought about it, then said, "Lizzy, I think I could arrange it for you."

A curious look crossed Lizzy's face. "Arrange what?"

"For you to meet Josh Ingram."

The librarian blinked. "Oh, I don't know," she said, all of a sudden flustered.

"Hey, don't give it a second thought. He's gonna love to meet you."

The librarian placed her hands on her cheeks and tears began to well up.

"C'mon . . . what are you doing?" Mary blurted out, and immediately wished she hadn't.

Startled, the librarian's look changed to one of embarrassment.

"Hey, I am sorry about that," Mary said. "Something about me and the emotional stuff . . . it kind of throws me off my game." An awkward silence filled the room, then Mary said, "If it's okay, I have some business to take care of. I guess what I am saying is, I'm gonna need access to any local and state newspapers you have dating back to the late 60s. That is, if you could show me where to look."

Lizzy touched Mary's arm. Her smile had returned. "That would be on microfiche. We started using digital storage about five years ago, so the old microfiche machines were moved to the basement."

Mary followed Lizzy down a long wide hallway, past a set of double wooden doors that opened to the library, then past several others that led to study areas and breakout rooms. At the end of the hall they took a flight of stairs down to the basement and came to a door with the word ARCHIVES stenciled in blue paint.

"I hope you don't mind spiders. The basement's full of them," Lizzy said, as she inserted a skeleton key and turned an oblong and tarnished brass knob. She glanced back at Mary and asked, "Are you all right?"

Mary's face had blanched. *Ahh, goddamn spiders,* Mary thought, and said, "Perfectly all right."

The door creaked open and the librarian flicked on the light switch. The room had a foul smell of old paper, dust, and mold. Mary couldn't care less about the odor, she was on the lookout for the hairy little bastards. Lizzy led the way, weaving them past brown metal desks, stacked plastic chairs, and piles of surplus shelving. Every few feet, Lizzy brushed away a cobweb or two that hung from the lights, while Mary kept brushing away anything, real or not. Near the center of the room was a cluster of filing cabinets. At one end of the cabinets sat three microfiche machines. Lizzy pulled a linen handkerchief from her pocket and wiped a thick layer of dust off one of the screens. She clicked it on, and a pale-blue light flooded the foot square screen, casting a sickly glow onto their faces. Mary got a brief refresher on how to search the microfiche, and how to send what she wanted copied to the printer. Then Lizzy left Mary to work alone.

The Harland Review and The Tampa Bay Post had both been microfiched. Mary chose July 2nd, 1968 as her starting point and worked her way forward, one day at a time. The first few weeks of headlines were typical small-town news. The Review: July 5th, *Electrocuted Raven causes black out.* July 13th, *Drunken boater loses limb to propeller.* July 16th, *Sheriff catches mayor duck hunting off-season.*

The Tampa Bay Post was quiet, nothing unusual to report.

Monday, July 29th, 1968 the headline on the front page of The Harland Review, read: *Myrna Washington found dead at the foot of Cranston Bridge.* Below the caption was a grainy black-and-white picture of her body impaled by a rebar rod that protruded a good twelve inches out her chest, her arms and legs hanging limp at her sides.

The Tampa Bay Post hadn't picked up the story.

The next day, the front page of The Harland Review, read:

t.g. brown

Cranston Bridge Tragedy

Still no answers in the death of teenager Myrna Washington. Her boyfriend Tyrrell Dodge is wanted for questioning and remains at large. Sheriff Barkley has asked that everyone remain calm and let the law do its job, and cautioned: "Just because Miss Washington was colored, is no reason to start finger-pointing. I must emphasize that any unlawful acts, will not be tolerated by this office."

Then on July 31st, on the front page of The Harland Review: *The search for Tyrrell Dodge continues.* And about halfway down the page, there was another story, it read: *Gerald Dennery and Larry Frank missing. Foul play not ruled out.* The article reported them as last seen on the same weekend that Myrna Washington died. Both were seniors at Sir Ralston High School, and both played on the football team, and both were white.

The next day The Tampa Bay Post got interested, and both newspapers went into full-coverage mode. At last, something to sink their teeth into. Blacks against Whites, and Whites against Blacks. The articles started with finger-pointing, but it didn't take long for pictures of looted stores and burning cars on Main Street to capture the headlines. After two full weeks of the crisis, and a final plea for calm from the governor, the military was sent in to settle things down. "Well . . . holy shit!"

Mary checked for coverage in a community rag and a religious periodical, though neither added much to the story. When it was clear she wasn't going to get more, she packed up her stuff, printed off the articles she wanted, and left the room.

She met Lizzy on the way out and thanked her, then stopped and thought for a second before asking, "Any chance you have copies of the high school yearbooks?"

"Yes, we do. After graduation most kids leave town to find work. They all come back though, for Thanksgiving and Christmas. It's usually the older ones who come in and ask for the yearbooks, looking for friends or old flames."

"How far back do they go?"

"Oh, way back to when the school first opened, September 1959. Would you like to see them?"

Lizzy led Mary down the hallway and into the office.

The office had one long counter. Behind it was a heavyset woman sitting on a stool passing books under a scanner, logging them back in. Along one wall of the office were the yearbooks, one for each year the school had been open.

"They're all in chronological order," Lizzy said. "Is there a specific year that you had in mind?"

"66 through 68," Mary said. "1968 in particular. I read there were two white boys who went missing that same summer as the black boy."

Lizzy raised an eyebrow. "Oh yes, those boys. Made for a heck of a summer." She walked to one end of the books, running her fingers along the spines before coming to a stop. She did a double take. "That's strange, all three years are missing," she said, and rubbed her swollen hands together. "I don't know how that can be. No one is allowed to take them out of the library." Then her face brightened. "Just a minute, here they are. Been misfiled, that's all," she said, looking relieved. She handed the three volumes to Mary, who put them on the counter and flipped open 1968.

Mary turned the pages, until she reached where the graduating class pictures should have been. "Someone's ripped out the entire class," Mary said, and shot a questioning glance at Lizzy.

"Oh my . . . how can that be? I've never seen anything like this before."

Mary opened the 1967 and 1966 yearbooks. The grade eleven and grade ten class pictures were ripped out as well. She frowned and looked at Lizzy.

"Who would do such a thing?" Lizzy asked, shaking her head. "And why take all those pictures?"

"Appears, someone wants to disappear."

A few minutes later, they said their good-byes and Mary thanked Lizzy again. Then Mary turned and headed for the high school.

Chapter 53

The land survey office was located on the north side of town, across from a dilapidated fruit distribution warehouse. Josh turned into an empty gravel parking lot situated next to the survey building's cinder-block wall. He bought a large, detailed map of the surrounding area, that included all the back roads, elevations, and where the wetland areas were located.

Once back at his hotel room, he spread the map out on the desk. He grabbed a cup saucer, turned it over and centered it on Cranston Bridge, then drew a red circle around the edge of the saucer with a ballpoint pen and lifted the saucer. *Somewhere in here lives the man with the scar running down his face.*

The main road through Cranston Bridge ran north and south, and was intersected by a smaller secondary road every two miles. Within the circle, Josh figured there were at least four main intersections to check, plus a few smaller intersections east and west. He decided the best plan would be to drive out to each intersection, stop at the closest house, and simply ask about the man with the scar. In the backwoods, neighbors would know anyone within a few miles of their home, and someone with a big scar on his face shouldn't be that difficult to remember.

He checked his watch; time to pick up Rachael.

Chapter 54

The deputy who tailed Josh from the survey office to the airport wasn't very good at it. Josh had just cleared the baggage claim area and glanced back. *Unbelievable . . . this guy blends in like a cowboy in a Shakespearean play.* Then he noticed Rachael sitting by an airport car rental kiosk and walked over.

"You have a friend I see," Rachael said.

"Yeah, he does a great job, I'm proud of him." Josh waved to the deputy.

The deputy's face slid into a frown, and he continued to stare.

Rachael turned and gasped when she got a good look at Josh's face. "Jesus, Josh have you been to see a doctor?"

Bluish rings tinged with yellow ran half-circles below his eyes, his upper lip had an angular scab on it, and one of his ears was scraped raw.

"Looks worse than it is," Josh said, not mentioning his sore ribs and bruised body. He changed the subject. "I'm parked out front, let's catch up along the way."

As they reached the bottom step to the sidewalk, Rachael grabbed his arm and turned him toward to her. "I am glad you're back."

"I'm glad I'm back too," he said, and started to lean toward her—when a horn went off beside them, yanking him right out of the moment, leaving him standing there, leaning in to her with a big dumb look on his face.

At the outskirts of town, Josh stopped at a roadside diner and used the washroom, then checked himself out in the mirror. *Ahhh man . . . you could've at least hugged her. You are such a moron.* He replayed the scene in his head, and a humiliated, pained look crossed his face. He took a moment to compose himself, then ran some cold water, splashed his face, dried with a paper towel and left the washroom. He grabbed a couple of coffees for the road, and they headed south out of town. First destination—Clinton Corner.

Rachael lowered her cell to her lap and sighed. "I have to be back in New York for a general meeting on O'Henry the day after tomorrow. I'm sorry Josh, that doesn't leave us much time." She took a deep breath then exhaled. "Let's hope it's enough."

Josh could see she was under a mountain of pressure. "So . . . Kingsley, is he getting ready to call you into kangaroo court?"

"He would like to. He thinks this is my swan song. . . . Who knows, he might be right. The jerk keeps kissing ass all the way up the food chain, making certain they're all fully aware of my lack of progress. Each day we come up with zilch, he gets braver and braver."

"Yeah, well, fuck him. It's always the same. There's never a break in a case unless we make one or get lucky. And we can't count on luck with O'Henry, he's too careful. So we're going to have to keep busting chops until something gives."

"Yeah, yeah, you're right I know. But it still makes my blood boil."

Josh gave Rachael a thumbnail sketch of the events in Guatemala, finishing with Walter's disclosure about the half picture. He left out the part about Anna.

"Mary's doing investigative work in the library. Checking old newspapers, looking for anything that could tie the Elherts to Myrna Washington's death." Josh glanced at Rachael who was looking straight ahead; he couldn't tell if she was listening.

Josh took an off-ramp onto a secondary road that ran parallel to the highway for about a mile, before heading southwest into the swamp country that ran along the coastline. Rachael unfolded the map on her lap and starting giving directions. They went another twelve miles to the intersection of RR 21 and Porcupine Road, also known as Clinton Corner. Josh eased back on the gas as they approached, threw the car into neutral and coasted up to the base of a dirt driveway. A hundred feet in was an abandoned shack, or at least it looked that way. They got out and made their way up the driveway.

The shack was sheltered from the wind on three sides by a thick growth of Florida gator bush. They walked in loose circles around the front yard, crisscrossing, looking for any sign that someone lived there. Rachael was knee-deep in broom grass, standing next to a rusted pickup, its doors removed, and its hood open. She held her arms in front of her, palms up, and shook her head as if to say, *nothing here.*

Josh headed around back. He stepped over a rotted out log, around a stack of old car batteries, before coming to an overgrown raspberry patch. In the center of the patch he found an opening large enough to slip through. On the other side was tall grass, weeds, a few rusting farm implements, and a boarded up outhouse. He scanned the area for another minute before meeting up with Rachael in the front yard. They climbed back into the car and left.

The next two intersections were equally unremarkable, and Josh was starting to think this whole thing had been a bad idea. At the fourth intersection the first signs of life appeared. There were two buildings. Up front, some twenty yards from the road, was a small home, a rancher. Its roof needed replacing, its shingles turned up at the corners, and strands of chickweed stuck out from its gutters. The home looked derelict, except for the fact it had a light on inside. The other building, a shed, was set thirty yards farther back, near a corner of the fenced yard. Josh could see gray smoke swirling out in loose curls from the shed's bent chimney.

It started with a dog's barking, a deep guttural sound. A moment later, the shed door swung open and a man who had to be in his late fifties stepped out. A large German Shepherd came out from behind him, cutting a path straight for Josh, then stopped a few feet short, its teeth gnashing like it was about to strike. Josh went to put his hand where his holster would have been, and called out. "I don't want to hurt your dog, mister. Tell him to back off."

The man didn't seem too interested in the fate of the dog, and as he stepped closer, Josh got a good look at him. He had on threadbare brown trousers, rolled down rubber boots and a wife-beater T-shirt. His sweat-stained straw cowboy hat was wrenched low on his forehead and he was carrying a pump-action 12-gauge shotgun. When he was within eye contact, the man's expression changed, his jaw muscles tightened and his mouth turned sour. He pumped a shell into the chamber, then yelled at his dog to shut up. The dog backed off a few feet and dropped to the ground next to a bald tire lying in the grass.

Josh stared at the man and thought to himself, *FUCK YOU*. Then he raised his right hand high in the air and said, "We come in peace." The effect was lost on the man. "Actually," Josh said, with a serious tone to his voice, "we would like to ask you a few questions about your wardrobe."

The man remained stone-faced, sizing up the situation. "You trying to be smart with me?"

Rachael glanced at Josh, a pained grin on her face, and showed her ID. "We are looking into an event that happened a long time ago, back in the late 60s. We need to find someone, and we're hoping you might be able to point us in the right direction," she said, pasting on a wide, glowing smile. "We'd like to ask you a few questions, if that's okay?"

The man shrugged, lowered the shotgun and pointed it at the ground. He just stared down, not focusing on anything in particular. It was clear he hadn't yet decided what to do.

Then the man looked up and asked, "What'd you want to know?"

"Do you know a man named Albert?" Josh asked. "We don't have a last name. He has a large scar that runs down his face. We were told he might live nearby, and we want to ask him a few questions."

"No one by that description or the name Albert lives

around here. What you wanna talk to him about?"

"We're investigating the death of a black girl, Myrna Washington, and the disappearance of her boyfriend, Tyrrell Dodge. It occurred in the summer of '68," Rachael said.

Josh could see the man considering what he was going to say. "Do you know what happened to those kids?" Josh asked, pressuring the man.

"What made you wanna ask me that?"

Pay dirt. He knows something. "Cranston Bridge is close by. Figured you might know what happened."

"Well, you've wasted your time, cause I don't know nuthin' about no kid being lost or being dead around here." The man's face grew cold and he straightened his back. "And I think you better be gettin' off my property." He raised his shotgun to waist level, pointing the barrel at Josh.

At that moment a siren went off; a sharp toot, followed by a long drawn out whine. A police cruiser pulled into the yard, followed by two other cruisers. A tall, paunchy man with a sheriff's badge got out the first cruiser and walked over. "Are these people bothering you, Boyd?"

"I was asking them to leave Sheriff. They've been nosing around some and they weren't invited."

The other car doors opened and a deputy from each cruiser got out. Both had their guns drawn, and positioned themselves behind their opened doors. Josh recognized the younger deputy from the airport.

Sheriff Stranton did not bother to ask for identification. He turned to Josh. "Boyd says he's asking that you leave his property, Ingram."

"Look Sheriff, I'm special agent Tanner." Rachael flashed her ID badge. "We're currently conducting a murder investigation."

"*Murder,*" the sheriff said and laughed. "What the hell are you talking about? There's been no murder around here. In fact, there's *never* been a murder around here as I recall. And I should know, I lived in these here parts all my life."

"We think the death of a black girl and her missing boyfriend in the late sixties might be in some way connected to a series of murders occurring in the New York area," Josh said. "We are following up on a lead that brought us here."

"Well, in that case, good old Boyd won't be any good to you. I've known him all his life and he's never traveled further than to town. Isn't that so, Boyd?"

"That's a fact, Sheriff."

Huh . . . your act could use some polishing boys, Josh said to himself. Even so, he could see Boyd was uncomfortable and wanted nothing to do with any of this. From the corner of his eye he saw the deputies were getting restless. *Why are they nervous? They have the drop on us. It's not adding up, a couple of high-strung deputies with their fingers on their triggers.*

"Look, Sheriff," Rachael said, sounding irritated. "This is an FBI investigation. Are you telling me that you are refusing to cooperate?"

Josh could see she was ready to unload on him. He cleared his throat and caught her attention, giving her a look that said, *let's get our asses out of here.*

Rachael hesitated for a second, then gave a shallow nod of recognition. Pointing her finger at the sheriff, she said, "We will be back. You can count on it."

"Sheriff, we're done here, so we'll be moving along now," Josh said, motioning for Rachael to get to the car.

Sheriff Stranton's eyes narrowed, and he called out, "Ingram, I want you and your little skirt on the next plane out of these parts. You hear me, boy? I catch you snooping again, there's gonna be trouble."

As they left the yard and turned onto the road, Josh could feel the sheriff and his men watching them.

"Thanks for saving me from myself," Rachael said. "I'd forgotten how small-town law enforcement has its own way of doing things."

"Yep, things that include a shovel and tight lips," Josh said.

Rachael didn't respond, she was already busy clicking away on her cell. A dozen miles passed before she spoke again. "I have to be back in New York tomorrow. The mayor's moved the meeting up a day. He wants an update on O'Henry, and Kingsley wants me there to take the heat. . . . Sorry Josh, I thought we'd have another day."

When they arrived back at the hotel, Josh turned to Rachael. "Mary and I are going to grab a bite to eat at the hotel bar at around seven."

"Oh yeah . . . I forgot she was here." Her voice sounded disappointed. "Sure, I'll see you later."

Chapter 55

It took Mary a total of five minutes to walk from the library to the high school. The school was bigger than she had expected, a 1950's style red brick two-story structure; its face carpeted with vines, except where the name, Sir Ralston High School, poked through. She paused for a second, taking it all in, and then climbed the three long flights of stairs to the entrance. The day was heating up, and she was already sweating by the time she reached the top stair.

Mary walked into the General Office and stepped up to the counter. She was met by a silver-haired woman who was well over six-feet in height. The woman's reading glasses hung on a long gold chain around her neck touching her name tag, which read: Sally Simmons (Office Manager). The office manager was trim, fit, and in control. She glanced down at Mary and did a double take.

Mary was about to introduce herself when the office manager cut her off, jutting the palm of her hand out in front of Mary's face.

"Oh please—just a moment, I'm very good with faces," she said, with an air of self-importance. "You know, I'm sure I recognize you . . . although for some reason I cannot place it. Tell me, what year did you graduate?"

Mary thought for a second. "1981, but I didn't attend

this school."

"Ohhh, I see," the office manager said, sounding a bit disappointed. "And *you* are?"

"My name's Mary Kowalski and I'm here with Josh Ingram, the writer."

"Yes, I've heard *he's* in town." Her voice now taking on a British accent. "News travels at the speed of light around here . . . you know."

Oh, I bet it does, Mary thought.

"I understand he's looking into some unseemly event from our past."

"We're looking into the death of a black girl and the disappearance of her boyfriend and two white youths who all went missing the same weekend," Mary said, matter-of-factly. "It happened in the summer of '68."

"Ohhh you're *assisting* him, are you?" the office manager asked, looking down her long skinny nose.

No, you emaciated giraffe, I'm here to chat with you all fucking day and bathe in your empty-headed drivel, Mary thought, but said, "Yes, it's an honor to be of service to such a great man." The words seemed to come out a little too sharp, and she could see the office manager trying to figure out if she had been offended.

Damn straight you have, yah treetop muncher, Mary thought, and smiled.

"Who could forget that summer," the office manager said, sounding as though she was back in control. "People still talk about it from time to time. Simply awful, those poor kids just up and disappearing. And those poor parents. You never get over such a thing you know . . ." She waited for Mary's reaction.

"No, you don't," Mary said, without emotion.

"But you didn't come here to discuss that, did you?"

"No, not really. I wish it was that straightforward. I was hoping you might be able to provide some information on the boys who went missing."

"Material for Mr. Ingram's new book, no doubt?"

"Something like that."

"Well, let me see . . ." the office manager said, and fell into a deep thinker bullshit look that immediately gnawed on Mary's nerves. "As I recall, the story goes that the two white boys were cousins. Their families, and I must be clear here, their families were said to be fine, churchgoing, God-fearing Christians." She stroked her chin. "Came from poor stock though. Not their fault of course . . ." Then she made an 'oops I just farted' gesture with her face, and said, "You understand what I'm saying."

"Of course." *You fucking moron.*

"As for the other missing boy, the boyfriend. Well, he didn't attend this school. He was colored, and in those days . . . you know, they had their own way of doing things," she said, and again waited for Mary to respond.

Mary remained silent for a moment before saying, "Maybe we could have a look at some of your yearbooks? 1968 in particular."

The office manager frowned and walked over to a long bookshelf where all the school's yearbooks were lined up. "As I recall, the cousins had graduated that year. What a shame. You raise your children, and just when they're ready to take flight . . ." She picked out the 1968 yearbook and flipped to the graduating class. "There they are. Gerald Dennery and Larry Frank, that's them." She handed the yearbook to Mary, pointing to their pictures.

If they weren't cousins they could've been twins, Mary thought.

"Only the Franks still live in town though. The Dennerys moved out a few years after the incident. Never got over their loss, you know."

"Do you mind if I spend awhile going through this?" Mary asked, pointing to the yearbook.

"Be my guest," the office manager said, and checked her watch. "I'll be going for lunch soon. Call me if you need anything else." Then she walked around behind the counter to the farthest desk, and picked up the phone.

Mary leafed through the yearbook, not knowing what else she was looking for. Near the back were photos of the students at various events. A couple of beefy guys with polka dot welder's caps were standing over the hood of a muscle car, with a caption below them that read: *Bring It On.* There were pictures from frosh night, the prom, and photos of kids in the hall posing in odd positions, pointing and laughing.

Mary could feel her heart sinking. She flipped back to the start, to the first of the five classes that made up the graduating class and scanned the students, one by one. When she again reached the page with the two cousins, she stopped. *Whatever happened to you two?* She studied their faces for a moment, then her eye caught the name Elhert in the bottom left-hand corner of the page. *William Elhert . . . well holy shit, you little bugger.* She peered at the office manager who was still on the phone, and then slipped a jackknife out of her pocket, opened it, and cut along the inner spine of the book. She peeled out the page, folded it, and stuck it into her back pocket, then replaced the yearbook into the bookcase, and waved good-bye on her way out.

As she exited the front doors she again felt the heat, and by the time she had reached the bottom flight of stairs, her shirt was soaked and stuck to her like wet toilet paper. At the base of the stairs she stopped and gazed up. The sheriff was standing there, his hands on his hips, a scowl on his face.

"You're with that Ingram feller, aren't ya?" the sheriff asked, but didn't wait for an answer. "I ran into him and his girl this morning. Snooping around just like you. And I told them they best not be poking their noses in other people's business." Then his face turned cold and he pointed his finger at Mary. "You listen up. My message is plain and simple. You and your friends are not welcome here. I want you all out of my town. . . . Are we clear on this?"

"Sheriff . . ." Mary said, and smiled, then curtsied and walked away. She decided to go back to the hotel, search the web and see if she could dig up anything else, and maybe even take a nap.

Chapter 56

Josh chose a table at the front of the bar facing out onto the street. He was on his second red ale when Mary came in and sat down across from him.

"So, where's Rachael?" Mary asked. "She got a *migraine*?"

Josh looked over Mary's shoulder. "There she is now."

Mary closed her eyes and let out a sigh.

Rachael walked up to the table, dressed in blue jeans and a lumberjack shirt.

Though he knew they'd talked on the phone before, Josh made the introductions, and Rachael took her seat.

"Dressing down?" Mary asked Rachael.

"Picked these up in town, thought it wouldn't hurt to blend in a little."

"Yeah okay," Mary said, which sounded like 'whatever'.

Josh stared at Mary, his brow furrowed and asked, "So what'd you find out?"

Mary returned the stare, her eyes saying, *what's your problem?* Then she took a deep breath and proceeded to fill them in on both the library and the high school. How there were two white boys, Gerald Dennery and Larry Frank, who also went missing the same weekend that

Myrna Washington died and Tyrrell Dodge went missing. Of how Myna Washington was found at the foot of Cranston Bridge, a rebar rod though her chest, and of the riots that followed. She told them of the pages torn out of the yearbooks at the library, and then finding an unspoiled yearbook at the high school that showed the cousins were in the same graduating class as William Elhert.

Mary thought for a moment, then said, "All I can say is, O'Henry's pointed us into one real mess. The Elhert family with all its connections, if they're somehow involved, they'd stop at nothing to keep a lid—" Mary's cell rang before she could finish. She held up her hand, then stood up and walked over next to the washrooms. It was Anwar; the power had gone out at Crawlies, the place was rocking and he was freaking out; a slow-pitch ball tournament had ended—and the women were thirsty. She told him to get to the backup generator, then went over the start-up procedure with him. Then she hung up, returned to the table and said that everything was okay. "Just a little power outage at Crawlies, that's all."

It was Josh's turn.

Josh filled Mary in about the man with the scar and the run-in he and Rachael had with Boyd and his dog. And of the Sheriff Stranton and his deputies arriving at Boyd's place and the averted showdown.

"Yeah, I met the sheriff outside the high school. A real charmer," Mary said.

After they ate, Josh could see both Mary and Rachael were bagged. With Rachael needing to catch a flight in the morning, they decided to call it a night.

Chapter 57

Back in his hotel room, Josh poured himself a brandy, then using the four-cup coffee maker supplied by the hotel he doubled up on the packets and made a pot. With a coffee in one hand, a half-full snifter and a cigar in the other, he stepped out onto the balcony, chose the wicker chair closest to the railing, put his feet up and lit the cigar. After a long indulgent drag, and a man-sized gulp of brandy, he laid his head back and said, "Ahhh . . . yesss . . ."

A massive maple had grown in close to the railing; its sturdy trunk illuminated by a 40-watt bulb set high on the wall. As Josh considered the rough, grooved bark and the thick twisted branches, he began to mull things over. *The sheriff is in it, no question about that. The only question is, how deep . . . ? He knows what happened to those kids, but he's smoke screening for someone. Could be for any number of rednecks, a relative or a buddy, or maybe . . . even him. And what's the Elhert family got to do with this? Not much would go down without them being aware. And even if they weren't involved, they would've got wind of what really happened.*

And why did O'Henry lead us to Harland? Is he playing us, sending us on a wild goose chase . . . or did he just needed time to set up his next kill, and this is all a di-

versionary tactic. Josh took another gulp. *Nah, I doubt it . . . there's more to it; this town has its secrets, and it wants to keep them.*

The puzzle kept looping through his brain until it was clear he wasn't coming up with any new material. Then his thoughts crossed over to his father. *What's he doing right now, at this very moment? Is he safe? Is he warm and dry? Ahh goddamnit, has he eaten, is he hungry?* "Ahhh hell!" Josh said, and poured himself another shot. Then his thoughts switched to Arthur and the terror of his friend struggling for his life . . . and then to Arthur in the ground, buried, cold—gone forever.

Josh gave his head a shake and polished off the rest of the brandy in one gulp. After a couple more minutes of trunk gazing, he was no longer contemplating much of anything, and he fell asleep.

The phone rang half a dozen times before he could get to it, so he had to wait for the message. When he saw the red light flashing, he hit play.

"Mr. Ingram, this is the Harland County Hospital. I am calling on behalf of one of our patients. I'm sorry to bother you at this hour, but he says he won't settle down until he has spoken to you, and only you. The patient's name is Harold Beamer. He's on Unit 34. And I should tell you, he isn't doing well. Please hurry."

The hospital was four blocks away and Josh arrived a few minutes later, sweating and short of breath. He pushed open a large glass door and walked over to a nurse who was leaning against the nursing station. The station was flanked by ten rooms running down either side, and he was told Harold was in the second room to the left. Josh poked his head in and saw the attending nurse busy taking Harold's vitals. A number of tubes and gadgets were attached to the old man, while a blue monitor fixed to a stainless steel pole beeped. The nurse played with a few dials, then rolled a small plastic switch on an intravenous line with her thumb, and the beeping stopped.

When she stepped back to leave, Harold's face and protruding ears came into view. He'd been beaten bad. His right eye was swollen shut, and a deep gash ran across his cheek. The gash had been sewn, but blood was seeping out along the stitching. His nose was broken, and his nostrils were stuffed with cotton, his face mapped in dark blotches of purple. The nurse whispered to Josh: "He's asleep now, he's had a rough few hours."

"Is he okay? I mean . . . *will* he be okay?" Josh asked.

"The doctor will be around later," the nurse said, "but I can tell you there's blood in his urine, and his pressure is dropping. It's good you came tonight." She put her hand on Josh's arm to comfort him. "I was the one who called you. Harold said he had to speak with you and no one else. Are you a relative?"

"An acquaintance," Josh said.

The nurse raised a questioning eyebrow.

"Is he able to talk?"

The nurse took a moment to respond. "His meds will start to wear off in the next hour or so, and his pain will return. He'll wake up then."

Josh thanked her and she left the room. He went down to the hospital restaurant in the basement and bought a coffee and a chocolate chip muffin, then stopped at the gift shop on the main floor and picked up a copy of The Harland Review. Catching the elevator to the third floor he returned to Harold's room. Almost two hours had gone by, and the sun was up and peeking over a neighboring roof line when Harold woke up. His one good eye opened to a mere slit. He rolled his head to the side to see Josh sitting beside him, and whispered, "I am glad you came."

"Who did this to you?" Josh asked, feeling an undercurrent of anger rising within him.

"The sheriff . . . and his deputies," Harold murmured. He coughed once, and a shot of pain racked his body. "Someone snitched me out," he said, talking through the pain. "Must've seen us in the alley. . . . Sheriff's a bad man. Wanted to teach me a lesson . . . not be shooting my mouth off and telling tales out of school . . ." He started drawing short, rapid breaths. "The doctor says I'm not doing so well, which means I might not make it. At least that's how I figure it." He moved his hand to his side, a couple of inches below his ribcage, and winced. "I got some information for you," he said, his eyes oily with despair.

"I'm listening," Josh said, as a wave of guilt rushed over him. *If not for me, the old guy would be dreaming of his next piece of pie, not flat out on this hospital bed.*

"I lied to you before . . . and I'm sorry about that," Harold said. "The man with the scar, he don't have a scar and his name isn't Albert . . . but I got his real name for you . . ."

Harold attempted to smile, then shifted his position and tried to get comfortable. "The man's name is Levi

Weiner. He's a friend of mine. He lives past Clinton Corner, about a mile-and-a-half, heading north. . . . He was under the bridge the night it happened."

"Can you tell me what happened?"

Harold swallowed. "He was there. Levi saw it. That black girl getting killed. He saw it all. Those two cousins, they were there too, before they all went missing."

"Okay . . . but, how does the sheriff fit into all this?"

"Not sure . . . back when it happened, the sheriff, he was just a deputy. He came around and talked to everyone, especially those that lived close to the bridge. . . . He made it clear as a bell, that if we knew anything, we were never to talk about it to nobody. And we all knew if we did, he'd be back and it weren't gonna be pleasant."

Josh thought for a moment. "You think Levi would be around if I was to pay him a visit?"

"Levi . . . he's always around. You can tell him I sent ya—" A wave of pain hit harder this time. Harold reached for his nightgown sleeve, trying to grab the call button, but his reflexes were off. Josh lifted Harold's arm, careful not to unhook anything, and found the button. He squeezed it and a small yellow light lit up on the headboard in the shape of a bell. "Thanks," Harold said.

"Thank you, Harold," Josh said, and a lump formed in his throat.

As Josh walked back to the hotel, his cell vibrated, it was Rachael. She had just finished talking to Kingsley. Her tone sounded low-keyed like she'd been red-carpeted. Kingsley was wearing her down. He told her about Levi

Weiner, and hoped to hear a glimmer of hope return to her voice. It wasn't happening, she was losing her confidence. A minute later, he rounded the last corner and saw Rachael standing under the shade of the hotel veranda, already clicking away on her cell. As he walked through the gate and climbed the steps she glanced up.

"Mary will be here in a minute. Can we give you a lift to the airport?" he asked.

"No, it's okay, a cab is on its way," she said, and sighed, slipping her cell into her pocket. "Jesus, Josh, I don't know if I'm healthy enough for office politics. Kingsley is such an ass. Sometimes I wish I was strictly back in the field, doing something useful, not playing these bureaucratic mind games."

Josh saw the cab pulling up. "Hey, you can't let him screw with your confidence, it's what he wants. Mary and I will finish up and be done here, tomorrow at the latest. Then I'll be on the next fight back to New York. Something *will* break, it's just a matter of time." He could see he wasn't making much of a dent and asked, "You okay?"

Rachael did her best to smile and said, "Yeah sure, I'm fine." Then she slipped into the cab. As the cab pulled away, a feeling of dread came over him, as though he may never see her again. *Ahhh man, stop thinking that way . . .*

He turned and saw Mary standing by the car, watching him and holding two coffees and what looked like a bag of pastries.

Chapter 58

Josh had finished most of his coffee and pounded down two glazed cinnamon rolls before they reached Clinton Corner. Passing by Boyd's place, he saw no sign of either Boyd or his dog. A half-mile farther along they crossed Cranston Bridge, then drove another mile-and-a-half before turning into a yard and cutting the engine. In front of them sat a doublewide trailer, a white and green two-tone job, nestled in a thicket of willow trees. The green paint had faded over the years, now speckled with bits of white seeping through. Its two side windows were wide open, and the ledges were blotched with black rot.

A short round man wearing too tight and dirty blue jeans was on the front porch. He had his back to them, bent over a bicycle, and furnished a crack in his ass that would make a room full of proctologists salivate. The man sneaked a peek under his arm, his eyes resting for a moment on Mary. He finished tightening a nut on the bicycle with a quarter-inch wrench, and then straightened himself up.

"We are looking for a man called Levi Weiner," Josh said.

"Why would you be doing that?" the man asked. He had a big, pie face, dime-sized eyes and an expansive mouth.

"We were told he might be able to help us," Mary said.

"He might be, depends on what you'd be asking about," the man said, and a wide grin spread across his face. "Aw shucks, I'm Levi . . . I guess you might of figured that out already . . . am I right? Course I am."

Mary shot Josh a questioning glance.

"Look around," Levi said. "This is not what one would call a densely populated neighborhood. In this here square mile, the population is two, that'd be me and that shit-head Boyd. Not many people want to talk to Boyd so much, so the way I see it, you're wanting to talk to me. Am I right? Course I'm right." Then he yanked his pants up, revealing his bare ankles. "And my guess is, you want to talk about my old buddy Harold . . . I got a call, hear he was hurt real bad." Levi's eyes grew moist, and a flash of anger sparked in them. "Sheriff Stranton—the motherfucker's brain is inversely proportional to the size of his gut. Mean as a tax collector and stupid as lead pipe. And that's one dynamite combination. Am I right? Course I'm right."

He paused and squeezed his hands together. "But where are my manners?" he said, and then padded off into the trailer, coming out a few seconds later with a brown gallon jug and a stack of plastic, colored cups. "You'll have to forgive the stemware, but the maid has the day off . . ." He chuckled.

He gave Mary a wink, then poured a couple of ounces of moonshine into each cup, passing one to her and one to Josh. He raised his cup to make a toast. "To old friends . . . may they live forever." Then he drained his glass and slammed it on the porch rail. "Oooeee!"

It was clear to Josh they were to follow Levi's lead, so he downed the contents of his cup in one gulp, instantly setting his throat on fire and turning his face a fire hydrant red. He gasped a few times, cleared his throat and turned to Mary, and smiled an innocent, schoolboy smile. She smirked at him and pursed her lips, then raised her orange plastic cup to her mouth. She took a long sip—then began to hit her thigh with her fist, and said in a deep, wheezy voice, as if she had just inhaled some lemon juice, *"It's soooo guud."*

Levi grinned, then walked to the other end of the porch and grabbed a small stack of white plastic chairs. Once they were all seated, he asked, "So, what is it you want to know?"

"I was with Harold at the hospital last night," Josh said. "He says you might be able to help us out. Back in the summer of '68, a teenage girl fell to her death at Cranston Bridge. Some say it was murder. Some say not. Harold told me you knew what happened that night, because you were there."

"Ohhh . . ." Levi said, and poured himself and Josh another generous shot. "That summer, such a gong show. You'd never seen such a ruckus. Copters buzzing overhead, people lined up, hundreds of them combing the woods. Little aluminum boats bobbing around in the swamp, sparkling in the sun. Always kinda stuck in my head that they were like diamonds. . . . Yeah, that black girl was murdered all right, I don't care what anyone says. Then there was that black boy, and them two white kids . . . they just up and disappeared. They're all dead too, I reckon."

"The two white boys, you think they were killed as

well?" Mary asked.

"Hell, those white boys weren't from rich families. Sad to say, but when the poor go missing they ain't going on some great adventure. They'd be sure as hell dead. That's what I say, anyway."

"So, there were four of them involved?" Mary asked. "The girl, her boyfriend, and the two white boys?"

"That'd be four all right. That is, the ones that either disappeared or died." Levi nodded to Josh. "Don't let this one slip away, she's a keeper. A natural born mathematician."

"So, how many others were there?" Mary continued, letting Levi's attempt at wit go over her head. "The ones that didn't disappear or die?"

"Well, there were two *ahhzers*." He stopped. "Sorry . . ." Levi said, looking embarrassed. "Damn shine makes my lips numb sometimes." He pursed his lips in and out a number of times, as though he was sucking on a pacifier. After a minute, maybe more, he stopped with his lip routine and looked to Mary.

"So, you're saying there were two *ahhzers*?" Mary asked, and grinned.

"Oh, you got a lip on ya, don't ya girl? Am I right? Course I'm right. Bet you're gonna give me your number, aren't ya?" He grinned, raising one eyebrow.

"Oh for Christ's sake Levi, just answer the question," Josh said. "Were . . . there . . . two *ahhzers*?" Then he and Mary laughed. A second later, Levi joined in.

After the laughter died down, Levi said, his voice slow and deliberate, "The two *others* . . . well, they were never mentioned in the press." Then he went quiet, as though that was all he had to say.

"Levi, you were under the bridge when the girl was killed, you must remember more," Mary said.

Levi poured himself another shot, then tilted the jug to her. She declined, but Josh accepted. Mary turned to Josh, and frowned, as if to say, *what are you doing?*

"Yeah, well I never told anybody the whole story, except Harold, and he was sworn to keep a lid on it," Levi said. "I guess what happened to him yesterday changed his view of things." He reached over and gave the bicycle wheel a spin. "You know, if I were to say anything to you, the sheriff and his deputies would want to drop by and pay their regards."

"I don't see any need for this to go any further than the three of us," Mary said, and nodded to Josh.

"We'll keep your name out of it," Josh said.

"I hope so," Levi said, and took notice of their car. "Any chance you could move your vehicle around back of the house, so as not to draw attention?"

When Josh returned to the porch and sat down, Levi was staring at the brown jug . . . then he started. "It was late in the day and it was a hot day, as I recall. I was under the bridge, trying to cool down, when these two black kids come along, crossing on foot. I wasn't able to see so good, but I could hear most of it. They were having a lover's quarrel, and Tyrrell—that's the girl's boyfriend—was in trouble and losing ground fast. He wanted her to come for dinner. She took offense to that, and told him something about his momma not liking her.

"I wanted to get a better view, so I climbed a bit and

got myself a better spot under the bridge. Didn't do me much good though, cause that's when a big old car drove onto the bridge. It followed them kids all the way to the other end, almost hit them, and that's when the girl hurt her ankle. Then the doors on the car swung open and four boys climbed out onto the bridge deck, drinking beer, smoking cigarettes, and laughing.

"I could tell them black kids were scared, and they had a right to be. It was the sixties, and being alone out here with a bunch of drunk white boys, well, that was not a fitting situation, no sir. Myrna, that'd be the girl, she wanted to get out of there in the worst way. Not Tyrrell though, he seemed to be offended and wouldn't run. Not that they'd get that far, on account of her ankle.

"Well, them boys then formed a half-circle around the black kids, and they were all still laughing when Myrna yelled at them.

"Whatever she told them, the tallest boy didn't seem to take to it, and he grabbed her chin and turned her face toward him. Tyrrell, he shouted and went to throw a punch, but the other boys held him back.

"That's when the tall boy grabbed Myrna by the waist and brought her in close. I could see her squirming and twisting, trying to get free. Then he reached down and hoisted her dress up, and ran his hand up her thigh. That's when Myrna must've kneed the boy, cause he buckled up faster than a three dollar pup tent. Then she turned and started to climb one of those bridge spans. She'd made it clear to the second level when the tall boy caught up to her and latched onto her ankle.

"Tyrrell, well he tried to break free, but the other boys would have none of that and put the boots to him good. After that he didn't move, he just laid there all curled up like a salted leech.

"And Myrna, well she just kept holding tight to that beam, squeezing her thighs, while that boy kept trying to pull her free. Then the boy stopped, and he put his hand to his nose, like he was smelling it. A second later, I heard him yell out, "Boys . . . she's pissing herself."

"That's when Myrna grabbed hold of a crossbeam barely within her reach, first one arm then the other. It was a huge mistake, cause all she did was hang there, dangling off the bridge. She tried to swing her legs back and forth so she could get a hold of the next beam. The poor girl, it didn't do her any good.

"By the time Tyrrell got to his feet, all he saw was his girl hanging from the side of the bridge. "Myrna!" I heard him call out.

"That's when it happened. First one of her hands let go and then the other, and then she dropped down the side of the bridge, past the tall boy, past the bridge deck, down to the foot of the bridge. She fell in silence, at least that's what it seemed like at the time, but when she reached the bottom, there came this slicing sound—and a heavy thud.

"Next I knew, Tyrrell was standing at the side of the bridge, screaming some *God awful* sound I'll never forget. Then he jumped over the guardrail and climbed down toward her, with them white boys all coming after him.

"When they had all run off into the forest chasing after Tyrrell, I went and checked on the girl. It was a gruesome sight. There was a rebar rod sticking straight out of her chest, and a puddle of blood surrounding it." Levi stopped, and shook his head.

"Did you recognize any of the boys from the car?" Mary asked.

"No. I wish I had've, but as I said, I was too far away . . . I would've loved to nail their asses to the wall, that's for sure. . . . I did get one thing though. A first name, that is. I heard it when one of them screamed it out. The name was Larry. Later, when I saw the name in the paper, I put two and two together and figured he had to be one of the missing cousins."

Josh was about to ask him why he didn't go to the police and then he remembered the sheriff.

"That's about all I can recall. I wish I had more, but it was a long time ago." Levi's focus turned to Josh. "Do you think Harold's gonna be okay?"

Another wave of guilt hit, and Josh swallowed. "I hope so."

After a few more minutes of probing, it was clear Levi was done, and Josh and Mary got up to leave. Josh shook Levi's hand before saying, "If anything else comes to mind, anything at all, call me." He handed Levi one of Rachael's cards with his number on the back.

On the way back to town, neither Josh nor Mary said a word. When they turned onto Main Street, Josh said, "I have a couple more leads I wanna follow."

"The Franks?"

"Yeah them and . . ."

"And . . . and what?"

Josh checked his watch. "You wanna stop for a bite to eat?"

"You're not going to tell me, are you?" Mary asked, studying him.

"That's right. I'm not going to tell you."

"Plausible deniability . . . ! God, Josh, you're not above the law, you know that. The sheriff would love to make an example out of you."

Josh's face was blank, he didn't respond. He had already tuned her out. He was planning his next move.

Chapter 59

It was late afternoon by the time Josh and Mary located the last member of the Frank family still living in town.

Happy Horizons Extended Care Facility had come about through government grants and private capital, and stank of boiled food and disinfectant. Bureaucrats and businessmen loved the place. It was cheaper than keeping the infirm and elderly in hospitals, and someone could still make a buck. Everyone loved Happy Horizons except the poor souls who had to live there.

Lillian Frank was in room 204.

Josh and Mary were told Lillian's unit was down the hall at the end, on the right, three doors past the open dining room. The fluorescent lights flickered as they made their way down the corridor, adding a perverse disco vibe to an already dismal atmosphere. In the kitchen, vegetables were bubbling in huge stainless steel pots, while red heat lamps glowed, keeping a pile of pork chops warm.

As they passed the dining room, Josh noticed a large round table fringed with gray-faced women. They all turned their heads and stared, and Josh felt his heart sink.

An aide was leaving Lillian's room as they arrived. She told them that Lillian was having a good day, but they shouldn't expect too much. Josh and Mary stepped in to see Lillian sitting by herself, tapping her fingers on a remote control. The black-and-white TV in front of her was off.

"Hello Lillian," Mary said.

Lillian did not respond.

Josh noticed Lillian's name tag, pinned to her blouse. A pink cartoon crocodile with a happy face had been stamped on either side of her name. The name tag reminded him of the first time he'd been called about his father. His father was in a hospital, and a woman who was part of hospital maintenance, a room cleaner, wore a similar name tag. She showed Josh into a room where his father was face down over a toilet. When his father raised his head and saw his son, a look of shame crossed his father's face, and he slid into a corner—his knees drawn to his chest. Josh remembered he hadn't seen a broken man. He'd seen a man who had taken him fishing and camping. A man who had shown him how to shake a hand, firm, like a man is supposed to. A man who got excited when his son came to visit, if only to sit and talk and laugh . . .

Mary spoke up, "Lillian, my name is Mary and this is Josh, and we've come to ask you a few questions. About your grandson, Larry."

Lillian blinked and turned to look at them.

"Can you tell us anything about his disappearance?" Mary asked, keeping her tone soft.

Lillian averted her gaze, staring off to the wall behind them, her eyes devoid of expression.

Ahh man, Josh thought. *She has nothing to live for.* He wanted to turn and leave, but instead, he said, "We understand Larry was never found. Could you tell us anything about that summer?"

Lillian continued to stare off at the wall, her hands now trembling on her lap.

Josh glanced at Mary and said, "Lillian, we know this is difficult for you, but we need you to focus. Can you remember anything about that summer your grandson, Larry, disappeared? Anything at all?"

Lillian's eyes teared up and she motioned with her hand for Josh to come closer. Then she whispered, "There are two laws . . . always been that way . . ." Then a tear ran down her cheek and she started to shake.

Mary sat down beside Lillian and put her arm around her.

Lillian remained silent, not another word was spoken.

A minute later, the aide came into the room and told them Lillian needed her rest.

As they left the building, Mary turned to Josh. "Now what?"

"There's one more lead I have to follow . . ."

"Yes, I know," Mary said. "And I'm coming with you—end of discussion."

Chapter 60

As they eased up to the front gate of George Elhert's estate, Josh lowered his window. The sentry station was dark and vacant, the gate closed. Josh climbed out, rolled one side of the gate open, and got back in the car.

Webbed veins of an electrical storm flashed on the horizon, and in the distance a muted roar rumbled across the sky.

"Storm's headed this way," Mary said.

"Uh-huh," Josh replied, as he scanned the area for electronic surveillance. All he saw was a single video camera, facing up into the sky, out of commission. As he dropped the car into gear and passed through the gate, another flash, closer this time, crossed the sky, and he caught a glimpse of the manor jutting out above the trees.

They were nearing the halfway mark when it occurred to him that, even though George Elhert had not lived here for years, the grounds were in perfect condition, manicured, trimmed, everything immaculate.

Mary glanced over at Josh. "Why is it that rich people, especially rich politicians, can go on and on about being one of 'the people' when they live in these obscene mansions? All while *the people* have to scrape out a shitty living on a stinking minimum wage. You know, it just pisses me off. . . . And, lordy lordy, if it isn't these rich bastards who are the first to call it outrageous should some poor schmucks want to raise the minimum wage a nickel. The rich are not of the people, they're privileged parasites that live off the toil of the downtrodden and disadvantaged."

Josh turned to Mary, and said, "Seat belt a little tight?"

"Fuck off," Mary said.

At the east side of the manor Josh saw a small service road, its entrance almost hidden by thirty-foot pyramid cedars set on either side. He rolled the car through the cedars, circled around back, and stopped in front of a pair of cellar doors at the back of the house.

He killed the engine. It was dark, the sun had set and the moon was hidden behind the advancing storm clouds.

"We'll go in through the cellar, less chance of tripping an alarm," Josh said.

Mary pulled a penlight from her purse and passed it to him. Josh clenched it in his front teeth, then bent down and gave the cellar door handles a hard tug. They didn't budge, then he saw why; an iron padlock was attached to the top of each door. He went back to the car, rummaged around in the trunk and returned with a tire iron. He inserted it into one of the padlocks, twisted hard, and the lock snapped open.

He led the way in, down a set of wooden stairs peppered in rat and bat shit. The air was dank, the stone walls wet and weeping. *Nice place,* he thought, as he ducked his head under a beam.

"Josh, I'm not so sure about this," Mary said. "This place has gotta be crawling with spiders."

Josh grabbed Mary's hand and they slipped between

two dust-covered boilers. One had a copper plaque on it that read, Beaver and Co. 1898. Sitting across from the boilers were three large, empty coal bins. Without warning, the penlight flickered and the room descended into utter darkness. Josh's gut instantly knotted. He tapped the penlight on the palm of his hand; at first it just blinked on and off, then stayed on—and he let out a sigh of relief. They pushed deeper into the cellar, until they came to an aluminum ladder and a bucket of tools blocking a door. He moved the ladder to the side, and saw a shiny, three-inch padlock on the door. He puffed out a short, forced breath, then fished around in the bucket and pulled out a twelve-inch screwdriver. He inserted it into the padlock and gave it a twist. The lock held tight, but the screws holding the metal clasp were set in rotted wood and the clasp gave way.

They entered into a wide set of stairs that turned sharp near the bottom, and then led straight up into the kitchen. Josh scanned the kitchen with the penlight. A matching pair of built-in wall ovens were on one wall, and a row of country sinks were set below windows facing out into the backyard. The narrow beam of the penlight caught a cupboard door that had been left ajar, and on the counter an open bag of flour had tipped over. A flash of lightning lit up the kitchen, and Josh spotted a light switch.

About half the lights in the kitchen were working, including a line of fluorescents under the cupboards, which flickered for a few seconds before growing into a full glow. That's when they heard it. The distinct, sharp beeping of a security alarm counting down.

"Shit!" Josh said.

"Jesus Christ . . . ! Josh, we gotta get the hell out of

here."

"Yeah, all right Mary," Josh said, and took a second to collect his thoughts, his adrenaline pumping. "Look, I need you to wait for me in the car with the engine running—but be ready to fly when I come out."

Mary stared at him, looking as if she was deciding what she should do, then she turned and made her way out the back door.

Josh ran down a long hallway that spilt into the main foyer. He located another light switch and again about half of them came on, including a massive candle chandelier hanging overhead. The foyer, paneled in oak, was circular in design and had numerous doors leading into different rooms. A spiral staircase rose from the center of the foyer to the second floor.

Josh knew he had about ninety seconds, tops, before the call went out to the security firm, and another five or six minutes before the sheriff's men would arrive. He dashed from room to room and had covered a third of them when he entered the library.

The room seemed familiar, and then it dawned on him. It was an exact duplicate of Elhert's library in New York. Same bookshelves, same stone fireplace, same oak desk. The only thing different was an octagonal crystal display cabinet set in the center of the room.

As he stepped near the case a light came on inside, illuminating a single hardback displayed on a copper bookstand. He stared at it and tried to remember. *What was it Walter said? Something about the picture always being in plain sight.* He tried the case, it was locked. With his elbow, he punched out a glass pane, shattering it, then reached in and lifted the book out of its cradle. He flipped through the pages, and quickly checked it over, then turned it upside-down and shook it. Nothing. Suddenly—the siren went off—blaring, jarring, overwhelming.

Josh stood there for a moment studying the cabinet, blocking out the noise as best he could, when he noticed the bookstand's base was made of a darker wood than that of the cabinet. He rushed to the desk and rifled through the drawers before returning with a letter opener. He stuck the knife edge between the darker wood and the cabinet, prying until the base popped up. He lifted the base out to find lying below, a photograph, cut in half, of three boys in front of a weigh scale. Josh examined it for a second, the siren still screaming. Something wasn't right. Then he did a double take. The black kid in the middle wasn't jumping, as the bottom half of the photo had suggested. The kid had something stuck in his chest holding him up. *What the . . .* Then his eyes shifted back to the scale. "Shit, they're weighing him." Josh stared at the photo for a few seconds, then folded it and slid it into his pocket.

Close to five minutes had elapsed when Josh burst out the back door. He was running full tilt across the porch when he tripped over a pipe wrench. He cleared the edge of the porch and landed on his back. He gazed up and saw the sheriff's face, just as a baseball bat cracked across his chest.

Chapter 61

Josh came to with his hands cuffed behind his back, lying on his side, his face in the dirt. He rolled his free eye to the side and saw Mary lying a few feet away. Startled, he took a short puff of air into his lungs and held it. Mary's eyes were closed, streaks of blood ran down from her hairline, and her face was lumped with huge welts. *God, she's barely recognizable. . . .* Then he saw her take a breath—and he exhaled.

The sound of shovels slicing into the earth was coming from behind him. As he rolled over to see, pain radiated across his ribcage so acutely he had to hold his breath to keep from screaming. He saw the sheriff's deputies standing hip deep in the ground. They were digging a hole, a large hole, and they were working flat out, wasting no time. The cruiser's headlights were on them; their faces were wet with sweat, and steam-like vapors were rising off their shirts. They looked tired and dirty, and Josh could tell they were almost finished.

Josh tugged on the cuffs, to see if there was any give, but they were on tight and only cut in deeper. He'd broken free of police handcuffs before . . . but under ideal conditions, in a classroom setting, and not with his hands behind his back. But if he could find a short length of wire, a pin or a metal clip, he knew he'd at least have a chance. He glanced around, scanning for anything usable. There was nothing. He thought about the tongue of his belt buckle, but given his predicament that was an impossibility.

The sheriff said something to his men then went around to the back of his cruiser.

Josh rolled over to face Mary, and another shot of pain ran through him. He took a few deep breaths and tried to collect himself. He needed to think . . . he needed to find a solution.

Despair was starting to creep its way in, tightening down hard on his thoughts, when he caught a glimpse of something; a small, thin object was dangling from a strand of her hair. Mary shifted her head an inch and whatever it was began to swing back and forth. It was black and had a shine to it. A piece of rotten straw? An insect? He couldn't tell. He wanted to try to wake her but could not take the chance. He wasn't even sure she would awake. Then it registered—*a bobby pin.*

Josh rolled back over to see Sheriff Stranton still standing behind the cruiser. After about a minute, the sheriff twisted his torso and looked over in their direction. Josh shut his eyes, held them closed for a few seconds, then peered out. The sheriff seemed to be reading a message on his cell, his lips tightly pressed together. After punching in what had to be a text message he turned back to his deputies. He told them to get their asses in gear and finish up. Josh calculated he had maybe a minute before the sheriff would look again in their direction.

A full minute had gone by and the sheriff turned toward them. Josh clamped his eyes shut and smiled to himself. His window of opportunity had been confirmed.

When Josh looked again the sheriff had turned and was facing his men. *Time to act,* Josh thought—sixty seconds. He rolled over a full three hundred and sixty degrees. Another sharp pain shot through his ribs as he came to a rest with his back touching Mary. His hands could feel her blouse, her breasts. Forty-five seconds. He wormed his body up, until his hand touched her nose. She didn't flinch. He walked his fingers over her face to her ear, like a giant spider, and there it was. His index finger touched the pin—and then it was gone. Fifteen seconds. He twisted his body and raked his fingers through the grass. Nothing. He tried again, combing the grass, and finally felt it. He pinched the pin between his index finger and thumb, then shifted it into his hand and closed his fist. Five seconds. *Oh shit . . . !* He pulled his legs up and rolled back into his original position, just as the sheriff was turning in his direction. Josh closed his eyes and froze. He waited another few seconds, nothing, only the sound of shovels cutting the earth. Then the sheriff told his men to wrap it up.

Josh maneuvered the bobby pin in his hands, spreading it open until it was nearly straight. With the index finger and thumb of one hand, he inserted the pin into the opposite handcuff, sliding it up between the cuff's teeth while applying pressure on the release mechanism. The cuff came loose and opened. He was ready.

Chapter 62

"Get over here and stand the woman up," Sheriff Stranton called out to his deputies. They both looked back in his direction, then put down their shovels and clomped over.

Reaching down, they grabbed Mary by her arms and lifted her to her feet. She was limp and hung on their hands, her head tipped forward. The deputies looked to their boss.

"Now, dump the bitch in the hole."

The deputies hesitated.

"Hurry the fuck up, while I watch this asshole."

Josh could hear Mary being dragged across the grass. One of the deputies made a guttural sound, a grunt, and a moment later there came a wet thud as her body landed in the grave's moist clay.

"Sheriff, ya want me to put a bullet in her?" the younger deputy asked.

Oh Christ! Josh thought, *I've waited too long.*

The sheriff scratched his ass for a second, then shook his head. "Hell no, she might one day get dug up. Don't want one of our bullets in her skull. Don't matter none, cause she ain't coming out of that hole alive. Now haul your asses over here and stand this sorry son-of-a-bitch up."

Josh willed his body to stay loose. He knew the timing of his decision to act, would decide Mary's fate. He had to hold off, and yet his mind screamed for revenge. So he swallowed and allowed the deputies to pull him to his feet, same as they did with Mary. This time, however, the work was harder, a lot harder, because they were now holding onto a 212 pound dead weight that readily accepted gravity.

The sheriff rubbed his face with his hands, holding them there for a moment. Then he grabbed a handful of Josh's hair and yanked his head up. "This fucker's gotta see it coming. Carson, give me your belt."

"Belt?" Carson asked, a puzzled look on his face. "What for?"

"Shut your pie hole son, and give me your goddamned belt."

The deputy frowned, then with one hand removed his belt and passed it over.

The sheriff played with it, running it through his fingers. The belt was a half-inch thick and made of soft leather. "Yeah, this will do," he said, and then slipped it over Josh's head, cinching it up tight around his neck.

"Now, watch this fucker beg for mercy," the sheriff said, then drew his gun and raised it high above his head. He held it there for a second, then brought the gun down fast—

Josh swung his hand out grabbing the sheriff's wrist, and the sheriff's eyes opened wide. Then Josh wrenched the sheriff's arm around his back and twisted his elbow until he heard him scream. Ripping the gun from the sheriff's hand, he jammed the barrel into the back of the sheriff's head, and cocked the gun.

The deputies stopped in their tracks, a look of disbelief on their faces.

Josh said, "Now gentlemen, using your index finger and thumb, carefully pick your gun out of its holster and drop it to the ground. Then back away, three full steps."

They hesitated and appeared confused. Josh rammed the gun into the soft flesh at the base of the sheriff's skull.

"Do as he says!" the sheriff cried out.

The deputies glanced at each other, then the older one slowly reached into his holster and dropped his gun to the ground. A moment later the other followed his lead. Then they both stepped back, three full steps.

"Now, go over by the grave," Josh said, eyeing the hole in the ground.

The deputies hesitated, again exchanging glances.

Josh repositioned the gun's barrel next to the sheriff's ear and fired a shot.

"Ahh God DAMN, my fuckin' ear!" the sheriff screamed.

The two deputies just stood there, dazed.

"*Do it* for Christ's sake!" the sheriff cried. "Just do it!"

The trance broke. And the deputies angled their way to the grave, their sight never leaving their boss.

"Now gentlemen," Josh said, in a calm voice. "I want you to lift my friend out of the grave. And then I want you to lay her on the ground by that tree . . . over there." He pointed in the direction of a maple some twenty feet away. "And be gentle with her . . ."

The deputies' expressions changed and they appeared relieved, as though they'd just received a pardon from the governor.

"What's that?" Josh asked. "Did you boys think I was

going to harm you?"

Neither one of them spoke, just glanced at each other before they dropped down into the hole. They lifted Mary's body out and carefully laid her down on the grass near the lip of the grave. As the deputies were crawling out of the grave and their bellies were rubbing on the damp earth, Josh looked at Mary's disfigured face, and a rage crackled in his brain. He nodded to the deputies, as if to say, a job well done—then smashed the butt of the gun against the back of the sheriff's head. The sheriff dropped to his knees, stunned, falling flat on his face. Then, in one clean motion, Josh raised the gun and squeezed off a round, putting a bullet through the skull of the younger deputy. Then he turned and caught the other deputy in the neck, blowing out a chunk of his esophagus, the force of the blow throwing him back into the grave.

Josh put his foot on the sheriff's shoulder and saw the back of his head was matted with blood. He glanced back at the grave, and saw the deputy with the neck wound had hoisted himself halfway out of the hole, his hand held tight to his neck. Josh stepped around the sheriff, walked over to the deputy, and field goal kicked him under the chin, crushing his jaw and tossing him back into the grave. As Josh looked down into the grave, he tilted his head; the deputy was on his back and had one hand held up, pleading. Josh pointed the gun and squeezed the trigger, planting a single round into the deputy's chest.

"You're gonna fry in hell for this!" the sheriff cried out, attempting to get to his feet.

Josh turned and said, "What makes you think . . . you're not already checked in?" Then he walked back to the sheriff, who had made it to one knee, and placed the barrel of the gun to the sheriff's forehead and pulled the trigger. Then he dragged the sheriff to the edge of the grave, wiped down the gun, put it into the sheriff's hand, clamping it to ensure good contact, then fired another round into the air. Then he dumped the sheriff and the younger deputy into the grave, tossing the gun in after them.

Josh loaded Mary into the passenger-seat of the sheriff's cruiser and strapped her in. A minute later the cruiser slipped through the tall cedars and into the backyard of the governor's mansion. He transferred Mary to the rental car, then gunned it for the hospital.

Chapter 63

A young doctor with shoulder-length blond hair, a stethoscope slung around his neck and wearing unlaced high-top sneakers, entered Mary's room. He had a set of X-ray films in his hand and said to Josh, "The X-rays look okay. There's no evidence of fractures." The doctor leaned in close to Mary and said in a raised voice, "Someone really went to work on you, Mary. You're lucky nothing more serious was damaged."

Mary blinked her eyes once in unison. Her head was wrapped in white bandages. Below each eye and her bottom lip blood had seeped through the gauze, giving her a ghoulish look.

The doctor turned back to Josh. "We need to keep her here for observation. The lump on her forehead is really quite large. This sort of blow to the skull can often cause internal swelling. . . . At present, she's stable. If there are no complications in the next twenty-four hours, she should be out of the woods. She'll need to stay a few more days after that, just to be safe."

"So, she'll be all right?" Josh asked.

"We'll take good care of her."

The door opened behind Josh, and Mary's eyes brightened. Josh turned to see a tall, thin, stooped woman standing in the doorway.

Mary motioned with the tips of her fingers for Josh to

come closer. He leaned over and put his ear to her lips. "Josh, this is a friend of mine," she whispered, and slid her gaze to the woman.

The woman reached out to shake Josh's hand. Her hands were twisted, her knuckles swollen. She introduced herself as Lizzy, the town's librarian.

"You've known Mary long?" Josh asked.

"No, we just met today. At the library," Lizzy said, now looking embarrassed that she'd dropped by.

"You must've made quite an impression. Mary's not one to make friends fast."

A smile broke out on Lizzy's face. "I volunteer here at the hospital. I like go around and talk to those that are stuck here for long stretches."

Mary tapped her index finger on Josh's arm, and said in a hushed tone, "I meant to tell you . . . I found a—" Then her eyes rolled up in her head. Suddenly, all the buzzers and chimes in the room went off. A moment later a crash cart team flung open the door, the lead physician ordering Josh and Lizzy to wait outside.

It was close to an hour later when the doctor emerged from the room. "She's out of trouble for now. But unfortunately she's suffered a stroke."

The word *stroke* rang in Josh's ears, and he sat back down.

"The blow to her head must have jarred her brain, which likely caused a blood clot to form, resulting in a blockage."

"So, she'll recover?" Josh asked.

"A positive thing about strokes these days, if there is such a thing, is that if you get to the clot fast, the damage can be minimal. Not a guarantee mind you, although if you're going to have a stroke, there is no better place to be than in a hospital." The doctor checked his pager.

"What about another stroke?" Josh asked.

"The drugs we've put her on should prevent another blood clot," the doctor said, and then left the room.

Lizzy patted Josh on the shoulder, and said she would fetch them something to drink. A couple of minutes later a nurse came out of Mary's room, clipboard in hand, and told Josh it would be all right to go in. The nurse stopped him at the door, handing him a folded piece of paper. "I don't know what to make of this. We found it in her back pocket."

Josh was unfolding the paper as Lizzy walked up.

"Oh, there they are," Lizzy said, her voice climbing. "That's it."

"What?"

"The missing page to the yearbook. Mary and I were going through the high school yearbooks, looking for the two white boys that went missing in the summer of '68. And there they are." She pointed to Gerald Dennery and Larry Frank.

"Yeah okay," Josh said, studying the boys' faces, his mind still thinking about Mary, when his eye caught the name William Elhert below his picture on the bottom corner of the page.

Josh's heart started to pound. Reaching into his breast pocket he pulled out the half photo of the three youths and held it up to the yearbook page—the white boy standing to the left of the dead black kid was William Elhert. "It's him. It's Elhert. An exact match." His gaze shifted to the other white boy. "Huh . . . Larry Frank," he said, pointing to the yearbook picture. He paused and frowned, *and the dead black boy . . . ah hell . . . Tyrrell Dodge, the missing boyfriend.*

He stepped over to the window to examine the half photo in better light. While both William Elhert and Larry Frank were smiling, their smiles seemed out of place. There was a sadness about them. Then it hit him. It wasn't sadness, it was fear. But fear of what? Fear for what they'd done? Or were they frightened by something else?

Then he thought of Rachael. "Oh God, I have to warn her."

"Warn who?" Lizzy asked.

"No time to explain," Josh said, and touched Lizzy's arm.

Lizzy smiled. "Do what you have to do, it's okay . . . I'll watch over Mary."

Josh nodded, then he ran out to the ward desk, grabbed a landline and dialed Rachael's number, and got her answering service. He paused and thought for a moment, then spotted a photocopier behind the desk, made a copy of the half photo and the yearbook page, grabbed a large envelope from the desk, and slid the originals into it. Then he folded the copies and stuffed them into his breast pocket.

Josh pushed open the front doors of the hospital and made a beeline for the parking garage. By the time he'd gotten the car started, he'd already left a message on Rachael's cell, asking her to call. He tried again. No answer. "*Rachael*, where the hell are you?" He fished a grocery receipt from his wallet, turned it over and punched in the cell number for Anakin. No answer. He punched in the number for Michal. Again, no answer. "This is such bullshit! Where the hell are you guys?" Then, he made a call to the operator and asked to be patched through to the New York FBI Special Investigations division. A few moments later he heard a ring on the other end and Vivian answered.

"Where is everybody?" Josh asked.

"Josh, is that you?"

"What's going on? I've been trying to get a hold of Rachael."

"Not much chance of that happening. Kingsley has had them all in a 'retreat' for most of the day, and now he has them locked away down the hall for the evening. For *Sensitivity Training. . . .*"

"Oh." Josh took a breath, relieved Rachael was okay. "Sensitivity Training . . . ?"

"Yes. Nothing more important than kicking ass, with a smile."

"Yeah right. Hey listen, I'm on my way back. There's a direct flight, I'll be there around eleven-thirty. When Rachael gets out, *don't* let her leave the office. It's very important. Understand?"

"Sure, no problem. They should be done by around ten. I'll let her know. . . . Josh, is everything all right?"

"Sort of . . . but I think we may have solved a forty-year-old murder, and the shit is gonna hit the stratosphere on this one. I need you to set up a meeting with Kingsley and the commissioner for tomorrow morning, first thing. And don't take any bullshit excuses. This can't wait. And tell Rachael I'll call her as soon as I touch down." Then he hung up.

Chapter 64

Rachael found it impossible to stifle a yawn as she rolled up to the front gate of the governor's mansion. She and her team had spent the day with Kingsley; and any day with Kingsley was never a good one, and always guaranteed to be a pain in the ass. So no matter how much her mind and body cried out for sleep, it still felt wonderful to be free of the office. Even if it was to meet with the governor.

The guardhouse didn't appear to be manned. Only the flicker of computer screens gave any clue that someone was there. Rachael tapped on the horn and a moment later she saw a fit-looking man about thirty years of age with jet-black hair, cut military style, come out of the back, zipping up his fly. He slid open the window to the booth, confirmed her ID, slipped her half a grin, and hit the gate button.

The black, wrought-iron gates, lit by a small spotlight, clanked and slowly retracted. As she passed through the gates an angular shadow crawled across the hood of the SUV, and a feeling of dread came over her. She was tired, and she knew her imagination could easily take over, so she decided to focus on good and safe things. With her forearm resting on the open window she took a deep breath and began to calm herself. The scent of autumn was rich, pungent, and real. It took her back to her grandfather's farm, to her childhood, to the fall, to the smell of decomposing cattails by the lake, to where her father first showed her how to fire a gun. It was a fine thought and a good memory to hold onto.

By the time she stopped in front of the manor her mind had shifted, again wondering if her career was over. Kingsley's posturing was eating away at her. She needed traction, a solid lead, and needed it fast or she knew she was finished. *God, let it be tonight,* she thought, but at the same time, hoped the meeting with the governor would be brief. Her mind felt sluggish, and her thoughts were beginning to turn sour. *I'll give it ten minutes, then I'm out of here.* She parked and got out.

She wasn't sure what to expect, but the governor had been adamant that he had important information regarding O'Henry. He was equally adamant that he couldn't give her the information over the phone. It had to be in person, and it had to be tonight. Tomorrow, he would be on the final leg of his campaign leading to election day. If she wanted the information, she would have to come out tonight. She had agreed to his request, but now, as she walked up to the front entrance, she wondered if it had been a bright idea.

A speaker hidden somewhere above came on, and a man's voice, an old voice, said he'd be down in a minute.

Rachael scanned the grounds and thought about O'Henry. It had been a full week since his last kill, and he had shut down all communication with her. She knew that if there was another seven-year gap, most, if not all, of the investigative team would've moved on. And when O'Henry did reappear, it would be as if a new file had been opened, which meant many more would die. A thump of anger flooded her mind. *That's not happening. If we're going to nail him, we're gonna do it now.*

She had grown weary of waiting and reached for the knocker just as the door opened.

"The governor is waiting for you down at the boathouse," Morgan the butler said, trying to sound comforting. "He's taking in the moon."

The butler appeared far older than the last time she had seen him; his face pale and drawn, dark half-circles under his eyes.

When they reached where the pathway sloped down to the boathouse, she stopped and thanked Morgan, telling him he should go back to bed. He smiled. "Thank you dear."

The pathway consisted of round slabs of slate set into the earth every two feet, ending at the top of a wooden staircase. Rachael descended the staircase and stepped out onto the veranda. She saw Governor Elhert at the far end seated in a wooden armchair, peering into a large refracting telescope. He turned his attention to her and smiled. It was a warm smile, a smile that seemed to say she was important. *Huh. No wonder people voted for you.*

The air was calm by the water, and she could hear the ocean lapping up against the pillars below. She decided it was a fine night for stargazing and started to relax. The moon had climbed halfway up the sky, shining bright, its buttery light bouncing off the water and wavering on each ripple. Rachael heard a clock inside the boathouse strike once, the sound absorbed into the thick stone walls. She glanced at her watch, it was half past eleven, then she took notice of the governor.

He was wearing dark-gray slacks, a light-blue silk shirt and a charcoal-gray sweater opened at the front. "Ah, Rachael. I'm so glad you could make it," he said, sounding refreshed and full of energy.

"Odd hours are part of the job description," she replied, trying to conceal her lack of vigor.

"Yes, of course, mine too . . . would you care to look? The moon is rather vivid tonight. The crater definition . . . outstanding."

Rachael walked over to the telescope, sat down in the wooden chair and peered into the eyepiece. She was surprised at how clearly she could see the surface of the craters. "You're right, it is amazing." After close to a minute, she broke her concentration and asked, "Do you think we'll ever colonize it?"

"Oh yes . . . yes, I think so. The bigger question of course is, will we all be around to see it happen?" He shrugged his shoulders and changed the subject. "Sorry about calling you out this late at night, though I suspect the information I have will interest you more than even the moon." He walked over to a set of French doors leading into the boathouse. "Would you care to join me? I do savor a shot of brandy late at night. It helps me unwind. A bit of a ritual I'm afraid."

"Sure . . . why not?" Rachael said, again feeling out of her comfort zone. *Not the smartest thing you've ever done.* With that lame thought circulating in her mind she rose out of the chair, and could have easily missed the tip of the pistol grip protruding from the chair's side pocket. She stood up straight, not letting on she had seen the gun and followed him into the boathouse.

The room was huge, with floor to ceiling windows,

two stories high, facing out across the ocean. It made her feel small, inconsequential, and a flash of anger rose from within her. She turned her attention back to the governor.

"Impressive. Beautiful," she said.

Governor Elhert was now standing next to a couple of wingback chairs that flanked a small round table in front of a stone fireplace. He gestured for her to come and take a seat. A modest fire had been lit and its crackling seemed to make the room more inviting.

It was late, and all she wanted was the information and to get out of there. But her team needed a break and she did too, so she swallowed hard and decided to play along, at least for a while. She took her seat and Elhert took his. He appeared pleased she had gone along with his request.

On the table was an ornate silver tray, a bottle of cognac and two snifters.

Rachael studied her host for a moment before saying, "Governor, I hope you haven't gone to a lot of trouble. You said on the phone you have information that can't wait. Maybe we should—"

"Yes, of course, you are right. But first . . . please join me in a little taste, then we'll get down to business, I promise." He poured a few ounces into each snifter.

Way too late for this bullshit, Rachael thought, and yet she could see the ritual was important to him, if not somewhat nonnegotiable. "All right, but then I have to cut loose. It's been a long, *long* day."

"I understand, you must be exhausted. Quite frankly, I don't know how you keep going. I mean, the stress of hunting killers, finding mutilated corpses. Unquestionably you must have trouble sleeping at night . . . knowing killers are out there, hunting their next prey. How *do* you do it? I would think you'd find no fun in it at all."

"Fun has nothing to do with it. And yes, my mother would agree with you. Why would any sane person do this job? I guess I just gravitated to it."

Elhert raised an eyebrow, then raised his snifter and gave a toast. "To the good and decent people of the world, may they make haste, and bring the monsters to their deserved graves."

Okay this is getting a little weird . . . Hoping to get back on track, back to O'Henry, she said, "At least in this case there is certainty."

"I'm not following you," Governor Elhert said, a furrow forming on his brow.

"With a serial killer, there is no gray area. He kills a number of people, usually one-by-one, in an often premeditated fashion. He kills because he needs to, and because he likes it—" Her cell phone vibrated in her purse and she reached in and grabbed it. She glanced over at the governor, who seemed less than pleased that she would take the call.

"Be only a second, the odd hours you know." She saw it was from Josh and felt relieved, and was a little amazed at just how relieved she was. She pressed a button and the screen lit up, and then it went blank. "Ahh—it's out of juice."

"Oh, that's a shame," Governor Elhert said, an amused look on his face. "You're free to use the landline."

She thought about it for a second. "No, no thanks. I'll charge it in my car on the way back and make the call then."

"As you wish. . . . So, you were saying that, with serial killers, there is certainty?"

"Governor, I don't want to bore you. The web has a ton of information on serial killers . . . all you have to do is go online."

"I know the web is a wonderful thing, but I am most interested in your experienced opinion," he stated in a calm, fatherly tone.

Rachael couldn't place what it was about the governor. Something was off, she could feel it, and he was starting to annoy her. "Okay, one observation, and then I must go."

Elhert took a sip of brandy and tilted his glass at her.

Rachael followed his lead and took a sip. *Strange* . . . Maybe it was due to her lack of sleep, yet she could feel its effect even before it reached her stomach. "One of the first tenets of any profiler's investigation is to ascertain if the perpetrator is disorganized or organized. In O'Henry's case, he fits the latter category to a T, which will ultimately lead to his downfall."

"Why is that? Correct me if I'm wrong, but being organized would seem to fall on the positive side of the ledger, would it not?"

"One would think, and yet by being organized he believes he is in control, and since he believes that, it makes him think he can outsmart those who are trying to stop him. Deep down he has a need to flaunt his superiority, which in turn makes him take chances. Only when he has humiliated his opponents does he feel in sufficient control of his world. It's a vicious loop."

"I see," Governor Elhert said, swirling his brandy.

Rachael checked her watch, took another small gulp and put down the snifter, letting him know she was done for the night.

"Well then," Governor Elhert said. "I suppose it's time to reveal why I had you come here tonight." He took a long draw on his brandy, then sat the snifter down on the table. "This evening I came across some information, or rather I should say, it was delivered to me."

Rachael said nothing, and cocked her head slightly to one side.

"Not so much information, really. Let's say . . . more of a statement."

Elhert opened a hidden drawer in the table and withdrew a folded, white piece of paper and handed it to her.

By now Rachael you must know that I have the deepest respect for you. Having your attention has provided me with tremendous strength and to that end I am indebted. I have enlisted the governor as a conduit which I believe affords a certain amount of credibility, as does my little gift box I've left for you. I thought you could use a little pick me up.
Ta ta, O

"This came with the note," Governor Elhert said, and reached back into the drawer and retrieved a tiny box, measuring one inch wide, two inches long and half-an-inch high. It was tied with a blue ribbon, curled at the ends. "Oh, and there was a card. . . . Hmm, it must have come loose. Oh, here it is," and he placed the card by the box. It was a simple card, similar to those used by flower shops. The inscription read: *For Josh Ingram's eyes only.*

Rachael felt her heart skip a beat, followed by a flutter in her chest. Elhert reached over and smiled at her as he handed her the box. She hesitated, then her fingertips touched his and an icy sensation ran through her—she flinched, gasped without showing it, and set the box down on the table.

She found herself being examined by Elhert, his gaze intense, without malice, a warmth in his eyes. She was receiving mixed signals. "I'll have to take this back to our forensic team. They'll need to go over it before it can be opened."

"Is that really necessary?" Governor Elhert asked, disappointment now registering on his face.

"I'm afraid so . . ."

"I guess you have to do, what you have to do."

"I'm glad you understand. And I want to thank you for contacting me this evening. But before I leave, I do have one question."

"Please . . . ask away?"

"Why you? Why was the note delivered through you? Why not just send it to me?"

"An excellent point, one that I've been asking myself. Perhaps it's because this is my state and he finds it more dramatic to go through me. His note does say he thinks it adds validity to the whole affair, whatever that means." He shrugged. "Really Rachael, I have no idea. Who knows what goes on in a troubled mind?"

Bullshit . . . ! She'd had enough for one night. "Well, I think I'd better get going." As she rose to her feet, the floor shifted under her, the corners of the room darkened and the walls started to fold in toward her. She grabbed her chair and steadied herself, and felt a rush of blood come to her head, a pounding in her ears—and then the darkness lifted.

"Are you all right?" Governor Elhert asked.

"I . . . I'm overtired that's all. I'm fine . . . just a little overtired."

"Yes, of course. May I walk you to your car?"

"No, really. I'll be fine," she said, and saw a worried look cross the governor's face. She wondered if he was concerned about her well-being or was something else troubling him.

"A good night's sleep will do wonders," he said.

She nodded.

Then they shook hands and said their good-byes.

As soon as she got into the safety of her vehicle she shuddered. *Time to get the hell out of here.* She inserted the key and the engine caught on the first turn. She dropped the drivetrain into gear and punched it.

After banking the SUV high through the first few bends in the driveway, she throttled down, rolled past the guardhouse, and turned onto the coastal road. As the distance between her and the governor's estate grew, she began to feel herself unwind.

She reached into the inside pocket of her jacket and withdrew her cell. She fiddled with the charger cord until she got it plugged in, then hit the message key. No response. She glanced at her phone—no power. *Ah c'mon.* She grabbed the charger plug and shifted it around in the socket, hoping to force a connection. Nothing.

She glanced up and saw a coyote skulking along the ditch, its tail between its legs. Without warning, it jumped onto the road in front of her and stopped, turned sideways, and just stared. She jammed on the brakes and the SUV came to an abrupt halt, throwing her cell phone into the air, bouncing it off the dash to the floor, landing it next to the gas pedal. Her purse was close behind, landing on the passenger-side of the floor.

She glared at the coyote for a moment, then hit the horn with the palms of her hands. The coyote blinked a few times, pranced around a bit, and then sauntered off the road, back into the ditch.

Rachael clenched the steering wheel, fear pumping through her veins—and yelled, "Goddamnit!"

On the floor she saw the contents of her purse: her lipstick, mascara, folding hairbrush, along with some coins and the ribboned box from O'Henry. She gathered it all up, dumped it back into her purse, and tossed the purse onto the passenger seat, and O'Henry's box fell back out. Then she dropped her cell into the cup holder and tried again to make a connection. No luck.

She took a few deep breaths and continued down the road, determined not to let any more drama enter her life. She followed the road for another few minutes, and then began to think she might have gone too far. "Do *not* miss the turn off . . ." she muttered. If she did, she knew, she'd soon find herself at Anton's place, where the road came to a dead end. She was done for night. She just wanted to get back to town and freshen up before Josh arrived.

Then her eyes caught sight of a flashing light up ahead. "Now what? A friggin' accident, at this time of night?" As she drew closer, she realized it was only a stalled van. Its left signal light was flashing and its side door was wide open. *No need to stop. Not out here, not in the middle of the night.*

Then something caught her eye. An object was dangling from the side door. She squinted, then rolled down her window and slowed to a crawl. She was still considering it when a crumpled bicycle, a mountain bike, came into view just a few feet from the van. *Had the van struck it? How can that be? Why would anyone be riding this late at night?* That's when she heard a woman call out. She had an accent, Russian she thought. The woman was crying. It was coming from inside the van. Then the dangling object came into focus, it was a woman's leg. Rachael slowed to a stop. *This is such a bad idea. . . . Do not open the fucking door. Don't be stupid.* She put her hand on the door handle, hesitated for a moment, then opened the door and stepped out. She drew her gun from its holster and released the safety. As she moved in closer, a new sound came from the van. At first it didn't register, then it became all too clear—a baby's cry. With her senses on high alert she raised her gun, edging herself toward the sliding door. The hairs on the back of her arms bristled. *This is all wrong, damn it! I should just leave, now, get the hell out of here.* She cocked her gun.

In the still of the night the baby's crying seemed to be getting louder, and Rachael's heart raced.

Oh my God . . . what am I doing? She inched her way forward until she stood at the side of the van, her back pressed up against the side panel. Switching the gun to her other hand, she reached down and gently touched the woman's leg. It was cold and hard, *not real.*

Rachael's heart froze.

Chapter 65

All Rachael felt was a pinch on her neck. The long, steel needle pierced her soft skin and slid into her carotid artery. A second later her heart ceased to beat, and darkness descended. She was letting go, all reason dissolving, her thoughts dispersing. Then her heart muscle clenched, a strong, life-clinging beat. But it came too late. Her legs had given out and she'd toppled forward, her upper body landing flat on the van floor.

O'Henry studied his catch for a moment, then reached down and slid his hands under her thighs, lifting the rest of her into the van. A grin surfaced on his face and his pulse jumped. The warmth of her thighs had seeped through his latex gloves and a current of pleasure shot through him—followed by a rush of guilt. He looked down at her: *Why Rachael, why couldn't you be the one . . . ?* Then he reached out and traced his index finger along the curve of her hip. *You won't change my mind, you know. Our game has come to its logical conclusion.* He paused and gave it some more thought before saying in a sad detached voice, "I'm so sorry. But I can't have you and Ingram ruin it all . . . now can I?" Then he rolled her onto her back and straightened out her legs. "I had wanted ours to be a long friendship. You're stronger, smarter than the others. You were the sly one. The one I chose to come along for the ride, the witness to my quest. And now my only regret is that it could not have lasted longer."

As he straightened her dress and smoothed out the creases his face went slack, his gaze unfocused. "You could've been perfect, you know . . . I would have liked that." Then a surge of anger brushed his heart and his eyes grew bitter. "No matter . . . your fate is sealed."

He walked back to Rachael's vehicle, dropped it into gear, and rolled it into the ditch.

As he climbed back into the cab of the van, he checked his watch. *Time to get home.*

Time to prepare for Ingram.

Chapter 66

It was 11:24 p.m. by the time the flight touched down. The atmosphere around LaGuardia was in slowdown mode for the day. The bulk of the late evening flights had arrived, and a few jet engines could still be heard winding down.

As his plane taxied up to the off-loading ramp, Josh tried Rachael's number again. It rang a few times then clicked over to her answering service. "Dammit," he mumbled. As he hung up he noticed a message on his cell. It had come in at 10:21 p.m. and with that realization, a sinking feeling took hold of him. He hit play.

"Josh, Rachael here. Got your messages. Hey, I know you wanted me to wait for you. Vivian tried her best to hold me down, but the governor called. He wants to see me tonight. He says he has received new information on O'Henry. He says I have to come tonight—right now . . . Josh I've gotta go, this could be the break we've been waiting for." Then her voice softened. "I'm thinking I should be back at the hotel around one. I've booked a room at the Broadview. If you could come up tonight, we could have a nightcap and I'll bring you up to speed . . . I know it's late but I really want to see you."

Ah hell, Rachael. Why couldn't you listen?

As he scrambled out of the terminal and onto the

street, Josh saw Vivian standing by an unmarked cruiser. She waved him over, then slipped into the driver's seat. He jogged over to her window and tapped on the glass, telling her he would drive. She frowned, then got out of the car, and said, "Josh, I tried to stop her, but she wouldn't listen."

"Yeah, I know you did," he said, then handed her the envelope with the originals inside. "Keep this safe, okay?" She gave a nod and walked around to the passenger-side. Josh jumped in, locked all the doors, and dropped the hammer. As he drove away, he could see Vivian in the rearview mirror flapping her arms and yelling.

Sorry Vivian . . . no witnesses . . . not tonight.

By the time he reached I-95 he'd had time to think, time to convince himself Rachael would be okay. *Elhert was involved in a murder, but . . . that was forty years ago. He's running for reelection in a few days, for governor for Christ's sake. He has no idea that I've got him nailed.* That side of the argument was working well for him, until his mind crossed over. *Shit . . . he did take part in the murder of that black boy. And with the election coming, and O'Henry bent on forcing a connection to the dead black girl and her boyfriend—the murdered boyfriend, Elhert's gotta be in panic mode. He needs O'Henry caught and killed, and he needs it now. He's desperate, he's capable of anything . . .*

Forty-five minutes later Josh got out of the cruiser and walked up to the sentry gate window. He showed his temporary ID. The guard peered at his clipboard, then frowned and went for the phone. Without hesitation Josh reached in and grabbed the guard by his collar, yanking him headfirst out through the open window, slamming him to the ground, and hitting him hard with one blow to the bridge of his nose. The guard was out cold.

As Josh pulled up in front of the manor, the only light that he saw was coming from the boathouse. He sprinted across the lawn and when he reached the slate steps, he stopped in his tracks. A man was standing on the veranda, looking up at him. It was the governor. He was on the phone and waving for Josh to come down.

"I was wondering when you'd show," Governor Elhert said, his tongue sounding thick as he clicked off his cell.

Josh stepped onto the veranda. "*Where* is Rachael?" he asked, barely able to control his anger.

"I'm afraid you just missed her, old boy," Governor Elhert said, and took a draw on his brandy. "Said she was tired, and needed a rest. Pity. I was so enjoying her company." He held up a bottle of brandy and pointed to it, and then pointed to Josh. "Care for a taste?"

Josh just glared at him.

"My guess is no . . ." Governor Elhert said, the timber of his voice thinning. "Look, that isn't necessary you know." He wagged his finger at Josh. "There's simply no need to be hostile. . . . Then again, maybe it's in the air. . . . I've just received disturbing word from Harland. Apparently, Sheriff Stranton and his deputies were all found dead this evening, piled into a freshly dug grave, located not too far from my father's home. I don't suppose you'd know anything about that?"

Josh said nothing.

"Of course not," Governor Elhert said, then sat down on the chair next to his telescope.

Josh reached into his jacket pocket, took out the folded half photo of the three boys and the yearbook page, and tossed them on the governor's lap.

As Elhert unfolded the photo, his face showed no sign of surprise. "Always thought it would have aged over time . . . and one would not be able to see who's who. . . . Oh well."

"Just so you know . . . I have the originals safely tucked away."

"I see," Governor Elhert said, his eyes narrowing. Then he studied Josh for a few seconds, and a knowing smile parted his lips. . . . "You don't know, do you? You don't get it . . ." He took a sip of brandy and smacked his lips. "And I thought you were the gifted one. So disappointing."

"What the hell are you babbling about?"

"Babbling." The governor's words were slurring more. "I'm not the one who's *babbling.*"

Josh grabbed Elhert by the collar, pulling him partway out of the chair, and in a calm voice said, "*Talk,* you son-of-a-bitch."

Elhert held up both hands as if he was surrendering. "Come now, old boy. You are missing the point. Who do you see in the photo? And then tell me, who don't you see?"

"What?" Josh asked, the domino already falling.

"Who do you think took the picture?" Governor Elhert asked.

Josh let go of Elhert, dropping him back down into the chair. "Anton."

Elhert smiled and clapped his hands together. "Yes. My dear troubled brother."

Josh stood there, speechless.

"He's been the family's dirty little secret for as long as

I can remember. He wasn't a nice boy. In a word, *cruel* would have to be the best way to describe him as a child. Of course, his hideous looks didn't allow him to grow up normal. God should certainly be spanked for that one. Imagine, allowing that unhappy brain and those hideous looks to grow up together."

Governor Elhert straightened himself out on the chair. "In Anton's defense, he did suffer in his teen years. Hormones raging, peer ridicule, rejection, all jumbled together, that sort of thing. He did eventually learn how to mask it, but oh my, in those early years, he was an open sore that kept the family busy."

Josh thought of the picture, and the frightened looks on the boys' faces. "You're telling me Anton murdered that black kid, and you and Larry Frank were innocent bystanders?"

"Innocent is such a strong word. Who among us is truly innocent?" Governor Elhert asked, as he handed the photo back to Josh. "You of all people must understand that."

Josh said nothing.

"Have it your way, old boy. As I see it, it's simply a matter of who believes his justification is the more valid one. A murderer is a murderer. It is what it is, and you are what *you* are."

Josh blinked, and said, "Something I don't understand, is how O'Henry fits into all this? Why did he want to dig up your past? Why point us in the direction of events that happened forty years ago? Why lead us to you?"

"To discredit me, I suppose. It's a question I've been asking myself," Governor Elhert said unconvincingly, and

401

then pointed to the half picture. "So what are you going to do with the *original* of that? Anton's not in it, and what good would it do to disgrace me now? Ruin my life, for what—some misguided sense that justice will be served?"

Josh hesitated for a moment, then said, "You said Anton has learned to hide his dark side. After seeing him the other day with Margaret, it's hard for me to believe he has a cruel side at all. In fact, he seemed very considerate."

"What can I say? Margaret brings out the best in people."

Josh's pulse picked up a beat. "How long has Margaret been taking lessons from him?"

"For some time now, close to seven years, I think. Yes . . . yes I'm certain of it. He'd had a spell with angina, his old ticker had been giving him some trouble. Still does, as I understand it. That's when Anton moved to the bay. He wanted to be closer to the family."

"In that time, has he ever had a harsh word with Margaret?"

"No, in fact. Margaret says he is a complete gentleman. To the point I would be jealous if it were any other man."

Josh thought for a moment and asked, "If O'Henry dislikes you, why stop at destroying your career? Why doesn't he just kill you?"

"Good point. . . . Perhaps he will try."

Josh pointed to the picture of the three boys, his fingertip on Larry Frank. "Both cousins went missing that weekend. Both of them were there, weren't they? Dennery was on the pier watching as well." At that moment, everything fell into place. "But Anton could only have witnesses he could trust. He could only trust family. And he knew he would need help if he was to get rid of both cousins. So you helped him—didn't you!"

At that instant, Elhert reached to the side of the chair and drew out his hand gun, a .45 caliber, and pointed it at Josh. "Well done, Mr. Ingram. Yes, of course, you are right. Anton decided to take the nigger out into the ocean and dump him. I have to tell you, it was a little dicey with all five of us crammed in that tiny boat. Once we'd cut the engine and dropped the nigger overboard, Anton wasted no time. He struck one of the cousins—Larry, I think it was—with a paddle, catching him on the side of his head, and over he went. I simply pushed the other cousin over the side. He couldn't swim, poor fellow . . . not that it would've done him much good, as we were in a strong current that day." He paused. "And now you've left me with no choice but having to dispose of you as well."

Josh stared at him and asked, "Answer me this. When did you first know that Anton was O'Henry?"

Elhert smiled. "Oh, I had no idea . . . none at all. Not until the note at the bridge showed up. That's when it first crossed my mind. You must understand, when Anton left to attend university he never came back. That is, not until seven years ago, when the drums of mortality started beating. We thought he wanted to reconnect. Make atonement for lost time."

"So, where is Anton tonight?"

"Where he always is. At his home."

Josh's pulse pounded. "How long ago did Rachael leave?"

"Ten minutes or so before you arrived, give or take."

"That can't be. I would've passed her on the way. . . ."

Elhert grinned.

Fuck! He's set her up. Without hesitation he kicked Elhert's gun out of his hand. It arced high into the air, landing at the edge of the veranda before splashing into the ocean. Then he spun around and round-housed Elhert on the side of the head, throwing him out of his chair and onto the deck, spread-eagled, face down and unconscious.

He fished out his cell and called the Broadview Hotel. "This is Josh Ingram of the FBI. I need to know—has Rachael Tanner come into the hotel in the last half hour . . . ? Are you *absolutely* sure!"

Chapter 67

The cruiser's headlights were following a long curve in the road, cutting through a fine mist, when Josh noticed a red flicker—a flash, *a reflector maybe?* He hit the brakes and slowed, and saw what appeared to be the top of a vehicle poking out of the ditch.

He stopped the car and ran to the side of the ditch, immediately recognizing the vehicle. "Rachael!" he cried.

He climbed down into the ditch, his heart pounding as he opened the SUV's door. It was empty, except for Rachael's purse on the passenger seat, and a small box lying beside it. He saw her cell and snatched it from the cup holder, unhooked it, and slipped it into his pants pocket. He stared at the tiny box for a second, and then picked it up.

As he jogged down the side of the road he hoped beyond all hope that he would see her, and she would be okay. He followed the road another fifty feet before seeing another set of vehicle tracks. The tracks were pressed deep into the hard sand. A truck, a three-quarter ton, or even a van, he guessed.

Next to the tire tracks he saw a faint footprint. It was a large boot print, maybe a hiking boot. *So what happened here, Rachael? You came across a vehicle on the side of the road and you stopped. You must have sensed some-*

one was in trouble. Bad trouble, or you wouldn't have done it. Not here . . . so what were you thinking?*

He searched the area for the next five minutes without finding a single clue, then he remembered the box. He retrieved it from his pocket, tugged at the ribbon, and removed the lid. Inside he found a card, folded, with a fine crease down its center.

He opened it and it read: END GAME.   O

"Son-of-a-bitch!"

Anton's house was lit up, every light in every room on, and every drape was drawn wide open. At a distance it looked to Josh like a very large and old dollhouse. Everything neat and tidy. Everything unreal.

As he turned into the driveway, Josh knew the security cameras would pick him up. But that no longer mattered—time had run out. He pulled up at the front of the house, then noticed a dirt road that branched off and ran along the side of the house, and decided to go in the back way. He followed the dirt road to the back where it sloped down for a short stretch, then cut left across a planked bridge that spanned a small creek. As the cruiser rolled to a stop at the back of the house, he killed the engine. In front of him, tucked in below the house, was a double car garage. A thin layer of fog was nudging up against the garage doors, and a hooded light bulb set above the doors cast a dull, unfiltered, almost granular yellow light onto the ground.

Josh got out and popped the trunk, rummaged around, and found an emergency kit—then spotted a folded blanket. Wrapped inside the blanket was a pump-action twelve-gauge shotgun. He checked the chamber. Empty. He quickly searched the trunk for cartridges, then went to the glove box. Nothing. He returned to the trunk and opened the emergency kit. He found a flashlight, a road flare, and some bandages. He clicked on the flashlight; it was dead. He stared at the flare for a moment, considered it, then stuck it into the waist of his pants and walked up to the garage doors. There he saw a fresh set of tire tracks. He bent down and ran his fingers across them. *Same as those that were on the side of the road . . .*

The garage doors were large and heavy and locked. Finding a side entrance door, he grabbed its handle and pushed. It swung open. . . .

Chapter 68

Rachael was flat on her back; her arms and torso strapped to the bench beneath her; her legs were spread, her knees bent, her ankles tied to the bottom of the bench legs with leather straps. A heavy oak collar straddled her neck and held her head in place.

Rachael opened her eyes and panic surged. She tried to raise her head—but couldn't, something was clamped over her neck, holding her down. It was thick and wooden. Nothing was making sense. "Who's there?" she called out, her voice echoing off the walls. No one answered. She called out, again and again, and still no one answered. She was sure she was not alone, someone else was in the room with her, she could feel it.

She squirmed and twisted, trying to find a weakness in the straps holding her, but soon realized she was not going anywhere. As she scanned the room, her heart pumped wildly, pressure building in her neck, blood pounding in her ears. *For God's sake, get a hold of yourself. Settle down and assess. You've been trained for this kind of shit—now use it.*

After a minute of controlled breathing she reopened her eyes, wider this time, and surveyed the chamber. The details of her captivity emerged. The walls, chiseled blocks of tan limestone, climbed a dozen feet or so to an ashen-gray slab ceiling. Candles were burning on small plates of pewter jutting out from the walls. From behind her she heard a flapping sound like that of a flag caught in an evening breeze. She rolled her eyes up, craned her chin back, and stretched her neck as far as the wooden collar would permit. She saw two large torches set into sconces on the wall behind her. They were burning bright and clean, the flames curling off the wrapped rags. The air smelled of ethanol and burnt sugar.

She straightened her neck and again looked straight up. At first, the object hanging high above her head didn't register. It was clinical by design, clean and shiny. The torchlight flickered on its black, polished finish and glinted on its razor edge. Steel, and quality steel at that, she figured. She calculated it to be a foot and a half in width, maybe a foot and a half high. *Difficult to tell from this angle, but a good two inches thick that's for sure, and it's gotta have the weight of an anvil.* Her mind danced around its name, refusing to fathom its gravity. A sense of dread crept in-and-out of her thoughts, and for a few insulated moments she managed to stay ahead of the inevitable and kept its name buried. Really, how could she allow it to surface? To do so was unthinkable, and yet the analytical side of her mind would not let up. It kept coming back to the one undeniable fact: all the decapitations had occurred with one clean slice. *Oh Christ . . . a guillotine.*

"Welcome back, Rachael," Anton said, standing just out of her sight. "I hope you don't mind, but I've taken the liberty of getting you ready."

She immediately recognized the voice. "Anton," she said, and waited for a reply. . . . "I know it's you. . . . What are we doing here, Anton? You know this isn't necessary. We can work something out . . . I can get you help."

"Oh, okay then, I guess I'll just let you go and we'll forget all about it," Anton said, and let out a short chuckle.

Then came a pause, a long, silent lull. All Rachael could hear was the sound of the torches burning behind her . . . flapping.

"Anton, what exactly are you doing back there? Let me have a look at you." She knew she had to get a conversation going, she had to buy time. "Are you standing there watching me? Maybe you're smiling and licking your lips? For all I know, you're standing at attention in your birthday suit—I'm curious, that's all. I'd have a look, but some asshole strapped my *fucking hands down!*"

"Oh, I'm not going to molest you," Anton said, and walked around into her field of view. "Though I must confess, I've thought about it. You being a near perfect specimen and all, but alas, I've made my choice."

"Lucky girl," Rachael said, and wished she hadn't, as a spasm of pain registered on Anton's face. "Come on Anton, untie me so we can talk. You're a smart man. There's a solution to every problem. We can work this out. I know you don't want to do this."

Anton smirked, his tiny lips forming an O around his childlike teeth.

Aw damn, I'm going to die . . .

"That's where you are wrong," Anton said. "There is nothing left to work out. I've taken care of all the details, we just have to sit back and wait. . . . Oh, that reminds me, I hope you don't mind . . . I do have an important call to make." He punched in a number on his cell and it rang several times before switching to the govenor's voice mail. He dropped the cell into his pocket and said, "As I had expected, our Mr. Ingram should be with us shortly. Yes, you see, I have taken care of that too."

Then he began to run his fingers down the grooves that would guide the blade to her neck. "Such a simple contraption. A work of art. At least I think so."

"Why, Anton? Why are you doing this?"

Anton kept tracing his fingertips along the guide rail. "You wouldn't understand. People like you don't." Then he reached over and touched her cheek with the back of his hand. She cringed.

"Get what?" Rachael asked, wanting to keep him talking. "What is it that I don't get?"

"Quite simply . . . the need for perfection. To have and hold beauty in your arms."

"Are you telling me this is all just about a *woman*?" Rachael blurted out, unable to control her sarcasm and anger.

"It's not a bright idea to piss off the man that's holding the lever," he said, giving her a fake pout.

"There's no such thing as perfection, Anton, you must know that."

"You are wrong, it's all around you. If you know where to look. The perfect diamond, the perfect rose, the perfect sunset. They're all there, waiting to be brought out into the open and appreciated."

"Bullshit. Humans are all imperfect. You, me, even God's imperfect, if you believe in such things. You've set yourself up for failure, Anton. You know you have."

Anton said nothing. He just stared at her.

"And what's this all about?" she asked, looking up. "A fucking *guillotine*?"

He blinked. "It's all about the process . . . final touches are what differentiate the great from the commonplace. Extraordinary from ordinary. Perfection from imperfection."

"And you think slicing off the heads of women makes you a grand conductor in the symphony of life? It makes you a sick lunatic in my book."

Anton tried to suppress a giggle, which ended up coming out in a distorted squeak. "Oh you . . . silly girl," he said, glaring down at her. "This black lever." And he pointed to it with his finger. "Is the throw switch. All I have to do is pull it down, and the blade is released. . . ." Then he brought his face down to within an inch of hers. "Perhaps I won't wait for Ingram after all." He paused for a long moment. "I did have a test for him, you see, an experiment in human behavior. But I see you aren't much of a conversationalist. And I must admit, this is growing tiresome." He stood up and reached for the lever, wrapping his fingers around it.

Oh Jesus! He's gonna do it. "And *ruin* the process?" Rachael's voice rang out. "Either you seek perfection or you don't. How can Josh witness your process if I'm dead?"

"Clever girl. Then again, I always knew you were. Why else would I arrange to bring you along on my quest?"

"What are you talking about?"

Anton got an amused look on his face. "Come now, did you really think you obtained your new job on your own merits? Oh please . . . let's just say, I have friends in high places."

Rachael grimaced. "Not true. How could you even

know that I'd applied?"

"I believe you're well acquainted with some of my Miami associates. Word travels . . . as they say. But this is getting rather dull, don't you think? Let's not dwell on trivialities, it'll spoil the moment. All I can say is, having you here to share my world, and . . ." he clapped his hands together. "And then, arranging for Ingram to join in . . . well, that was priceless."

"What?" Rachael asked.

Anton cocked his head, a questioning look on his face. "Well . . . Arthur, of course."

Rachael thought for a moment. "Anton, are you saying you arranged for Arthur's murder just to bring Josh on board?"

"It was one of my finer moments, I must admit. I couldn't be sure Ingram would come out of his self-imposed retirement unless I gave him sufficient reason to do so. Now, I simply could've had Arthur killed, but there were other considerations. I needed Ingram to focus his attention in the direction of my brother. So I slipped the old book, with the contract and the half picture, into the auction bag and Arthur took it home. Then I let nature take its course."

A puzzled look crossed her face.

"The bag," Anton said. "The surplus book bag that Arthur purchased at the auction."

Oh my God, he's orchestrated everything . . . She wanted to scream, but knew she had to keep him talking. It was her only hope. "So. You've been killing successful beautiful women. Why? Because you found them imperfect?"

"It is when I study them that I come to understand

413

their flaws." He pointed to the cage on the other side of the room. "There were times, I must confess, when I saw their faults early on. But then again, what's a boy to do? Once they'd captured my attention, I had to act. I mean, what choice did I have?" He rubbed his belly a few times and smiled. "Truth be told, I found my perfect match some time ago . . . seven years ago to be precise. I thought I'd find another, a replacement if you will. I tried. I really did. Still, somehow they always found a way to disappoint me. Sadly, I came to the conclusion that they always would."

Rachael eyes narrowed. "If that's the case, that you've found her—your perfect one—and there could never be a replacement, then why in God's name would you start this latest killing spree?"

Anton looked at Rachael with a look of disbelief on his face. "Oh, I have *never* stopped killing my dear. Why would I do such a thing?"

Ahh no . . . "Then why would you have O'Henry resurface?"

"To bring you and Josh onboard of course, and to point you in the right direction," Anton said, matter-of-factly.

"*Why . . . ?* Why would you do that, you sick bastard?" she cried.

"To set my plan into action," he replied, then stopped and tilted his head. "You *are* getting yourself all worked up my dear. It rattles me to think you haven't figured it out. . . . Oh, all right, I'll explain. My plan was simple. Have Josh locate the other half of the old photo he's been carrying around, which, I might add, was ultimately placed in his hands by yours truly. You may be interested to know, the completed picture shows my smiling brother standing next to a dead Negro, who is being weighed on a scale—a prized catch if you will. Rather outlandish of course, and needless to say, that photo would be the ruination of the good governor should it suddenly appear. I must confess, I had tremendous faith in our Mr. Ingram. I mean, a man of his talents. I figured if he could not locate the missing half, the half that would destroy my brother, then no one could."

"So, your plan all along has been . . . to ruin your brother?" Rachael asked, knowing the answer.

"Correct."

"And, what if Josh could not find the other half of the photo?"

"Then I would be forced to go to plan B."

"Which is?"

"Sadly . . . I would have to kill my own brother."

"Because he's in your way?" Rachael asked, a strained look on her face.

"Correct again."

Then it clicked. "Oh my God! The perfect woman . . . is Margaret!" Rachael blurted out, her voice shrill and incredulous. She then saw the muscles in Anton's forearm tense. He turned his gaze toward the blade, his face grim. *Shit, he's gonna throw it . . .*

Anton's hand tightened on the lever, and the pin holding the blade suspended began to retreat. Looking down at her, he grinned and said, "You need to shut your trap . . ."

Chapter 69

Two cargo vans were parked inside the garage: one white, one dark-blue. Josh squeezed in past the white van and found himself standing at the entrance to an underground passageway. He peered into the tunnel and noticed a long row of oil lamps placed high on each side. They were unlit, yet the accumulated soot on the flared glass appeared fresh.

He entered the tunnel and had not made it in more than twenty feet or so, before the last of the light coming from the garage petered out. Now, standing alone in the dark, his skin began to chill, and he could again smell the rot of the root cellar.

He quickly withdrew the flare from his waistband, removed the cap and struck the end. The brilliant flash cut at his eyes.

So much for stealth, he thought. He continued in another thirty feet with the flare held high above his head, and stopped when he came to a solid wooden door. The door was black and had been left ajar.

He dropped the flare onto the hardened clay, opened the door and stepped through into a long, narrow entryway. A large cabinet was pushed up against one wall. It measured a foot in depth, stood ten feet tall, and ran the length of the narrow room. Its glass doors were frosted.

Josh reached out and touched the glass, and felt the frost melt on his fingertips. Using the palm of his hand he rubbed in a circular motion until a small section of the glass became transparent. Looking out at him from within the cabinet was a woman's head, frozen, her eyes gouged out. "Ahh Christ," he said, and took a step back, watching the glass cloud over. Then he moved forward, rubbed the glass again, and this time put his nose to the cold surface and peered inside. He counted six shelves, all with heads lined up in neat rows, their noses an inch from the glass. All were frozen. All were without eyes.

As he turned his head away, a burning rage rose from deep within him. He paused for a second and tried to clear his mind, then noticed a flickering light coming from the next room, and he shouted, "Anton . . . if you've harmed Rachael, I'm going to hurt you in ways you never thought possible. You got that? You sick fuck!"

"Josh, my dear . . . you are really in no position to lose your cool," Anton said. "But please, come in. We've been expecting you."

Josh considered his options then decided to walk straight in. If Anton wanted him killed, he would've already tried. With that thought in mind, he stepped around the corner and there they were. Rachael strapped to the bench of a guillotine, her mouth duct taped, a large wooden collar straddling her neck, with Anton standing at her side, his hand on some kind of lever.

"Not another step, Ingram," Anton said, the pitch of his voice rising.

Josh noticed a leather strap tied to Anton's wrist, securing his wrist to the lever. His sight followed a cable running from the lever to the guillotine. The cable looped around a pulley, then turned ninety degrees and ran along the top of a crossbar, attaching itself to a long pin that held the blade in place.

"Anton . . . come on . . . what are we doing here?" Josh said. "You don't need Rachael. She's not the one you want. *I'm* your adversary, you know that. Let Rachael go and take me instead."

"Do you . . . think this is a negotiable item?" Anton asked. "It is noble of you, but really, you must know me better than that."

"Then what do you want?"

"Direct to the point. No nonsense Ingram. Now that's much better. . . . But no, I don't think I'll let her go . . . not now anyway. Maybe . . ." Anton said, looking as though he had a smile that was itching to come to the surface.

Josh decided not to bite and stared at Anton, and waited.

"Very well," Anton said, and reached down with his free hand and ripped the gray duct tape off of Rachael's mouth, then stuck the tape to the side of the guillotine. Rachael took a deep breath.

"Rachael, are you all right?"

"Yes . . . but Josh, his hand is tied to that lever—"

"If I could interrupt," Anton said, sounding carefree, like he was interrupting dinner guests. "I thought it was high time we got a woman's perspective. And, yes, yes of course, you are both in a hell of a predicament." He nodded at his hand. "You will note that if I am moved, fall, or whatever, the pin will be released and off goes Rachael's head. Oh, but enough of the mundane triviality of it all. I do so want you both to hear me out. I have a proposition."

Josh said nothing.

"Josh, you're a believer in predictability, are you not? For instance, if you take certain ingredients and bake them at a certain temperature, you get a certain type of cake. It's what you expect and it's what you get. Humans are like that, predictable. Take the character of an individual and put him in a certain set of circumstances, and he will act in a predicable way. Am I right?"

"Josh, whatever he's about to say. You know it's all bullshit," Rachael said.

Anton turned to Rachael. "Rachael my dear, I've invited you to this party, however, if you are going to be rude, I'm afraid I'm going to have to slap that tape back on."

"What's your game?" Josh asked, wanting to keep the focus on him.

"I'm a humane man with a heart that beats, same as yours," Anton said, and then waited for a few seconds. "And to prove it, I will grant Rachael a thirty day extension on her life . . . no, let's make that thirty-one days, like a long calendar month." Then he nodded in the direction of the cage. "Who knows, a lot can change in a month. Perhaps I'll change my mind."

"Josh, you know he's lying," Rachael cried. "Do whatever you can to save yourself and take him out."

"Oh my, this *is* a heartbreaking scene," Anton said, turning to Rachael. "My sweet girl . . . Josh is the epitome of the handsome knight in shining armor. He'd gladly sacrifice himself just to give you a chance. He's a bit naïve, but then again, aren't all gallant men?" Anton turned to Josh. "But I like you Ingram, always have. That's why I chose you to work with Rachael." And he gave her a wink.

"So I'm going to give you a chance to prove yourself to the one you love."

Josh said nothing, feeling a calm come over him, his mind cold and calculating.

"You should be thankful for this opportunity. As I understand it, you didn't get this chance to save your poor wife. *Ellen* was her name, I believe. A sad story, you getting there too late to be of any help. . . . Yes, yes, I know, it's as if it's happening all over again." He grinned. "This would be twice you've been off on your timing. The newspapers will carry the story. I can see the headlines, in big bold type. *Two too late Ingram. He doesn't do it again.* Two too late Ingram, kind of has a ring to it."

"Fuck you," Josh said, his eyes now dead pools.

"A lot of repressed anger coming from over there," Anton said. "Do you want to hear my proposal or not?" Then he gave Josh a pouting look. "Really, it's all the same to me." And with that said, he reached down with his free hand and picked up a 9mm that had been perched on an inner ledge of the guillotine. "I could simply shoot you and pull the lever. It is getting late and to tell the truth, I am starting to feel a bit peckish. So, if you don't feel you're up to it—"

"Let's hear it," Josh said.

"Don't you *dare* listen to this asshole," Rachael pleaded. "Josh, you save yourself. I'm already dead. You know he only wants to see you lose."

"You see that round table?" Anton asked, pointing to a small table about six or seven feet to his left. "On its top is a gray handkerchief that is draped over what looks like a rather large lump. The lump is a .357 magnum revolver."

Josh glanced over at the handkerchief. "Yeah, I see

it."

"I want you to go to the table and pick up the gun. And just so there is no mistake. So there's no heroic, I'm-going-to-save-the-day bravado coming from you. May I remind you that my wrist is fastened to this lever. And should, for any reason my arm drop, a split second later your dear Rachael's head will roll, and her last thoughts will be about basket weaving."

Josh could see Rachael trembling, her chin held high—defiant.

Josh stepped over to the table, and noticed it had been positioned to ensure all three of them had an unobstructed and intimate view of one another. "Now what?" he asked.

"Jesus . . . Josh don't be a fool!" Rachael shouted.

"I want you to lift the revolver and point it up under your chin, and then cock it."

Josh picked up the gun as he was told, and pressed the end of the barrel under his chin, and slowly pulled back the hammer with his thumb until—it clicked.

"This is where you get to show how valiant you are. Your moment of redemption. You couldn't carry out this one small act for your precious wife," Anton said, his voice now filled with excitement. "But you can now. Now you can redeem yourself."

"Josh, *please* listen to me," Rachael cried. "He's not going to grant me extra time. He wants me to witness you blowing your brains out. You know there are no rules. There is no deal."

"What's it going to be, Ingram? Does your woman get another thirty—"

Josh squeezed on the trigger, the pressure then transferred to the release mechanism. He knew the next sound would be that of the hammer striking the firing pin. Then in one motion he turned the gun on Anton and shot him an inch above his right eye. Anton's expression froze as large chunks of his brain blew out the back of his head and he dropped, and his arm came down. The cable tightened around the pulley and the pin slid back and the blade dropped.

At the same moment, Josh fired at the blade's guide rail. The bullet tore deep into the rail groove, mangling it, twisting the metal guide. A split second later, the blade caught, digging into the blown out rail, and came to an abrupt halt with a loud *cracking* sound that shook the entire frame of the guillotine, stopping it a foot above Rachael's neck. Her eyes sealed tight, her fists clenched.

Josh unlocked the latches to the wooden collar, removed the straps across her chest and quickly untied her ankles. Slipping his hand under her neck he lifted her out from below the blade, then sat down on the bench with her curled up on his lap, her head pressed against his chest.

Looking straight ahead, he began to gently rock back-and-forth, and felt a warm tear run down his cheek.

Chapter 70

Josh entered McClinty's at a little past nine p.m. It was Monday and the place was buzzing. Rachael's team had taken a middle booth. Vivian sat at the end of the bench, newspaper in hand, reviewing yesterday's race results. Michal was nursing a Vodka and looked like he'd had a few. Anakin was holding his cell an inch from his ear, getting shit for something. And Charley had a hand full of potato chips he was stuffing into his face as he watched a game on an overhead flat screen. Rachael was seated in the middle and smiled as he approached.

Oh my God, Rachael, you are so beautiful, Josh thought, and took a breath. *You're actually making my heart ache.*

"Glad you could make it," Rachael said. The team stopped what they were doing and took notice.

Josh studied their faces for a moment. "Guys I wish I could stay, but I have to get back to the marina."

"You're leaving right now, tonight?" Rachael asked. "Stay . . . and at least have a drink."

"I wish I could . . . but I have to go. I just wanted to say, thank you. To all of you."

"For what?" Anakin asked. "If it wasn't for you, that lunatic would still be in circulation and Rachael wouldn't."

Josh grinned. "Hey, I do hope our paths cross again," he said, and then focused on Rachael. "Can we talk for a second?"

They walked out onto the front steps of McClinty's. There was a light breeze. The air was cool and smelled as if somewhere to the north it was snowing.

"So . . . when will I see you again?" Rachael asked, a deep sadness in her voice.

"I need to go back to the marina. Work out what I'm to do with the rest of my life."

"I wish you would stay . . ." she said, and tears began to well.

Josh reached out and touched her cheek with his fingertips, then leaned in toward her. He looked into her eyes, and Rachael raised herself up onto her toes, and they kissed, a soft gentle kiss.

Josh climbed into a waiting cab, and as it pulled away he turned and looked out the side window. Rachael waved good-bye and tried to smile. He did the same.

Chapter 71

Anna handed off her quarter horse to the ranch foreman and walked back to the house. She took a chair on the covered veranda and sat down across from her mother. Her mother passed her a fresh glass of lemonade, packed high with ice. It was another hot, muggy evening in Guatemala and the lemonade tasted good.

"A police officer was around to see you," her mother said. "He said a security camera picked up your plates at the training airport. He said he had some routine questions for you. Word is, someone stole an airplane from the hangar last week."

Anna took a sip of her lemonade.

"I told him he should check with your father." Her mother put down her drink and looked out over the mango orchard. "I think that's the last we'll hear from him." Then she slid a package across the table to Anna. "It was delivered this afternoon. It has your name on it."

Anna held the package for a moment in her hand and then ripped off the brown packing paper. Glancing over at her mother, she smiled, the book's green leather cover was unmistakable.

Chapter 72

The sun was going down for the night over the marina. Josh stood on the top step outside Crawlies and inhaled the salted air. He heard seagulls squawking below him on the boardwalk, and saw they were fighting over the remains of a discarded cheeseburger. It was good to be home.

He opened the door and walked in. The others were already seated at the card table. All except Mary. He scanned the room for a moment and there she was, filling a pint of ale for an old man seated at the bar.

As he walked over, Mary took notice, and said, "Love gone askew for you? You big lump of emotional excrement."

"I've missed you too, Mary," he said. "Busy night?"

"Same as usual . . . the four stooges have been asking about you." She nodded in the direction of the card table. Anwar Nasser, Little Bob, and the two cousins looked over and waved.

Josh caught a whiff of fried bacon, onions and garlic, and he grinned.

"Go sit with the *boys*, and I'll bring you your usual." Then she tapped a pint of red ale and handed it to him. Josh walked over to the card table, and Anwar tried for a high-five and missed.

Mary wiped down the bar with a wet rag and smiled.

ABOUT THE AUTHOR

t.g. brown grew up in Edmonton, Alberta, and attended the University of Alberta. He and his wife live in British Columbia.

Made in the USA
Lexington, KY
30 March 2015